PRAISE FOR JODI PICOULT

"In her remarkable and vibrant first novel, Jodi Picoult displays near perfect pitch. *Songs of the Humpback Whale* is ingeniously structured and reminiscent of early Anne Tyler."

—Mary Morris

"Charming and poignant, Picoult's novel is even better after a second reading."

—*Library Journal*

"As Picoult uses five voices to tell a complex tale of love, friendship, and a Faulknerian family history, her mastery of language strongly individuates her characters. . . . This powerful and affecting novel demonstrates that there are as many truths to a story as there are people to tell it."

—*Publishers Weekly*

"[My *Sister's Keeper*] grabs the reader from the first page and never lets go. This is a beautiful, heartbreaking, controversial, and honest book."

—*Booklist* (starred review)

"[*Second Glance*] is a fast-paced, densely layered exploration of love, the pull of family and the power of both to transcend time. Bottom line: Great ghost story."

—*People* (Critic's Choice)

"[I]t is impossible not to be held spellbound by the way she forces us to think, hard, about right and wrong."

—*The Washington Post*

Also by Jodi Picoult

Handle with Care

Change of Heart

Nineteen Minutes

The Tenth Circle

Vanishing Acts

My Sister's Keeper

Second Glance

Perfect Match

Salem Falls

Plain Truth

Keeping Faith

The Pact

Mercy

Picture Perfect

Harvesting the Heart

Songs *of the* Humpback Whale

A Novel in Five Voices

Jodi Picoult

Washington Square Press
New York London Toronto Sydney

This book is a work of fiction. Names, characters, places and incidents are products of the author's imagination or are used fictitiously. Any resemblance to actual events or locales or persons, living or dead, is entirely coincidental.

Dr. Roger Payne's name is used by courtesy of the Whale and Dolphin Conservation Society USA, 191 Weston Road, Lincoln MA 01773

Oliver's article for *The Journal of Mammology* has been excerpted from an actual article in the *Journal*: "Humpback Whale Songs on a North Atlantic Feeding Ground," written by David K. Mattila, Linda N. Guinee and Charles A. Mayo. It is reprinted by courtesy of the American Society of Mammologists.

A Washington Square Press Publication
1230 Avenue of the Americas, New York, NY 10020

ISBN-13: 978-0-7434-3101-9
ISBN-10: 0-7434-3101-4

First Pocket Books trade paperback printing October 2001

40 39 38 37 36 35 34 33 32 31

Interior design by Nancy Singer Olaguera

Printed in the U.S.A.

To Tim, for everything you've given me

Acknowledgments

The author is grateful to many people and institutions for the detailed information they provided: Sarah Genman, the librarian at the New England Aquarium; the Provincetown Center for Coastal Studies; the Long Term Research Institute in Lincoln; Honeypot Orchards and Shelburne Farm in Stow. Special thanks to Katie Desmond and her tireless work at the Xerox machine, to everyone in my family who read the manuscript and supported my efforts, and to those people whose lives and experiences I borrowed to create fiction. Finally, this book would not have been published without the help of Laura Gross, my agent, who always believed in me; and Fiona McCrae, my editor, whose expertise and faith were invaluable. For this special paperback edition, I'd also like to thank Emily Bestler, who had the delightful idea that my fans would want to read everything I'd written, and then made it possible.

SONGS *of the* HUMPBACK WHALE

Prologue

Rebecca *November 1990*

In the upper right hand corner of the photo is a miniature airplane that looks as if it is flying right into my forehead. It is very tiny and steel-blue, a long bloated oval cut in the middle with its own wings. It is the shape, really, of the Cross. It was the first thing my mother noticed when we received the photo in Massachusetts. "You see, Rebecca," she said. "It's a sign."

When I was three and a half, I survived a plane crash. Ever since, my mother has told me I am destined for something special. I can't say I agree with her. I do not even remember. She and my father had had a fight—one that ended with my mother crying into the garbage disposal and my father taking all of the original paintings off the walls and stashing them in the trunk of his Impala for safekeeping. As a result, my mother took me out to my grandparents' breezy yellow home near Boston. My father kept calling. He threatened to send the FBI if she didn't send me back home. So she did, but she told me she couldn't go with me. She actually said, "I'm sorry, honey, but I can't stand that man." Then she dressed me in a little lemon knit outfit with white gloves. She turned me over to a stewardess at the airport, kissed me goodbye, and said, "Now don't lose the gloves. I paid a bundle."

I don't remember much about the crash. The plane broke all around me; it split in half right before row number eight. All I recall was trying so hard to hold tight onto those gloves, and the way people didn't move, and not being sure if it was all right to breathe.

I don't remember much about the crash. But when I was old enough to understand, my mother told me that I was one of five survivors. She said that my picture was on the cover of *Time*—me crying in a burnt little yellow outfit with my arms outstretched. A farmhand had taken the photo with a Brownie camera and it had gone out to press and into the hearts of millions of people in America. She told me about fires that reached the sky and singed the clouds. She told me how insignificant the fight with my father was.

A trucker took this photo of us the day we left California. In the corner is that airplane. My mother's hair is tied up in a ponytail. Her arm is casually draped around my shoulder, but her fingers rest unnaturally tight on my neck as if she is trying to keep me from running away. She is smiling. She is wearing one of my father's shirts. I'm not smiling. I'm not even looking at the camera.

The trucker's name was Flex. He had a red beard and no moustache. He said we were the best scenery he'd seen since Nebraska. Flex used his own camera—we'd left in too big a hurry to take ours. He said, "I'll take your picture and you give me your address and I'll send it." My mother said what the hell, it was her brother's rental address. If Flex turned out to be a lunatic and burned the place down no one would really be hurt.

Flex sent the photo to us care of Uncle Joley. It came in a used, readdressed manila envelope snaked with a line of twenty-five one-cent stamps. He attached a Post-it note for my mother that she did not let me read.

I'm telling you the story of our trip because I'm the only one who has really put it all together. It involved all of us—Mom, Daddy, Uncle Joley, Sam, even Hadley—but we all see it different ways. Me, I see it going backward. Like a rewinding movie. I don't know why I see it like this. I know, for example, that my mother doesn't.

When we got the photo from Flex, we all stood around the kitchen table looking at it—me, Mom, Joley and Sam. Joley said it was a nice picture of me, and where did we take it? Sam shook his head and stepped back. "There's nothing there," he said. "No trees, no canyons, nothing."

"We're there," my mother said.

"That's not why you took that picture," Sam said. His voice hung at the edges of the kitchen like thin silver. "There's more. We just all can't see it." And like that, he walked out of the room.

My mother and I turned to each other, surprised. This had

been our secret. We both looked instinctively at a spot in the highway to the right of our bodies. It is the place where California becomes Arizona—a change that truckers can sense in the pavement; that for everyone else remains unmarked.

1 JANE

The night before I got married I woke up, screaming, from my sleep. My parents came into the room and put their arms around me; they patted my head and smoothed my hair, fine, and I still couldn't stop screaming. Even with my mouth closed, I continued—the high, shrill note of a nocturnal animal.

My parents were beside themselves. We lived in a button-down suburb of Boston, and we were waking up the neighbors one by one. I watched the lights come on in different houses—blue and yellow, blinking like Christmas—and wondered what was happening to me.

This wasn't a common occurrence. I was barely nineteen, a straight-A student fresh out of Wellesley College and in 1976 that was still an accomplishment. I was marrying the man of my dreams in a prototypical white clapboard New England church, and the reception—a lavish one with white-gloved waiters and Beluga caviar—was going to be held in my parents' backyard. I had a job waiting for me when I returned from my honeymoon. There was no foreseeable problem that I could articulate.

To this day, I don't know why that happened to me. As mysteriously as it all started, the screaming went away and the next morning I married Oliver Jones—*the* Oliver Jones—and we just about lived happily ever after.

I am the only speech pathologist in this town, which means I get shuttled back and forth to different elementary schools in the San Diego suburbs. It's not such a big deal now that Rebecca is old enough to take care of herself, and since Oliver is away so much of the time, I have less to do at home. I enjoy my work but certainly not the way Oliver enjoys his work. Oliver would be content to live in a sailcloth tent on the coast of Argentina, watching his whales sound in warm water.

My job is to help children find their voices—kinds that come to school mute, or with lisps or cleft palates. At first, they come into my little makeshift classroom one at a time and they shuffle their Keds on the floor and shyly glance at the formidable recording equipment and they are absolutely silent. Sometimes I stay silent too, until the student breaks the ice and asks what he or she is supposed to do. Some students cover their mouths with their hands at this point; I have even seen one little girl cry: they cannot stand to hear their own voices, pieces of themselves that they have been told are ugly. My role is to show them there's someone who is ready to listen to what they have to say and the way they have to say it.

When I was seven, I tell these kids, I used to whistle every time I said the letter S. In school I got teased and because of this I did not have many friends and I did not talk very much. One day my teacher told the class we'd be putting on a play and that everyone had to participate. I was so nervous about reading aloud in front of everyone else that I pretended I was sick. I faked a fever by holding the thermometer up to a light bulb when my mother left the room. I was allowed to stay home for three days, until my teacher called, and my mother figured out what I was doing. When I went back to school, my teacher called me aside. All of the parts had been taken in the play, she said, but she had saved a special role for me, offstage. I was going to be the Manager of Sound Effects, just like in the movies. I practiced with my teacher every day after school for three weeks. In time I discovered I could become a fire engine, a bird, a mouse, a bee, and many other things because of my lisp. When the night of the play came, I was given a black robe and a microphone. The other students got to be just one part, but I became the voice of several animals and machines. And my father was so proud of me; it was the only time I remember him telling me so.

That's the story I give at those Coastal Studies cocktail parties

Oliver and I go to. We rub shoulders with people who'll give grant money. We introduce ourselves as Dr. and Dr. Jones, although I'm still ABD. We sneak out when everyone is going to sit down to the main course, and we run to the car and make fun of people's sequined dresses and dinner jackets. Inside, I curl up against Oliver as he drives, and I listen to him tell me stories I have heard a million times before—about an era when you could spot whales in every ocean.

In spite of it all, there's just *something* about Oliver. You know what I'm talking about—he was the first man who truly took my breath away, and sometimes he still can. He's the one person I feel comfortable enough with to share a home, a life, a child. He can take me back fifteen years with a smile. In spite of differences, Oliver and I have Oliver and I.

In this one school where I spend Tuesdays, my office is a janitorial closet. Sometime after noon the secretary of the school knocks on the door and tells me Dr. Jones is on the phone. Now this is truly a surprise. Oliver is at home this week, putting together some research, but he usually has neither the time nor the inclination to call me. He never asks what school I head to on a given day. "Tell him I'm with a student," I say, and I push the play button on my tape recorder. Vowel sounds fill the room: *AAAAA EEEEEIIIII*. I know Oliver too well to play his games. *OOOOO UUUUU*. Oh, you. Oh, you.

Oliver is Very Famous. He wasn't when we met, but today he is one of the leading researchers of whales and whale behavior. He has made discoveries that have rocked the scientific world. He is so well known that people take pictures of our mailbox, as if to say, "I've been to the place where Dr. Jones lives." Oliver's most important research has been on whale songs. It appears that whole groupings of whales sing the same ones—Oliver has recorded this—and pass the songs down over generations. I don't understand much about his work, but that is just as much my fault as Oliver's. He never tells me about the ideas burning in his mind anymore, and I sometimes forget to ask.

Naturally Oliver's career has come first. He moved us to California to take a job with the San Diego Center for Coastal Studies, only to find out East Coast humpbacks were his true passion. The minute I got to San Diego I wanted to leave, but I didn't tell Oliver that. For better or for worse, I had said. Oliver got to fly back to Boston and I stayed here with an infant, in a climate that is always summer, that never smells like snow.

I'm not taking his phone call.

I'm not taking this again, period.

It is one thing for me to play second fiddle; it is another thing to see it happen to Rebecca. At fourteen she has the ability to take a survey of her life from a higher vantage point—an ability I haven't mastered at thirty-five—and I do not believe she likes what she is seeing. When Oliver is home, which is rare, he spends more time in his study than with us. He doesn't take an interest in anything that isn't tied to the seas. The way he treats me is one matter: we have a history; I hold myself accountable for falling in love in the first place. But Rebecca will not take him on faith, just because he is her father. Rebecca expects.

I've heard about teenagers who run away, or get pregnant or drop out of school, and I have heard these things linked to problems at home. So I offered Oliver an ultimatum. Rebecca's fifteenth birthday next week coincides with Oliver's planned visit to a humpback breeding ground off the coast of South America. Oliver intends to go. I told him to be here.

What I wanted to say is: This is your daughter. Even if we have grown so far apart that we don't recognize each other when we pass, we have this life, this block of time, and what do you think about that?

One reason I keep my mouth shut is Rebecca's accident. It was the result of a fight with Oliver, and I've been doing my best to keep something like that from happening again. I don't remember what that argument was about, but I gave him a piece of my mind and he hit me. I picked up my baby (Rebecca was three and a half at the time) and flew to my parents. I told my mother I was going to divorce Oliver; he was a lunatic and on top of this he'd hit me. Oliver called and said he didn't care what I did but I had no right to keep his daughter. He threatened legal action. So I took Rebecca to the airport and told her, "I'm sorry, honey, but I can't stand that man." I bribed a stewardess with a hundred dollars to take her on the plane, and it crashed in Des Moines. The next thing I knew I was standing in a farmer's cornfield, watching the wreckage smoke. It still seemed to be moving. The wind sang through the plane's limbs, voices I couldn't place. And behind me was Rebecca, singed but intact, one of five survivors, curled in her father's arms. She has Oliver's yellow hair and freckles. Like him, she's beautiful. Oliver and I looked at each other and I knew right then why fate had made me fall in love with a man like Oliver Jones: some combination of him and of me had created a child who could charm even unyielding earth.

2 Oliver

Hawaiian and West Indian humpbacks seem less unhappy to me than the whales off the coast of New England. Their songs are playful, staccato, lively. Violins, rather than oboes. When you see them diving and surfacing there is a certain grace, a feeling of triumph. Their slick bodies twist through a funnel of sea, reach toward the sky; with flippers outstretched, they rise from the pits of the ocean like the second coming of Christ. But the humpbacks in Stellwagen Bank sing songs that fill you to the core, that swell inside you. They are the whales with which I fell in love when I first heard the calls—eerie, splayed, the haunted sound your heart beats when you are afraid of being alone. Sometimes when I play the tapes of the Northern Atlantic stock, I find myself sobbing.

I began working with Roger Payne in 1969, in Bermuda, when he and colleague Scott McVay concluded that the sounds made by humpbacks—*megaptera novaeangliae*—are actually songs. Of course there is a lot of leeway in the definition of "song," but a general consensus may be "a string of sounds put together in a pattern by its singer." Whale songs are structured like this: One or several sounds make up a phrase, the phrase is repeated and becomes a theme, and several themes make up a song. On the average songs last from seven to thirty minutes, the singer will repeat the song in its same order. There are seven basic types of sounds, each with variations: moans, cries, chirps, yups, oos, ratchets, and snores. Whales from different populations sing different songs. Songs change gradually over the years according to the general laws of change; all whales learn the changes. Whales do not sing mechanically but compose as they go, incorporating new pieces into old songs—a skill previously attributed solely to man.

Of course, these are only theories.

I did not always study whales. I began my career in zoology looking at bugs, then progressed to bats, then owls, then whales. The first time I heard a whale was years ago, when I had taken a rowboat off a larger ship and found myself sitting directly over a humpback, listening to its song vibrate against the bottom of my boat.

My contribution to the field was discovering that only the male whales sing. This had been hypothesized, but to get concrete evidence required some way of determining a whale's sex at sea. Viewing the undersides of whales was possible but dangerous. Taking a clue from genetics, I began to consider the feasibility of cell samples. Eventually I created a biopsy dart, fired from a modified harpoon gun. When the dart hit the whale, a piece of skin a quarter inch thick was removed and retrieved by a line. The dart was covered with an antibiotic, to prevent infection in the whale. After many unsuccessful attempts I finally amassed a body of evidence. To this day, the only recorded singers in the whale community are male; no female has ever been recorded.

Twenty years later we know a lot about the varied songs of humpbacks but little about their purpose. Since the songs are passed down through generations of males and are sung in entirety only at the breeding grounds, they are seen as a possible method of attracting females. Knowing a given stock's song may be the prerequisite for sex, and variations and flourishes may be an added inducement. This would account for the complexity of whale songs, the need to know the song currently in fashion—females choose a mate depending on the song they have to sing. Another theory for the purpose of the songs is attracting not females, but other males—acoustic swords, if you will, that allow male whales to fight over a female. Indeed, many male whales bear the scars of competition from mating.

Whatever the message behind the beautiful sounds, they have led to much speculation, and much information about the humpback whale's behavior. If a whale is a member of a specific population, he will sing a certain song. Thus if the songs of each whale population are known, a singing whale can be traced to its origins no matter where the song is taped. Whale songs provide a new method of tracking whales—an alternative to tagging, or to newer photographic fluke identification. We can group male whales by the songs they sing; we can connect females to these groups by attending to the songs to which they listen.

This is my latest professional question: Should we be paying more attention to the individual singer? Won't the personal histories—who the whale is, where he has been sighted, with whom he has been sighted—tell us something about why he sings the way he does?

I have conducted exhaustive research. I have been featured in *Newsweek,* the *Christian Science Monitor* and the *New York Times.* Along the way I got married and had a child. After that, I never felt like I was giving enough time to my family *or* my career. In limbo, that's what I call it. In limbo. Whales never sleep, you know. They are voluntary-breathing mammals, and have to constantly come up for air. They drift in the depths of ocean, unable to rest.

I used to try to mix the two. I took Rebecca and Jane on tracking voyages; I played tapes of the New England humpbacks in the house, piping the melodies into the kitchen and the bathroom. And then one day I found Jane hacking at a speaker in the kitchen with a carving knife. She said she couldn't listen anymore.

Once, when Rebecca was five, all of us sailed to Bermuda to observe the breeding grounds of the East Coast humpbacks. It was warm then, and Rebecca pointed at porpoises we passed on our way out to the reefs. Jane was wearing my rain gear—I remember this because there wasn't a cloud in the sky, but she preferred it to the goosebumps she got from the wet wind. She stood at the railing of *Voyager,* my hired boat, with the sun beating down on her hair, turning her scalp a shade of pink. She gripped the rail tightly; she never was firm-footed on the water. When we docked she'd walk with tentative steps to convince herself she was on solid ground.

Whales play. When we got to the exact spot and lowered the hydrophone into the ocean, there was a group of whales several hundred yards away. Although we were recording a whale singing way below the surface, we couldn't help but watch the others. Their flukes slapped against the water; they rolled, languorous, stroking each other with their dorsal fins. They shot out of the water, ballistic. They slipped in and out of the waves, marbled in ebony, white.

When the melancholy notes of the whale's song filled the boat, it became clear that we were watching a ballet, executed artfully, except we didn't know the story being told. The boat pitched from left to right and I watched Rebecca grab Jane's leg for support. I thought, My two girls, have they ever been so beautiful?

Although she was only five, Rebecca remembers many things from our trip to Bermuda. The whales are not one of them. She can tell you of the texture of pink sand; about Devil's Hole, where sharks swim below your feet; of an estate's pond with an island shaped the same as the actual island of Bermuda. She cannot remember her mother in yellow rain gear, or the slow-moving humpbacks that frolicked, or even the repeated cries of the whale below, to which she asked, Daddy, why can't we *help* him? I don't recall if Jane offered her opinion. In regard to whales, she has largely remained silent.

3 JANE

My daughter is the family stoic. By this I mean that while I fly off the handle in given situations, Rebecca tends to hold it all inside. Case in point: the first time she experienced death (a beloved guinea pig, Butterscotch). She was the one to clean out the cage, to bury the small stiff form in the backyard, while I cried beside her. She did not cry for eight and a half days, and then I found her washing dishes in the kitchen, sobbing, as if the world had ended. She had just dropped a serving platter on the floor, and shards of pottery radiated from around Rebecca's feet, like the rays of the sun. "Don't you see," she said to me, "how beautiful it was?"

Rebecca is in the living room when I get home from work. This summer she's working as a lifeguard and her shift ends at two, so she's already home when I get home. She's eating carrot sticks and watching "Wheel of Fortune." She gets the answers before the contestants do. She waves to me. "A Tale of Two Cities," she says, and on the TV, bells ring.

Rebecca pads into the kitchen in her bare feet. She is wearing a red bathing suit that says GUARD across her bust and an old baseball cap. She looks much older than fourteen and a half, in fact sometimes people think we are sisters. After all, how many thirty-five-year-old women do you know who are just having their first babies? "Daddy's home," Rebecca warns.

"I know. He tried to call me this morning." Our eyes connect.

Rebecca shrugs. Her eyes, the shape of Oliver's, dart past my shoulder but seem to have trouble finding an object of focus. "Well, we'll do what we always do. We'll go to a movie he wouldn't like anyway, and then we'll eat a pint of ice cream." She opens the door of the refrigerator lazily. "We don't have any food."

It's true. We're even out of milk. "Wouldn't you rather do something different? It's your birthday."

"It's not that big a deal." Suddenly she turns to the door, where Oliver is standing.

He shifts from one foot to the other, a stranger in his own home. As an afterthought, he reaches for me and kisses my cheek. "I've got some bad news," he says, smiling.

Oliver has the same effect on me each time I see him: he's soothing. He's very handsome—for someone who spends so much time outside, his skin isn't dry and leathery, it is the color of iced coffee, smooth as velvet. His eyes are bright, like paint that hasn't dried, and his hands are large and strong. When I see him, his frame filling the doorway, I do not feel passion, excitement. I can't remember if I ever have. He makes me feel comfortable, like a favorite pair of shoes.

I smile at him, grateful for the calm before the storm.

"You don't have to say it, Daddy. I knew you wouldn't be here for my birthday."

Oliver beams at me, as if to say, See? There's no reason to make a fuss. Turning to Rebecca he says, "I'm sorry, kiddo. But you know the way it is—it's really in everyone's best interests if I go."

"Everyone who?" I'm surprised I say it out loud.

Oliver turns to me. His eyes have gone flat and dispassionate, the way one looks at a stranger in a subway.

I slip out of my heels and pick them up in my right hand. "Forget it. It's done."

Rebecca touches my arm on her way into the living room. "It's all *right*," she whispers, stressing the words as she passes.

"I'll make it up to you," Oliver says. "Wait till you see your birthday present!" Rebecca doesn't seem to hear him. She turns up the volume on the TV, and leaves me alone with my husband.

"What are you getting her?" I ask.

"I don't know. I'll think of something."

I press my fingers together—this is a habit I've acquired for dealing with Oliver—and head up the stairs. At the first landing I turn around to find Oliver following me. I think about asking when he is going to leave, but what comes out of my mouth instead is unexpected. "God damn you," I say, and I actually mean it.

There is not much of the old Oliver left. The first time I saw him was in Cape Cod when I was waiting with my parents for the ferry to Martha's Vineyard. He was twenty, working for the Woods Hole Oceanographic Institute. He had straight blond hair that fell asymmetrically across his left eye, and he smelled like fish. Like a normal fifteen-year-old, I saw him and waited for sparks to fly, but it never happened. I stood dumb as a cow near the dock where he was working, hoping he'd notice me. I didn't know I'd have to give him something to notice.

That might have been the end of it except he was there when we came back over on the ferry two days later. I had wised up. I tossed my purse overboard, knowing it would float with the current in his direction. Two days later he called me at home, saying he'd found my wallet and would I like it back. When we started dating, I told my mother and father it was Fate.

He was into tide pools back then, and I listened to him talk of mollusks and sea urchins and entire ecosystems that were ruined at the whim of an ocean wave. Back then Oliver's face would light up when he shared his marine discoveries. Now he only gets excited when he's locked in his little study, examining data by himself. By the time he tells the rest of the world, he's transformed from Oliver into Dr. Jones. Back then, I was the first person he told when something wonderful cropped up in his research. Today I'm not even fifth in line.

At the second landing I turn to Oliver. "What are you going to look for?"

"Where?"

"In South America." I try to scratch an itch in my back and when I can't reach it Oliver does.

"The winter breeding grounds. For whales," he says. "Humpbacks." As if I am a total moron. I give him a look. "I'd tell you, Jane, but it's complicated."

Pedantic asshole. "I'll remind you that I am an educator, and one thing I have learned is that anyone can understand anything. You just have to know how to present your information."

I find myself listening to my own words, like I tell my students, to hear where the cadences change. It is as if I am having an out-of-body experience, watching this weird one-act performance between a self-absorbed professor and his nutty wife. I am somewhat surprised at the character Jane. Jane is supposed to back down. Jane listens to Oliver. I find myself thinking, this is not my voice. This is not me.

I know this house so well. I know how many steps there are to get upstairs, I know where the carpet has become worn, I know to feel for the spot where Rebecca carved all of our initials into the banister. She did that when she was ten, so that our family would have a legacy.

Oliver's footsteps trail off into his study. I walk down the hall into our room and throw myself onto the bed. I try to invent ways to celebrate Rebecca's birthday. A circus, maybe, but that's too juvenile. A dinner at Le Cirque; a shopping spree at Saks—both have been done before. A trip to San Francisco, or Portland, Oregon, or Portland, Maine—I wouldn't know where to go. Honestly, I don't know what my own daughter likes. After all, what did I want when I was fifteen? Oliver.

I undress and go to hang up my suit. When I open my closet I find my shoe boxes missing. They have been replaced by cartons labeled with dates: Oliver's research. He has already filled his own closet; he keeps his clothes folded in the bathroom linen closet. I don't even care where my shoes are at this point. The real issue is that Oliver has infringed on my space.

With energy I didn't know I had, I lift the heavy boxes and throw them onto the bedroom floor. There are over twenty; they hold maps and charts and in some cases transcriptions of tapes. The bottom of one of the boxes breaks as I lift it, and the contents flutter like goosedown over my feet.

The heavy thuds reach Oliver. He comes into the bedroom just as I am arranging a wall of these boxes outside the bedroom door. The boxes reach his hips but he manages to scale them. "I'm sorry," I tell him. "These can't stay."

"What's the problem? Your shoes are under the bathroom sink."

"Look, it's not the shoes, it's the space. I don't want you in my closet. I don't want your whale tapes—" here I kick a nearby box, "—your whale records, your whales *period,* in my closet."

"I don't understand," Oliver says softly, and I know I've hurt him. He touches the box closest to my right foot, and his quiet eyes hold the contents, these ruffled papers, checking their safety with a naked tenderness I am not accustomed to seeing.

This is how it goes for several minutes: I take a carton and stack it in the hall; Oliver picks it up and moves it back inside the bedroom. Out of the corner of my eye I see Rebecca, a shadow behind the wall of cartons in the hall.

"Jane," Oliver says, clearing his throat, "that's enough."

Imperceptibly, I snap. I pick up some of the papers from the broken carton and throw them at Oliver, who flinches, as if they have substantial weight. "Get these out of my sight. I'm tired of this, Oliver, and I'm tired of you, don't you get it?"

Oliver says, "Sit down." I don't. He pushes me down by my shoulders, and I squirm away and with my feet shove three or four cartons into the hall. Again I seem to take a vantage point high above, in the balcony, watching the show. Seeing the fight from this angle, instead of as a participant, absolves me of responsibility; I do not have to wonder about what part of my body or mind my belligerence came from, why shutting my eyes cannot control the howling. I see myself wrench away from Oliver's hold, which is truly amazing because he has pinned me with his weight. I pick up a carton and with all my strength hold it over the banister. Its contents, according to the labels, include samples of baleen. I am doing this because I know it will drive Oliver crazy.

"Don't," he says, pushing past the boxes in the hall. "I mean it."

I shake the box, which feels like it is getting heavier. At this point I cannot remember what our argument is about. The bottom of the carton splits; its contents fall two stories.

Oliver and I grip the banister, watching the material drift through the air—paper like feathers and heavier samples in Ziploc bags that bounce when they hit the ceramic tile below. From where we stand we cannot tell how much has been broken.

"I'm sorry," I whisper, frightened to look at Oliver. "I didn't expect that to happen." Oliver doesn't respond. "I'll clean it all up. I'll organize it. Keep it in my closet, whatever." I make an effort to scoop nearby files into my arms, gathering them like a harvest. I do not look at Oliver and I do not see him coming for me.

"You bitch." He grabs my wrists in his hands.

The way he looks at me cuts inside me, says I am violated, insignificant. I have seen these eyes before and I am trying to place them but it is so hard when I can feel myself dying. I have seen these eyes before. *Bitch*, he said.

It is in me, and it has been waiting for years.

As my knees sink, as red welts form on my wrists, I begin to take ownership of my own soul, something that has been missing since childhood. Strength that could move a city, that could heal a heart and resurrect the dead pushes and shoots and stands and *(bitch)* concentrates. With the sheer power of everything I used to dream I could be, I break away from Oliver's hold and strike his face as hard as I can.

Oliver drops my other wrist, and takes a step backward. I hear a cry and I realize afterward it has come from me.

He rubs his hand across his cheek, red, and he throws his head back to protect his pride. When he looks at me again, he is smiling, but his lips are slack like a carnival clown's. "I suppose it was inevitable," he says. "Like father, like daughter."

It is only when he has said this, the unspeakable, that I can feel my fingers striking his skin, leaving an impression. It is only then that I feel the pain spreading like blood from my knuckles to my wrist to my gut.

I never imagined there could be anything worse than the time Oliver struck me; the time that I had taken my baby and left him; the event that precipitated Rebecca's plane crash. I believed the reason there was a God was to prevent such atrocities from happening to the same person twice. But nothing prepared me for this: I have done what I've sworn I could never do; I have become my own nightmare.

I push past Oliver and run down the stairs. I am afraid to look back, or to speak. I have lost control.

From the dirty laundry pile I quickly grab an old shirt of Oliver's and a pair of shorts. I find my car keys. I pull a Rolodex card with Joley's address and walk out the side door. I don't look back, I slam the door behind me, and still wearing only a bra and a slip, climb into the cool refuge of my old station wagon.

It is easy to get away from Oliver, I think. But how do I get away from my own self?

I run my fingers over the leather of the seat, raking my fingernails into pits and tears that have developed over the years. In the rearview mirror, I see my face and I have trouble placing it. Several seconds later I realize that someone is echoing my breathing.

My daughter holds a small suitcase on her lap. She is crying. "I have everything," she tells me. Rebecca touches my hand; the hand that struck her father, that struck my own husband, that resurrected those dead and buried gaps.

4 JANE

When I was ten I was old enough to go hunting with my father. Every year when goose season came, when the leaves began to turn, my father became a different person. He'd take his shotgun out of the locked closet and clean the entire gun, down to the insides of the barrels. He'd go to the town hall and get a hunting license, a stamp with a picture of a bird so pretty it made me want to cry. He'd talk about that roast goose dinner he was going to get us, and then early on a Saturday he'd return with a fluffy grey bird, and he'd show Joley and me the place where the shot went in.

Mama came into my room at four A.M. and said if I was going goose hunting I'd have to get up. It was still pitch dark when Daddy and I left the house. We drove in his Ford to a field, owned by a buddy, that was used to grow field corn in the summer, which—Daddy told me—is what geese love the most. The field, which had sported stalks of corn much taller than me just weeks before, had been razed; there were false pillows of dust caught between stumps of corn left from summer.

My father opened the trunk and extracted the leather case that held the gun and the funny goose decoys Joley and I used as hurdles when we played Obstacle Course. He scattered them through the field, and then he took a pile of dead stalks and created a little hutch for me, and one for himself. "You sit under there," he told me. "Don't breathe; don't even *think* about getting up."

I squatted down like he did and watched the sun paint the sky as it slowly turned into Saturday. I counted my fingers and I took quiet, shallow breaths, as I'd been told. From time to time I stole a glance at my father, who rocked back and forth on his heels and absentmindedly stroked the barrel of his gun.

After about an hour my legs hurt. I wanted to get up and run around, let free that dizzy feeling behind the eyes that comes when you don't get enough sleep. But I knew better. I stayed perfectly still, even when I had to go to the bathroom.

By the time the geese actually arrived (which according to my father, *never* took this long), the pressure on my bladder caused by squatting was unbearable. I waited patiently until the geese were feeding on the cornfield, and then I cried out, "Daddy! I have to pee!"

The geese flew into the air, deafening, a hundred wings beating like just one heart. I had never seen anything like it, this mass of grey wings blotting the sky like a cloud; I thought surely this was why he had wanted me to come hunting.

But my father, startled by my cry, missed his opportunity at a good shot. He fired twice but nothing happened. He turned to me; he didn't say a word, and I knew I was in trouble.

I was allowed to go to the woods that edged the cornfield to pee, and, amazed that my father hadn't given me any toilet-paper substitute, I pulled up my underpants and overalls feeling dirty. I settled quietly under my cornstalk hutch, much better. My father said under his breath, "I could kill you."

We waited two more hours, hearing thunderous shots miles away, but did not see any more geese. "You blew it," my father said, remarkably calm. "You have no idea what hunting is like." We were about to leave when a flock of crows passed overhead. My father raised his gun and fired, and one black bird fluttered to the ground. It hopped around in circles; my father had shot off part of its wing.

"Why did you do that, Daddy?" I whispered, watching the crow. I had thought the purpose of hunting was to eat the game. You couldn't eat crow. My father picked up the bird and carried it farther away. Horrified, I watched him wrench the crow's neck and toss it to the ground. When he came back, he was smiling. "You tell Mama about that and I'll give you a good spanking, understand? Don't tell your brother either. This is between me and my big girl, okay?" And he gently placed his shotgun, still smoking, in its leather case.

5 JANE

"Okay," I tell Rebecca. "I know what we're doing." Adjusting my side mirror, I pull out of the development and onto the freeway that leads to the beach at La Jolla. Rebecca, sensing that we are in for a long drive, rolls down her window and hangs her feet out the window. A million times I have told her that it is not safe for her to do that, but then again I don't even know if it is safe for her to be with me anymore, so I pretend I don't see her. Rebecca turns off the radio, and we listen to the hum and grind of the old car's symphony, the salt air singing across the front seat.

By the time we reach the public beach, the sun is pushing scarlet against the underedge of a cloud, stretching it like a hammock. I park the car along the span of sidewalk that lines the beach, diagonally across from a late-afternoon volleyball game. Seven young men—I wouldn't place any of them past twenty—arch and dive against the backdrop of the ocean. Rebecca is watching them, smiling.

"I'll be back," I say, and when Rebecca offers to go with me, I tell her no. I walk away from the game, down the beach, feeling the sand seep into the lace holes of my tennis shoes. It grits cool between my toes and forms a second sole beneath my foot. Standing straight, I shade my eyes and wonder how far out you have to be to see Hawaii. Or for that matter, how many miles off the California coast you must be before you can see land.

Oliver said once that at certain places south of San Diego you can see whales from the coast, without binoculars. When I asked him where they were going, he laughed. Where would you go? he said, but I was afraid to tell him. In time, I learned. I discovered that Alaska to Hawaii and Nova Scotia to Bermuda were the parallel paths of two humpback whale stocks. I learned that the West Coast whales and the East Coast whales did not cross paths.

Where would you go?

At thirty-five, I still refer to Massachusetts as home. I always have. I tell colleagues I'm from Massachusetts, although I have been living in California for fifteen years. I watch for the regional weather in the Northeast when I watch the national news. I am jealous of my brother, who roamed the whole world and by divine providence was allowed to settle back home.

But then again, things always come easily to Joley.

A seagull comes to a screeching hover above me. Batting its wings, it seems enormous, unnatural. Then it dives into the water and, having caught carrion, it surfaces and flies away. How amazing, I think, that it can move so effortlessly between air and sea and land.

There was one summer when we were kids that my parents rented a house on Plum Island, on the north shore of Massachusetts. From the outside it seemed pregnant, a tiny turret on top that seemed to distend into a bulbous lower level. It was red and needed a paint job, and contained framed posters of tabby kittens and nautical trivia. Its icebox was a relic from the turn of the century, with a fan and a motor. Joley and I spent very little time in the house, being seven and eleven, respectively. We would be outside before breakfast and come in only when the night seemed to blend into the line of the ocean that we considered our backyard.

Late in the summer, there were rumors of a hurricane, and like all the other kids on the beach we insisted on swimming in the ten-foot waves. Joley and I stood at the shore and watched columns of water rising like icons from the ocean. The waves taunted: Come here, come here, we wouldn't hurt you. When we got up enough courage, Joley and I swam out beyond the waves and rode them in on our bellies, getting pounded into the beach so forcefully that handfuls of sand got trapped in the pockets of our bathing suits. At one point, Joley couldn't seem to catch a wave. Floating several hundred yards out in the ocean, he tried and swam as hard as he could, but at seven he didn't have the strength. He got tired quickly, and there I was, my feet buried by the undertow, watching monstrous swells form a fence that kept us apart.

It was so quick that no one noticed, no other kids and no parents, but as soon as Joley began to cry, I dove under the water and frogkicked until I was well behind him; I burst to the surface, wrapped my arms around him and swam with all my power into the next wave. Joley swallowed some sand, landing face down on the rocky beach. Daddy came out to get us, asking what the hell were we doing out here in this weather. Joley and I dried off and watched the hurricane through the cross-taped windows of the cottage. The next day, which was bright and sunny, and every day after that, I did not go into the water. At least not past my chest, which is what I will only do now. My parents assumed it was the hurricane that had scared me, but that wasn't it at all. I didn't want to offer myself so easily to the entity that had almost taken away the only family member I loved.

I inch towards the water, trying not to get wet, but my sneakers get soaked when I hold my wrists into the water. For July it is fairly cool, and it feels good where my skin is still burning. If I swam far out, over my head, would I soothe the part of me that hates? The part that hits?

I cannot remember the first time it happened to me, but Joley can.

Rebecca's voice pulls me. "Mom," she says. "Tell me what happened."

I would like to tell her everything, beginning at the very beginning, but there are some things that are better left unsaid. So I tell her about the shoe boxes and Oliver's records, about the broken carton, about the shattered baleen samples, the ruined files. I tell her that I hit her father, but I do not tell her what Oliver said to me.

Rebecca's face falls, and I can tell she is trying to decide whether or not to believe me. Then she smiles. "Is that all? I was expecting something really big." She reaches into the sand, shyly, and winds a piece of dried seaweed around her fingers. "He deserved it."

"Rebecca, this is my problem, not yours—"

"Well it's true," she insists.

I can't really disagree with her. "Anyway."

Rebecca sits on the sand and crosses her legs Indian-style. "Are you going to go back?"

I sigh. How do you explain marriage to a fifteen-year-old? "You don't just pack up and run away, Rebecca. Your father and I have a *commitment*. Besides, I have a job."

"You'll take me, won't you?"

I shake my head. "Rebecca."

"It's obvious, Mom. You need *space*—" here Rebecca makes a sweeping gesture with her arms. "You need room to reconsider. And don't worry about me. Everyone's parents are doing it. Reconsidering. It's the age of separation."

"That's ludicrous. And I wouldn't take you even if I *were* leaving. You're his daughter too. Answer me this," I say, looking hard at her. "What did your father ever do to you to deserve you leaving?"

Rebecca picks up a rock, a perfect stone for skimming, and bounces it across the ocean six, no, seven times. "What did he ever do to deserve me staying?" She looks at me and jumps to her feet. "Let's go now," she says, "while we can still outsmart him. He's a scientist and he tracks things for a living, so we need as much of a head start as we can get. We can go anywhere—anywhere!" Rebecca points towards the parking lot. "We only have a limited supply of money, so we'll have to budget, and I can call up Mrs. Nulty at the pool and tell her I have mono or something, and you can call up the superintendent and tell him you caught mono from me. And I'm up for anything, as long as we drive. I have this thing about air travel . . ." She lets her voice trail off, giggling, and then she scrambles towards me, falling on her knees. "How does that sound, Mom?"

"I want you to listen to me, and listen carefully. Do you understand what happened this afternoon? *I . . . hit . . . your . . . father.* I don't know where that came from, or why I did it. I just snapped. I could do it again—"

"No you won't."

I begin to walk down the beach. "I don't know what happened, Rebecca, but I got angry enough and they say these things happen over and over; they say it's a cycle and it's passed down, do you follow? What if I hit you by mistake?" The words cough out of my mouth like stones. "What if I hit my baby?"

Rebecca throws her arms around me, burying her face in my chest. I can tell that she is crying too. Someone near the volleyball net shouts, "Yeah, man, that's game!" and I draw her closer to me.

"I could never be afraid of you," Rebecca says so quietly that I think for a minute it may be the sea. "I feel safe with you."

I hold her face between my hands and I think: this time around, I am in a position to change things. Rebecca hugs me, her hands knotted into fists, and I do not have to question what she is grasping so tight: my daughter is holding our future.

"I have no idea where to go," I tell Rebecca. "But your uncle will." Thinking about Joley it is easy to forget Oliver. My brother is the only person I have ever truly trusted with my life. We think each other's ideas, we can finish each other's sentences. And because he was there when this all began, he will be able to understand.

Suddenly I break free from Rebecca and sprint down the beach, kicking sand up behind me, like I used to do with Joley. *You can run but you can't hide*, I think. Oh yes, but I can try. I feel air catch in my lungs and I get a cramp in my side and this pain, this wonderful physical pain that I can place, reminds me that after all I am still alive.

6 REBECCA *August 2, 1990*

Sam, who has never in his life left Massachusetts, tells me about a Chinese ritual of death, minutes before I leave his apple orchard. We are sitting in the dark cellar of the Big House, on rusted milk cans from the early 1900s. We have adjusted to the heavy air, the white mice and the wet smell of apples that has been built into the foundation of this place: mortar mixed with cider to form sweet cement. Sam's back is pressed against my back to help me sit up; I am still not feeling one hundred percent. When he breathes in, I can feel his heartbeat. It is the closest to him I've been since we arrived in Stow. I am beginning to understand my mother.

There are thick beams in the cellar walls, and forgotten cane rockers and cracked canning jars. I can make out the jaws of the animal traps. Sam says, "In China, a person cannot be buried until an adequate number of people have paid their respects." I do not doubt him, and I do not ask how he knows of this. With Sam, you take things for granted. He reads a lot. "Even tourists can go into the funeral parlor and bow to the widow of a dead man, and they count. It doesn't matter if you knew the person who has died."

A small square of light sits in the center of the dirt floor. It comes from the only window in the cellar, which has been padlocked shut the entire time we've been here.

"Meanwhile, outside the funeral parlor, relatives sit on the sidewalk and fold paper into the shapes of castles and cars and fine clothing. They fold it into jewelry and coins."

"Origami," I say.

"I guess. They make piles and piles of these, you know, things that the dead person didn't have when he was alive, and then when they cremate the body they add all these paper possessions to the fire. The idea is that the person will have all these things when he gets to his next life."

Someone starts a tractor outside. I am amazed that the orchard is still business as usual with all that has happened. "Why are you telling me this?" I ask.

"Because I can't tell your mother."

I wonder if he expects me to tell her, then. I wonder if I can remember the way he told it. The exact words would mean so much to her.

Sam stands abruptly and the imbalance knocks me off the milk can. He looks down at me on the floor but makes no effort to pick me up. He hands me the flannel shirt—Hadley's—that I have let him hold for a few minutes. "I loved him too. He was my best friend," Sam says. "Oh, God. I'm sorry."

At the mention of this, I begin to cry.

Uncle Joley's face appears in the square of the cellar window. He raps on the glass with such force I think the pane will shatter. I wipe my nose on Hadley's beautiful blue shirt.

Uncle Joley has been outside with my parents. He must have been the one to talk my mother into going back to California. No one else here has that much power over her, except maybe Sam, and he wouldn't tell her to go.

Sam picks me up in his arms. I am exhausted. I lean my head

in the crook of his shoulder and try to clear my mind. Outside is too bright. I shade my eyes, partly because of this and partly because everyone who works at the orchard has come from the fields to see the spectacle, to see me.

My father is the only one who is smiling. He touches my hair and opens the door of the shiny Lincoln Town Car. He is careful not to get too close to Sam; after all, he is not a stupid man. I look at my father briefly. "Hey, kiddo," he says under his breath. I feel nothing.

Sam stretches me on the back seat on top of old horsehair blankets I recognize from the barn. These remind me of Hadley. He looked nothing like Sam—Hadley had choppy fair hair and pale brown eyes like the wet sands in Carolina. His lip dipped down a little too far in the middle. "These are yours now," Sam says. He puts a hand to my forehead. "No fever," he adds, real matter-of-fact. Then he puts his lips to my forehead like I know he's seen my mother do. He pretends it is to check my temperature.

When he closes the car door he cuts off the sound from outside. All I hear is my own breathing, still rasping. I crane my neck so that I can watch out the window.

It is like a beautiful mime. Sam and my father stand at opposite sides of the stage. There is a backdrop of willow trees and a green John Deere tractor. My mother holds both of Uncle Joley's hands. She is crying. Uncle Joley lifts her chin with his finger and then she puts her arms around his neck. My mother tries to smile, she really tries. Then Uncle Joley points somewhere I can't see and claps my father on the back. He propels my father out of my range of vision. My father turns his head. He tries to catch a glimpse of my mother, whom he has left behind.

Sam and my mother stand inches apart. They do not touch each other. I get the feeling that if they did, a blue spark would appear. Sam says something, and my mother looks towards the car. Even from this distance, in her eyes I can see myself.

I turn away to give them privacy. Then Uncle Joley is at the window, rapping for me to roll it down. He reaches halfway into the back seat with his lanky arms and pulls me forward by the collar of my shirt. "You take care of her," he says.

When he says that, I start to see how lost I am. "I don't know what to do," I tell him. And I don't. I don't know the first thing about holding together a family, especially one that resembles an heirloom vase, shattered but glued back together for its beauty, and no one mentions that you can see the cracks as plain as day.

"You know more than you think you do," Uncle Joley says. "Why else would Hadley have fallen for a kid?" He smiles, and I know he is teasing. Still, he has admitted that Hadley did fall, that I did fall. Because of this simple thing I sink back against the seat. Now I am certain that I will finally sleep through a night.

When the front doors open it sounds like the metal seal breaking on a new can of tennis balls. My mother and father slide into their seats simultaneously. On my father's side of the car, Uncle Joley is giving directions. "Just take one-seventeen all the way down," he says. "You'll hit a highway."

Any highway, I think. They all take you to the same place, don't they?

Sam stands across from my mother's open window. His eyes have paled clear and blue, which gives the illusion that he has spaces in his head through which the sky shows. It is an eerie thing to see, but it holds my mother.

My father starts the car and adjusts his headrest. "We're in for a long ride," he says. He is as casual as I've ever heard him be. He is trying but it is too late. As he eases the car forward, dust foams at the wheels. My mother and Sam are still staring at each other. "I think we're going to be just fine," he says. He reaches behind his seat to pat my foot.

As my father pulls down the driveway my mother's head turns to watch Sam's eyes.

"You two have really been on some trip," my father says. "You had me all over the place." He keeps up his monologue but I lose track of the words. My mother, who has turned halfway around in her seat, closes her eyes.

I am reminded of a time that I watched Hadley bud grafting. He took a bud from a flowering apple tree and grafted it to the branch of an old tree that hadn't been bearing fruit. With a sharp knife, he made a T-shaped cut in the bark of the old tree. He said it was very important to cut only the bark, not the wood of the tree. Then like a whittler, he pried away the folds of bark. He had the branch from the younger tree in a plastic baggie. He sliced off a middle-section bud, taking a little piece of the meat of the branch. To my surprise there was a leaf inside—I never really gave much thought to where the leaves were before they actually came out. Hadley cut off the leaf and gave it to me and then pushed the bud under the bark flaps of the old tree. He wrapped it tight with a greenish tape the way you might wrap a sprained ankle.

I asked him when this would start to grow, and he told me in about two weeks they'd know if the bud had taken. If it did, the stub of the leaf stem would be green. If it didn't, both the bud and the leaf would have dried up. Even if the graft took, the bud wouldn't branch until next spring. He told me that the great thing about grafting like this was that an old tree, a dead tree, could be made into something new. Whatever strain of apple was grafted would grow on that particular branch. So in theory you could have four or five different apple varieties coming off of one tree, all different from the original fruit the tree used to bear.

I pull away a blanket from the floor of the back seat. Underneath someone—Sam?—has put bushels of apples: Cortlands and Jonathans and Bellflowers and Macouns and Bottle Greenings. I am amazed that I can pick all these out by sight. Intuition tells me there are more in the trunk, and cider. All of these things to take with us to California.

I reach for a Cortland and take a large, loud bite. I interrupt my father, who is still talking. "Oh," he says, "you took some with you, did you?" He has been saying something about the air quality in Massachusetts versus in L.A. He continues to talk, but neither my mother nor I listen. She is hungrily watching me with this apple.

I stretch out the other half to her. She smiles. She takes a bite even bigger than mine. Juice runs down the side of her mouth but she makes no effort to wipe it away. She finishes the apple down to its core. Then she unrolls the window and tosses it onto the road. She leans her head out the window. Her hair blows into her face, hiding parts of it and illuminating others.

A motorcycle swerves on the other side of the road. It comes close enough to alarm my father and to break my concentration. The Doppler effect, I think, listening to the engine scream lower and lower as it disappears. But it doesn't really disappear. It just leaves my field of vision, temporarily.

My mother catches my eye: Be strong for me. Be strong for me. This silent chant fills the car. There is something to be said for the fact that my father cannot hear a thing. My mother's thoughts come in waves, pulling me towards her like a tide: I love you. I love you.

7 SAM

You are not going to believe this, but when I was a kid my father had this old radio upstairs in the barn that didn't work, and I always figured if we ever got it going we'd hear all those old radio things: Amos and Andy, Pepsodent commercials, fireside chats. I imagined the voices would crackle like lousy phone connections, swallowing their own syllables. I used to bug my father daily to twist a green wire around a yellow one, or to poke at the huge pitted speaker, but he'd tell me to do whatever else I was supposed to be doing and that was the end of that.

My dad was almost fifty when I was born, and this radio was a thing from his heyday, I don't know, but he wouldn't let me touch it. It looked just like you are picturing it: large, wooden carved, slick shiny mahogany inlaid with brass, a speaker bigger than my face, a dial that was cracked by a fall. My father, knotted, patient, would follow me up to the hayloft to the ledge where the radio sat, impressive as a contemporary jukebox. I begged him to tinker with it, to make it run as he had the tractor and the hand-pump (he was like that), I begged because I wanted to hear his story.

My father had told me time and time again he had no patience for electric things, as he called them. He told me to put my time to better use. But this radio, it had mystery. What it was doing in a hayloft, I don't know.

When I was fourteen I took a book on electronics out of the library and began to fidget with all the black and red snaked wires I could find in my house. I became fascinated with tangles. I took apart my alarm clock and put it back together. I took apart the telephone and put it back together. I even dismantled the conveyor belt we used to sort the apples for market. I began to wonder about the insides of other things. I did all this without attracting the attention of my father. Then I removed the back panel of the radio one Sunday and, scared of going further, left it right next to the radio for the next day.

But that was the night that the apples began to rot. It was the strangest thing. We had a hundred acres, and this disease, it was a plague, really, spread from east to west, slowly, hitting about twenty acres overnight, our best trees. We spent the next day spraying and pruning and trying all the other tricks in the book. The second night, the Macouns began to fall from the trees. My father took up smoking, which he'd quit. He checked the balance in the savings account. In the middle of the night I sneaked up to the hayloft. I lay in the piles of dry grass and timothy, imagining the Big Band swing sounds, the sweet Andrews Sisters, filling the arched roof and settling over the pickled beams. Then I screwed the back plate onto the radio.

Don't expect miracles, we lost half our crop that year. It had nothing to do with the damn radio; it was a parasite whose scientific name I have forgotten. At fourteen, what did I know? Little white things, like potato bugs, only more deadly. When my parents moved to Florida six years ago I had the radio fixed. I was twenty, I still expected to hear Herb Alpert, and I got Madonna. I laughed when I heard her, garbled, like an old gramophone.

It had nothing to do with the apples, did I say that already?

8 Oliver

(From an article Oliver sits down to write for the Journal of Mammology:)

I hope they never come back.

Detailed analysis of humpback whale songs from the low- to mid-latitude waters of the eastern North Pacific (Payne *et al.*, 1983) and the western North Atlantic have shown that the songs change rapidly and progressively over time, obeying unwritten laws of change.

Previously, humpback whales were thought to sing only during the winter months, when they occupy low-latitude wintering grounds, and during migration to and from these grounds (Thompson *et al.*, 1979, and others). Our observations between June and August in the high-latitude feeding area of Stellwagen Bank seemed to confirm these reports. In approximately 14h of recording during the mid-season, we heard only unpatterned sounds and no songs.

She must be coming back, or she wouldn't have taken Rebecca. But you won't find Oliver Jones apologizing. She's the one at fault here. She's the one who is to blame. I still have her mark on my face.

Until recently the only complete humpback whale songs recorded on high-latitude feeding grounds in any season were those reported by McSweeney *et al.* (1983) from two recordings made in southeast Alaskan waters in late August and early September. These recordings, which were the result of listening for 155 days during five summers, showed abbreviated versions of the wintering ground song of humpback whales from the eastern North Pacific, and contained the same material sung in the same order as the Hawaiian songs from the surrounding winter seasons.

I don't know what has gotten into her lately. She isn't acting like she usually does. Lately she has been there when I least expect her, demanding, anticipating things I cannot give. She should know what this all means to a scientist—the hunt, the track, the thrill of it. And now. She struck me—hard.

The strange thing: her face, after she hit me. She was in greater pain than I. You could see it in her eyes—like she had been violated in some way that broke her own image.

We report here the first recordings of complete humpback whale songs on the high-latitude feeding grounds in the North Atlantic, along with evidence to suggest that a) whales apparently start singing before migration and b) singing on the high-latitude feeding grounds is common in autumn. Our observations and recordings were made near Stellwagen Bank, Massachusetts, an elongate region of shallows lying north of Cape Cod in the southern Gulf of Maine. Each year this area is occupied by a seasonally returning population of humpback whales (Mayo, 1982,3) that feeds in the region (Hain *et al.*, 1981).

The last time it was autumn. It was late September when she left and took the child. After the crash, when I saw her at the hospital, she looked broken, that's the turn of phrase, like tempered glass that has been splintered. Who would have believed it: happening again. But this husband kept his promise. Oliver Jones did not hit her. She gave herself reason to leave. What was it—run it back through your mind like a cassette, get to the point where the outbreak occurred: the sting, my laughter. Then come the words, the affirmation of the past she tries to run from: like father like daughter like father like daughter.

We described song structure using established terminology: briefly, humpback whale songs are composed of a sequence of discrete themes that are repeated in a predicable order; each sequence of themes is considered a song; and all songs sung by a single whale without a break longer than one minute make up a song session (Jones, 1970).

I know her past and it has remained largely unspoken, but the truth is the truth. Like father, like daughter—I surprise myself—it sounds malicious. For every action there is an equal and opposite reaction. She strikes me, I strike her. Is it possible one can physically move a person with one's words?

Preliminary analysis of the recordings from the three days in autumn of 1988 shows that all three contain complete humpback whale songs. Comparisons with songs from March, the end of the winter season, show that the November songs closely resemble the song from the end of the winter season before, which agrees with the hypothesis (Jones, 1983) that songs change primarily when they are being sung and not during the quiet summer.

Picture this: Oliver Jones, sitting on the steps in his sumptuous San Diego home, trying to write an article for a professional journal and being distracted by headlights that pass by. Oliver Jones, deserted by his family for reasons he cannot comprehend. Oliver Jones, defending himself from a crazed wife with the power of language. With a single sentence fragment. Oliver Jones. Scientist. Researcher. Betrayer. What a life she has had. Is there any one thing Jane could say to me that could compel me to leave?

Because we have considerable data about many of the seasonally resident individuals in the Gulf of Maine study area and a collection of humpback whale songs from the western North Atlantic wintering grounds dating back to 1952, these studies should help illuminate the function of the high-latitude feeding ground songs and their relationship to those on the wintering grounds. With further study we hope to determine how much singing occurs on the feeding grounds, who the singers are, and in what context they sing.

This time she must come home. She must so that I can tell her that I know why she left. That it is possible I was the one at fault. And if she does not come home I will go and find her. Tracking is what this scientist built his name upon.

9 JANE

Instead of fighting when we were growing up, Joley and I went through a ritual of saving each other. I was the one who lied for him when he first ran away from home and surfaced again in Alaska, working for an oil rigger. I was the one who bailed him out of jail in Santa Fe, when he had assaulted a traffic cop. When research in college convinced him the Holy Grail was buried in Mexico, I drove him to Guadalajara. I talked him out of swimming the English Channel; I answered all his calls, his letters. During all the time Joley tried to find a corner of this world in which he felt comfortable, I was the one who kept track of him.

And in return, he has been my biggest fan. He believed in me with such faith that at times I began to believe in myself too.

Rebecca is inside the 7-Eleven, getting something to eat. I told her to be sparing, because the bottom line is, we don't have a lot of cash, and there's only so far we can go on Oliver's credit cards before he cancels them. The operator makes a collect call to Stow, Massachusetts, which is accepted by someone named Hadley. The man who has answered has a voice as smooth as syrup. "Jane," he says. "Joley's mentioned you before."

"Oh," I say, unsure how to respond. "Good."

He goes out to find Joley, who is in the field. I hold the receiver away from my ear and count the holes in the mouthpiece.

"Jane!" This welcome, this big hello. I pull the receiver close.

"Hi, Joley," I say, and there is absolute silence. I panic, and press the buttons—numbers one and nine and six—wondering if I have been disconnected.

"Tell me what's the matter," my brother says, and if it had been anyone else but Joley I would have asked him how he knew.

"It's Oliver," I begin, and then I shake my head. "No, it's me. I left Oliver. I took Rebecca and I left and I'm in a 7-Eleven in La Jolla and I haven't the first idea what to do or where to go."

Three thousand miles away, Joley sighs. "Why did you leave?"

I try to think of a joke, or a witty way to say it. It's already a punch line, I think, and in spite of myself I smile. "Joley, I hit him. I hit Oliver."

"You hit Oliver—"

"Yes!" I whisper, trying to quiet him, as if the entire nation between us can hear.

Joley laughs. "He probably deserved it."

"That's not the point." I see Rebecca come up to the counter inside the 7-Eleven, carrying Yodels.

"So who are you running from?"

My hands start to shake, so I tuck the phone into the crook of my neck. I don't say anything, and I hope that he will fill in the answer for me.

"I need to see you," Joley says, serious. "I need to see you to help you. Can you get to Massachusetts?"

"I don't think so." I mean it. Joley has traveled the whole world, its caverns, rolling oceans, and its boundaries, but I have never been far from suburbia on the East or the West Coast. I have lived in two pockets disconnected from a whole. I have no idea where Wyoming is, or Iowa, or if it takes days or weeks to travel across the country. I haven't the slightest sense of direction when it comes to things like this.

"Listen to me. Take Highway Eight east to Gila Bend, Arizona. Rebecca can help you, she's a quick kid. In the morning, go to the post office in town and ask for a letter in your name. I'll write and tell you where to go next, and I won't give you more than one step at a time, and Jane?"

"Yes?"

"I just wanted to make sure you were listening. It's all right," he says, and his voice caresses. "I'm here, and I'm going to write you cross-country."

Rebecca comes outside to the phone booth and offers me a Yodel. "I don't know, Joley. I don't have faith in the U.S. Postal Service."

"Have I ever let you down?"

No, and because he hasn't, I start to cry. "Talk to me," I say.

So my brother begins to talk, endless and lovely and interconnected. "Rebecca will love it here. It's an orchard, a hundred acres. And Sam won't mind that you're coming—he owns the place—awfully young for a controlling farmer but his parents have retired to Florida. I've learned a lot from Sam." I motion to Rebecca to come closer, and when she does I hold the phone between us so that she can hear. "We grow Prairie Spys, Cortlands, Imperials, Lobos, McIntosh, Regents, Delicious, Empire, Northern Spy, Prima, Priscillas,

Yellow Delicious, Winesaps. At night when you go to bed, you hear the bleating of sheep. In the morning when you lean out your window, you smell cider and sweet grass."

Rebecca closes her eyes and leans against the gum-studded phone booth. "It sounds terrific," I say, and to my surprise, my voice is no longer quivering. "I can't wait to see you."

"Take your time. I'm not going to chart your course by the fastest highways. I'm going to send you to places I think you need to go."

"What if—"

"Oliver won't find you. *Trust me.*"

I listen to Joley's breathing on the other end of the line. The atmosphere changes in La Jolla. The salt in the air turns molecular; the wind reverses its course. Two boys in the back seat of a Jeep sniff at the night sky like bloodhounds.

"I know you're scared," Joley says. He understands. And with that admission, I feel myself slip, limp, into the careful hands of my brother.

"So when we get to Gila Bend," Rebecca says, "Uncle Joley is going to meet us?" She is trying to work out the particulars; she is that kind of girl. Every fifty miles or so, when she can't get anything but static on the AM radio, she asks me another logistical question.

"No, he's going to send us a letter. I guess we're going to see the sights on the way to Massachusetts."

Rebecca slips her feet out of her sneakers and presses her toes against the front window. Frost halos form around her pinkies. "That doesn't make any sense. Daddy will find us by then."

"Daddy will look for the shortest distance between two points, don't you think? He wouldn't head for Gila Bend, he'd head for Vegas." I am impressed with myself—Vegas was a shot in the dark for me, but from Rebecca's face I can tell I have given a more direct location.

"What if there's no letter? What if this takes us forever?" She scrunches down in the seat so that her neck folds into several chins. "What if they find us, weeks from now, dying of dysentery or lice or heartworm in the back seat of a Chevy wagon?"

"Humans don't get heartworm. I don't think."

I catch Rebecca staring at my wrists, which rest against the large steering wheel. They have flowered into bruises, saffron and violet, like big bangle bracelets that cannot be removed. "Well," I say quietly, "you should see what his cheek looks like."

She slides across the seat and cranes her neck to see the driver's perspective. "I hope I never have to." She is beautiful at almost-fifteen. Rebecca has straw-straight yellow hair that springs to the crest of her shoulders; her summer skin is the color of hazelnuts. And her eyes are the strangest combination of Oliver's blue and my grey—they are a violent sort of green, like the hue of a computer screen, transparent, alarming. She is in this for the adventure. She hasn't considered what it means to leave your father behind, for a little while or forever. What she sees is the drama—the explosion, the slamming doors, the once-in-a-lifetime opportunity to live out the plot of a young-adult novel. I cannot say I blame her, and I cannot condone bringing her along. But leaving her behind was not a viable alternative.

I'm crazy about her. Since day one, she has depended on me, and, remarkably, I have yet to let her down.

"Mom," Rebecca says, annoyed. "Earth to Mom."

I smile at her. "Sorry."

"Can we pull over?" She looks at her watch, a leather and gold Concord, a gift from Oliver several Christmases ago. "It's only nine-thirty, and we'll be there by midnight, and I really need to pee."

I don't know how Rebecca has figured on midnight, but she's been calculating with a ruler and a little road map she found wedged in the back seat. Geography, Mom, she told me. We all have to take it in Social Studies.

We pull aside when the road develops a shoulder and lock up the car. I go with Rebecca into the woods to go to the bathroom—I'm not about to let her out on the side of the road in the middle of night. We hold hands and try not to step on poison ivy. "Nice out," Rebecca says, as she is peeing. I'm holding her forearms for balance. "Isn't it warmer than usual?"

"I forget you're a California girl. I have no idea if it's warmer than usual. Usual on the East Coast is fifty-five degrees at night."

"What am I going to use?" Rebecca says, and I look at her blankly. "Toilet paper?"

"I don't know." She reaches for leaves on the ground and I grab her wrist. "No! You don't know what that stuff is; it could be sumac, or God knows what, and that's the last thing you need: not to be able to sit on a driving trip cross-country."

"So what do I do?"

I will not leave her alone. "Sing," I tell her.

"What?"

"Sing. You sing and I'll run up to the car for a tissue and if I hear you stop singing I know you're in trouble."

"That's stupid," Rebecca says. "This is Arizona, not L.A. No one's out here."

"All the more reason." Rebecca stares at me, incredulous, and then begins to sing a rap song. "No," I tell her, "sing something I know, something where I know the order so I won't get confused."

"I don't believe this. What's in your repertoire, Mom?" She loses her balance for a moment, and stumbles, cursing.

I think for a moment, but there is little we have in common in the realm of music. "Try the Beach Boys," I suggest, figuring that after fifteen years in California something has to stick.

"Well, the East Coast girls are hip," Rebecca warbles, "I really dig those clothes they wear . . ."

"That's great," I say, "and the northern girls?"

"With the way they kiss . . ."

I sing with her, walking backward as far as I can, calling on her to raise the volume of her voice as I get farther and farther away. When she forgets the words, she sings syllables, da-da-da. When I can see the car I break into a run, and find a tissue that I'd used to blot lipstick, and bring it back to Rebecca.

"I wish they all could be California girls," she says, as I run up to her. "You see? No one came near me."

"Better safe than sorry."

We lie down on the hood of the Chevy, our backs on the slope of the windshield. I try to listen for the bends of the Colorado

River, which we passed several miles back. Rebecca tells me she is going to try to count the stars.

We pass the last Yodel between us like a joint, taking smaller and smaller bites at the end so that neither one of us will be accused of finishing it. We argue about whether or not a helicopter's lights are a shooting star (no) and if Cassiopeia is out at this time of year (yes). When the cars are not passing us, it is almost quiet, save for the hum of the vibrating highway.

"I wonder what it is like here during the day," I say aloud.

"Probably a lot like it is now. Dusty, red. Hotter." Rebecca takes the Yodel out of my fingers. "You want it?" She pops it into her mouth and squashes it against her front teeth with her tongue. "I know, disgusting. You think it gets really hot here, hot like in L.A., where the roads breathe when you step on them?"

Together we stare at the sky, as if we are waiting for something to happen.

"You know," Rebecca says, "I think you're taking all this really well."

I lean up on one elbow. "You think?"

"Yeah. Really. I mean, you could be falling apart, you know? You could be the type who doesn't stop crying, or who won't drive on highways."

"Well I can't be," I say, honestly, "I have to take care of you."

"Take care of *me?* I can take care of myself."

"That's what I'm afraid of," I say, laughing, and I'm only half joking. It is easy to see that in two or three years this daughter of mine will be a knockout. This year in school she read *Romeo and Juliet,* and she told me pragmatically that Romeo was a wimp. He should have just taken Juliet and run away with her, swallowed his pride and worked at some medieval McDonald's. What about the poetry, I asked her. What about the tragedy? And Rebecca told me that that's all very well and good but it isn't the way things happen in real life.

"Please," Rebecca says, "you're getting that weepy cow look again."

I would like to lie here for days with my daughter, watching her grow up in front of me, but since I am running away from my own problems I don't have that luxury. "Come on," I say, nudging her off the hood of the car. "You can hang your head out the window while we drive and finish counting."

By the time we reach the signs for Gila Bend the soil turns brick red, veined with night shadows of cacti. The sides of the road level around us so that it seems we should be able to see the town and yet there is nothing but dust. Rebecca twists around in her seat to double-check that we have read the green sign correctly. "So where is this place?"

We travel several miles without seeing traces of a civilized town. Finally I pull to the side of the road and turn off the ignition. "We could always sleep in the car," I tell Rebecca. "It's warm enough."

"No chance! There are coyotes and things here."

"This coming from the girl who was willing to go to the bathroom with all the lunatics hiding in the woods?"

"May I help you?"

The sound startles us; for three and a half hours we have heard only the patterns of each other's voices. Standing beside Rebecca's window is a woman with a tattered grey braid hanging down her back. "Car trouble?"

"I'm sorry. If this is your property, we can move the car."

"Why bother," the woman says, "no one else has." She tells us that we have come to the Indian Reservation in Gila Bend, the smaller one, and points out furry lavender shapes in the distance that indeed are houses. "There's a larger reservation about six miles east, but the tourist traps are here." Her name is Hilda, and she invites us to her apartment.

She lives in a two-story brick building that smells like a dormitory—federally subsidized housing, she explains. She has left all the lights on, and it is only when we are inside that I realize she has been carrying a paper bag. I expect her to pull out gin, whiskey—I have heard stories—but she takes out a carton of milk and offers to make Rebecca an egg cream.

On the walls are woven mats in all the colors of the southwestern rainbow, and charcoal drawings of bulls and canyons. "What do you think of her," I ask Rebecca, when Hilda is in the makeshift bathroom/kitchen.

"Honest?" Rebecca says, and I nod. "Well, I can't believe you're here. Have you lost your mind? It's midnight, and some person you've never seen in your life comes up to the car, and says, Hey, come to my place, and she's an *Indian* to boot, and you just pick up your things and go. Whatever happened to never taking candy from strangers?"

"Egg creams," I say. "She hasn't offered us candy."

"Jesus."

Hilda comes out with a wicker tray that carries three foamy glasses and ripe plums. She holds one up and tells us they are grown locally by her step-brother. I thank her, sipping at my egg cream. "So tell me how you came to be on Dog Forked Road at midnight."

"Is that what we were on?" I turn to Rebecca. "I thought it was Route Eight."

"We turned *off* Route Eight," Rebecca says. She turns to Hilda. "It's a long story."

"I have all the time in the world. I'm an insomniac. That's what I was doing on Dog Forked Road at midnight. Milk's the only thing to soothe my heartburn."

I nod sympathetically. "We've come from California. I guess you could say we've run away from home." I try to laugh, to make light of the situation, but I can see this woman whom I hardly know staring at the bruises on my wrists.

"I see," she says.

Rebecca asks if there is some place she can lie down, and Hilda excuses herself to fix up a fold-out couch in the other room. She collects pillows from one closet and sheets colored with Peanuts characters from the kitchen pantry. "Get some sleep, Mom," Rebecca says, sitting beside me on the loveseat. "I worry about you." Hilda ushers her into the bedroom, and from my angle I can see Rebecca slip in between the sheets, sighing the way you do when you run your ankles along all the cool spots. Hilda stands in the doorway until my daughter falls asleep, and then she steps back and presents me with Rebecca's face, in profile, lit silver and traced with the grace of the moon.

10 Joley

Dear Jane—

Do you remember when I was four and you were eight, when Mama and Daddy took us to the circus? Daddy bought us small flashlights with red tips that we could swing around and around when the clowns came out, and peanuts—so many! the shells we stuffed in our pockets. We saw a lady stick her head inside the jaws of a tiger; and a man dive into a small bucket from a place way up in the air that I thought must be Heaven. We saw brown-skinned midgets flipping over each other, catapulted by ordinary seesaws like the one in our backyard, and Mama said, Now don't you two do this at home. And Mama held Daddy's hand when the acrobats did their most difficult trick, swinging on a silver trapeze and locking in midair like mating falcons for just a moment, before they grabbed another trapeze and went separate ways. I missed the trick because I was so busy looking at Mama's hand; the way her fingers twisted between Daddy's as if they had a right to be there; her diamond engagement ring holding all the colors I had ever seen.

Then there was a kind of intermission, do they call it that at a circus? And a man in a green coat began to mill through our seating section, peering into the faces of the children. And suddenly a woman was standing in front of me, calling TOM! TOM! and pointing. She bent down and told Mama I was the most adorable little boy she'd ever seen, ever. And Mama said that's why she named me Joley, after joli*—French for "pretty"—as if Mama fancied herself to be French. And then the man in the green coat came over and squatted down. He said, Boy, would you like to ride on an elephant? Mama said that you were my sister and that one couldn't go without the other, and they gave you a quick once-over and said, Well, all right, if that's that, but the boy sits up front. They took us backstage (there's another word—is there a backstage at the circus?), and we crunched peanut shells with the toes of our* *shoes until a lady wearing sequins all over her body picked us up one by one and told us to straddle the elephant.*

Sheba (that was the name of the elephant) moved in sections, in quarters. Her right front hunched forward, then her right rear. Left front, left rear. Her skin felt like soft cardboard and the hair sticking through her saddle itched my legs. Then we entered the ring, me sitting in front of you. Flash cubes popped and a thundering announcer, a man I thought was God, told everyone our names and ages. I saw washes of color spinning by in the audience. I tried to find Mama and Daddy. You held me tight around the ribs. You said, I don't want you to fall off.

If you are reading this you've made it to Gila Bend and I'm sure you've gotten yourself a good meal and a decent night's rest. When you leave the P.O. you'll see an apothecary on your right. The owner of the store is named Joe. Ask him how to get to Route 17. You're heading towards the Grand Canyon. It's something you ought to see. Tell Joe I sent you, and he'll set you straight.

It's an eight-hour drive. Same thing: Find a place to stay and go to the P.O. in the morning—the one closest to the northernmost point of the canyon. There'll be a letter waiting to take you somewhere else.

About the circus: They took pictures of us riding that elephant, but you never knew. One where most of your face was hidden became the poster for Ringling Bros. the next year. It came in the mail when you were at school; I had been let out early from kindergarten. Mama showed me and wanted to hang it up on the wall of my bedroom. My pretty boy, *she called me. I wouldn't let her hang it up. I couldn't stand seeing your hands around my waist but your face lost in the shadows. In the end she threw it out, or she said she did. She sat me down and said that I had been given my looks by God and that I'd have to get used to it. I told her, flat out, that I didn't understand. They made me ride up front because of how I look, I told her. But don't they know Jane is the beautiful one?*

Love to you and Rebecca.
Joley

11 Rebecca *July 29, 1990*

A clamshell of color snaps open and shut several inches from my face flashes lights and the sounds of animals that are dying what has happened I ask you what has happened? sometimes it comes to me times like this when the world has turned black and white sometimes it comes and it will not leave it does not leave no matter how many times I scream or I pray.

I saw people ripped in two flesh split like broken dolls in what used to be an aisle outside the sky had shattered and the world which I had always imagined as soft cotton blue was angry and stained with pain.

Do you see I had witnessed the end of the world I saw heaven and earth trade places I knew where devils came from I was so young at three and a half with the weight of my life on my brow I knew for sure my head would burst.

At the end of it all row nine sailed inches away like a glider in the night and over its rotten edge I watched the fireworks diamond glass explosions and in spite of myself I started to cry.

There is a sound that the mute make when they are murdered I learned this years later on the evening news their vocal cords cannot vibrate so what the listener hears instead is the air quivering pushing in pushing out a wall of silence this is the voice of terror in a vacuum.

For days I have felt a leopard crouching on my chest. I breathe in the stale air it exhales. It scratches at the inside of my chin and it kisses my neck. When it shifts its weight, my own ribs move.

"She's coming to," I hear, the first words in a long time.

I open my eyes and see in this order: my mother, my father, and the tiny attic room of the Big House. I squeeze my eyes shut. Something isn't right: I have been expecting the house in San Diego. I have forgotten entirely about Massachusetts.

I try to sit up but the leopard screams and claws at me.

"What's the matter with her?" my father is saying. "Help her, Jane. What's the matter." My mother presses cold towels against my forehead but does not notice this monster at all.

"Can't you see it," I say, but it comes out a whisper. I am drowning in fluid. I cough and phlegm comes up, and keeps coming. My father holds tissues into my palm. My mother is crying. Neither one of them understands that if the leopard will just move, I will be fine.

"We're going to go home," my father says. "We're getting out of here."

He is wearing the wrong clothes, the wrong face to be on this farm. I search my mother's face for an answer to this. "Let me be with her a minute, Oliver."

"We need to work this out together," my father says.

My mother puts her hand on his shoulder. It looks cool, like a ladyslipper or a corner of the hayloft. "Please."

The hayloft. "Tell me this," I say. I try to sit up. "Hadley is dead."

My mother and father look at each other and without a word my father leaves the room. "Yes," my mother says. Her eyes spill over with tears. "I'm so sorry, Rebecca." She reaches across the heart-sewn quilt. She buries her face in the cave of my stomach, in the breast fur of this leopard. "I am so sorry." The animal stands and stretches and vanishes.

To my surprise I do not cry. "Tell me everything you know."

My mother sits up, shocked at my bravery. She says that Hadley broke his neck in the fall. The doctors said he died instantaneously. It has been three days, but it took this long to raise his body from the gorge.

"What have I been doing for three days?" I whisper. I am embarrassed that I do not know the answer.

"You have pneumonia. You've been sleeping most of the time. You were gone when your father first arrived here—you'd run off after Hadley. He insisted on going with Sam to find you—" She looks away. "He didn't like the idea of Sam staying here with me."

So he knows, I think. How interesting. "What does he mean, 'We're going home'?"

My mother holds her hand to my head. "Back to California. What did you think?"

I am missing something. "What have we been doing here?"

"You don't have to hear this now. You need to rest."

I pull the quilt away from myself and gag. All over my legs are bruises and scrapes and yellowed gauze wrappings. My bare chest is crossed with raked furrows of dried blood. "When Hadley fell, you tried to climb down after him," my mother says. "Sam pulled you away, and you started to scratch at yourself. You wouldn't stop, no matter how many things they wrapped around you, or how much sedation you'd been given." She starts to cry again. "You kept saying you were trying to tear your heart out."

"I don't know why I bothered," I whisper. "You'd already done that."

She walks to the other side of the room, as far away as she can possibly get. "What do you want me to say, Rebecca? What do you want me to say?"

I don't know. She can't change what has been done. I begin to realize how things are different when you grow up. When I was little, she would sing to me when I was sick. She would bring me red Jell-O and sleep curled beside me to listen for changes in my breathing. She would pretend I was a princess locked in a tower by a wicked magician, and she acted as my lady-in-waiting. Together we would watch the door for my shining white knight.

"Why do you want me to forgive you?" I say. "What do you get out of it?" I turn away and Sam's sheep, all seven, scuttle down the path they've carved in the middle field.

"Why do I want you to forgive me? Because I never forgave my father, and I know what it will do to you. When I was growing up my father would hit me. He hit me and he hit my mother and I tried to keep him from hitting Joley. He broke my heart and eventually he broke me. I never believed I could be anything important—why else would my own father hurt me? And then I forgot about it. And I married Oliver and three years later he hit me. That's when I left the first time."

"The plane crash," I say, and she nods.

"I went back to him because of you. I knew that more than anything else I had to make sure you grew up feeling safe. And then I hit your father, and it all came back again." She buries her face in her hands. "It all came back again, and this time it was part of me. No matter how far I run, no matter how many states or countries I cross I can't get it out of myself. I never forgave him. He won. He's in me, Rebecca."

She picks up an antique marbled pitcher that has been in Sam's family for a long time. Without even really noticing, she lets it slip out of her grasp and shatter on the floor. "I came here and I was so happy, for a little while, I forgot again. I forgot about your father, and I forgot about you. I was so crazy in love—" she smiles, far away, "—that I didn't believe anyone else could feel the way I did. Including—*especially*—my own daughter. If you could fall in love with someone who was twenty-five, and it was all right, then it couldn't possibly be all right for me to fall in love with someone who was twenty-five. Can you see?"

I have seen my mother with Sam in the shadow of the orchard; they're joined at the mind. That is what has been different about these weeks: I have never seen her like this. I have never enjoyed being with her so much. I don't understand what my father is doing here or why he wants her back. The woman he wants isn't here. That woman doesn't exist anymore.

"But I've watched you with him," I say.

"If it was right, Rebecca," my mother says, "it would have happened years ago."

I don't have to ask her why she is going home, anymore. I already know the answer. My mother thinks she has failed: not just my father, but me. She can't have Sam; it's her punishment. In the real world, the best of circumstances don't always come to be. In the real world, "forever" may only be a weekend.

My mother looks at me. When our eyes connect there are more words that come in silence. What you cannot have, I cannot have. My life created yours, and because of this my life depends on yours. How strange, I think. I learned about love's Catch-22 before my own mother. *I* taught this lesson to *her.*

She smiles at me and she lifts the sheet of gauze from my chest. "Sometimes I can't believe you're only fifteen," she murmurs. She runs her fingers across my nipples and over my breasts. As my mother touches me the wounds begin to close on themselves. We watch in silence as split skin heals and bruises diffuse. Still, there will be scars.

When he comes into the room in the middle of the night I am expecting him. He is the only one who hasn't come to see me since I regained consciousness. First the door opens a crack, then I see the flashlight's head, and by the time Uncle Joley makes his way to the bed, I know where we are headed.

"If we drive now, we'll be there in plenty of time," he tells me, "and no one will have figured out where we've gone."

He carries me in his arms to an old blue pickup truck that didn't have an engine for several weeks. He jump starts it by rolling it in neutral down the hill of the driveway. He has provided me with a cape—orange with fuschia pom-poms, a throwback to the seventies. Sitting between us on the cracked leather seat is a thermos of black coffee and an oat-raisin muffin.

"I don't suppose you're feeling like yourself yet." When I shake my head he turns on the windshield wipers. He squirts washer fluid, which fires over the back of the truck. It trickles into the flatbed, spurting like a water gun. "So much for that," Joley says.

He is a handsome man in a faded kind of way. His hair curls at his ears, even after he's just had a haircut. The first thing you notice about his face is the space between his eyes—so narrow that it makes him look either mongoloid or very intelligent, depending on your frame of reference. And then there are his lips, which are full like a girl's and as pink as zinnias. If you take your favorite Mel Gibson poster, and fold it up and put it in the pocket of your jeans and then send them through the washer and dryer, the picture you'd wind up with would be kinder, less startling, and smooth at the edges. Uncle Joley.

The sun comes up as we cross the New Hampshire border. "I

don't remember much of this," I tell him. "I spent a good deal of the trip in the back of a truck."

"Let me guess," he says. "Refrigerated?"

He makes me smile. When my father and Sam found us, I was running a 104-degree fever.

Uncle Joley doesn't talk much. He knows it is not what I need. He asks every now and then if I will pour him a cup of coffee, and I do, holding it to his lips like he is the one who is sick.

We pass the brown road sign that delineates the White Mountain region. "It's beautiful here," I say, "isn't it?"

"Do you think it's beautiful?" my uncle asks. He catches me off guard.

I survey the peaks and the gulleys. In Southern California, the land is flat and offers no surprises. "Well, yes."

"Then it is," he says.

We drive on roads that I have never seen. I doubt they are even really roads. They snake through the woods and look more like two tracks left from winter skiers than a path for a car, but they do provide a short cut. The truck bounces back and forth, spilling the coffee and rolling the untouched muffin under the seat. We end up in Hadley's mother's backyard, which I can't help but recognize. We park the truck like a peace offering in the small space between the house and Mount Deception.

"I'm glad you could come," Mrs. Slegg says. She opens the screen door. "I heard what happened to you."

She puts her arms around me and helps me into her toasty kitchen. I am so ashamed. Her son is the one who has died, and here she is fussing over my scratches. "I'm sorry." I stumble over the words Joley has coached me to say. "I'm sorry for your loss."

Hadley's mother's eyes widen, as if she is shocked to hear any phrase like this at all. "Sugar, it was your loss too." She sits down on the ladderback chair beside mine. She covers my hand with her own puffy fingers. She is wearing a blue housecoat and a loud apron with an appliquéd raspberry. "I know just what the two of you need. Where have my wits been? You come all the way from Massachusetts and I'm sitting here like a tub of butter." She opens the breadbox and takes out fresh rolls and crullers and sesame cakes.

"Thanks, Mrs. Slegg, but I'm not very hungry yet."

"You call me Mother Slegg," she urges. "And no wonder, a little thing like you. You can probably barely stand alone in a wind, much less take this kind of pain standing tall."

Uncle Joley walks over to the window. He peers out at the mountain. "Where is the funeral going to be?"

"Not far from here. A cemetery where my husband is buried, God rest his soul. We have a family plot." She says it so casually that I start to watch her for signs: did she not love her own son? Is she a closet mourner, tearing at her hair when everyone leaves?

A boy comes into the kitchen. He takes the milk out of the refrigerator before acknowledging us. When he turns, he looks so much like Hadley I feel as if I have been punched. "You Rebecca?"

I nod, speechless. "You're—"

"Cal," he says. "I'm the younger one. Well, I was." He turns to his mother. "Should we go?" He is wearing a flannel shirt and jeans.

Cal, two of Hadley's friends from high school and Uncle Joley are asked to be the pallbearers at the cemetery. There is a preacher who gives a nice, respectable service. In the middle of it all a robin lands on the casket. It begins to peck at the ring of flowers. After ten seconds of watching this peacefully, Mrs. Slegg screams to the preacher to stop. She falls onto the ground and crawls towards the casket to grab the flowers. In the flurry of noise the bird flies away. Someone leads Hadley's mother away.

I do not cry throughout the entire ceremony. No matter where I turn I can see that mountain, waiting to claim Hadley again when he is part of the earth. *Here I will remain with worms that are thy chambermaids,* I find myself thinking, and for the life of me I cannot place the quote. It must be something I have learned in school but it is hard to believe. It seems so long ago, and I was such a different person.

The four men step forward and lower the leather straps that drop the casket slowly into the ground. I turn away. Up until this point I have pretended that Hadley is not in there at all; that this is just a token and he is waiting back at the Big House for me. But I see the struggle of muscles in Uncle Joley's back and the sinews in Cal's fingers. I am convinced that there is indeed something in the rough mustard box.

I cover my ears so that I do not hear him hit the bottom. The cape falls away from my chest and exposes what has happened to me. Nobody notices except for Mrs. Slegg. She is some distance away, and she only cries a little bit harder.

Before we leave the cemetery, Cal presents me with the shirt Hadley was wearing the night before he died. The one I wrapped around myself when my father and Sam came. It is blue flannel checked with black. He folds it into triangles, like a flag. Then he tucks in the corners and hands it to me. I do not thank him. I do not say goodbye to Hadley's grieving mother. Instead, I let my uncle escort me to the truck. In near silence, he drives me back, where everyone else is waiting for their world to end.

12 OLIVER

I head to the Institute as if nothing has happened at all. I do not go in every day, and I have no real reason for going today of all days, except for the fact that as I walk through the halls I hear reverential acknowledgments of my presence—"Dr. Jones, Dr. Jones"—and this is somehow life-affirming.

When I couldn't sleep last night, I took the videotapes of the last trip to Maui and played them over and over on the VCR in the bedroom. On these tapes the humpbacks rise majestically out of the water, arch in midair, and slip back into the ocean, opening holes that weren't there. Under the water you can see them, anticipate when they will break through the strained surface; their fins glistening and their flukes pulsing, and for that blessed moment before the magic ends, Jesus, they become pure beauty.

I had watched the tape several times before the sun came up, and when it did I inexplicably found myself wondering how many months it had been since Jane and I had made love, and I am disappointed to say I could not come up with a concrete number.

At the Institute, my office overlooks the San Diego Marina. There are three walls of glass, if you can imagine, and then one oak paneled door. It had been blond wood, but I decided to stain it to better see the grain of the wood, and Jane, who was up for a project at the time, insisted on doing it for me. She came into my office for an entire week, trying patches of stains on different pieces of the door molding: names like Colonial Cohasset and Mahogany Sheen and Natural, which seemed to me an irony. Finally she picked a shade called Golden Oak which was more brown than gold. I was at my desk the day she arrived with a squeegee and a disposable brush and a gallon of the stuff, although a quart would have done the job. She was very methodical, so much so that I was proud of her, working from the bottom to the top to avoid dripping, blotting the door after each coat. In truth she was quite lovely to watch. Then, when she finished, she stepped back from the door towards my desk. "What do you think—" she started to say, and then she covered her mouth. She ran to the door and began to scrape at the drying stain with the squeegee. I ran up and put my arms around her, trying to calm her down. "Don't you see it," she insisted, gesturing wildly. She pointed to several lines in the grain of the wood.

"It looks beautiful." Indeed the grain stood out.

"You don't see it," she cried. "There. It's plain as day now. The face of the devil."

Jane has not come to my office since then, since I refused to have the door stripped. I sort of like it. I close the door behind me, and twisting my head this way and that, I try to make out this face.

It is obvious that she is headed to her brother's, and that she is doing this via automobile or train—she can't get Rebecca to fly. Most likely she is not taking a train; it would be too easy for me to trace the tickets. I could second-guess her and take a plane to Boston, and be there by the time she arrives. But then again her godforsaken brother would already be there, and he would find some way to warn Jane. They have this telepathic connection that, although astounding, frustrates.

Second option: I can contact the police after a matter of time, and have an APB put out. After all, I did not do anything illegal that would make Jane leave, and I can bring her in on charges of kidnapping. Of course then I lose the freedom to act on my own.

Third option: I can go after her myself. Somewhat like trying to put a butterfly on a leash and take it for a walk, but I imagine if I got the knack of the route I could catch her.

I have never written a conclusion without collecting data to ground the hypothesis. And I have never been stumped scientifically. Perhaps you just go, and take inventory along the way. Perhaps you catch her and then decide what you are going to say.

"Shirley." I buzz my secretary, a tall woman with dyed red hair who I imagine has a crush on me.

She swings open the oak door. "Yes, Dr. Jones?"

"I have a problem that I'm afraid you are going to have to take care of." Her lips set in a straight line, ready for the responsibility. "In regards to the trip to Venezuela . . . I need you to cancel."

"The trip?"

I nod. "Do anything you have to do. Lie, cheat, anything. I need at least a month of personal time. Tell them that. Personal." I lean across my desk and I take her wrists *(her wrists)* in my hands. "I'm counting on you," I say softly. "Our secret." The Institute will eat the coast of this trip, and I'm afraid to say in the frenzy, poor Shirley will lose her job. I must remember to send her something when this is over.

She nods, a brave soldier. "Dr. Jones, will you be calling in for your messages?"

"Twice a day," I lie. I would rather wrap this mess up quickly and get entrenched in my research again than do a mediocre job, ten minutes here and ten minutes there. I will not call until I have found Jane.

When the secretary leaves, I switch off the overhead lights

and pull the blinds. I put on the Stellwagen tapes, the haunting, tortuous medley from the floor of the ocean. In the late 1970s, the *Voyager* spacecraft went into orbit carrying greetings in fifty-five languages, music from Bach, Mozart and a rock group, and these songs of the humpback whale.

The map of the United States I pull out of my drawer is faded but functional. It looks foreign; I am accustomed to the swirls and eddies of navigational charts. With a ruler and a red marker I draw a three-inch radius, and then expand that into a circle. This is as far as they could have gone last night. Phoenix, or Vegas, or Sacramento, or Guaylas, Mexico. My parameters.

If I can track whales, which I hardly know at all, then I can surely track my wife.

Except this requires thinking like Jane: sporadic, eclectic, impossible. With whales we have clues. We have currents, feeding grounds and sightings. We know the starting place of their journey and the end point. We work forward, connecting the incremental pieces that we find. It is not much different from navigation by sonar—the process used by whales, in which sound waves are bounced off of geological formations underwater to chart a clear course.

If Jane and Rebecca are headed to Massachusetts, they will not be going via Mexico or Sacramento. With a green highlighter I cross off those two cities. This leaves the circumference segment between Phoenix and Vegas. And they could truly be anywhere.

Resting my cheek against the cool marble of my desk, I give myself to the melody of the whale songs. There are no lyrics, no refrains. They are more like the chants of African tribes: the pattern, though regular, is foreign to our culture. Not chordal, not symphonic. Themes that you least expect recur, patterns you have heard twice already come through yet again. Sometimes the whales sing together, and sometimes, dramatically, they cry through the ink of the ocean, bemoaning alone.

I find myself humming along. To think like Jane. To think like Jane.

I prop my head up on my elbows. Whales don't have vocal cords. We don't know how it is that they make these sounds. It is not through the expulsion of air; there are no bubbles surrounding whales when they sing. And still there are these clicks, these whistles, these cello groans.

Jane's door faces me. Without warning, immersed in the sounds of the sea, I can clearly see her devil.

13 SAM

The apple, I tell them, came before Adam and Eve in the story of Creation. It had to have been there at least three years because that's how long it takes for a new tree to bear fruit, much less carnal knowledge.

That's the first line of the talk I give every year at my old alma mater, the voc-tech high school in Lexington. I'm a big draw at the school. I'm the head of one of the only profitable apple orchards left in Massachusetts, I have a staff of fifty, one hundred thriving acres, a good rapport with the buyers for Sudbury Farms and Purity Foodstores, and U-Pick-Em fields that attract the public on weekends from as far away as New York. I kind of fell into the position when my father retired after his heart surgery, but I leave that part out of my speech.

The kids seem to get younger every year, although I suppose you could make a case that I am getting older. This time, there aren't as many of them as there used to be because of the economy; they all want to go into steel production or microchip processing—farming doesn't pay. I watch them filter into the auditorium and they are still ninety-nine percent male, which I understand. It's not that I have anything against women's lib, but working at an orchard requires grit and muscle that few ladies have. My mother, maybe, but she was an exception.

I don't plan to talk about running an orchard, or profitability margins, or scabs or even textbook examples of management. I'll tell them what they are least expecting to hear, and I try to draw them into my life. The stories my father told me when I was growing up, when we would sit on the porch and all around us the scent of cider would make us dizzy;

these are the very things that bred pomology into my mind. I never made it past high school and I may not have the smarts of a high-style manager; I admit there are many things I do not understand, and I will not waste their time. Instead, I tell them what I know best.

In reality the apple mentioned in the Bible probably wasn't an apple. Apples didn't grow in Palestine, but the first translations of the Bible were done in some northern country, and the apple comes from England, so there you go. I have heard that there are shells fossilized in the peaks of the Rocky Mountains, left from a time when the water reached that high on the earth. Well, apples have been fossilized too. Archaeologists have found remains of apples, charred in the mud in prehistoric excavations sites near Switzerland. Imagine.

The apple spread west, and it spread fast. It grows from a seed. Toss an apple core into the ground and in a couple of years you'll have a sapling. When I was a kid, apple trees sprung up on the farms of my parents' friends, in just about every place where there wasn't something growing. The trees would fight against the cows that grazed on their leaves, and after a few years they'd get above the cows' necks and drop the fruit at their bases. Then the cows would cluster at the bottom and eat the sweet apples, inadvertently planting new seeds. In our own cow pasture we had a tree that grew apples as red as fire, that made pies almost as good as Macouns. Never did figure out that variety, or market it . . . if I had I probably would be a lot richer than I am today.

You can find apples in Norse mythology, Greek mythology and fairy tales. My father told me all the stories. There's Snow White's poisoned apple and Eve's fall from grace. In Scandinavia, a character called Iduna kept a box of apples that, when tasted by the gods, gave them new youth. As late as the 1800s in England, fertility salutes were dedicated to apple trees to ensure a bountiful harvest. And here in New England, when little girls peeled apples, they tossed a long curl over their shoulders to see what letter it would make when it fell—the initial of their future lover.

At this point I ask Hadley—who graduated from Minuteman Tech with me and has been working at the orchard since—to pass out the apples I've brought. When these kids taste for themselves what the work and patience of human hands can do, well, they understand a lot more than I could ever tell them. I open the floor up for questions, and then I have no problem giving information. Lectures I have trouble with. But questions are a different story. I have always found myself to be a much better listener than talker.

"Are you hiring?" kids ask. "Do you break even?" One industrious boy asks something about the merits of scion grafting versus bud grafting, the official names of which I didn't learn until about two years ago. But the question I will like best will come from the kid in the back, way in the last row, who hasn't said a word. I jump off the podium and walk down the aisle and lean over towards him, and he turns red. "What do you want to ask?" I say softly so no one else can hear. "I know there's something."

There is, it's in his eyes. "What is your favorite?" he asks, and I know what he means. Spitzenburgs, I say, but they've about died out now. So suppose I have to say Jonathans. It's the question I never got to ask when my own father gave this speech, when I was still a student.

Afterward, I send Hadley back with the truck. Me and Joellen, a math teacher at the school and my first girlfriend, go out on the town. There's a Chinese place we like; I don't get to eat too much of that in Stow. I order her a Mai Tai, which comes in a porcelain coconut with two pink umbrellas, and I get a Suffering Bastard myself. When Joellen gets a little drunk, she forgets that she hates me for some reason or another, and like last year we will probably wind up in the back seat of her Ford Escort, on top of textbooks and abacuses, clawing at each other and bringing back the past.

I do not love Joellen. I never have, I think, which may be the reason she thinks she hates me.

"So what you been up to, Sam?" she says, leaning across the Peking fried chicken wings. She is a year younger than me but she's looked thirty for as long as I can remember.

"Pruning, pretty much. Getting ready for the troops in the fall." In late September we open the orchard up to the public. Sometimes I can gross over a thousand dollars in one Sunday, between bushels of apples and fresh-pressed cider and retail-pricing wholesale Vermont cheddar cheese.

Joellen grew up in Concord, one of three or four fairly poor families living in a trailer park, and she came to Minuteman Tech to be a beauty stylist. She has a reputation for doing nails. "Find your own variety yet?"

For years I have been working in a greenhouse, grafting and splitting buds in hopes of coming up with something really incredible, some apple that will set the world on edge. My own form of genetic engineering, I'm trying to bring back a Spitzenburg, or something like it that is easier to grow and more adaptable to our climate, so that this time it won't die out quite so fast. I can't tell if Joellen is interested, or mocking me. I have always been a lousy judge of character.

Joellen dips her finger into the duck sauce and deliberately sucks it clean between her lips. She holds her hands out to me. "Notice anything?"

Her nails, which are what I have been trained to look at first, are covered with tiny caricatures of Sesame Street characters. Big Bird, Ernie, Snuffelupagus, Oscar the Grouch. "That's good. Where'd you learn that?"

"Kids' Band-Aids," she sighs, exasperated. "I can copy pretty good. But that's not it. Look again." She wiggles her fingers, so I start to look for new creases in her skin, cuticle damage, anything. "The ring," she says finally. "For God's sake."

Christ, she's engaged. "Well, that's great, Joellen. I'm happy for you." I don't know if I really am, but I know it is what I am supposed to say. "Who is it?"

"You don't know him. He's a Marine. Doesn't look a thing like you, either. We're getting married in September, and of course you'll be invited to the wedding."

"Oh," I say, making a mental note not to come. I resist the urge to check if she is pregnant. "What's his name?"

While Joellen tells me the life history of Edwin Cubbles, hailing from Chevy Chase, Maryland, I finish the food on the table, my drink and Joellen's drink. I order two more drinks and finish those too. While she is telling me the story of how they met at a costume party on the fourth of July (he was a walrus, and she was Scarlett O'Hara), I try to make the umbrellas stand upright in the thick and seeded duck sauce.

Last year when I came to speak at the high school we drove to the place where we both lost our virginity—a field in some conservation land that turns purple with fireweed at the end of the summer. We sat on the hood of her little car and drank Yoo-Hoo from a convenience store and then I lay down in the grass to watch the night come. Joellen sat between my legs, using my bent knees as a kind of armchair, and she leaned back against me so that I could feel the hooks of her bra through her shirt and mine. She told me again how sorry she was that she had broken up with me, and I reminded her that it was me who did it—one day I had just realized I didn't feel the way I used to. Like barbecue coals, I said, you know the way they're orange one minute and then you turn around they've just become grey dust? As I told her this I cupped my hands around her breasts; she didn't stop me. Then she flipped herself over and began to kiss me, and rub her hands up and down the legs of my good khaki pants, and as I got hard she said to me, "Now Sam, I thought you didn't feel the same way."

Joellen is still going on about Edwin. I interrupt her. "You're the only girlfriend I've ever had who's gotten married."

Joellen looks at me and she is truly surprised. "You've had other girlfriends?"

Although we haven't had our main course yet I signal for the check. I'll pick it up as an engagement present; we usually go dutch. She doesn't seem to notice that the lo mein and the beef with pea pods haven't come, but then again she hasn't really eaten much of anything. "Don't worry about driving me home," I tell her, feeling my face turn red. "I can get Joley or Hadley to take a run out here."

The waiter, I notice, is a hunchback, and because I feel bad I take a couple of dollars extra out of my wallet. He has brought pineapple spears and fortune cookies with the check. Joellen looks at me and I realize she is waiting for me to pick a cookie. "After you," I say.

Like a kid, she dives into the puddle of pineapple juice and uses her nail as a chisel to crack it. "Great beauty and fortune dwell in your smile," she reads, pleased with the outcome. "What's yours?"

I break my cookie in half. "You will find success at every turn," I read, lying through my teeth. Really, it says something dumb about visitors from afar.

As we walk out of the restaurant Joellen takes my arm.

"Edwin is lucky," I say.

"I call him Eddie." And then, "You really think so?"

She insists on driving me back to Stow; she says it could be the last time she sees me as a single woman, and I can't argue with her there. About halfway, in Maynard, she pulls into the parking lot of a church, an old New

England white clapboard church with pillars and a steeple, you name it. Joellen reclines her seat all the way and rolls back the moonroof in the car.

I get the feeling I have to leave. Fidgeting, I open the glove compartment and riffle through the contents. A map of Maine, lipstick, two rulers, a tire gauge and three Trojans. "Why are you stopping?"

"Jeez, Sam. I'm doing all the driving. Can't I take a little rest?"

"Why don't I drive? You get out and sit over here and I'll drive. You've got the whole way back to drive, anyhow."

Joellen's hand wanders across the console, like a crab, and comes to rest on my thigh. "Oh, I'm not in a hurry." She stretches, deliberately, so that her ribs rise and her breasts get flat under her blouse.

"Look, I can't do this."

"Do what," Joellen says. "I don't know what we're doing." She reaches across to loosen my tie and unbutton my shirt. Pulling the tie through the buttoned collar, she wraps it like cord around her hands, and slips it over my head to rest on the back of my neck. Then, drawing me in, she kisses me.

God can she kiss. "You're engaged," I say, and when my lips move hers move with me, pressed on mine, like an echo.

"But I'm not married." With amazing skill she swings her leg over the center console, pivoting, coming to sit spread-eagled on my lap.

I am losing control, I think, and I try not to touch her. I wrap my fingers around the plastic fixtures of the seat belt until she takes my hands and holds them up to her chest. "What's stopping you, Sam? It's the same old me."

What's stopping you? Her words stay, frosted on the window. Morals, maybe. Idiocy? There is a buzzing in my ears, fueled by the way she is rubbing against me. She slides her hand down my shorts and I can feel her nails.

There is this buzzing and *what is stopping you?* My head keeps ringing and at some point I realize that I cannot be held accountable for what is happening, for my hands ripping at her and the taste of the skin on her nipples, and she closes on me, closes and holds from the inside. Remember when it was you and me, baby, in this field, at fifteen, with life laid out in front of us like a treasure chest; and love was something to breathe in your girl's ear. Do you remember how easy it was to say forever?

When it is over her hair is free and our clothes are puddled around us on the front seat. She hands me her underwear to wipe myself clean and smiles with her eyes slitted shut as she climbs back into the driver's seat. "It was nice seeing you again, Sam," she says, although we are still seven miles from my place. Joellen puts on her blouse but leaves her bra in the back seat with her teaching tools, and insists on driving naked from the waist down. She says no one will see but me, and then she asks for my undershirt, on the floor, to sit on so she won't drip onto the red velveteen seats.

I do not kiss her goodbye when she pulls into the driveway. In fact I don't say a word, I just get out of her car. "I can keep the shirt?" she asks, and I don't bother to answer. I'm not about to wish her a nice wedding, either, I'd expect lightning to come out of the sky and strike me. Chrissake, we were in the parking lot of a *church.*

When I walk into the Big House, Hadley and Joley are still at the kitchen table playing Hearts. Neither of them looks up when I come in and throw my tie on the floor. I strip off my shirt too and toss it so it slides across the linoleum. "So," Hadley says, grinning. "You get any?"

"Shut the fuck up," I tell him, and walk upstairs. In the shower I use up an entire bar of soap and all the hot water, but I imagine it will take some days before I feel truly clean.

14 JANE

It spreads out in front of us like a pit of fire, flamed red, gold and orange in layers of rock. It is so big that you can look from left to right and wonder if the land will ever come together again. I have seen this from a plane, but so far away it was like a thumbprint on the window. I keep expecting someone to take down the painted backdrop: that's all folks, you can go home now—but nobody does.

There are plenty of other cars parked at this "PICTURE SPOT" along the highway that borders the Grand Canyon. People popping flash cubes in the afternoon light, mothers pulling toddlers away from the protective railing. Rebecca is sitting on the railing. She has her hands on either side of her hips, a brace. "It's huge," she says, when she can sense me behind her. "I wish we could go into it."

So we try to find out about burro rides, the ones where they take pictures of you on the donkey to put on your living room table when you get home. The last tour, however, has left for the day—which doesn't really upset me since I have little desire to ride on a burro. I agree with Rebecca, though. It is hard to grasp like this. You feel inclined to take it apart, to see it pieced like a jigsaw puzzle before you consider its entirety.

I find myself thinking about the river that carved this art, the sun that painted its colors. I wonder how many millions of years this whole thing took, and who got to wake up one morning and say, "Oh, so there is a canyon."

"Mom," Rebecca says, missing the beauty, "I'm getting hungry." At her feet is a gaggle of tiny Japanese children all wearing the same blue school uniform. They carry little one-step cameras, and half take pictures of the canyon, while the other half take pictures of my daughter.

Reaching over the children, I pull Rebecca off the railing; she is making me nervous anyway. "All right. We'll find a diner." I walk towards the car but on second thought step back to the railing for a final look. Enormous. Anonymous. I could hurtle myself down the walls of this chasm, and never be found.

Rebecca is waiting for me in the car, arms folded tight across her chest. "All we had for breakfast was that beef jerky from Hilda."

"It was free," I point out. Rebecca rolls her eyes. When she gets hungry, she gets irritable. "Did you see signs for anything on the way?"

"I didn't see anything. Miles and miles of sand."

I sigh and start the car. "You'd better get used to it. I hear driving in the Midwest is lousy."

"Can we *just go*," Rebecca says. "Please."

After a few miles we pass a blue metal sign that says JAKE'S, with an arrow. Rebecca shrugs, which means Yes, let's turn. "Jake's is the name of a diner if I've ever heard one," I say.

The interesting thing about the environs surrounding the Grand Canyon is that they're ugly. Dusty, plain, as if all their splendor has been sucked out by the area's main attraction. You can drive, even on a highway, for miles without spotting desert vegetation or the hint of color.

"*Jake's!*" Rebecca screams, and I slam my brakes. We do a 180-degree turn in the dust, which points us towards the little shack I've passed. There are no other cars, in fact there isn't even a diner. What is there is an airfield, and a tiny plane in the distance, puttering.

A man with very short yellow hair and spectacles approaches the car. "Hello. Interested in a ride?"

"No," Rebecca says quickly.

He holds his hand out to her across my chest. "Name's Jake Feathers. Honest to God."

"Let's go," Rebecca says. "This isn't a diner."

"I fly over the canyon," Jake says, as if we are listening. "Cheapest deal you'll find. Unlike anything you'll ever see." He winks at Rebecca. "Fifty dollars apiece."

"How long?" I ask.

"*Mom,*" Rebecca says. "Please."

"As long as it takes," Jake tells me. I get out of the car and stand up. I hear Rebecca swear and recline her seat. The plane, in the distance, seems as if it is rolling forward.

"You ain't seen the Canyon unless you've seen it from the inside. You won't believe it till you do it."

I have been thinking this very thing. "We don't have the money," Rebecca whines.

I stick my head in the window. "You don't have to go."

"I'm not getting on that plane."

"I understand. But do you mind if I do?" I lean in closer for privacy. "I mean, we can't ride the burros, and I think one of us ought to see it. We came all the way here, and you know, you can't say you've seen it—"

"—if you don't see it from the inside," Jake says, finishing my sentence. He tips an imaginary hat.

Rebecca sighs and closes her eyes. "Ask if he has any food."

Minutes later, with my daughter waving from the hood of the car, Jake takes me up in his Cessna. I do not believe this contraption is going to fly, with its rusted studs and notched propellers. The control panel—something I've always conceived of with flashing lights and radar gadgets—is no more complex than the dashboard of the station wagon. Even the throttle Jake uses for takeoff resembles the knobs for the air-conditioning.

As we lift off the ground my head whacks against the metal of the airplane's frame. I am surprised at the roughness of the flight, the way the plane chugs as if there could be bumps in the air. Next time, I think, a Dramamine. Jake says something to me, but I can't hear him over the engine.

Inside this plastic bubble I can see panoramically—the trees, the highway, Rebecca, getting smaller, disappearing. I watch the ground run behind us and then suddenly there is nothing there at all.

We've fallen off a cliff, I think, panicking, but there's no drop. We turn to the right and I see the perimeter of this beautiful gully in a way I haven't seen—ridges and textures so close they become real. We pass lakes in the valley of the canyon, emeralds that grow larger as we inch farther down. We fly over peaks and past furrows; we hum across carved rocks. Under us at one point is a green village, a trembling ledge dotted with the red roofs of homes and minute fenced-in farms. I find myself wanting to go to this village; I want to know what it is like to live in the shadow of natural walls.

Too quickly we turn around, letting the sun wash us full-force, so powerful I have to shade my eyes. I breathe deeply, trying to internalize this amazing open space where there is no firm footing, where there once was water. When we fly back over the edge of ordinary ground, I see Rebecca sitting on the hood of our station wagon. As Jake lands I wonder what cities and sculptures lie millions of miles beneath the sea.

15 JOLEY

Dear Jane,

I was cleaning out my closet in anticipation of your arrival, and do you know what I found? The wave machine, which incidentally still works. Remember? Plug it into the wall and the sound of the ocean fills your room, pounding against the walls. Mama got it for me when I started to lose sleep. It was new in its day—a machine that simulated the way nature should be, that drowned the sounds of a house falling apart at its foundations.

When I was nine and you were thirteen the arguments began to get louder—so loud the attic rattled and the moon sank. You bitch, Daddy screamed, you whore—you had to spell that word for me, and learn about the meaning from the bad girls at school. On Mondays and Thursdays, Daddy came home drunk, his breath smelling like silage. He'd slam the door open and he'd walk so heavily the ceiling (our bedroom floors) shook. And when you're nine and you're in a room with tall ships stenciled on the walls that begin to move out of fear or shock or both—the last thing you want is to be alone. I'd wait until the coast was clear—when Mama's crying carpeted my footsteps—and I'd run into your room, which was soft and pink and full of you.

You waited for me, awake. You pulled back the covers and let me crawl in, hugging me when I needed it. Sometimes we turned on the lights and played Old Maid. Sometimes we made up ghost stories, or sang TV commercials, and sometimes we couldn't help but listen. And then when we heard Mama creep up the stairs and close her bedroom door behind her, followed by Daddy, thunderous, minutes later, we covered our ears. We snuck out of your bedroom and tiptoed downstairs, looking for traces—a broken vase, a bloody tissue—that might keep our attention a little longer. Most of the time we found nothing at all, just our living room, where we were allowed to buy into the fantasy that we were your average happy American kids.

When Mama found me in your room some months later—on a morning we had happened to sleep later than her—she didn't tell Daddy. She half-carried me, asleep, into my own room and told me I must never never go in there again at night. But when it all happened again and I was forced to cry just to keep myself from listening, Daddy ran upstairs and threw open my door. Before I had time to consider the consequences you squeezed under his arm and ran to my side. Get away, Daddy, you said. You don't know what you're doing.

Mama bought me the wave machine the next day. To some extent it worked, I didn't hear a lot of the fighting. But I couldn't curl into the small of your neck—baby shampoo and talcum powder—and I couldn't hear your voice singing me kangaroo lullabies. All that I had was the solace of a wall that connected our rooms, where I could scratch a pattern you'd know how to answer. That was all I had, that and the sound of water where there was none, insisting I push from my mind the hollow sounds of Daddy hitting Mama, and then hitting you, again. Take Route 89 to Salt Lake City. There's water there you can't see. Give my love to Rebecca. As always,

Joley

16 REBECCA *July 25, 1990*

When I see myself in the reflection of the truck's window, I understand why nobody has stopped to pick me up. I've been in the rain for three hours, and I haven't even reached the highway yet. My hair is plastered against my head, and my features remind me of a soft-boiled egg. Mud is caked on my arms and legs in paisley shapes: I don't look like a hitchhiker; I look like a Vietnam vet.

"Thank God," I say under my breath, and I blow a cloud of frost between my teeth. Massachusetts is not California. It can't be more than fifty degrees out here, although it's July, and the sun's barely set.

I am not put off by truckers anymore, not since coming cross-country. They look worse than they are, for the most part, like the so-called tough guys in school who refuse to throw the first punch. The man in the cab of this truck is shaved bald, with a tattoo of a snake running from the crown of his head down his neck. So I smile at him. "I'm trying to get to New Hampshire."

The trucker stares at me blankly, as if I have mentioned a state he's never heard of. He says something out loud, and it's not directed to me, and suddenly I see another person appear in the passenger seat. I cannot tell if it is a boy or a girl but it seems this person had just woken up. She—no, he—runs a hand through his hair and sniffs in to clear his nose. My shoulders begin to shiver again; I can see there isn't room for me.

"Listen," the driver says, "you ain't running away from home."

"Okay. I'm not."

"Is she thick, or what." He squints at me. "We can't stow away minors."

"Minors? I'm eighteen. I just don't look it right now. I've been on the road for hours."

The boy in the passenger seat, who is wearing a White Snake shirt with cut-off sleeves, turns my way. He grins. He is missing his two front teeth. "Eighteen, hey?" For the first time I understand what it is like to be undressed by someone's eyes. I cross my hands in front of me. "Let her get in the back, Spud. She can ride with the rest of the meat." The two of them start to laugh hysterically.

"The back?"

The White Snake boy points with his thumb. "Lift the hatch and make sure you lock it from the inside. And," he leans out the window so that I can smell the chocolate curdles of his breath. "We'll stop for a little rest, baby. Real soon." He slaps the driver high five, rolls up his window.

It is an unmarked white truck so I don't know what to expect from its contents. I have to swing myself up on the steel frame to unhook the latch, then swing down and pull the handle with me. I know they are in a hurry so I climb back inside and pull the doors shut with the strings someone has attached to the padded inside.

There are no windows. It is pitch-dark, and freezing. I reach around me like I am blind and feel the shapes of chickens shrink-wrapped in plastic, the T-bones in steaks. The truck begins to bounce. Through a wall of raw flesh I can hear the boy with the White Snake shirt, singing along to a tape of Guns 'n' Roses.

I am going to die, I think, and I am much more terrified than I was walking along the road at night. I am going to freeze to death and when they open this hatch two hours from now I'll be blue and curled like an embryo. Think, I tell myself. Think. How in God's name do the Eskimos live?

Then I remember. Way back, in fifth grade we studied them—the Inuit—and I had asked Miss Cleary how they stay warm in a home made of ice. Well, they have fires, she said. But believe it or not the ice is a house. A strange house but a house indeed. It traps their body heat.

There is not much room to move in here but it is enough. I squat, wary of standing in a moving truck. Little by little I move meat away from the wall of the truck and pile it back up, leaving a tiny enclosure for my own body. It gets easier as my eyes adjust to the dark. I find that if I layer chicken with tenderloins, the walls don't come tumbling down.

"What you doing back there, baby," I hear. "You getting yourself ready for me?"

And then the rough voice of the driver: "You gonna shut up Earl, or I'll have to throw you back there to cool down."

I curl into the small space I've created and wrap my arms tight around myself. Soon, I think, there'll be someone else to do this for me. I don't know that it is any warmer, but in my head I think it is and that really makes a difference.

I know it was her. I know that she was the one who told Sam to get rid of Hadley, or else why would Hadley go? He was happy there, Sam was happy with him there, there weren't any problems. It was my mother; she gets in her head an idea that she can run the world for everyone and she actually thinks she's right.

It's okay for her to run around giggling like an idiot with Sam, right? But if I fall in love—real love, you know—it's the end of the world. Hadley and I really have something. I know what I'm talking about, too. I've had boyfriends for a week or so in school, and this is nothing like it. Hadley's told me about the way his father died working in front of him; about the time he almost drowned in a frozen pond. He's told me about the time he stole a pack of Twinkies from the Wal-Mart, and couldn't sleep till he gave it back. He's cried, sometimes, telling me these things. He's said there's no one quite like me.

We'll get married—isn't it Mississippi or someplace like that where fifteen is legal?—and we'll live on a farm of our own. We'll have strawberries and wax beans and cherry tomatoes and apples, I suppose, and absolutely no rhubarb. We'll have five kids, and if they all look like Hadley that's fine with me, as long as I have one little girl to myself. I've always wanted someone like me.

I'll invite my father for the weekend—that'll drive my mother crazy. And when she and Sam come to visit we won't let them in. We'll post Dobermans trained for her scent. And when she stands outside her car and calls to us, begging forgiveness, we'll turn on the outside stereo speakers and flood away her voice with Tracy Chapman, Buffalo Springfield and those other ballads Hadley likes.

He came to me before he left. He sneaked into my room and pressed his hand against my mouth before I could speak. He told me he had to leave and then he slipped off his boots and got under the covers. He put his hands up my nightgown. I told him they were cold, but he just laughed and pressed them against my belly until he caught my heat. "I don't understand," he whispered. "Sam and me have been together for almost fifteen years. He's more my brother than my brother. This is more my home." I thought he might be crying and that was something I did not want to see, so I didn't turn to face him. He said, "I'll be back to get you, Rebecca, I mean that. I've never been with anyone like you." Those, I think, were the exact words.

But I wasn't going to sit around and wait for him, watching my mother coring Macs with Sam in the kitchen or rubbing his feet after dinner. I wasn't going to watch that and pretend like nothing had happened. Obviously, she doesn't care about me, or she wouldn't have pushed Hadley away.

Once I said to Hadley, "You know you're almost old enough to be my father." I mean, ten years is some difference. And he told me I was no ordinary fifteen-year-old. Fifteen-year-olds in Stow read *Tiger Beat* and go to the Boston malls to see visiting soap opera stars. I told him that Stow was about three years behind, then—in San Diego that's what twelve-year-olds do. And Hadley said, "Well, maybe these kids are twelve after all."

I believe in love. I think it just hits you and pulls the rug out from underneath you and, like a baby, demands your attention every minute of the day. When I get close to Hadley I breathe faster. My knees shake. If I rub my eyes hard, I can see his image in the corners. We've been together one whole week.

We haven't done it yet. We've come awfully close—like that time in the hay on the horse blankets. But he's the one who keeps pushing me away, what do you make of that? I thought all guys wanted was sex—which is another reason I'm crazy about him. He said to me, "Don't you want to be a kid for a couple of days longer?"

My mother told me about sex when I was four. She started by saying, "When a man and a woman love each other very much . . ." and then she stopped herself and said, "When a man and a woman are married and love each other very much . . ." I don't think she knows I caught the slip. I'm not supposed to have sex until I'm married, which doesn't make any sense to me. Number one, most girls in high school have done it by the time they graduate and very few get pregnant—we aren't stupid. And number two, it's not like marriage is the peak of your life. You can be married, I think, but that doesn't necessarily mean you are in love.

Maybe I fall asleep for a while in this chicken igloo. When I wake up I am not sure if it is my eyes blinking or the door opening that lets in a slice of light. Whatever it is it goes away very quickly, and it is several seconds too late when I notice we aren't moving.

The boy is there, tossing away the wall of ice with the force of a superhero. In the darkness his teeth are blue like lightning. I can see his ribs. "You been quiet," he says, revealing me.

I am not as frightened as I should be. I consider playing dead but I am not sure that will stop him.

"Let's play a game. I'll go first." He strips off his T-shirt, to show his skin, which glows.

"Where are we?" I hope it is a McDonald's, where, if I scream, I have a chance of being heard.

"If you're real good I'll let you out to take a look." He thinks about what he's said and then he laughs, and takes a step forward. "Real good." He pokes my shoulder. "It's your turn, baby. The shirt. Take off the shirt."

I collect all the saliva I can and spit at his chest. "You," I say, "are a pig."

Because his eyes are still adjusting to the light I have the advantage. While he is trying to figure out what I've done I push past him and lunge for the latch on the door. He grabs me by the hair and, pinning me by the throat, presses me up against the cold, cold wall. With his free hand he grabs mine and holds it against his crotch. Through his jeans, I can feel him twitch.

I bring my knee up with power that surprises me and crush it against him. He falls back on the broiler-fryers and the strip streaks, clutching his groin. "You little fuck!" he yells. I throw open the latch and tear into the fast-food restaurant.

I hide in the ladies' room, figuring that is the safest place. Inside the stall I lock the door and crouch on the toilet seat. I count to five hundred and try to ignore the people who rattle the lock to see if there is someone inside. I will not ride with men, I vow. I can't afford to.

When the coast is clear I come out of the stall and stand in front of the sink area. I wash the mud off my arms and legs with warm industrial soap and scrub my face; then I hold my head under the air blower to dry my hair. There are icicles in the scalp. As I poke my head out the bathroom door, an older woman wearing a green wool suit with a matching fedora and a strand of pearls goes inside.

They are gone. I survey the walls of the restaurant to see what town we are in but these places all look the same. Employee of the Month: Vera Cruces. We use eighty-five percent lean beef, flame-broiled not fried. The well-dressed woman comes out of the bathroom.

"Please," I say, sidelining her. "Can you help me?"

She glances at my clothing, evaluating whether or not to speak to me. She reaches for her purse.

"Oh, no, no money," I say. "You see, I'm trying to get to New Hampshire. My mother lives there and she's very ill and my boyfriend was driving me from our boarding school, but we've had a fight, and he left me here." I turn away, and catch my breath like I've been sobbing.

"Where do you go to school, dear?" the woman asks.

I am stumped. The only prep schools I know are in California. "Boston," I tell her, smiling. To distract her, I sway a little, and lean against the wall. She reaches out to support me and I take her warm, bony hand. "I'm sorry. I'm not feeling all that well."

"I can imagine. I'll take you as far as Laconia, and we'll see if we can put you on a bus."

The truth is, I'm not feeling all that well. I didn't exactly fake it when I swooned. My eyes are burning something awful, and there is the taste of blood in my mouth. When this woman, who introduces herself as Mrs. Phipps, offers me her arm on the way to the car I am happy to take it. Inside, I stretch across the back seat with a Dior jacket as a blanket and fall asleep.

When I wake up Mrs. Phipps is peering at me in the rearview mirror. "Hello, dear. It's just past ten o'clock." She smiles; she reminds me of a wren. "Do you feel better?"

"Marvelous much," I answer. It's a phrase I heard once in an old movie and I have always wanted to use it.

"Looks as if you have a fever," she observes, detached. "Your face is red as a beet." I sit up and look into the mirror; she's right. "Now, I've been thinking. You look like a Windsor girl. Am I right?"

I have no idea what a Windsor girl looks like. I smile. "You bet."

"I went to Miss Porter's. But that was years ago, of course." She pulls the car into a shopping center with an odd kiosk in the middle. "This is Laconia," she says. "You slept most of the way. Now where is your mother?"

I stare at her for a second until I remember what I've said. "Carroll, in the White Mountains."

Mrs. Phipps nods and tells me to stay in the car. She comes back with a bus ticket and a crisp ten dollar bill. "You take this, dear. In case you need anything along the way." When I get out of the car she pats me as you might pat a disinterested cat and gives me directions for the trip. Her face is a wrinkled plum. She wishes my mother the best, and then gets in her Toyota and drives away, waving. I feel bad, watching her go. I feel bad that I have lied; I feel bad that this kind old woman is driving alone at ten at night, on the same roadways as violent, perverted truckers.

Hadley's house, 114 Sandcastle Lane according to the phone book, is a long and simple avocado-colored ranch that looks as if it was tossed by a tornado at the base of a huge mountain. This mountain is Hadley's backyard, and if you stand a little too close you get the impression that the house is built against a natural wall of rock. There isn't a doorbell, just a knocker in the shape of a frog. I know Hadley will answer, because I've come all this distance.

I see his eyes first—soft and brown as earth, the color of thunderstorms. They get wider as they see me. "What are you doing here?" Hadley says, grinning. He swings open the screen door and steps onto the porch in front of me. This object of my affection. He takes me into his arms and lifts me off my feet, holding me level with himself.

"Surprised?"

"Hell, yes." Hadley touches my face with the pads of his fingers. "I can't believe you're here." He cranes his neck around the pillars of the porch. "Who's with you?"

"I came myself. I ran away."

"Oh, no, Rebecca." He straddles a rusted iron stool. "You can't stay here. Where do you think they'll come looking first?"

At this realization I sway again, thinking this has all been for nothing. "I almost got raped coming here," I say, starting to cry. "And I think I'm sick, and I don't want to be at Sam's without you." My nose starts to run, and I wipe it on my sleeve. "Don't you want me here?"

"Sssh." He pulls me closer so I am standing between his legs. He locks his ankles behind me. "Of course I want you here." He kisses my lips, my eyes and my forehead. "You're burning. What's happened to you?"

I tell him the story, the entire story, which makes him punch the doorframe at one point and laugh at another. "I've still got to get you away from here," he says. "Sam'll come looking." He tells me to wait here, and he disappears back into the house. Through the corner of the window I see a television set turned to *The Twilight Zone,* fuzzy pink slippers propped on an ottoman, and a square of quilted orange robe.

"Who was it?" I hear someone say.

Hadley comes back with two blankets, a loaf of bread, a plastic cup and three cans of Chef Boyardee pasta. He stuffs all this into a knapsack. "I told my mother you were a friend of mine, and we were going out to a bar. That way she won't worry, and she won't know a thing if they come to ask her questions."

Hadley takes my hand and leads me into the backyard, up to the face of this mountain. "This way," he says. He places my foot in a crevice and shows me what to do.

Mount Deception is not particularly hard to climb. It levels off and becomes a flat plain for a while, then rises ten feet again, and so on until you get to the top. From an aerial view it must look like the pyramids in Egypt. Hadley carries the knapsack and climbs behind me in case I fall, which I'm proud to say I do not do. We continue like this for about an hour, using the moon as a torch.

Hadley takes me to a small clearing in a knot of pine trees. He walks me around the parameters of this space, and then holds me by the waist as we come to the north corner. There is a straight drop, a hundred feet maybe, to a cavern below with a stuttering river.

While Hadley makes us a home, I sit on the edge of this cliff, dangling my feet. I am not afraid of heights; they fascinate me. I drop twigs and stones, progressively larger, and try to hear how long it takes before they hit the rocks.

"Dinner," Hadley says, so I turn back to the clearing. He has stretched one blanket over pine needles to form a surprisingly soft mattress. In the center is a candle (I hadn't seen him carrying that, it must have been in his pocket) and a can of Raviolios. "I forgot utensils," he says. He picks up the can and feeds me a piece of pasta with his fingers. It tastes cold and tinny, absolutely delicious. "Now, you promise you won't get up in the middle of the night to pee and take a wrong turn?" Hadley rubs my arms, which are puckered with the cold. My teeth chatter.

"I won't go anywhere without you," I say. "I mean it."

"Sssh." Hadley stares at me as if he knows he will be tested on how well he remembers the shape of my mouth, the color of my eyes. "They don't know you like I do," he says. "They don't understand how it is." He lies down on his stomach and leans his cheek on my thigh. "Here's the plan. We'll stay here overnight, and then I'll get the truck in the morning, and we'll take a drive down to Stow again. If you talk to your mom about all this—if she sees we came back of our own free will—I think it will work out."

"I'm not going back there," I tell him. "I hate what she did."

"Come on, Rebecca, everyone makes mistakes. Do you blame her? If your daughter was dating a guy ten years older wouldn't you be a little worried?"

The moon dances across his hair. "Whose side are you on?" I say, but he's kissing my knee, that ticklish spot, and I can't really stay angry at him.

I lie down beside him and feel his arms close around me and for the first time in hours I get warm. He takes off his jacket and wraps it around my shoulders awkwardly, and when our foreheads bump together we laugh. As he kisses me I think about the smells of the cider press and the way summer feels when you know it is going to end.

I unbutton Hadley's flannel shirt and hold it soft against my skin. The hair on his chest is an unlikely shade of red. It circles in spirals that remind me of my father's nautical maps. I rub my fingers across them, the opposite way, making the hair stand on end. He sings to me.

Soon we are at that point we have been at before, naked

except for each other. Hadley's outstretched hands can cover the length of my spine. "Please," I say to him. "I don't want to be a kid anymore."

Hadley smiles. He pushes the hair back from my forehead. "You aren't." He kisses my neck and then he kisses my breasts and my stomach and my hips and then down there. "What are you doing," I whisper, but I am really speaking to myself. I feel something starting, some energy, that draws blood from my fingertips and begins unexpectedly to open. I pull back on Hadley's hair and scratch at his neck. I am afraid I will never get to see his face again. But then he slides up my body and in and we move like a sail, like a wind; he kisses me, full, on the lips, and to my great surprise I taste like the ocean.

Because we were asleep we did not hear them coming. But in the spotlight of the morning, they are standing over us: a park ranger, Sam, my father.

"Jesus, Hadley," Sam says, and Hadley jumps up. He's wearing his boxers. I pull his shirt over me and roll a blanket around my legs. I cannot see everyone clearly; there is some kind of fire behind my eyes.

"Hadley." My voice is not my own. "This is my father."

Unsure of what to do, Hadley holds out his hand. My father does not take it. I'm puzzled seeing my father in this environment. He is wearing suit pants and a polo shirt and brown loafers. I am amazed that he could climb up here with a sole like that.

My head is throbbing so heavily I lie back down. The park ranger—the only person here who has been paying attention to me—kneels down and asks if I am all right. "To tell you the truth," I say, "I don't really know." I try to sit up with his help, but there are shooting pains in my ears and in my eyes. Hadley kneels down beside me. He tells the ranger to get me away from everyone, where there's air.

"Get the hell away from her," my father says. "Don't touch her."

Sam, standing beside him, tells Hadley it might be best.

"What do you know?" Hadley shouts at Sam.

I am having a great deal of trouble concentrating on the scene at hand. When people speak, I can't hear the actual words until several seconds later. The sun swims in between their faces, bleaching them like overexposed photos. I try very hard to focus on Sam's eyes, the brightest color of anything in front of me. Beside Sam, my father seems small and two-dimensional, like a paper doll.

"Rebecca," my father's voice comes to me through a tunnel. "Are you all right? Did he hurt you?"

"He wouldn't hurt her." Sam leans in close to me with a face curved like a camera lens. "Can you stand up?"

I shake my head. Hadley takes my shoulders in his hands, regardless of what my father has said, which I do not remember anyway. He places his head so close to mine I can read his mind. He is thinking: I love you. Don't forget that. "Let me talk," I whisper, but nobody seems to hear me.

"Look, she came to me. She hitched. We were headed to your place today to work this all out." His words are too loud.

"Hadley," Sam says slowly, "I think you'd better let Rebecca come home with us. And I think you'd better stay here for a while."

Let me talk, I say again, but I am ignored. It occurs to me I may not be speaking at all.

Hadley stands up and walks away from the clearing. He has his hands on his hips. When he turns around the veins in his forehead are strained and blue, and he stares at Sam. "You know me. You've known me forever. I can't believe," here he looks at my father, "I cannot believe that you—*you*—would doubt me. You're my friend, Sam. You're like my brother. I didn't tell her to come here—I wouldn't do that. But I'm not just gonna turn my back and let you take her away. Jesus, Sam," he takes a step backward. "I love her."

With all the energy I have I lunge towards Hadley, not quite standing and not quite crawling. He catches me in his arms and presses my face into his chest. He whispers into my hair things I cannot make out.

"Let go of her, you bastard," my father mutters. Sam lays a hand on his arm but he shakes it off and yells into the sky. "Let go of my daughter!"

"Give her to us, Hadley," Sam says softly.

"Sir," the ranger says, the first word I hear without the static of the trees.

"No," I whisper to Hadley.

He kneels down and takes my face in his hands. "Don't cry, now. You look like an onion when you cry, your nose gets all long . . ." I look up at him. "There you go. Now I said I'd come for you, didn't I, and your father came a long way to see you. Go on home." His voice cracks, and he swallows hard. I trace his Adam's apple with my finger. "You need a doctor. Go back to Sam's and get better, and I'll come for you. We'll work this all out like I said. You go with them."

"Give her to us," Sam says again.

I know as sure as I know myself that if I leave that mountain without Hadley I will never see him again. "I can't," I tell Hadley, and it's true. Except for him, I don't have anyone left who will love me. I wrap my arms around his waist and pull myself closer.

"You have to go with them," he says gently. "Don't you want to make me happy? Don't you see?"

"No," I say, pulling myself to Hadley.

"Go, Rebecca," Hadley says, a little louder. He loosens my grip on his waist and holds my hands.

"I won't." Tears are running down my face and my nose is running and I don't give a damn. I will not, I tell myself. I will not.

Hadley looks at the sky and with great force pushes me away by my wrists. He pushes so hard that I land several feet away on the rocks and the dirt. He pushes so hard that, without me beside him, he loses his balance.

I try to grab at him but I am too far away. I catch the air, and he falls over the edge of the cliff.

He falls so slowly, twisting in a somersault like a rough-cut acrobat, and I hear the rush of the river I heard last night before there was the beating of his heart in my hand. Thick as breath, I hear his spine hit the rocks and the water below.

After this, everything that has built up inside me spills out. It is nonverbal. It is a chord that comes when a knife cleaves your soul. And only now, with this sound surrounding, does everyone choose to listen.

17 OLIVER

My car runs out of gas in Carefree, Arizona, of all places, and I am forced to walk a sweltering half-mile to find a gas station. It is not the mom-and-pop operation I am expecting, but rather a respectable steel and chrome Texaco. Only one attendant is there.

"Hey," he says as I walk up. He doesn't really look at me, so I have the opportunity to survey him first. He has long brown hair and terrible acne; I place him at seventeen. "You're not from around here."

"Oh," I say, more sarcastic than I have to be. "How can you tell?"

The boy laughs through his nose and shrugs. He seems to actually be thinking up an answer to my rhetorical statement. "I know everyone in this town, I guess."

"That's astute of you." I smile.

"Astute," he repeats, trying the word on for size. As if he remembers his occupation, he jumps off the ten-gallon drum he has been resting on and asks if I'd like some help.

"Some unleaded," I tell him. "My car is down the road."

He focuses his attention on my gas can, a gift from the bank where Jane and I have a savings account. Marine Midland Bank, it is called, and its logo is a streamlined cartoon whale—we chose the institution for obvious emotional reasons.

"Hey," the boy says. "I seen one of these."

"A gas can? I'd imagine so."

"No, a whale can. You know, this picture thing here. There was one in here yesterday being filled up. Some lady who filled her tank and then found out we took credit cards and asked if we could fill up the spare can too."

Jane, I recall, has a can like it. The second year we were banking with Midland, we chose another gas can. We already had a nice toaster.

"What did this woman look like?" I can feel my neck getting flushed and the hair on the back of my neck standing. "Was there anyone with her?"

"Shit, I don't know. We get a million people in here a day." He looks up at me, and to my complete embarrassment I recognize this as a look of pity. "They weren't from this town though, I can tell you that."

I grab him by the shirt collar and hold him pinned to the diesel fuel tank. "Listen to me," I say, enunciating clearly. "I am looking for my wife and that may be her. Now you think about it and try to remember what she looks like. You try to remember if she had a little girl with her. If you talked to her about where she was going."

"Okay, okay," the boy says, pushing me away. He gives me a sideways look and makes a slow circle around the self-service island. "I think she had dark hair," he says, looking at my face to see if he is getting the answer right. He smacks his hands on his thighs, then. "The girl was pretty. A real fox, you know? Blond and a tight little ass. She asked for the key to the bathroom," he laughs, "and I told her I'd give her the key to my house too, if she met me there after work."

This is the best news I have heard in hours. Nothing is certain with such a vague description, but in a situation such as this some hint of evidence is better than nothing. "Where were they headed?" I ask, as calm as I can be given the circumstances.

"Route Seventeen," he says. "They asked how you get back to Route Seventeen. Maybe they're headed to the Canyon."

Of course they were going to the Grand Canyon. Jane was with Rebecca, and Rebecca would want to see as much as possible, each tourist trap en route. An angle I hadn't considered.

"Thank you," I say to the boy. "You have made my day."

The boy grins. He needs braces. "That's a buck twenty-five," he says. "Hell. It's on the house."

I run from the gas station without thanking the boy. I do not notice the heat or the distance on the journey back. The Grand Canyon. I feed in the gas and turn the ignition, imagining this union of Jane, Rebecca and the majestic red walls that were cut by the Colorado River.

18 SAM

In my opinion, if you leave things to their natural course, they go bad. Apples that grow wild along the shores of brooks tend towards blight. I'm not saying that you can't get a perfect apple without chemical help, but I'll tell you it's not easy.

The reason I keep sheep at the orchard is so that I don't have to spray so much. I don't know; I never liked the idea of pesticides. Guthion, Thiodan, Dieldin, Elgetol—they don't sound right, do they? I'm caught in the system, though—as a commercial grower I have to produce fruit that is competitive with other commercial orchards, or else the supermarkets won't buy. So I try to use the less toxic ones that I've heard of: dodine instead of parathion to prevent apple scab and mildew; Guthion sprayed only once, so I risk bull's-eye rot. I completely avoid 2,4-D—I can't stand things without real word names—and that's what I use my sheep for. They graze on the grass and weeds around the trees, like lawnmowers, so I don't need chemicals. And although it kills me, I spray the trees that are cordoned off for the supermarkets with Ethrel and NAA before the harvest, because quite frankly if mine aren't as red and as ripe as everyone else's, I'll go under.

Joley is in the barn mixing up the Thiodan: it's time to spray for the woolly aphid; nobody wants an apple with a worm in it. He's the first person I've seen since the night before, the night with Joellen, and I'm glad it's him and not Hadley. Joley's a good guy; he knows when to leave you alone and when not to. "Morning, Sam," he says to me, without looking up.

"You know to only spray the northwest half of the orchard?" Even without being told, Joley is a natural farmer. He's older than I am—I'm not quite sure how much—but I have no trouble getting on with him. Hadley talks back from time to time, but Joley wouldn't. Absolutely no farming experience, and he's a natural, did I say that?

He came in a couple of seasons ago, a Sunday U-Pick-Em day, when there were little kids all over the place. Like mosquitoes, they get in places you don't want them, and when you slap at them to make them go away, they hover in front of your face to bug you a little bit more. We get lots of the Boston crowd because we've got a good reputation, and since he looked like another one of those button-down preppies I assumed he'd come out here to get a bushel or two, to bring them home to some condo on the Harbor. But he came into the retail outlet we open for the fall. He stood in front of the dormant conveyors we use to sort the best from the mediocre apples, and he just kept fingering the gears over and over. He stood there for so long I thought he was sick, and then I thought maybe he was slow-witted so I didn't go over to him. Finally he walked into the orchards, and, fascinated, I followed him.

I've never told anyone this but it was the most amazing thing I have ever seen. I've been working on this orchard my entire life. I learned how to walk by hanging on the low branches of the apple trees. And I have never done the things that I saw him do that day. Joley just walked past the crowds, way past to the roped-off area we keep for the commercial apples, and stood in front of a tree. I held back from yelling at him; instead I followed him, hiding behind trees. Joley stopped at a tree—Mac, I believe—and cupped his hands around a small pink blossom. It was a young tree, grafted maybe two seasons ago, and so it wasn't bearing fruit yet. Or so I thought. He held this blossom in his hands and he rubbed the petal with his fingers, he touched the soft throat of the inside and then he knotted his hands around it, like he was praying. He stood like this for a few minutes and I was too spooked to make a sound. Then he opened his palms. Inside was a smooth, round, red apple, plain as day. The guy's a magician, I thought. Incredible. It hung from the still-thin branch, which bent under the unnatural weight. Joley picked it and turned around to face me as if he knew I was there all along. He held out the apple to me.

I don't think I ever officially offered him the job, or that I even knew I was looking for someone. But Joley stayed on the rest of that day and after that, moving into one of the extra bedrooms of the Big House. He became as good a worker as Hadley, who grew up on a farm in New Hampshire before his dad died and his mom sold out to a real estate developer. All you'd have to do is show Joley once, and he became an expert. He's a better grafter than I am, now. His specialty, though, is pruning. He can cut branches off a young tree without a second thought, without feeling like he's killing the thing, and just a season later it is the most beautiful umbrella of leaves you've ever seen.

"Did someone pen up the sheep?" I ask. They can't get near this stuff. Joley nods and hands me a hose and a nozzle. The really big orchards have machines for this stuff, but I like to work with my hands. It makes me feel, when I pick the fruit, like it actually came from me.

We head up towards the early Macs and the Miltons, which will come to harvest in late August and September. I wonder how long it will take before he asks me about last night.

"I've got a favor, Sam," Joley says, aiming at a middle-size tree. "I need your permission for something."

"Well, shit, Joley. You can just about do anything you want around here. You know that."

Joley turns the nozzle so that the pesticide dribbles at his feet. It makes me nervous. He keeps staring at me, and finally, noticing, he gives the nozzle a hard twist to the left to shut the flow. "My sister and niece are in trouble and I need a place for them to stay a while. I invited them here. I don't know how long they'll stay."

"Oh." I don't know what I had expected, but somehow it was worse. "I don't think that's a problem. What kind of trouble?" I don't want to pry, but I feel like I ought to know. If it's illegal, I may have to reconsider.

"She left her husband. She belted him, and she took the kid and left."

I try to place Joley's sister; I know he has talked about her in the past. I'd always pictured her like Joley—thin and dark, honest, easy. I pictured her the way I picture most girls from Newton where I know Joley grew up—dressed well, smelling like lilac, their hair smooth and heavy. The girls I knew from the Boston suburbs were rich and stuckup. They'd shake my hand if introduced to me, and then check when they thought I wasn't looking to see if they had gotten dirty. A farmer, they'd say. How *interesting.* Meaning: I didn't know there were any left in Massachusetts.

But girls like this didn't leave their husbands, and especially didn't hit their husbands. They got quiet divorces and half the summer homes. Maybe she's fat and looks like a sumo wrestler, I think. Because of Joley, I always gave this unknown woman the benefit of the doubt. He's talked about her a lot, a little bit at a time, and you get the sense she's his hero.

"So where is she?" I ask.

"Headed towards Salt Lake City," Joley says. "I'm writing her across the country. She doesn't have a super sense of direction." He pauses. "Hey. If her husband calls, just tell him you don't know a thing."

Husband. The whale guy. I am starting to remember bits and pieces of a person. Rebecca, the girl's name. A picture in Joley's room of a beautiful little boy (himself) and a thin, pale girl holding him tight, beside her. A plain girl I had asked about, and was surprised to find out was related. "She's the one in San Diego," I say, and Joley nods.

"She isn't going to go back there," Joley says, and I wonder how he knows with such conviction. He reaches under the tree, holding the pesticide stream away, to pick up a fallen branch. He tucks it into a back pocket. "The guy she married is an idiot. I never understood what it was about him she couldn't live without. Goddamned humpback whales."

"Whales," I say. "Wow." I've never heard Joley get so emotional about anything. Most of the time I've been with him, he moves in shadows, quiet, keeping in his thoughts. He lifts the stream of chemicals into the sky, letting it come down, artificial rain, on the top of a neighboring tree.

Joley cuts the line of spray and drops the can softly onto the lawn. "Why do you spray, anyway? Isn't there something you can use that's natural?"

I sit down on a dry patch of grass and stretch out on my back. "You wouldn't believe the crap that goes on with the commercial crop when you don't spray. Aphids and worms and scabs and all kinds of other things. There's just too many of them to take care of individually." I shade the sun from my eyes. "You leave it up to nature, and the whole thing goes to shit."

"Yeah," says Joley. "Tell me about it." He comes to sit down beside me. "You'll like her. You remind me of her, a little."

I think about asking, In what way? but I am not sure that I want to know the answer. Maybe it's the way I've taken him in, I think. I find myself wanting to know more about this Jane, what she looks like and the kinds of books she reads and where she got the nerve to hit her own husband. She sounds like, as my father would say, hell on wheels. "Women don't know what they want anymore. They tell you they're getting married, and then they jump you. Go figure."

Joley laughs. "Jane always knew she wanted Oliver. The rest of us just couldn't understand why." He leans up on one elbow. "Sam, you gotta see this guy. He's your classic scientist, you know? In a fog the whole day, and then he sees his daughter, and he's lucky if he can remember her name. Talks and talks about these fucking tapes he makes of whale songs—"

"Joley, if I didn't know better I'd say you were jealous."

He pulls a thistle from the ground beside him. "Maybe I am," he says, sighing. "See, here's this great person. And Oliver gets to make her over in his own image, you know? He didn't ever care about what a great person she was to begin with. If she had stayed with me—well, I know it doesn't work like that, but in *theory*—she'd be totally different now. She'd be like she used to be. For one thing, she wouldn't be scared of her own shadow." He stretches out on his back again. "I'll put it in your terms. She used to be an Astrachan, and now she's a crab apple."

I smile at him. Crab apples are tart, almost inedible, except in jellies. But Astrachans, well, they're the best all-arounds—sweet in cooking, sweet when eaten raw. I roll away from Joley, anxious to change the conversation. I feel weird talking like this to him. It is one thing if we are talking about the orchard, or my own life, but he is older than me, and when I remember that, I don't feel right about giving him advice. About all I can do is listen.

"So you going to tell us what happened last night?" Joley says, my way out.

"You heard me." I sit up and hug my knees, wiping off grass stains on my jeans. "Joellen's getting married. She tells me this and then she comes on to me."

"You've got to be kidding."

"Would I joke about something like that?" I mean it as a light remark but Joley stares at my face, as if he is trying to evaluate me before making a decision.

"I'm not going to ask you what happened," Joley says, laughing.

"You don't want to know–"

"Oh, I don't?"

I shake my head, grinning. Getting it out, saying it in the freedom of this great spread of land, my own land, somehow makes it seem all right. Once it is out, I can forget about it. I turn to Joley. "This kind of shit ever happen to you, or is it me?"

He laughs and stands up, leaning against a tree that he recently grafted. "I only fell in love once in my life," he says, "so I'm no expert."

"Some help you are." He offers me a hand to pull myself up. We pick up the hose and the spray bottle and head farther into the commercial half of the orchard. I walk ahead and stand at the crest of the hill, surveying the four corners of this place. There are men pruning younger trees straight ahead of me, and farther along in the commercial section I can make out Hadley, supervising the spraying of more Thiodan. Now that it's July all the leaves and blossoms are out, reaching against the sky like fingers.

Joley hands me the fallen branch he picked up earlier, a likely candidate for late-summer bud-grafting. "Cheer up, Sam," he tells me. "If you're lucky, I'll introduce you to my big sister."

19 Rebecca *July 22, 1990*

While we are waiting in line for our ice cream, my mother brings up the subject of Sam. "So," she says to me. "What do you think? Really."

I have to say, I have been expecting this. They haven't argued all day. In fact, most of the times I have seen my mother this morning, she has been in the company of Sam, strolling through the south corner of the orchard, or snapping beans with him on the porch as the sun beats down, or just talking. I've wondered what they are saying—Sam having no experience in speech disorders, and my mother knowing next to nothing about agriculture. I figure they talk about Uncle Joley, their common ground. Once or twice, I've pretended they are talking about me.

"I don't know him really well," I say. "He seems nice enough."

My mother steps in front of my line of vision so that all I can see is her. "Nice enough for what?"

What does she expect me to say? She stares so hard that I know she demands a better answer, a right answer, and I haven't any idea what that could be. "If you mean, Should I screw him, then, if you want to, yes."

"Rebecca!" My mother says it so loudly that the woman in front of us, Hadley, Joley and Sam himself all turn around. She smiles, and waves them all away. Then she says more quietly, "I don't know what has gotten into you here. Sometimes I think you aren't the same kid I brought out East."

I'm not, I want to say, I'm crazy in love. But you don't tell your mother that, especially when she's all of a sudden best friends with a different guy who happens to be the same age as the guy you love. My mother turns to Uncle Joley. "She wants a small chocolate. I'll have a javaberry. Can you order, we're going to walk a ways."

I pull my arm away from her grasp. "I don't want chocolate," I tell my uncle, although that was what I had planned to order. "She doesn't know what I want." I shook a look at my mother. "Creamsicle sherbert."

"Creamsicle? You hate creamsicle. You told me last year it reminds you of St. Joseph's children's aspirin."

"Creamsicle," I repeat. "That's what I want." To avoid a scene, I walk with my mother. When we leave, Hadley and Sam are pointing at an all-terrain bicycle.

"What is it?" I say, figuring if I get it out into the open then this will all be over. I know it is about Hadley, and how much time I have been spending with him. For all I know, maybe she found out about us in the barn.

I have worked this all out in my mind, the product of several nights that I have lain awake missing the sounds of California. You don't hear passing cars, or Big Wheels on the sidewalk, or the surf from miles away. Instead there are cicadas (peepers, Hadley says), and the wind in the branches and blossoms and the bleating of sheep. I swear you can hear headlights here. I cannot see the drive from my bedroom; at least three times I have run to the window at the end of the upper hall to survey the cars below—count them, and make sure my father hasn't come yet. The only thing I can imagine worse than confronting my mother about Hadley is confronting my father about this entire trip.

This is what I am going to say to my mother: I know you think that I am young. But I was old enough to come here with you. And I was old enough to know what was going on between you and Daddy, and what was better for us in the long run. So don't tell me I don't know what I am doing. After all, you weren't any older than I am when you began to date Daddy.

What my mother says is: "I know you think I'm betraying your father."

I stare up at her in amazement. This isn't about me at all. She hasn't even *noticed* me and Hadley.

"I know that I am still married to him. Don't you think every time I see you in the morning I think about what I've left behind in California? A whole life, Rebecca, I left my whole life. I left a man who, at least in some ways, depends on me. And that's why sometimes I wonder what I'm doing out here, in this godforsaken farm zone—" she waves her arm in the air, "—with this—"

When her voice falls off, I interrupt her. "This what?"

"This absolutely incredible man," she says.

An absolutely incredible man?

My mother stops walking. "You're pissed off at me."

"No I'm not."

"I can tell."

"I'm not. Really."

"You don't have to lie . . ."

"Mom," I say, louder. "I'm not lying." Am I? I face her and put my hands on my hips. I think, who is the child here? "So what's been going on between you and Sam, anyway?"

My mother turns beet red. Beet red, on my own mother! "Nothing," she admits. "But I've been having some crazy thoughts. It's nothing. Absolutely nothing."

My own mother. Who would have thought. "I didn't think you two got along."

"Well, neither did I," she says. "But I guess compatibility isn't the issue." She stares in the direction of Hadley and Sam, who are waiting with Uncle Joley at the front of the ice cream line. This place is different from the one we went to yesterday, back when my mother and Sam didn't like each other. This place makes its own ice cream. It has only seven flavors and Sam says it's always busy. "We should head back," my mother says, without any real determination.

When we first got here, Sam wanted nothing to do with my mother. After the whole sheep-shearing fiasco, which was a lousy first impression, he'd told Hadley my mother was some uptown bitch with a lot to learn about real life. And when Hadley told me, and I'd told my mother, she'd snorted and said that an apple farm in East Jesus wasn't real life.

And then last night they just started hanging around together. When I first saw it I couldn't believe it; I thought that my mother found Sam to be such a hick, she had to see it for herself. In truth, I didn't pay much attention. I had been spending time with Hadley—we'd hit it off immediately, and then after last night, well, who knew what would come of this. Hadley, who was so fascinating. He could do things that I had never seen anyone do: make seedlings grow, plane a rough tree into a board, build things that would last forever. He was absolutely incredible.

Absolutely incredible. All this time, whether she knows it or not, my mother has been falling in love.

"I think you've got the hots for Sam," I say, testing the idea out loud.

"Oh, please. I'm a married lady, remember?"

I stare at her. "*Do* you remember?" I wouldn't blame her if she didn't. I could barely conjure a picture of my father's face, and I had less of a reason to want to be away from him. When I thought about him really hard, I could see his eyes—wide, blue, unbelievably tired. His eyes, and the lines around his mouth (although not his mouth itself) and the bend of his knuckles holding a pen. That's it, the memory of fifteen years.

"Of course I remember," my mother says, annoyed. "I've been married to your father for fifteen years. Aren't you supposed to love the person you marry?"

"You tell me."

This stops my mother dead in her tracks. "Yes, you are supposed to." She says the words slowly. She seems to be trying to convince herself. "Sam is just a friend." She waves her hand in front of us, as if she's clearing away everything else she's said. "My friend," she repeats. Then she looks at me with such confusion I think she's forgotten that she has been speaking to me all along. "I just wanted you to know that's where things stand."

"Well, I appreciate that," I say, and I try not to laugh. I don't imagine that's what she wants to hear. "Our ice cream is going to melt." She grabs my hand to take me back to the counter. I shake her away, because Hadley is watching. "Please, Mom. I'm not three."

I walk over to Hadley and offer him some of my cone. He smiles and pulls me to sit on his lap while he winds his tongue along the ridges made by the soft ice cream machine. We end up trading our cones, because after all I do not like creamsicle.

My mother is standing almost diagonally across from us. She is feeding Sam her cone while Sam is feeding her his cone. Sam misjudges the distance and dots a little vanilla on my mother's nose. She giggles and mashes her cone onto Sam's chin. Watching them, you have to smile. She's acting like a kid, I think. She's acting like me.

Uncle Joley, Hadley and I ride in the back of the red pickup on our way to Pickerel Pond. It's the place where Sam learned how to swim when he was a kid, a few miles away from the orchard. In the fifties, Sam yells from the cab of the truck, there was only this one pond. It's the one we'll see with lily pads that's still stocked with fish. But then the residents in the area chipped in and they dug a huge hole beside it, added sand for the bottom, and built swimming docks. For a summer fee, your whole family could come and swim whenever.

It is a perfect Sunday. The sun has scalded the metal of the flatbed and all three of us are sitting on our T-shirts. There isn't much of a wind, but there seems to be a breeze when you find yourself thinking about it. The air smells like luck. "I think you'll like this place," Hadley says over the roar of tires. "No undertow."

Maybe my mother will even swim. I've always assumed that it's the current of the ocean that keeps her from venturing into the water. In fact, she has been very optimistic about coming here for a picnic. She packed the lunch herself and keeps talking about how nice it will be to cool off.

The sun beats on the crown of my head. I hold my palm up against it for a minute of shade. "It's like fire," I tell Hadley, and I make him touch it too.

Uncle Joley, who has brought a ukulele, is trying to play the beginning bars of "Stairway to Heaven." He has almost got the notes right, but it sounds like sick luau music. To me it is not soothing, but it lulls Hadley to sleep. His head rests in my lap. The entire trip, Uncle Joley strums unlikely songs: "Happy Birthday," the Mickey Mouse Club theme song, "Blue Velvet," "Twist and Shout."

Sam pulls into what looks like a thicket, but it opens up to a dirt path and then becomes a road. At the end is a parking lot with a metal gate and rusted hinges. "They tried to lock up here at night for a few years," Sam yells to us. "But kids kept jumping the fence to party on the beach. When they left the gates open at night, all the kids stopped coming here."

Hadley, who has woken up, says, "That's 'cause it wasn't fun anymore. You only want to make trouble at a place that's off limits."

Sam leans his head out his window and tries to look at Hadley. "You used to come here?" He laughs. "Figures."

Sam and my mother carry the cooler to the pond, and I take the towels, the paddle games and the yellow kickball. Uncle Joley brings his ukulele. At a green post, Sam signs his name on a clipboard.

The pond is much larger than I had envisioned. It is almost perfectly square, but then again it was man-made. Adjacent to the swimming pond is the real pond, Pickerel Pond, and it is so large that I cannot see one of its edges. There are two Sunfishes, a muddy paddle-boat and a metal rowboat on the shore of the big pond, all labeled PPA, Pickerel Pond Association.

Sam comes up behind me. "You can take out the boats if no one else is using them." He turns to my mother, pointing out the sights that are missing at this swimming pond, twenty years after its creation. "There used to be a diving board off that dock. And over here? Second Dock here didn't always connect to the shore. If you wanted to get to it you had to swim to it. And when you're a little kid, you have to take a swimming test each summer to be allowed to swim beyond the buoys."

Hadley and Uncle Joley, who apparently have this all planned, take the towels and the ball from my arms. They grab me, kicking and screaming, and toss me on the count of three off First Dock. Somewhere, a fat lifeguard yells at us. No throwing. Not off that dock.

Hadley jumps in after me and grabs my ankle. He pulls me under. The water is murky, colored with some blue dye, and colder in some spots than others. I tread water, trying to find a warm place where Hadley will not try to drown me again.

Uncle Joley, who has been speaking with the lifeguard, does a swan-dive into the pond. He surfaces, already talking. "The reason this place looks like a giant Tid-E-Bowl is because of chemicals. They put the blue in to cloud the water so algae doesn't grow as easily."

"Algae," I say, "yuck." I am sure there is algae or something worse at the beaches of San Diego, but there you rest assured it keeps going out with the tide.

My mother keeps herself busy by spreading our towels on the small stretch of beach. It's funny, it isn't a beach at all. It's more like a couple of bulldozer dumps of sand, raked nicely. These people, I think. We could teach them a thing or two.

My mother creates a colony of towels. She borders the striped with the pink one, the *Les Miserables* promo towel with the Ralph Lauren. At the edge of all four of these she lays a big plaid blanket. I wonder who will get to lie there. She pays no attention at all to the position of the sun. "Hey," she calls to Sam, but he is out of her range.

In fact, at the exact moment she calls, Sam's body hits the water in a double somersault. For someone without the aid of a diving board he has an awfully good amount of height and spring. All the rest of us, already in the water, clap. Sam pulls himself onto Second Dock and takes a bow.

His body, unlike Hadley's, is compact. He has dark hair on his chest that grows in the shape of a heart. The hair on his legs, surprisingly, isn't as coarse. Sam has broad shoulders and a small waist, strong arms (all that lifting) and muscular thighs. I remember hearing something at the dinner table about him having trouble buying jeans—the legs always too tight, the waist too big, or something like that.

"Come on," Hadley says, swimming up behind me. "Let's race." He begins to do a vigorous crawl across the pond. He almost collides with Uncle Joley, who is swimming a lazy backstroke and chanting something in another language. Swimming, I remember, is a sort of religious thing for Uncle Joley. My mother says she has no idea where he got *that* from.

Hadley and I tie on the other side of the pond. "It's because you've got ten years on me."

"Give me a break," I laugh. "You just want an excuse."

"Oh, do I?" he says, pulling my hair and holding me under the water. I open my eyes, and massage his legs. When he lets me go, I swim between them, running my fingers along the inside. "That's cheating," he says.

We move to the shallow end, where a bunch of kids are on the shore, spooning sloppy sand into pails. Hadley and I sit on the bottom of the pond, letting the water play at our wrists. "I used to do that all the time. Sand castles."

"You grew up on a beach. You must have gotten pretty good," he says.

"I hated it. One minute you've got the pride of two hours' work; the next minute a wave knocks it all down."

"So you decided not to go to the beach. Toddler boycott?"

I turn to him, shocked. "How'd you know? I refused to go. I'd throw tantrums every weekend as my parents loaded up the car with floats and towels and coolers."

Hadley laughs. "Lucky guess. You must have been a ballsy little kid."

"Must have been? Everyone tells me I still *am.*"

"You're ballsy all right," Hadley says. "But you're no kid. You've got more sense in your head than almost anyone I know, and you sure as hell don't act like I did when I was fifteen."

"Back when there were dinosaurs."

"Yeah," Hadley grins. "Back when there were dinosaurs."

I would have loved to see Hadley when he was my age. I pretend to bury a pebble. "How did you act?" I ask.

"I cursed a lot and took up smoking. Sam and me were peeping toms in the girls' locker room in gym," Hadley says. "I wasn't quite as focused as you."

Focused. In Hadley's eyes there is a perfect, round reflection of the sun. "I guess I'm pretty focused."

Hadley and I play with the paddle game in the shallow end of the pond and try to catch bullfrogs in our hands. We dig flat stones from the sandy bottom with our toes and see who can skim them further. Sometimes, we just stretch out on the slick wet wood of First Dock, and, holding hands, we sleep. From time to time I catch my mother's eye. I do not know if she is looking at us in particular, or if it is just chance. She speaks to Sam at one point when he comes out of the pond to rest. Sam looks in our direction, and shrugs.

At lunch my mother completely forgets to serve Hadley and pretends that it is an accident. Then, she makes a big deal about giving him a beer, and not giving one to me. "Some of us," she says, staring at me, "are still too young to drink."

Hadley gives me half of his anyway when my mother gets up to go to the bathroom. Uncle Joley tells me to ignore her when she gets like this.

After lunch, my mother insists on cleaning up the picnic. She double-bags the garbage and rearranges the leftovers. She refolds used napkins. She shakes the towels off to get rid of crumbs. Sam, who has been waiting for her, jumps into the pond and swims the perimeter twice while she is doing all this. Apparently she said she would go in after lunch.

Finally Sam comes over to the oasis she's created. She is standing in front of it trying to find something else to do. Uncle Joley, Hadley and I kneel in the shallow end, waiting to see what will happen. Hadley has his hands spread across my rib cage, pressing me back against the floating pockets of his bathing suit.

Sam picks my mother up in his arms and begins to carry her towards the shallow end. She is still wearing her shorts.

"No," she says, laughing at first. She kicks her heels, and people around the pond smile, thinking this is some kind of joke. I lean against Hadley and wonder when she is going to snap.

"Sam," she says, more insistent. They have passed the edge of Second Dock; they are almost at the edge of the water. "I can't."

Sam stops for a moment, serious. "Can you swim?"

"Well, no," my mother says. Big mistake.

Sam's feet hit the water and my mother begins to shout. "No, Sam! No!"

"Good for him," Uncle Joley says, to no one in particular.

Sam begins to wade deeper. The water hits my mother's shorts, spreading like a stain. She stops kicking when she realizes it only makes her more wet. At one point I think she has almost resigned herself to what is going to happen. Sam, a man with a mission, continues to walk into the water.

"Don't do this to me," she whispers to Sam, but we can all make out the words.

"Don't worry," Sam says, and my mother clutches her arms tighter around him. He stares directly at her, like he has blocked out the rest of the watching world. "If you don't want to go—really don't want to go—then I'll take you back. Now. Just say the word."

My mother looks terrified. I am starting to feel sorry for her.

"I'll be with you," Sam says. "I'm not going to let anything happen."

She closes her eyes. "Go ahead. Maybe this is what I need after all."

With measured steps, Sam inches farther into the water until it reaches my mother's chin. Then, telling her to focus on his eyes, *right here*—he says—*my eyes*—he ducks under the surface.

It seems like a very long time. Everyone on the shore of the pond is watching. Several industrious kids with scuba masks swim out closer and peek underwater to see what is going on. Then my mother and Sam burst out of the water in unison, gasping for air. "Oh!" my mother cries. "It's so wonderful!" Her eyelashes blink back water, and her arms make wide circles in front of her, with ripples that reach us. Sam is triumphant. He winks at Uncle Joley and stays beside her, a personal lifeguard, fulfilling his promise to my mother. Nothing is going to happen, after all, as long as he is there. Well it's about time, I think. Hadley and I, bored by all the theatrics, check into taking a canoe out onto the larger pond. As we go, my mother is doing the crawl.

At one point my mother and I are the only two awake. We lie on the towels on our backs and try to find pictures in the clouds. I see a llama and a paper clip. She sees a kerosene lamp and a kangaroo. We both look for a chameleon, but there is none to be found.

"About Hadley," my mother says, "I've been thinking."

I feel my shoulders tense. "We have a lot of fun together."

"I've noticed. Sam says Hadley likes you a lot."

I lean on one elbow. "He said that?"

"In not so many words. He said he's a very responsible person." She picks grass absentmindedly with her left hand.

"Well he is. He takes care of just about everything on the farm that Sam doesn't. He's his right-hand man."

"Man," my mother says. "Exactly. You're a kid."

"I'm fifteen," I remind her. "I'm not a kid."

"You're a kid."

"How old were you when you started to go out with Daddy?"

My mother rolls onto her stomach and pushes her chin into the sand. I can barely understand her. I think she says, "It was different then."

"It's not different. You can't just keep yourself from falling for a person. You can't turn off your emotions like a faucet."

"Oh, you're an expert?"

I think about saying, *Neither are you,* but decide against it.

"You can't keep yourself from falling in love," she says, "but you *can* steer yourself away from the wrong people. That's all I'm trying to say. I'm just warning you before it's too late."

I roll away from her. Doesn't she know it's too late already?

Sam, awake, sits up between us. To keep up a conversation we'd have to talk across him. My mother, probably against her better judgment, gives me a look. We'll continue this later, she is saying.

They decide to go fishing in the metal rowboat, and leave me to watch over Uncle Joley, Hadley and the cooler. I take out a nectarine and eat it slowly. The juice drips down my neck and dries sticky.

My mother doesn't know what she is talking about. I don't believe I have a thing for "older men." I think I have a thing for Hadley. I reach down and swat a fly from his ear. He has three birthmarks on his lobe, three I hadn't noticed before. I count them, twice, fascinated. When I am with him, I don't know who I am. I don't know and I don't care; it must be someone wonderful because he seems to be having such a good time. And he holds me the way I used to hold china dolls as a child. They were so beautiful, their painted faces, that I only let myself take them off the shelves in my bedroom for minutes at a time.

Uncle Joley doesn't snore, but he breathes heavily when he sleeps. It drives me crazy. It's a raspy noise that comes in currents. You get into a rhythm listening to him, and then all of a sudden he alters the pattern, and you find yourself hanging, waiting for him to complete what he's started. After about three minutes of listening to this I stand and stretch. I walk around the pond, dipping my toes in the water and writing my initials in the sand. H.S. + R.J. I realize there won't be any tide to wash this away.

On the far end of the pond are a thatch of reeds and cattails. They are wheat-yellow and as high as I am. The area is off-limits, a swamp. When the lifeguard isn't looking I step behind the first row. Once I do this, I am hidden. I take a last look at Hadley; I sift through the reeds with my arms.

The ground is a sponge that closes up around my ankles. I keep walking. I want to know where I will end up. Somewhere, there must be water.

The cry of a cormorant tells me I have reached the edge. I can't actually see a shore; I have to part the thickest growth here with my hands. I have come to a part of Pickerel Pond that I couldn't see from the swimming area. It is an inlet shaded by willow trees. In the middle is a rowboat, my mother and Sam.

My mother has just caught a fish, I have no idea what kind it is. Its spine is a series of spikes that grow shorter and shorter; the hook seems to be caught in its cheek. My mother holds the fishing line while Sam smoothes the spikes of the fish and gently removes the hook. As he does this I hear a faint pluck. He holds the fish into the water and they both watch it swim away at an amazing pace. I myself did not know fish could move that quickly. When I look up at my mother and Sam, they seem quite pleased with themselves.

Sam has propped the oars on my mother's seat. She has her hands on the gunwale of the rowboat and is leaning back slightly. Sam, balancing, comes forward and catches his arms around her waist. When she sits up she doesn't look startled. She leans forward and kisses him.

I feel my heart beating faster and I think about leaving, but they will hear me then. I consciously try to think of my father, expecting him to jump to mind. But all I can remember is my own reaction, last Mother's Day, when my father cooked breakfast in bed for her. He woke me up to ask about my mother's favorite type of eggs and I looked at him as if he were crazy. He was married to her, after all. Didn't he know she doesn't eat eggs?

Sam cups his hand around my mother's right breast and kisses her neck. He says something to her I cannot hear. His thumb keeps rubbing and like magic I see her nipple appear. My mother tightens her grip on the edge of the boat. She opens her eyes to look at him. As the boat turns in the wind I see Sam. His eyes—well, they look like they are growing deeper. I can't describe it any better than that. He kisses her again, and from this new angle I see her mouth meet his, her tongue meet his.

They move so slowly. I do not know if this is something that has to do with the balance of the rowboat, or with what is happening. My head is pounding now and I don't know why. I cannot decide if I should be angry at her. I cannot decide if I should try to leave. All I know for sure is that I have never seen my mother like this. It crosses my mind: maybe this is not my mother; check again.

I turn around and run as fast as I can through the swamp. I trip across the chained "KEEP OUT" sign and cut my thigh. Ignoring the lifeguard's whistle I dive into that cool, anonymous pond. I open my eyes as wide as I can. I imagine water rushing into the back of my head. When I reach the other side I hide under the dock until I am ready. Then I throw myself down on my towel, beside Hadley, as if I really do not care at all.

20 JANE

It's seven in the morning and I'm driving on a humming highway with no other cars around me when suddenly I see a big pink truck approaching in the rearview mirror. I think, Oh good, some company. And this thing, this *thing*, gets closer and pulls next to me and—honest to God—it's a hot dog on wheels. Well it's a car, I suppose, but it's covered with a papier-mâché façade shaped like a large frankfurter in a roll. It has a squiggle of mustard on it too. Etched on the side of the bun is professional sign-painter's lettering, which says OSCAR MAYER. "Incredible," I say.

The driver, whom I can see through a little square cut out of the papier-mâché for side visibility, grins at me, showing all his teeth.

"Rebecca," I say, nudging her. "Get up. Look at this, will you? If you don't see this you won't believe me."

She sits up a little and blinks twice. Then she closes her eyes again. "You're dreaming," she tells me.

"I am not, I'm driving." I say it loud enough to make her open her eyes again. This time the driver waves at Rebecca.

Rebecca, alert, crawls into the back seat. "My bologna has a first name," she sings. "It's O-S-C-A-R." She doesn't finish the song. "What *is* this thing?" She is looking for a telltale freezer door, a disclaimer, anything that explains this vehicle.

"Maybe I should slow down and let him pass."

"No way!" Rebecca cries. "Go faster. See if he can match us with a wiener on the roof."

So I push the gas pedal a little harder. The hot dog car can keep up with us at seventy-five, eighty, even ninety miles per hour. "Remarkable. It's aerodynamic."

Rebecca climbs back into the passenger seat. "Maybe we should get one."

Then the driver of the hot dog car cuts me off, which makes me really angry because the tail of the hot dog grazes the luggage rack of my station wagon. Then he swerves into the breakdown lane so suddenly I shoot past him, but he quickly catches up to us. He rolls down his window and motions for Rebecca to do the same. He has a nice face, so I tell her it's okay.

"Want to stop for breakfast?" he yells across the rushing air. He points to a blue highway sign that indicates food is available at the next exit.

"I don't know," I say to Rebecca. "What do you think?"

"I think maybe he'll let us drive the car. *Okay!*" Rebecca yells to him, and she smiles like she has all the charm in the world tucked into her back pocket.

We follow his car into the parking lot of the Pillar O'Salt diner. There are two windows boarded up, and only one other car, the chef's, I imagine. However, there does not seem to be a warning from the Department of Health. Do they have one out here, I wonder?

Rebecca gets out of the car first and runs over to touch the material that makes up the bun of the hot dog truck. It is rough and stubbly, a disappointment. The driver gets out of the cab. "Hello," he says, in a voice that sounds oddly prepubescent. "Nice of you to join me for breakfast. I'm Ernie Barb."

"Lila Moss," I say, offering my hand. "And my daughter, Pearl." Rebecca, somewhat surprised, curtsies.

"Pretty nice truck, eh?" he says to Rebecca.

"Nice isn't the word." She reaches to feel the lettering on the bun. The O itself is larger than her head.

"It's a promo truck. Not real functional but it gets people to notice."

"That it does," I tell him. "Do you work for Oscar Mayer?"

"I sure do. I drive across the country just drumming up interest. Recognition is a big factor in the sales of processed meats, you know."

I nod. "I can imagine." Ernie touches my shoulder to lead me towards the diner. "Have you eaten here?"

"Oh, lots of times. It's better than it looks." Ernie walks first, then me, then Rebecca, through the swinging saloon doors of the diner. I find myself wondering how they lock them at night.

Ernie has a yellow crew cut spiked in a haphazard halo around his face. Although I can only see the stubs of his hair it seems to grow thicker in some patches than in others. His skin is oily and he has three or four chins. "Annabelle!" he calls, and a short fat woman in the clipped dress of a waitress lumbers out of the men's room, of all places. "I'm back, sugar."

"Oh," she says, in a gravelly voice that makes Rebecca jump. "And to what do we owe this honor?" Then, as if on second thought, she kisses him directly on the mouth and murmurs, "It's good to see you."

"This is Lulu and Pearl," Ernie says.

"Lila," I correct him, and he repeats the word, rolling it around his mouth like a marble. "We were together on the highway."

"Good for you," Annabelle says, another mood shift. She slaps three menus on our table and leaves in an unexplained huff.

Except for Annabelle and an absent chef (unless, I think, she *is* the absent chef . . .), we are the only people in the diner. It's early, but somehow I get the feeling no one ever really comes to the Pillar O'Salt. Its decor is just a little off: homey ruffled curtains, but cut in a sick green plaid; sturdy wooden tables that have been painted the hazard shade of orange.

"It's nice to have a meal *with* people for a change," Ernie says, and Rebecca and I smile politely. "Lonely on the road." We nod. Rebecca tries to explode the beads of water on her glass with her finger. "Pearl," Ernie says, but Rebecca doesn't need the clue. "Pearl!" It is the noise, not the name, that sparks Rebecca's attention. "How old are you, girl?"

"Almost fifteen. I'll be fifteen next week." She looks at me, asking if this, like our names, is privileged information she shouldn't be telling a stranger.

"Glory," says Ernie. "This calls for something." He squeezes out of his chair and walks into the men's room, which from Annabelle's actions, I've deduced, must connect to the kitchen. He comes out a minute later, carrying our meals. Rebecca's scrambled eggs support a birthday candle that systematically drips onto her hash browns. Ernie sings "Happy Birthday" by himself.

"Isn't that nice, Pearl," I say. "An early present."

"And it truly is," Ernie says. "This meal's on me."

"Thank you, Mr. Barb." Rebecca picks up her fork and Ernie tells her to make a wish—which she does, blowing the candle onto a napkin and starting a small fire that Ernie douses with tomato juice.

Throughout the meal Ernie discusses his job: how he got it (an uncle in corporate); how he likes it (he does); how he's been rewarded (HOT DOG! Publicity Award, 1986 and 1987). Finally he asks us where we're from (Arizona) and where we're headed (my sister Greta's in Salt Lake City). Rebecca kicks me under the table every time I lie, but she doesn't know any better. Oliver can be a very smart man.

This is what Ernie eats: a stack of raspberry pancakes, three eggs, with sausage, a side order of hash browns, four slices of toast, an English muffin, two blintzes, two grapefruit halves, smoked mackerel. It is only during his mushroom omelette that he says he feels stuffed. In the kitchen, Annabelle drops something that breaks.

In the end, Ernie doesn't even pay for the meal; Annabelle insists it's on the house. She stands at the doorway as we walk back to Ernie's hot-dog car. "Ladies," he says, "a pleasure." He gives me his card, which has no home address, only the number for his car phone.

Rebecca and I stand in front of the diner, watching the fabricated hot dog disappear at a point on the horizon. We stand just far enough apart to not be able to touch each other.

"It was too red to look real," Rebecca says, turning. "Did you notice?"

21 JANE

Rebecca is looking out the window at the flat field of white. It's mesmerizing. "Do you think this is what Heaven is like?" Rebecca asks.

"I hope not," I say. "I like a little color."

It would be easy to be fooled into believing the Great Salt Plains are covered with snow, if it weren't for the ninety-five-degree temperatures and the gusts of hot wind that hit my face like someone's breath. Salt Lake City, dwarfed by the huge Mormon Church, is not a place where I feel comfortable. In fact, I feel like I am sinking deeper into this different religion, this different climate, this different architecture. My clothes stick to me. I want to get Joley's letter and leave.

But the postmaster, a thin middle-aged man with a sagging moustache, insists there is no letter for a Jane Jones. Or a Rebecca Jones. No Joneses at all, he says.

"Look again. Please." Rebecca is sitting on the front steps of the post office when I come out. I could swear I see heat waving up from the pavement. "We're in trouble," I say, sitting beside her. Rebecca's shirt is stuck to her back, too, and there are circles of sweat under her arms. "Joley's letter isn't here."

"So let's call him."

She doesn't understand the pull of Joley's words like I do. It's not his directions I need, it's his voice. I don't care what he says, just that he says it. "There are two branch post offices. I'm going to try there."

But the two branch offices have no mail for me either. I think about throwing a tantrum but that won't do anyone any good. Instead, I pace the anteroom of the post office, then I walk out onto the blazing sidewalk, where Rebecca stands, accusatory.

"Well," Rebecca says.

"It should have been here." I look up at the sun, which seems to have exploded in the past minute. "Joley wouldn't do this to me." I feel like crying and I am weighing the consequences when I look at the sun again and, hissing, it comes hurtling down at me and my world turns black.

"She's coming around," someone says, and there are hands; hands with cool water pressing against my neck and my forehead, my wrists. This face, too big, looms into view.

Oliver? I try to say but I can't remember where my voice is.

"Mom. Mom." It's Rebecca, I can smell her. I open my eyes wide and see my daughter leaning over me, the ends of her hair grazing my chin like silk. "You fainted."

"You hit your head, Mrs. Jones," says the displaced voice I heard before. "It's just a cut, no stitches needed."

"Where am I?"

"You're in the post office," that other voice says, and then a man squats in front of me. He smiles. He is handsome. "Are you feeling all right?"

"Okay." I turn my head. Three young women with washcloths are on my right. One of them says, "Now don't sit up too fast."

Rebecca squeezes my hand. "Eric was nearby when you collapsed. He helped me carry you in here, and his wives helped you cool off." She looks frightened, I don't blame her.

"Wives. Oh."

One of the women gives Rebecca a little jar and tells her to hang onto it in case this happens again. "The heat is dry here," Eric tells me. "This happens to visitors a lot."

"We're not visiting, we're just passing through," I say, as if it matters. "What did I do to my head?"

"You fell on it," Rebecca says, matter-of-fact.

"Maybe I should go to the hospital."

"I think you'll be fine," says the middle wife. She has long black hair woven into a French braid. "I'm a nurse, and Eric's a doctor. A pediatrician, but he knows about fainting."

"You picked a lucky bunch to fall in front of," Eric says, and the women laugh.

I try to stand up and I realize my knees aren't up to it. Eric grabs me quickly and loops my arm around his neck. The sky is spinning. "Sit her down," Eric commands. "Listen," he turns to Rebecca. "Let us take you to the lake. We're on our way anyway, and it might do your mother some good to cool off."

"Is that okay, Mom?" Rebecca says. "Did you hear?" She is shouting.

"I'm not deaf. Fine. Great." I am lifted to my feet by Rebecca, Eric and two wives. The third carries my purse.

In the back of Eric's minivan are rubber floats and towels that get pushed out of the way for Rebecca and me. Eric positions me lying down, with my feet propped up on an inner tube. From time to time I take sips of cold water from a thermos. I have no idea where this lake is and I'm too tired to find out.

But when we stop at the shores of the Great Salt Lake I am impressed. You can see across it for miles; it might as well have been an ocean. Eric carries me to the lake down a steep embankment, surprising for someone who is relatively slight. There are many people swimming here. I sit on the sandy bottom of the lake, in a shallow spot that wets my shorts and half my T-shirt. I beg not to go in farther than this; I don't like to swim, or to feel that my feet cannot reach the bottom.

I am wondering how my clothes will ever dry, when it occurs to me I keep floating up to the surface. I have to bury my arms in the sand to keep sitting. This takes all the energy I have. Eric and two wives paddle past me on a raft. "How do you feel?" he says.

"Better," I lie, but I *am* beginning to cool off. My skin no longer feels like it is raw and splitting. I duck my head under the water to wet my scalp.

Rebecca runs past me, splashing. "Isn't this excellent!" She dives and surfaces like an otter. I've forgotten how much she loves to swim, since I hardly ever take her to the water.

Rebecca moves a little farther out and says, "Hey Mom, no hands." She sticks her arms and legs into the air, buoyant on her back.

"It's the salt," Eric tells me, gently helping me to my feet. "You float better than you do in an ocean. Not bad, for a landlocked state."

Rebecca tells me to lie on my back. "I'll swim you out. I'm a lifeguard, remember?" She wraps her arm across my chest and vigorously scissor-kicks. Because I am in her arms, her care, I don't try to protest. Also because I am still feeling fairly sick.

After a second, when I have the courage to open my eyes, I see the clouds passing by, lazy and liquid. I listen to the way my daughter breathes. I concentrate on being weightless.

"Look, Mom," Rebecca says, dancing in front of me. "You're doing it by yourself. Yourself!" She is no longer holding me. In the center of this great lake, forces I can't even see keep me afloat.

22 Rebecca *July 21, 1990*

"What's the matter with you!" I shout at Hadley. He walks down the hill out of my range of vision. For the life of me I cannot figure out what I have done.

This is the way it has been all day. Hadley was already out when I woke up. He was with the sheep, feeding them. Sheep grain, Hadley said, is made of oats and molasses and corn and barley. Stick your nose in the bin, he said, it smells great. So I held my head in the cool metal storage trough and I breathed in this honey smell. When I lifted my head, Hadley had gone without saying goodbye.

Just now I came upon him on the hill drinking from an army canteen. All I did was put my hand on his arm, real light, so I wouldn't startle him. But Hadley jumped a foot and spilled water on his shirt. "For Chrissake," he yelled, and he shook his arm away. "Can't you just leave me be?"

I don't understand. He's been so nice to me the three days we've been here. He was the one who offered to take me on a tour of the orchard. He showed me what the different types of apple were. He let me wrap grafting tape around his hand to practice at it. He showed me the way to make cider. I didn't even ask, and he did all this for me.

Yesterday when he took me out on the tractor I told him about my father. I told him the kind of work he does. I told him what my father looks like when he talks about his work. His lips twitch and his cheeks flush. When he talks about me, it is like he is talking about nothing at all.

During our talk, Hadley had said, "I'm sure you can remember when you had a good time with him." So I thought. But I could only remember when he had bought me a bicycle. He came with me into the street to show me how to ride it. He told me how to pedal and what balance was, scientifically. A couple of times he ran down the street beside me, yelling, *You've got it! You've got it!* Then he seemed to fall back. I kept pedaling and pedaling but I reached a hill I could not manage. I kept thinking, I want Daddy to notice me, how well I do. When I fell off the bicycle I watched it roll down the hill, dented and busted, and I did not notice I was bleeding. I needed stitches in my wrist and forehead that Christmas. My father had gone inside to take a business call.

Hadley didn't say anything at all when I told him that. He changed the topic. He told me if you handle apples like eggs and pack them just right, they will not bruise.

I tried to talk about it again. Once I had gotten started, there was no stopping me. I told him about the time Daddy hit my mother, and about the plane crash. He stopped the tractor in the middle of the field to listen. I told him that I didn't love my father.

"Everyone loves their father."

"Why," I had asked. "Who says that they've got that coming to them?"

And Hadley started the tractor again and didn't say much for the rest of the afternoon. He didn't eat dinner with us. And now this.

He thinks that I am a spoiled brat. That there is something wrong with me. Maybe there *is* something wrong with me. Maybe you are supposed to love your parents, no matter what.

It is easier with my mother; it has to do with the way we both think. I feel I must be following in her footsteps, because every time I turn around she knows exactly where I stand. She doesn't really judge me like my friends' mothers do; she just takes me the way I am. Sometimes she really seems to like that, too. We're more like equals, I suppose. She listens to me, but not because she's my mother. She listens to me because she expects me to listen to her.

When I was little I used to pretend my father had a pet name for me. He called me cookiepie and he would tuck me in at night, every other night, alternating with my mother. I believed in this so hard that I would shut my eyes tight under the covers until I heard footsteps, and someone stuffing the sheets under the mattress. Then I'd peek, and it was always my mother.

As I got older I tried to see what held his interest. I'd snoop through the drawers in his study, holding charts this way and that. I'd steal his whale tapes and play them on my Walkman. Once I spent a week looking up all the words I didn't get in an article he'd written. When he came home from his trip and saw that I had gone through his drawers he called me into the study. He made me bend over his knee and he spanked me. I was twelve.

I went through a period then where I tried to see what other things might possibly hold his attention. I watched the way he moved around my mother. I expected to see it—love—but it was strange. They lived in the same house and could go for an entire day without saying anything to each other. I tried to see what I could do to make him notice me. I wore skirts that were too tight. I insisted on wearing makeup to school. I had my best friend's older sister buy me a pack of cigarettes and I left them on top of my textbooks, right where my father would see it, but in the end he said nothing to me at all. In the end, it was my mother who grounded me for a month.

There is only one time that I can remember my father in command of a situation. When I was five we sailed to Bermuda as a family—my father for work and my mother and I for pleasure. We visited many tourist attractions and we roasted hot dogs on the beach. We went out on my father's rented boat to record the whales one day. My mother held onto the rail and I held onto my mother. My father ran around the boat, calling to the men who worked for him to change course and to raise the speed to so many knots. He paused only for a moment at the bow with his binoculars and when he saw what he was looking for he smiled so wide. He smiled like I had never seen him smile. I got scared and buried my face in my mother's side.

Without Hadley around there's nothing for me to do at this orchard. Uncle Joley has gone to town with Sam and I don't know any of the other workers by name. They are polite, but they don't take time to explain.

I've been walking aimlessly, and to my surprise I find my mother in the commercial section of the orchard. My mother, who doesn't know and doesn't care about farming at all. It's a lazy kind of day. "You can feel the heat just hanging here, can't you," she says when she sees me. "It's enough to make you want to go back to California."

She is sitting with her back pressed against a tree, one that I know has been sprayed recently. It will make her pretty cotton skirt smell like citronella. I don't mention this, though. It is already too late. "Where have you been hiding yourself at this wonderful Club Med?"

"Not much to do, is there? I was off with Hadley but he's ignoring me today." I try to sound nonchalant. "Acting like a big shot with Sam gone."

"Oh, please," my mother says. She lolls her head backward so that her chin points into the breeze. "Don't even mention his name."

"Sam?"

"The man is a fool. No social graces whatsoever. And rude—" she rubs her neck with her right hand, "—rude like I can't tell you. I was in the bathroom this morning, and you know the way there's no lock? Three guesses who comes waltzing in when I'm in the shower. And he has the audacity to stand in front of the mirror and lather his whole face with shaving cream before I can say, Excuse me. So when I do he turns around—turns around!—and looks at me. He gets all pissed off and says he isn't used to having women around who spend half their lives in the bathroom."

I think this is hilarious. "Did he see you?"

"Of course he saw me."

"No," I say. "Did he *see* you?"

"How should I know? And why should I care?"

"Uncle Joley says Sam's a really good businessman. He's made the place three times as profitable as it was when his father was around."

"He may be a great businessman for all I care, but he's a lousy host."

"We didn't exactly come here invited."

"That's not the point." I want to ask her what the point is, but I decide to let it be.

My mother stands up and twirls the cotton skirt. Citronella. She doesn't seem to notice. "What do you think?"

She had been raiding a closet in the room she's sleeping in—Sam's mother's, I assume, all her extra clothes she didn't take to Florida. The two women are not the same size; my mother has been wearing most things with a belt of Sam's that she added another hole to.

"Mom," I ask, "why do you and Sam hate each other? You don't know him well enough for that."

"Oh yes I do. Sam and I grew up with these stereotypes, you know? In Newton we used to make fun of all the tech kids who couldn't get into colleges—not even state schools. It seemed every mechanic and carpenter had come from Minuteman and was proud of it, and we couldn't understand it; you know the value of a good education. There's no denying that Sam Hansen is an intelligent man. But don't you think he could do a lot better than this—" She sweeps her arm out over these one hundred acres, green and wild and polka-dotted with the heads of early apples. "If he's so smart, why is he happy running a tractor all day?"

"That's not what he does all day," I protest. "You haven't even walked around this place. They work so hard! And it's all orchestrated, you know? Season by season. You couldn't do it."

"Of course I could. I just don't want to."

"You have got some chip on your shoulder. Honestly." I roll over onto my stomach, breathing clover. "I don't think that's why you hate Sam. My theory is you hate him because he is so unbelievably happy."

"That's ridiculous."

"He knows exactly what he wants, and he goes and gets it. You may not want the same thing, but he's still a step ahead of you." I stare up at her. "And that is driving you crazy."

"Thank you, Dr. Freud." My mother sits down on the cool grass and hugs her knees to her chest. "I'm not here to see Sam. I'm here to see Joley. And we're having a wonderful time together."

"So now what?"

When she begins to speak she stutters. "We'll just stay for a little while. Stay and figure out some things, and then we'll come to a decision."

"In other words," I say, "you have absolutely no idea when we're leaving."

My mother shoots me a look that suggests she still has the power to punish me. "What is this all about, Rebecca? Do you miss your father?"

"What makes you think that?"

"I don't know. You can tell me if you do. I mean, he *is* your father. It's natural."

"I don't miss Daddy." My voice goes flat. "I don't." Humidity slides across the hills and hangs on the tree branches. It presses against my throat and makes me choke a little. I don't miss my father, not even when I am trying to miss him.

"Sssh," my other says, pulling me closer. We sit beneath the heavy arms of an old McIntosh tree that has been grafted to bear Spartans. She is holding me for the wrong reasons and still it feels nice. Far away, I see the Jeep drive up with Sam and Uncle Joley. They get out and begin walking towards where we are sitting. At a certain point, Uncle Joley notices my mother and me. He says something to Sam and points. They stop walking and Sam's eyes connect with my mother's for a moment. Uncle Joley continues to walk towards us but Sam turns sharply to the left. He does not follow.

At dinner that night, Uncle Joley tells us about the buyer for Purity, a woman named Regalia Clippe. Although Sam had mentioned her, Uncle Joley hadn't met her until today. She was five feet tall and weighed over two hundred pounds. She loved gossip and the story today was about herself: she had just returned from getting married at the Church of the Living Gospel in Reno, Nevada. Her brand new husband ran the only sod farm in New Hampshire and (could they tell from the circles beneath her eyes?) she hadn't been getting a lot of sleep.

"I don't know, Joley," my mother said, laughing. "I think people like that follow you around. You've met more than your fair share."

Hadley, who had come for dinner, asked me to pass the zucchini. It was more than he'd said to me all day.

"*I* met Regalia Clippe. She's my buyer. It has nothing to do with Joley," Sam says.

"I didn't mean anything by it." My mother looks at me.

"The Church of the Living Gospel," Uncle Joley says, and my mother laughs. He leans his elbows on the table. "You've got a really nice laugh, Jane. Like bells."

"Church of the Living Gospel Bells?' Sam says, and everyone cracks up. I try to catch Hadley's eye, but he's staring at his food like it's something he has never seen before.

"We've got to do something about the weeds in the west corner," Hadley says to Sam. "They're out of control. If you want we can let the sheep in—now that they're sheared there's no reason to keep them penned." Sam nods, and Hadley grins at his plate. He is pleased, I can tell, to have made that decision.

"Well, the good news," Sam says, "is that Regalia Clippe renewed our contract for Red Delicious."

"That's great," I say.

Hadley looks up. "Yeah, but how many others is she buying from, Sam?"

"Sure, Hadley, just knock the wind out of my sails." Sam is smiling; he is not really angry. "I don't know. I didn't ask her. But she was real happy to have us back again and last year we made up Collins' shipment when the aphids hit him, so that's that."

For dinner we are having zucchini and almonds, fried chicken, peas and mashed potatoes. It is really very good. Sam cooked it all in a matter of minutes. Hadley says Sam always does the cooking.

"So what did you two do today?" Uncle Joley asks. My mother is about to answer when she notices that Uncle Joley is staring right at Hadley and me. Hadley's face turns bright red. My mother folds her hands in her lap.

Sam drops his fork, which clatters on the edge of his plate. Finally Hadley looks up at my uncle. "We didn't do anything, all right? I had a lot of stuff I had to get done." He rolls his napkin into a ball and whips it across the room. It misses the garbage pail; instead, it hits the dog. "I've got somewhere I have to go," Hadley mutters. He scrapes his chair back and runs out of the kitchen.

"What's his problem?" Sam helps himself to a mountain of potatoes and shakes his head.

"Sam," my mother says, "I was wondering why you don't grow anything but apples here?"

I kick her under the table. It isn't any of her business.

"Apples take a lot of time and effort." I get the feeling he has been asked this before.

"But couldn't you make more money if you diversify?"

"Excuse me," Sam says quietly, "but who the hell are you? You come in here and two days later you're telling me how to run things?"

"I wasn't—"

"If you knew a damn thing about farming maybe I'd listen."

"I don't have to take this." My mother is near tears, I can tell by the thick of her voice. "I was just making conversation."

"You were making trouble," Sam says, "plain and simple."

My mother's voice gets husky. I remember a story she likes to tell, about when she worked placing classified ads for the *Boston Globe* as a college kid, and one man fell in love with her voice. He sold his boat the first week but he'd keep calling her to hear her talk. He placed his ad the entire summer just so he could listen to my mother.

"Sam." Uncle Joey touches my mother's arm. She stands up and runs towards the barn.

The three of us—Sam, Uncle Joley and me—sit in silence for a moment.

"Want any more chicken?" Sam offers.

"I think you overreacted," Uncle Joley says. "Maybe you could apologize."

"Jesus, Joley," Sam sighs, leaning back. "She's your sister. *You* invited her here. Look. She just doesn't belong in a place like this. She should be wearing high-heeled shoes and clicking along some marble parlor in L.A."

"That's not fair," I protest. "You don't even know her."

"I know plenty like her," Sam says. "Would it make it all right if I went out there and apologized? Shit. For a little peace and quiet." He stands up and pushes away his plate. "So much for a happy little family dinner."

Uncle Joley and I finish the zucchini. Then we finish the potatoes. We don't say anything. My foot taps on the linoleum, fast. "I'm going out there."

"Leave them alone, Rebecca. They'll work it all out. They need to."

He may be right but this is my mother we are talking about. I have visions of her like a hellcat, clawing at Sam and leaving him with raw scratch marks on his cheeks and arms. Then I picture Sam's strength getting the best of her. Would he do that? Or is that only my father?

I hear their voices long before I see them, behind the shed that holds the tractor and the rototiller. Because Uncle Joley may be right, I decide I should not interfere. I slouch down and feel splinters crack through my shirt.

"I told you I was sorry," Sam says. "What more can I do?"

My mother's voice is farther away. "You're right. It's your house, your farm, and I shouldn't be here. Joley imposed on you. He shouldn't have asked you to do something like this."

"I know what 'imposed' means."

"I didn't mean it like that. I don't mean anything the way you take it. It's like every sentence I say goes through your head the reverse of the way I intended it."

Sam leans against the wall of the shed so heavily I think he may be able to feel me there. "When my father ran this place he was real haphazard about it. A stock here, another stock there. Commercial trees mixed right in with retail. Since I was eleven I told him this wasn't the way to run an apple orchard. He told me I didn't know what I was talking about, and no matter how much schoolwork I did on the subject I didn't have as much experience running the place as he did. How could I? So when he retired to Florida, I dug up the younger trees and replanted them the way I wanted them. I lost a couple, and I knew I was taking a hell of a risk. He hasn't been up here since he retired, and when he calls I pretend the place still looks the way it was when he left."

"I get your point, Sam."

"No, you don't. I don't give a shit if you think this orchard should grow watermelons and cabbage. Go tell Joley and tell Rebecca and whoever the hell you want. And the day I die if you can convince everyone else, go ahead and replant the place. But don't you ever tell me to my face what I've done so far is wrong. This farm—it's the best thing I've ever done. It's like—it's like me telling you your daughter is no good."

My mother doesn't answer. "I wouldn't plant watermelons," she says finally, and Sam laughs.

"Let's start over. I'm Sam Hansen. And you're—?"

"Jane. Jane Jones. God," my mother says, "I sound like the most boring person on earth."

"Oh, I doubt it." I hear, quite clearly, the sound of their fingers pressed into a handshake. It is quiet as night.

Their footsteps come in fours, and they get closer to where I am sitting. In a panic I crawl to the other side of the shed, away from their voices. The only place to go is into the barn. I try to be quiet when my sneakers scratch against the hay. I press my belly to the floor and pull myself in on my fingertips.

When I sit up the first thing I see is a bat. It is dark and folded into the corner of the hayloft. I consider screaming but what good would that do me?

The bat screeches and flies past me. I put my hands up to shield my face and something catches my wrists. When I turn around, it is Hadley.

"What are you doing here?" I say, terrified.

"I live here," Hadley says. "What are *you* doing here?"

"I was eavesdropping. Did you hear them?"

Hadley nods. He picks a stalk from the hay bales lining the wall and puts it between his front teeth. "I was hoping for a knock-out in the first round."

"You're awful," I tell him, but I laugh. In this light, he looks taller than usual. And his lips, the way they come down so far in the front. I hold out my hand. I want to touch him. Embarrassed, I pull away. "Did you get all your stuff done?"

"What stuff?"

"Dinner. What you were saying to my uncle."

"Oh," Hadley says. He shuffles his boots on the loose hay. "That."

He doesn't say anything for such a long time I think something might be wrong. I turn around and stare at him. "What's the matter with me?"

"There's nothing the matter with you," Hadley says. "You're a very pretty little girl."

"I'm not a little girl." I hold my chin higher.

"I know how old you are. I asked Joley."

So much for that. "Well I don't get it. I was having a really good time with you the other day, and then clear out of the blue you act like I have the plague."

"I just can't spend a lot of time with you." He paces back and forth in the little square of light the moon makes on the floor of the barn. "I get paid for this, Rebecca. This is my job, you know?"

"No, I don't know. I don't know about jobs at all, but I have a pretty good idea of the way you're supposed to treat a friend."

"Don't do this to me," Hadley said.

I clench my fists at my sides. Do *what?* I haven't done anything at all.

He takes a step closer and my heart jumps, just like that. I take a step backward.

Pressed up against the stack of hay bales, I start to hyperventilate. I'm breathing in all this awful dry grass and it is getting to my lungs. Hadley leans in close to me, and I see my face reflected in his eyes.

I push my hand against his chest and walk to the other side of the barn. "So you have to get rid of the weeds, is that it? That's what you were talking to Sam about. When do those apples drop—September?" I talk a mile a minute about a subject I do not know.

"What are you going to do tomorrow? I was thinking, maybe I'll walk into Stow Center tomorrow. I haven't been there yet and Uncle Joley says there's this record store I'd really like with a lot of neon and stuff. Did I ask you what you're going to do tomorrow?"

"This," Hadley says, and he wraps his arms around my waist and he kisses me.

I used to think that the best feeling in the world was flying on my bicycle down a hill that I had worked so hard to climb, flying faster than the speed of sound, with my arms and my hair waving. I'd cup one hand and try to catch the air and when I got to the bottom, after all that, there was nothing in my hand.

I think of this in the moments that Hadley is pressed up against me and I keep my eyes wide open, afraid that I'll find nothing there when I am so convinced. He sees me, at one point, and smiles with my lips still touching his. "What are you looking at?" he whispers.

"You," I tell him.

23 JOLEY

My father died three years before my mother. The doctor said it was a heart attack but Jane and I had our doubts. It had yet to be proven that my father had a heart at all.

Jane was living in San Diego by then, and I was in Mexico. I had been doing research on Cortèz, which turned into research on the Holy Grail, which turned into research about I don't know what. Jane was the only person who knew where I was—in a little village near Tepehuanas that was so small it didn't have a name of its own. I lived with a pregnant housekeeper named Maria and her three cats. I dug a small excavation site in the wilds of the mountains. I found nothing, but I told that to nobody but Jane.

My mother, of course, called Jane first. She would have called me, I imagine, but she didn't know my address, or how to dial an international call. She said that just like that my father had dropped dead. The hospital kept asking her if he had complained of gas or made sounds during the night, but my mother did not know. She got used to sleeping with earplugs many years ago to combat my father's snoring, and she always went to bed before he did.

"Do you think," Jane said noncommittally on the flight to Boston, "they have had sex during this decade?"

"I don't know," I told her. "I don't know what they do."

Did I mention this all happened the weekend before Easter?

When we arrived at the house my mother was sitting on the front lawn. She was wearing a familiar purple bathrobe and Dearfoam slippers, although it was past noon. "Mama," Jane said, rushing into her arms. My mother hugged Jane the way she always did: looking over her shoulder at me. I wondered, and I still do, if she looked at Jane when I was in her arms. For Jane's sake, I always hoped so. "It's over," Jane said.

And my mother looked at her as if she was crazy. "What do you mean it's over?"

Jane looked at me. "Nothing, Ma." She pulled me aside as we climbed up the steps to the house. "What is *it with her?" Jane said. "Or is it me?"*

I wouldn't know. I was the only person in that household my father did not inflict violence upon, thanks largely to my sister's interference. Jane had given up her childhood for me, really, so what else could I say? "It's not you," I told her.

Jane and I were sent out to get a party platter for the guests after the funeral. Daddy's body had been set on ice for three days now; no church would hold a service because of Easter. But now, with the funeral set for Monday, preparations had to be made. Jane and I went to Star Market's deli counter; it was the closest and honestly neither of us cared about the caliber of the food. "Hey, honey," said the burly man at the counter. "You having relatives over for Easter?"

While my mother went through the ritual of crying, pulling at her hair and stroking old photos, Jane and I sat upstairs in what used to be our rooms. We talked about everything we could remember that might help us put it all behind. I touched the places on Jane where there used to be bruises. I let her talk about the very worst time, but she only hinted at what had happened that night she was driven to leave.

We slept in our respective beds the night before the funeral, with the doors open in case Mama needed us. A little after three Jane came into my room. She shut the door, sat on the edge of the bed, and then she handed me a picture of the two of us, one she had found trapped between the headboard of her bed and the wall. "I've been thinking there's something wrong with me," she whispered. "I don't feel anything. I'm going through the motions, you know, but I couldn't care less that he's dead."

I held her hand. She was wearing an old nightgown of our mother's. I found myself wondering what she wore at night, next to Oliver, in her own home. She would never sleep naked like I did. She did not like the feeling. "There's nothing wrong with you. Considering the circumstances."

"But she's *crying.* She's *upset. And he was worse with her than he was with me." She let those last words run together and then she got into bed beside me. Her feet were very cold, and the strange thing was, they stayed like that the entire night.*

At the funeral, the reverend talked about how my father had been such a pillar of the community. He mentioned that he was a doting husband and father. I held Jane's hand. Neither of us cried, or pretended to for the sake of decency.

It was an open casket. My mother wanted it that way. Jane accepted everyone's condolences and I kept my arm around my mother's shoulders, holding her up most of the time. I brought her juice and biscuits and did everything my maiden aunts suggested, to help her through such a difficult time.

By the time all our relatives and assumed friends left for the graveyard it was mid-afternoon. The funeral manager gave Jane the bill and then she disappeared. When I asked him where she had gone he pointed to the anteroom, the place they had the coffin on display. I watched her standing over his image, this wax mask that carried none of the terror and the power I knew. She ran her finger over the silk that lined the box. She touched my father's blue ancient matter tie. Then she raised her arm. Her wrist was shaking when she whipped her hand through the air, the hand that I caught before she struck a dead man.

24 SAM

If you look real carefully, you can see the scars on my eyes. I was born cross-eyed, and the first operation was done when I was so young I cannot remember. Medically speaking, the procedure involved tightening up the slack muscles that let my eye wander. Invisible stitches, I guess. There's hardly anything there now, twenty-four years later, except a thin line of film in each eye, like a yellow eyelash. You can see this when I look out the corner of my eye.

Until I had the second operation I wore thick Coke-bottle glasses; round ones that made me look something like a bullfrog or a lawyer. I did not have many friends, and during recess I'd sit alone behind the swings and eat the sandwich my mother had packed in my lunch box. Sometimes the other kids came up, called me four-eyes or crossed their eyes to make fun of me. If I came home from school crying, my mother would bury my face in her apron—it smelled of fresh flour—and tell me how handsome I was. I wanted to believe her, but I couldn't. I took to looking down at my shoes.

My teachers began to say I was shy, and they called up my mother, concerned. One day my parents told me I was going to have an operation. I would stay in a hospital, and I would have patches on my eyes for a while, and when it was all over my eyes would look just like everyone else's. Like I said, I do not remember my first operation, but the second is very clear. I was scared it would change the way I'd see things. I wondered if when the bandages were removed, I would look the way I thought I looked. If the colors I saw would be the same.

The day after the operation I heard my mother's voice at the foot of the bed. "Sam, honey, how do you feel?"

My father touched my shoulder and handed me a wrapped package. "See if you can tell what it is." I ripped off the paper and ran my hands along the soft leather folds of a soccer ball. Best of all—I knew exactly what it would look like.

I asked to hold the soccer ball when my bandages were removed. The doctor smelled like aftershave and told me what he was doing every step of the way. Finally he told me to open my eyes.

When I did, everything was fuzzy, but I could make out the black and white boxes of the soccer ball. Black was still black and white was still white. As I blinked, everything started to come clear—clearer than it was before the operation, in fact. I smiled when I saw my mother. "It's you," I said, and she laughed.

"Who did you expect?" she asked.

Sometimes when I look in the mirror now I still see my eyes crossed. I've dated ladies who tell me how nice my eyes are: the most unusual color, reminds them of the fog in summer, things like that. I let the words roll right off my back. I'm no more handsome than the next guy, really. In a lot of ways I'm still four-eyes, eating lunch behind the swings at school.

My mother burned all the photos she had of me with my eyes crossed. Said we didn't need a reminder of that around the house, now that I had the operation. So at this point all I have left is this faulty perception, from time to time, and the scars. I also have that soccer ball. I keep it in my closet, because I don't think that's the kind of thing you should ever get rid of.

25 JANE

Oliver is the only man who has ever made love to me. I know, I grew up during the generation of sex and drugs and peace, but I was never like that. I'd met Oliver when I was fifteen, and dated him until we were married. We built up a repertoire over the years, but we always stopped at a critical point. I talked about sex with my friends and pretended I had done it. Since no one ever corrected me, I assumed I was saying the right things.

As for Oliver, he did not really pressure me. I assumed he had slept with other women, like all the other guys I had known, but he never asked me to do anything I didn't want to. The perfect gentleman, I told my friends. We would sit for hours on the docks downtown in Boston, and all we'd do is hold hands. He would kiss me goodnight, but perfunctorily, as if he were holding back much more.

My best friend in college, a girl named Ellen, told me in excruciating detail about all the sexual positions she and her boyfriend Roger had mastered in the cramped quarters of a VW bug. She'd come into class early and stretch her legs out in front of her seat, complaining how tight the muscles in her calves were. I had been dating Oliver for five years, and we never came close to the unbridled passion Ellen discussed as casually as she talked about her pantyhose size. I began to think it was me.

One night when Oliver and I went to a movie, I asked if we could sit in the back row. The movie was *The Way We Were*. As soon as the opening credits rolled on the screen, I handed Oliver the popcorn and began to trace my thumb along the inseam of his jeans. I thought, if that doesn't get him excited, what will? But Oliver took my hand and clasped it between his own.

I tried once more during the movie. I took a deep breath and started to kiss Oliver's neck, the edge of his ear. I did all the things I had heard Ellen talk about that I thought might work in a public theater. I unbuttoned a middle button of Oliver's oxford shirt, and slipped my hand inside. I rubbed my palm over his smooth, olive chest, his strong shoulders. The entire time, mind you, I was staring at the movie screen like I was really watching.

Oh, Oliver was gorgeous. He had thick blond hair and a smile that ruined me. His pale eyes gave him the air of being somewhere else. I wanted him to really see me, to stake a claim.

During the scene where Robert Redford and Barbara Streisand take a walk on the beach and discuss names for the baby, Oliver grabbed my hand and withdrew it from his shirt. He buttoned himself up again and gave me a sidelong look. He pulled me out of the theater.

Oliver didn't look at me. He waited for the popcorn attendant to turn the other way. When she did, he slipped up the stairs to the balcony, which was closed for the night.

The balcony was empty and cordoned off with golden silk ties. Oliver pressed against me from behind. He had removed his shirt and was silhouetted against the satin wall of the theater. "Do you know what you do to me?" Oliver said.

He unbuttoned my cotton blouse and ripped the zipper of my jeans. When I was standing before him in my bra and panties, he took a step back, and just looked. I began to worry about the people below us, if they would turn around and see this show instead. And like he could read my mind (which I think he could do back then), Oliver pulled me down to sit on his lap.

We sat on the aisle seat in the back, me straddling him and blindly facing the projection booth; him glassy-eyed, facing the movie. He lowered my bra straps from my shoulders and held my breasts in his hands, like a scale. He held them very lightly, like he didn't quite know what to do with them. He let my bra fall to my waist and then he unbuttoned the fly of his jeans. With some acrobatics, we pushed his pants down around his ankles, and I didn't even have to stand up. In the background I heard the characters talking.

"Do you love me?" I whispered into his neck, unsure if he would hear.

Oliver looked at me, absolutely looked at me, the first time I was sure I had one hundred percent of his attention. "Actually," he answered, "I think I do."

I started to do the things that Ellen told me about, pressing against him and rocking my hips slowly, then faster. I felt the crotch of my panties becoming damp. The tip of Oliver's penis peeked through the fly of his boxers, swollen pink. Gingerly, I brushed it with my index finger. It jumped.

When Oliver touched me I thought I would faint. The back of the chair in front of us supported me, otherwise I am sure I would have fallen. He pulled aside the crotch of my underwear and then with his free hand pushed himself through his shorts. I was riveted; I watched this pulsing, knotted arrow and completely forgot that it was attached to Oliver. I watched the entire time while Oliver positioned himself and then lifted my hips and in an awful siren of pain I saw him disappear inside of me. Ellen did not tell me that this would hurt. I didn't scream, though, or cry, because of all the people below. I kept my eyes wide and stared at the satin curtain of the back wall. Only then did Oliver say, "Have you ever done this?"

When I shook my head I expected him to stop but by then it was too late. Not sure of what I was doing, I moved with him in a primitive sort of dance, a bump and grind, and I watched Oliver's eyes close in disbelief. At the last moment he grabbed at my hips with the force of Atlas and pushed me off. He crushed me against his chest, but not before I saw him, red and slick, distended, quivering. He ejaculated in a fountain of heat, a sticky glue that matted our stomachs together and made a rude noise when I tried to sit back.

I managed to walk out of the movie theater that night but I was sore for several days. I stopped asking Ellen about her dates with Roger. Oliver started to call me two or three times a day, when he knew perfectly well I was in class.

We bought condoms and began to do this regularly, enough so that it stopped hurting, although I did not think I had had the orgasm that Ellen told me about. We did it in my dorm room, in Oliver's car, on the grass near the Wellesley pond, in the locker room of the gym. It seemed the more illicit we got, the more fun we had. I saw Oliver every night, and every night we had sex. I started to tell Ellen about things we had done.

One night Oliver did not make a move to take off my clothes. I asked him if he was feeling all right, and he told me yes, he just didn't feel like doing it. That night I cried. I was certain this heralded the beginning of the end of our relationship. The next night I wore the dress that Oliver liked best, even though I knew we were going bowling. In the car that night, I didn't give Oliver a chance to refuse me. I unzipped his fly as we were driving back to the dorm and made him pull over onto a dark sidestreet. No matter what I did, however, Oliver did not get involved. He was going through the motions. Finally I asked him what the problem was. "I just don't feel like it tonight, Jane. Do we have to do this every night?"

I didn't see why not. As far as I was concerned, sex was love. If you had sex you had love. If Oliver didn't want me all of the time, there was some problem. I told Ellen that he was getting ready to break up with me and when she asked how I knew I told her why. She was shocked. She said all guys wanted to have sex, all the time. I locked myself in my dorm room and cried for two days, in preparation.

What Oliver returned with, however, was a diamond ring. He got down on one knee, just like in the movies, and he proposed. He said he wanted me with him forever. It was a half-carat, and nearly flawless, he said. We set a date for that summer, the day after graduation. Then, on the rough carpet of my dorm room (with my roommate due back momentarily), we made love.

I do not know how many months into it I started to realize that sex did not equate with love. Oliver and I, once married, had different schedules. We went to sleep at different times and he was reticent about having sex in broad daylight. Sometimes the patterns of our lives kept us apart for a couple of months, and then we'd have sex again and drift our separate ways. Rarely did we both want to make love at the same time. Things had changed so much since college; Rebecca was conceived on a night when I was wishing Oliver would just leave me alone so that I could sleep.

When I told Rebecca about sex I made sure I mentioned it was something you do when you are married. It was not said to be hypocritical. Rather, it was a way of ensuring that she might feel this fire in marriage, and not just the heat of its ashes.

26 REBECCA *July 19, 1990*

The sign for Hansen's orchard—a white one with hand-painted apples as a border—is on the left-hand side of the road. My mother sees it without me having to point it out. We turn into the driveway and our tires creak against the gravel. Lining the path are two stone walls, imperfect enough to let you know they were crafted by hand. There are pits in the driveway, filled with rainwater.

We drive to the top of a hill, and everywhere I look there are neat rows of apple trees. Well, I know they are apples because of Uncle Joley, but I wouldn't be able to tell otherwise. Most are almost bare and scrawny. Far away, on just one tree, I think I can make out tiny green apples. Somehow, I expected to see fruit on every single one, all at the same time.

My mother parks on a mound of grass that looks just big enough for a car. Several hundred yards away is a garage with an old station wagon that looks like our old one, and a big green tractor. There are all kinds of machines and gadgets in there that I do not recognize. Opposite the garage is a large red barn. On the hayloft is a Pennsylvania Dutch Hex sign.

"I don't know where Joley is," my mother says. "I mean, we're on time." She looks at me, and then at the unbelievable view. Below the barn, below the acres and acres of apple trees, is a field of tall grass that comes right to the edge of a lake. Even from up here, you can tell how clear the water is, how sandy the bottom.

On the crest of the hill is a huge house, white with green trim. It has a double porch and a hammock swing and factory doors with wavy glass. From its outside I just know it has a long spiral staircase inside. There are four windows on the second floor alone. "I don't see why we don't take a look around," I suggest, and I make a move towards the house.

"Rebecca, you can't just walk into someone's house you don't know. We'll walk around out here, and see if we can't find Joley." She links her arm through mine.

We walk down the slope of the hill to the back side of the barn, and as we get closer there is a buzzing sound. I unlatch the hinge of the fence that leads into this penned-in area. There are little pellets everywhere—you don't have to be a genius to know manure. Under the ledge of the barn is a man with a power tool of some kind, which is attached by a cord to an outlet somewhere above him. He has a sheep sitting like a human, on its rear end, and he is standing behind it and holding its front legs. At first glance, it looks like they are performing a sort of dance. The man takes the tool—it's a razor—and begins to run over the matted coat of the sheep. Funny, I think. It doesn't look at all like a cloud, like sheep are supposed to. The coat falls off in a thick blanket; it lands in the hay and dirt. As the sheep gets progressively naked, I notice its potbelly and tired eyes. From time to time the man wrestles with the sheep, the razor waving. He pushes with one foot and twists the body of the animal so that it lies this way or that. It always lands the way he seems to want it to land. When the man does this, the muscles in his arms stand out.

Finally he turns off the humming razor and helps the sheep to its feet. It looks at him like it has been betrayed. It doesn't resemble a sheep at all anymore, but a goat. It runs down a rocky path towards the apple trees. The man wipes his forehead with the sleeve of his T-shirt.

"Excuse me," my mother says, "do you work here?"

The man smiles. "I suppose you could say that."

My mother takes a step closer. She watches her feet to see where she is stepping. "Do you know someone named Joley Lipton? He works here too."

"I'll take you to him in a minute, if you'd like. I've got one more to shear."

"Oh," my mother says, disappointed. "All right." She leans against the fence and crosses her arms.

"If you can help me out this will go faster. Just give me a hand in here bringing out the last ewe." He opens a door I did not notice, one that must lead to a pen inside the barn. My mother rolls her eyes at me but follows the man inside. I can hear him saying things softly to the sheep. Then they appear at the door, all three of them, and the man motions towards the ledge where he was shearing before.

My mother's shirt is falling off her right shoulder, where she is bent down. Her arms look tight and uncomfortable. "What would you like me to do with this?"

The man tells her to walk the sheep to where the other one was. She does and then the man lets go on his side to pick up the razor. As he does this, my mother lets go of the sheep on *her* side. "What are you doing?" the man yells, and the sheep bolts away. "Catch it," he yells to me, but every time I take a step towards it, it runs in the other direction.

He glares at my mother, as if he has never seen anyone so stupid in his life. "I thought it would just stay put," she says. Then she runs to a corner of the pen and tries to grab the sheep by the wool of its neck. She comes close but she slips on wet hay and lands in a pile of manure. "Oh," she says, on the verge of tears. "Rebecca, get over here."

In the end it is the man who catches the sheep and who shears it single-handedly. He either pretends he has not seen my mother fall or he just doesn't care. He runs the razor over the body of this sheep in minutes, leaving a soft fleece on the ground like snow. My mother stands up and tries to shake off manure. She doesn't want to touch it with her hands, so she rubs up against the fence. The man, who sees this, laughs.

When he has let the sheep run free, he closes the hinge door on the pen inside the barn and unplugs the razor. He walks over to where my mother and I are standing. "Tough break," he says, trying not to crack up.

My mother is furious. "I'm sure this isn't appropriate behavior for a field hand. When I tell Joley about this, he'll report you to the person who runs the place."

The man holds out his hand, and then on second thought withdraws it. "I'm not too worried about that," he says. "I'm Sam Hansen. You must be Joley's sister."

I think this is hilarious. I start to laugh and my mother glares at me. "Could she clean up before we find Uncle Joley?" I say, and then I hold out my own hand. "I'm Rebecca. Joley's niece."

Sam takes us up to the house on the hill, which he calls the Big House. He says it was built in the 1800s. It is decorated with very simple country-style furniture: lots of light-colored wood and blue and red. Sam takes us to our respective rooms (up the spiral staircase). My room used to be his as a kid, he says. And my mother is staying in his parents' old bedroom.

My mother washes off and changes and comes back downstairs holding her dirty clothes. "What should I do with these?"

"Wash them," Sam suggests. He starts to walk outside and leaves my mother standing beside me, gaping.

"He's a hell of a host," she says to me.

Sam explains the different sections of the orchard as we walk through it en route to see my uncle. The top, which we drove past, is the commercial section, which gets sold to supermarket chains. The bottom is retail, which ripens later and gets sold to local farmstands and the general public. Each section is sectioned again according to the type of apples grown. The lake down at the edge of the orchard is Lake Boon, and yes, you can swim in it.

At one point he calls to a tall man who is cutting branches off one tree. "Hadley," Sam says, "come meet Joley's relatives."

When the man approaches us I see that he isn't old at all. He has sunny hair cut irregularly, and soft brown eyes. Like the cows, I think. He smiles at me first. Then he shakes my mother's hand and introduces himself. "Hadley Slegg. It's nice to meet you, ma'am."

"Ma'am," my mother whispers to me. She raises her eyebrows.

Hadley drops behind Sam and my mother so that he can speak to me as we are walking. "You must be Rebecca." I am thrilled that he knows me. I don't even ask how. "What do you think of Massachusetts?"

"It's pretty," I tell him. "Much more quiet than California."

"I've never been to California. I've heard things, of course, but I've never been." I'd like him to tell me what he's heard but he doesn't elaborate. "You still in school?"

Nobody has asked me about school in the longest time. "Are you?"

Hadley laughs. "God, no. I finished with that a long time ago. I wasn't the best student, if you know what I mean." He waves his hand out over the trees we're passing. "But I like what I'm doing, and I've got a good job thanks to Sam." He looks at me a little more closely. "So you're a swimmer?"

"How did you know that?" I say, amazed.

"I can see it through your shirt." How stupid of me. I am wearing my "GUARD" bathing suit under this T-shirt because it is so hot today.

"I was a lifeguard in San Diego. Not a real ocean guard, but just at a pool." I look at him, but I get embarrassed and turn away.

"That's tough work," Hadley says, "a lot of responsibility." He raises his hand to his head and ruffles his fingers through his hair. I smell strawberries. "You know, I could take you around and show you how this place works. It's kind of interesting, really."

"I'd like that." I had been wondering what I would do all day on a farm full of busy people. "I could help, if there's something I'd be able to do."

Hadley smiles at me. "Hey Sam, we've got some cheap labor. Rebecca is going to work for free."

Sam, who has been talking to my mother on and off, twists around so he can see me. "Okay. You can shear the sheep next time they need it." He grins. "Unless your mom wants to do it."

At this point, my mother starts to run across the field. "It's Joley," she shouts. "Joley!"

Uncle Joley is standing on a ladder, wrapping green tape around a branch of a tree. He sees my mother but makes no motion to stop wrapping the tape. He winds it slowly and carefully, and I watch Sam smile as he does this. Then he holds his hands to the branch for a moment, and closes his eyes. Finally he climbs down the ladder to where my mother is waiting, and hugs her.

"Looks like you survived the trip, Rebecca," Uncle Joley says to me when he walks closer. He kisses me on the forehead. He has not changed a bit. He turns to Sam and Hadley. "I assume you've all met."

"Unfortunately," my mother mutters, looking at Sam, and I'm positive he can hear her.

Joley looks from Sam to my mother, but neither one says anything else. "Well, it's great that you're here. We've got a lot of catching up to do."

Sam says, "Why don't you take the rest of the afternoon, Joley. On account of you never see your sister."

Joley thanks him and takes my mother's hand. "Are you all right?" he says, looking deep at her, as if the rest of us have disappeared. It makes us uncomfortable, though, and Sam starts to head back to the sheep pen. Hadley watches Sam leave and asks if I want to stay with Joley or learn abut pruning. I consider staying—I haven't seen my uncle in a long time, after all—but on second thought I tell Hadley I'd like to go with him.

Hadley takes me through the retail orchard, pointing out various types of apples by tree. Some of the names I recognize: Golden Delicious, McIntosh, Cortlands. Most are foreign: Gravensteins, Miltons. "They sound like the names of mailboxes on a very rich street," I tell Hadley, and he laughs. He stands very tall when he walks, and from my position it looks like he touches the sun.

He takes a deep breath as we come to the corner where the lake hits the orchard. "Smell it?" he asks, and there is mint all around. "It grows wild here."

"Did you grow up in Stow? You know so much."

Hadley smiles. "I grew up on a farm in Massachusetts. Hudson. But my mom sold the place when my dad died. She lives in New Hampshire now. In the mountains." He turns to me. "You grew up in San Diego?"

I glance up at him. "Do I look it?"

He picks a reed from the water's edge and clamps it between his front teeth. "I don't know. What do people from San Diego look like?"

"Well, they're usually blond and skinny and real airheads."

I mean it as a joke, but Hadley stares at me so intently that I think he will burn a hole through my shirt. He starts at my feet and winds up looking at my eyes. "Two out of three," Hadley says. "I won't tell you which two."

We walk for a while along the shore of Lake Boon, letting the cattails whip around our knees. At one point Hadley reaches down and very casually plucks a tick from my thigh. He tells me about Uncle Joley, and about Sam. "Joley just came in here one day, and I have to tell you I was a little jealous—I'd been working with Sam for seven years and here this city boy struts into the place and can work miracles. But it's true, no doubt about it. Your uncle—God that sounds funny—can heal things. He's saved more dying trees single-handedly than I don't know what."

I am impressed. I want to try to touch a tree myself, to see if this skill might be inherited. Hadley keeps talking. His voice had a strange twang to it—a Boston accent, I guess it's called—with weird *A* sounds and missing *R*s. "Sam took over the orchard when his dad had the heart attack. Parents live in Fort Lauderdale now, in Florida. He'd had ideas though, for a while. His dad walked out the front door of the Big House, and that very day Sam had tractors uprooting and moving trees." He surveys the land up the hill. "I mean, it looks good now, and it turned out all right, but that's not something *I* would have done. Sam's like that."

"Like what?"

"A kind of gambler, I guess. It's a real risk to move around well-rooted trees, and he knew that—he's smarter than me when it comes to agriculture. But the way it was here, well, it just wasn't the way he saw it in his mind. And he had to make all the pieces fit together."

Hadley sits down on a cluster of rocks on the edge of the lake and points to the tree overhead. "You hear that cardinal?"

There is a noise like a squeaky toy—high and low and high and low and high and low. Then out of the branches flies a bright red bird. The things this guy knows, I think.

"It's really nice of Sam to let us stay here," I say, making conversation.

"No insult to you and your mom, but he's doing it for Joley.

Sam isn't really big on visitors, especially women from California. He's been griping about it all week, actually." He stops and looks at me. "I guess I shouldn't be telling you this."

"Well, that's all right. He seems to have it out for my mother. She fell into a pile of manure before and he didn't do anything to help her."

Hadley laughs. "Not much you *can* do if someone falls in a pile of shit," he says. "Didn't your mom grow up around here?"

"Newton. Is it close by?"

Hadley whistles through his teeth. "Close in miles but a world away. Sam's got this chip on his shoulder about the suburbs in Boston. They're the ones with all the power who always vote down local aid to farms, but they haven't got any idea what kind of work we do here. Newton girls, when we were in school, were the ones who used to giggle when we walked by, you know, come on to us but not let us near them. Like we were always dirty, because we worked with our hands instead of pushing a pencil. Some of them were really hot, too. Drove Sam nuts."

Hadley turns to face me. He is smiling and about to say something but when he looks at me his smile falls away and he is just left staring. "You have really pretty eyes."

"Oh, they're a mutation," I say. "In biology we had to go around class and tell our genetic combinations—you know, big *B,* little *b,* et cetera. So all the blue-eyed kids said little *b,* little *b,* and all the brown-eyed kids said big *B,* little *b,* or big *B,* big *B,* and when the teacher came to me I said 'I have green eyes,' and the teacher said that green eyes are a mutation of blue. Like a radioactive monster."

"Well, they're a really nice mutation, then." Hadley grins at me and I think I have never seen anyone with such an open smile. It's like he's saying, *Come with me, come along, we have all the time in the world.*

We walk for a little while along the edge of the lake (Hadley says it's stocked with freshwater bass, thanks to him and Sam when they were kids), and then we cut up the north side of the orchard. Finally, far away from the house, I begin to see apple trees that really have apples hanging on them. Hadley tells me these are the Puritans and

Quintes—a little tart for eating but great for cooking. As we come closer, I see Sam and Uncle Joley and my mother.

"Where have you guys been?" Uncle Joley says. "We were getting ready to have lunch."

Hadley pushes me gently between the shoulder blades so that I take a step forward. "We've been down by the lake. Rebecca was telling me all the stupid things you did at family Christmas parties," Hadley says, and everyone laughs.

"Sam," my mother says, "Joley says you have one hundred acres?"

Sam nods, but you can tell from the look on his face he doesn't want to talk about it. I wonder if it is the subject, or my mother. "You know anything about apples?" he says, and my mother shakes her head. "Then it wouldn't really interest you."

"Sure it would. What varieties do you grow here?"

Sam ignores her, so Joley and Hadley take turns reeling off the names of the different apples growing at the orchard.

"And what are these?" My mother reaches out to the tree we are passing and picks one of these early apples—a Puritan, Hadley had said. It all happens very fast, the way she holds it to the sun to observe and then lowers it to her teeth, ready to bite into it. Suddenly Sam, who is walking behind her, throws his arm over her shoulder and knocks the apple out of her hand. It rolls on the clipped grass and settles under a different tree.

"What in God's name is your *problem?"* my mother hisses.

Sam's eyes darken until they are the color of a thunderstorm. "They were sprayed today," he says finally. "You eat it, you die." He pushed past her and walks ahead of us towards the Big House. As he passes the fallen apple he steps on it with his work boot. My mother holds her throat. For several seconds we stare at the pulp of this apple, ruined.

27 Oliver

I have never been to Salt Lake City, which worries me. What if this impromptu trip was motivated by my own subconscious desires, rather than tapping into the quality of Jane? What if Jane and Rebecca are well into, or through, Colorado by now? If I miss them in Colorado, I will catch up with them in Kentucky. Or Indiana, wherever. As long as I reach them before they get to Massachusetts; as long as I have a chance to offer my side of the story before Joley begins brainwashing Jane again.

Joley Lipton, the bane of my existence. We have never really understood each other. Even after I had won over Jane's parents—a twenty-year-old dating their teenage baby—I never got her brother's approval. Not then, not years later. He almost refused to attend the wedding, until he saw his stubbornness was literally wasting Jane away. So he did come, but sat in a corner throughout the ceremony and the reception. He belched loudly (I assume it was he) when we were pronounced man and wife. He did not offer me congratulations; he never has. He spread a rumor that the salmon mousse was rancid. And he left early.

In my opinion he is terribly in love with his sister, beyond the usual parameters of a brother-sister relationship. He has always been a drifter, and Jane has always been fiercely loyal to him. I don't find him deserving of such support; I have heard about their childhood and it seems he was the one to get off the proverbial hook. Yet, there is something about him. Perhaps he annoys me because of this: I cannot pin down my emotions about him. He instigates. He fills Jane's head with ridiculous notions about the institution of marriage—he, whom I have never seen with a woman. He calls at the wrong times and shows up unexpected. If Jane gets to Joley before I reach her, she may never come back. She will have been conditioned otherwise. She will most certainly not listen to me.

This blinding whiteness hits me quickly, a desert of salt. Suddenly I am in its midst, driving, a blot against this expanse. I know better; it is not colorless. White is all the colors in the rainbow, reflected at once.

I pull the car into the shoulder of the road, where several other tourists have stopped to take photographs. The terrain is flat and sweeping. If not for the record heat, I could easily be convinced I am seeing snow. A woman taps me on the shoulder. "Sir, would you mind?" She waves a camera in my face and motions where I have to push the button. Then she runs to the guardrail where her traveling companion—an elderly man in green overalls—is already sitting. "One, two, *three,*" I say, and the flash cube goes off. The man has no teeth, I see this when he smiles.

I have always wanted to see the Great Salt Lake because of its incongruity. The idea of it: saltwater in a landlocked state, an ocean away from the ocean. I have heard that it is so large it may as well be an ocean (a small one, anyway). I look at my watch—5:20. There is not much I will do today, anyway. I can go to the lake, take a look around and check into a motel for the night. If I must travel across America, I might as well enjoy myself.

I try to avoid the route through the city, since there might be a rush hour; if Mormons have rush hours. Instead I skirt the perimeter, bordered on both sides of the road by white earth. From time to time a breeze or a passing truck blows salt onto the asphalt, which swirls in front of the car like a wailing ghost. There are no signs for the lake and I do not want to waste the time to ask at a service station, so I follow the other cars on the road in front of me. Surely one of them, maybe more than one, will be going to the Great Salt Lake. I pass cars earnestly, searching the windows for children or watermelon floats or shining inner tubes, the telltale symbols.

The seventh car has someone in a bathing suit. From my point of view, the passenger is young, female, and wearing a red suit criss-crossed in the back, much like Rebecca's GUARD suit. It is a station wagon just like Jane's—same color, same dent in the fender. I try to pull alongside the car because my blood begins to beat in my ears. Who is the driver? I cannot tell, but as I advance I see that the girl has long blond hair, wrapped into a knot of some kind at the back of her neck. *Rebecca.* I accelerate, my foot pushing hard against the floor of the car, weaving around a slower car in front of me. I pass them, and then swerve into their lane, relying on the rearview mirror. When I lift my eyes, I expect to see Jane, her fingers drumming on the steering wheel, her sunglasses slanted and reflective. Instead I see a burly man with a black beard and a tattoo on his chest that reads COME TO MAMA. The girl is not Rebecca at all, and the driver honks at me for cutting him off.

They are, however, going to the Great Salt Lake, and I follow them until I can see the lake from the car. Then I drive another half-mile down its edge, so that I will not have to face them in person. I park the car in a no-parking zone and walk to the edge of the water.

As far as the eye can see there is water. Deep and calm, marble-blue, with the tiny waves one finds on the Great Lakes. Well, it could be the ocean. I sit on the shore and pull off my shoes and socks. Leaning back on my elbows, I try to imagine a whale surfacing in the center of this lake, black and white, like a picture show. Then I listen to the wind and imagine instead it is that tearing sound whales make as they break through the water's surface, and then the hollow moan through the blowhole, clearing. The sun, on its way down, beats a steady rhythm. What a day, I think. What a day.

I have second thoughts about it but I roll up my pants and take off my shirt, leaving it with my shoes and socks on the banks of the lake. Then I wade in, letting the water mat my underwear against my thighs. I dive underneath and swim as hard as I can to the spot where I pictured that whale.

Amazing, the salt content of this lake. It tastes like the ocean, feels like the ocean, buoys like the ocean. In some places it probably reaches great depths. Children play along its edges, but there is hardly anyone where I stop and tread water. I shake my hair from my eyes and survey the shore. People are starting to leave; it's dinnertime. I should go too, and rent a room somewhere, so that I can get an early start tomorrow. To wherever it is that I am supposed to be going.

I float face down in the water and then jackknife at the waist, plunging headfirst towards the bottom of the lake. I would love to see what is there: fire coral or anemone or even white-bellied sharks and continental ridges. I kick my feet vigorously until the pressure of the depth threatens to break my eardrums. At this point all I can see is a milky black. I pivot and begin to swim to the surface, breaking with the force of a whale and embracing the air with a skeletal gasp.

A biplane comes remarkably close to the surface of the water and then circles towards the sun. It is the same sun, I realize with relief, that Jane and Rebecca are watching, wherever they may be. For a moment the plane hovers in silhouette like an artificial eagle. Well, I think, at least I don't have to worry about them leaving the country. Jane couldn't get Rebecca on a plane come hell or high water.

For a while after the crash we took Rebecca to a local military airport that ran programs for people who were afraid to fly. Behavior modification, really: the patrons would become proficient at a small task and then work their way up to actually flying. The first step was to come to the airport, just to look at it. Then you gave your ticket into the reservations desk the next week. Then came sitting in the terminal, and then walking outside to look at the plane. After that achievements came very gradually: getting onto the stairs of the plane (two weeks' time), walking onto the plane (two weeks' time), sitting for an hour on the immobile plane (four weeks). Eventually the plane took off for a fifteen-minute flight around the Bay area.

We took Rebecca although she was very young because the psychiatrist who had treated her recommended the program. She told us that events such as these are the most scarring to children, even though we may not be able to see it. The perfectly adjusted child might one day snap because of an unarticulated fear of flying. So Rebecca (the youngest by far) went to phobia classes. She was everyone's darling, the other women would fight to hold her and make sure she was all right and that she understood the instructions. Rebecca herself did not mind the attention. After she left the hospital in Des Moines, she did not mention the accident and she did not give any indications of having been involved in such a catastrophe, and because of this we also shied away from the subject. We told her these classes were just a fun thing, like other little girls took ballet or piano lessons. Jane was the one who actually drove her there; I was usually away on business.

I was away on business the time Rebecca temporarily lost control—during the second week of the plane-sitting excursion. The first week, Jane told me over a crackling Chilean phone connection, Rebecca had been fine. And then all of a sudden this Saturday she was uncontrollable, throwing herself across the seats and screaming and crying. The psychiatrist told us we should continue to bring her to the phobia class, in spite of her outburst. She said that the outburst was a manifestation of fear, and as a scientist I was inclined to agree. But Jane refused to take her, and since I was in South America, I hadn't any leverage. Rebecca was four then, and she has yet to set foot on a plane since.

Of course. They will go to Iowa.

I float, staring up at the sun. How stupid of me. I should have realized this earlier. I was so busy concentrating on Jane that I neglected to see that Rebecca herself is one of Jane's biggest clues. Where Rebecca goes Jane will follow. And at her age, Rebecca will want to see the site of the crash; to jog her memory, maybe, or to put it all behind her. Wherever else they choose to go en route to Massachusetts is incidental. Iowa will be the midpoint; Iowa is the sure thing.

Suddenly I am overwhelmed with relief. I will meet them in What Cheer, Iowa; I will stake out the cornfield where the wreckage still sits, until I see them, and then we shall talk. I am one step ahead. I start to smile, and then grin wider, and before I can stop myself I am laughing aloud.

28 Joley

Dear Jane—

Are you enjoying Fishtrap? It's a great little place to get away from it all, particularly civilization. Montana is quite beautiful, and overlooked. Take your time getting across it. What matters isn't when *you get here, but* how *you get here.*

I have been doing a lot of thinking about your visit, and you, and me. In particular I have been remembering the night before your wedding to Oliver, when we were on the back porch in Newton. You were wearing the yellow dress you always thought made you look fat in the hips, and you had your hair pulled back in a ponytail. You had matching yellow shoes—I've never forgotten that, because it gave you this look of absolute completion. You came out on the porch, holding a bottle of Coke, and you offered it to me without even looking me in the eye. But we hadn't been doing a lot of speaking those days, not since I told you I wasn't going to come to the wedding.

It had nothing to do with you, I suppose you understand that by now. But I was sixteen and nobody was listening to me, including you. I had these feelings about Oliver, I can't be any more specific than that. Feelings that made me wake in the middle of the night, sweating, ripping the sheets on the bed. And dreams, which I have not told you or anyone.

This is what you said: You're just a kid, Joley. You don't know what it's like to be in love. When it's right, you know it. Why, look at how long I've been dating Oliver. If it wasn't meant to be, it would have ended a long time ago.

You told me this months before the wedding, while you were cooking dinner—it was a fricassee, I remember because the oil kept spattering you in the face while you were speaking. You told me this after I begged you to give Oliver back his engagement ring. And I was a kid, and maybe I didn't know anything about love, but I would hazard a guess that you knew just as little as I did. The difference being you thought *you knew. Anyway, when you set the date, I announced that I wasn't coming to the wedding, it being against my principles.*

Then you stopped eating entirely. I thought at first it was pre-wedding jitters but when you couldn't fit into any of your clothes, or Mama's, and when we had to belt your tightest pair of jeans just to hold them up, I knew that the cause had nothing to do with your marriage. Oh, Jane, I wanted to tell you that I didn't mean it, that

I'd go back on my word, but I was afraid you might take it as a blessing for your marriage, and I wasn't about to give that.

And that night, before the wedding, you came onto the porch. I was looking at the lawn, or what was left of it after all the striped pink tents had been set up. There were white ribbons and crêpe de chine *festooned all over the yard. It looked like a circus was coming, not a bride, and I won't make any jokes about that. You gave me a Coke. "Joley," you said, "you're going to have to get used to him."*

And I turned to you, trying not to catch your eye. "I don't have to get used to anything," I said. You had always trusted me before, and I didn't know why you wouldn't trust me now. Even to this day I cannot put into words what it was about Oliver that set me off. Maybe it was the combination: Oliver and you.

You began to reel off a list of all the things about Oliver that were kind and gentle and important. You told me that best of all, Oliver would get you out of this house. I nodded, and wondered to myself, at what price?

That's when the hawks came. They circled above us, rare in Massachusetts even then. Their talons stretched behind them, orange spears, and their beaks broke the blue of the sky. They alternated between beating the air and coasting, a foreign cursive alphabet.

"Oh, Joley," you said, squeezing my hand, "what do you think of that?"

I thought it was an omen, and I decided that I would let whatever those hawks did determine my actions for the wedding. I have always prided myself on reading signs: the tickle in Mama's voice that betrayed her composure; the showers you took at midnight and that nightgown you tore to shreds; Oliver; those hawks. We both watched as the birds flew together, connecting like acrobats. Four wings beat to block out the sun, and when the mating was over they ripped like a broken heart, one hawk flying east and one flying north. I turned to you and said, "Yes, I will come to your wedding."

So you might say that I have betrayed you because I knew all these years that your marriage would not last. I did not tell you because you had no reason to believe me, until now. I also did not tell you the dream that I had over and over every night until the wedding. In it, I saw you and Oliver making love—a very difficult thing for a brother to envision his sister doing, I might add. Your legs were wrapped around Oliver's lower back, and then suddenly you cracked down the middle like a Russian doll and split into two halves. Inside was another you, a smaller you. Oliver did not seem to notice. He was still thrusting when again you cracked down the middle, splitting to reveal an even smaller person. And so on and so on until you were so tiny that I could barely make out your face. I was terrified to see what would happen, and because of this, maybe, I always woke up. But the night before the wedding the dream continued all the way to the end, and as Oliver finally came, you cracked down the middle and split again and this time there was nothing inside at all; there was just Oliver, exposed.

When I woke up the night before the wedding, I heard you screaming, and you continued to do that until the sun came up.

You are going to be here sooner than you realize—another week at the most. Please wish Rebecca a happy birthday. Head north on Rte. 15 to Rte. 2, and take that east into Towner, North Dakota. It may take you a couple of days but it is a straight shot. There's only one P.O. in Towner.

God, I can't wait to see you.

Love,
Joley

29 JANE

After Utah, Rebecca and I rip up a piece of paper Oliver used to track our miles per gallon and write the names of five states on the back: Nevada, Colorado, New Mexico, Wyoming and Idaho. We stuff these in one of Rebecca's sneakers, and then I give her the honor of choosing our destination. And in Idaho, as I expect, Joley's letters find us again, guiding us through the plains.

We decide to sell the car in Poplar, Montana. Well, not sell it, really, but trade it in for a less expensive car and get some cash. I have credit cards but I am leery of using them; Oliver must be well on his way, and since the cards are in his name, American Express would gladly give him a record of the last purchases, their dates and locations. The last time I used a credit card was just at the border of California and Arizona, to get gas. And in truth we have stretched our several hundred dollars a third of the way across America, which deserves mention. Why couldn't we have run out in Palm Springs of Aspen, a town steeped in an inflated economy and populated by the rich? Why Montana?

"Poplar," Rebecca says. She is in charge of reading the small brown road signs that line Route 2. The Missouri River runs on her side of the car, right alongside the highway. When we were bored earlier we tried to outrace it. She is sitting cross-legged, her hair flying wildly around her face. She hasn't brushed it yet today—we had to sleep in the car last night since we had no money for a motel, and thank God it was warm enough. We put down the back seat and spread an old blanket across the rusty hinges. We used the spare tire as a pillow. It was nice, actually, the way we could see the stars. "I can't see the place from here," Rebecca says. "Maybe we'd better turn off."

We are looking for a town that seems well populated, which is a fifty-fifty toss-up this far north in Montana. We gave up trying to find a car dealership hours ago. Apparently, many gas stations double as dealerships in Montana.

I've promised Rebecca she can pick the car. After all, her birthday is tomorrow and she didn't even complain about sleeping in the back of the wagon. We had a long discussion about the most practical type of car and our dream cars (Mercedes for me, Miata for her) and the likelihood of finding any vehicle in Montana that will actually start.

I pull off the exit and brake at the end of a dusty dirt road. There is no sign, no more road, nothing. I haven't any idea which way to turn, so I look at Rebecca. "Looks like Poplar isn't too pop'lar," she says, and giggles.

To my left is a heavily wooded area. To my right is a purple mountain. The only place to go would be straight ahead, which means crossing through a field of some sort that is laced with red wildflowers and yellow berries. "Hang on," I warn Rebecca, and then shifting the station wagon into overdrive, I roll its thick tires over the weeds and tall grass.

The grass is so tall that I cannot see out the windshield. I am afraid of running over a little kid, or a cow, or crashing into a combine. It is a little like driving through a car wash, where those wet cloths massage the surface of your car like a million lapping tongues, except here we are in a tunnel of soft silver brushes. We roll along, five miles per hour, with our fingers crossed.

"This is wild," Rebecca says. "We don't have towns like this around San Diego."

"No," I admit, not quite certain if that is for better or for worse.

"I could get out," she suggests. "I could scope for you. You know, tell you if you're about to hit a woodchuck or something."

"I don't want you leaving this car. Then there's the chance I'll hit you."

Rebecca sighs and resigns herself to slumping down in her seat again. She starts to French-braid her hair, an incredible feat to me, since she has no mirror for reference. She braids all the way to the bottom but she has lost her ponytail holder. Rummaging through the garbage trapped between the seats she comes up with a trash bag twist-tie, and improvises.

Suddenly the field opens and I am inches away from a Coke machine. I slam my foot on the brake and send Rebecca crashing into the windshield. "Shit," she says, rubbing her forehead. "What are you trying to do to me?" Then she looks out the windshield. "What is that doing here?"

I back up several feet so that I can maneuver the car around the vending machine. As I break through the last row of reeds, the car rolls, free, onto the blacktop of a gas station. There is only one pump and a small concrete building, not large enough for service.

However, at least ten cars are lined up in a row diagonally across from where we are parked, which leads me to believe they may be for sale. An old man with white hair braided down his back is leaning against the pump, doing a crossword puzzle. He looks at us but doesn't seem surprised that we have driven out of a field. He says, "What's a five letter word for 'irritate'?"

"Annoy." I step out of the car.

The man makes no effort to look at me. He fills in the word I've given him. "It fits. What can I do for you?"

Rebecca gets out of the car and slams the passenger door. She stands back and surveys the station wagon and starts to laugh. It is wreathed with berries and black-eyed Susans, which have become tangled in the overhead rack and the antenna during the journey across the field. It looks as if the car has been at a 1960s commune. Rebecca begins to pull off the long, knotted stems of the plants.

"To tell you the truth, we're looking to get a new car," I say. "Something a little flashier."

The man makes a strange noise through his nose, and then removes a handkerchief from his pocket and wipes it across his forehead. "Flashy," he says, circling the car. He makes that noise again. "Won't be hard to get flashier than this."

"It's a very good car. Solid, and reliable, and there's only thirty thousand miles on it. A cream puff." I smile at him, but he is inspecting the tires.

"If it's so damn good, why are you looking to get rid of it?"

I give Rebecca a look that tells her to keep quiet. "May I speak to you alone for a moment, Mr.—?"

"Tall Neck. The name is Joseph Tall Neck."

Alibis and excuses race through my mind, but when I begin to speak I find that I am telling him the truth.

". . . So we left my husband in California, and we're driving across America and quite honestly we need a car *and* we need cash, which brought us to you."

This man looks at me with his coal-colored eyes, and he doesn't believe a word I've said. "Tell it to me straight, lady."

"Okay," I say. "Okay. This is it: my daughter's birthday is tomorrow. All her life she's been taking these tap dancing lessons, and there's an audition for a movie in L.A., and she asked if I would take her to it for her birthday present. Her dream is to be a big star, but frankly we haven't got the money to spend on a fancy costume or a big car or anything else that will make the bigwigs in Hollywood notice her. So we talked it over and decided we would sell the car and get something a little cheaper, and then with the extra cash we'd buy nice clothes and rent a limo to go to the audition." I say this all in one breath and then lean against the gas pump, spent. When I look up, the man had walked over to Rebecca. His eyes are glowing.

"Dance," he commands.

I don't know where she picked it up, because Rebecca has never taken a tap dancing lesson in her life. But she starts shuffling and doing a soft shoe in the red earth of the field we've driven through, using the flattened tire tracks as a makeshift stage. "I can sing, too," she says, grinning.

Tall Neck is entranced, you can see it in his face. "You are really something. Who knows? You could be the next Shirley Temple." The man leads Rebecca over to the line of cars in the front corner of the station. "Which one do you like?"

Rebecca bites her lower lip. "Oh, I don't know. Mama? Come over here. What do you think?"

When I stand next to her, she elbows me gently. "Well, honey," I say, "I want you to pick. It's all part of your birthday present."

Rebecca clasps her hands in front of her. She doesn't have much of a choice: several beat-up Cadillacs, a blue Jeep, a dusty Chevy Nova.

"How about that one?" Rebecca says, pointing to a little MG I hadn't noticed. I have always steered away from cars that small, because of the safety risk. It is half-hidden behind the gas price sign, red with rust spots over each tire. The interior is ripped in many places.

"The convertible top is automatic," Tall Neck says, "and still works." Rebecca jumps over the door of the car and lands in an awkward split on the front seat, one foot wedged into a hole of foam where the vinyl has cracked.

"How much?" I ask, and Rebecca and Tall Neck both jump as if they have forgotten I am there. "And how much will you give me for the wagon?"

Tall Neck gives me a sour smile and walks back to the station wagon. He pulls a wild daisy from the side mirror. "I'll give you three thousand, although it isn't worth that much."

"Are you joking?" I explode. "It's only four years old! It's worth twice that!"

"Not here it isn't," he says, and he walks back to the MG. "This car here I'll give you for one thousand."

Rebecca turns to me with incredibly sad eyes, meant for Tall Neck to see. "It's too much money, isn't it, Mama?"

"It's okay, honey. We can go somewhere else. There's lots of places to stop on the way to Hollywood."

"Five hundred," Tall Neck says, "and that is my last offer."

A woman drives into the station in a lemon-colored van and pulls in front of the gas pump. Tall Neck excuses himself to fill the tank. Rebecca beckons me closer to the car, and I climb over the door less agilely than she did, and sit in the driver's seat. "Where did you learn to tap dance?" I asked.

"School. Gym class. I had a choice of tetherball or tap." She leans against my shoulder. "So you think I'll make it on Broadway?"

"I don't know if you'd make it in Poplar, to tell you the truth. But you did a nice job of snowing this guy." I begin to fiddle with the radio dial (broken) and the shift (sticks on reverse). Rebecca opens up the glove compartment, which is empty, and reaches under the seat to find a lever for moving it back. She pulls out a manila envelope, dusty, which has been wedged into the springs underneath.

"What's this," she says, opening the clasp. She pulls out bills—twenties, all of them, and as her eyes grow wide I grab the envelope from her.

I start to count quickly, before Tall Neck finishes his transaction. "There's over six hundred here," I tell Rebecca. "That's what I call cash back financing." Rebecca, who sees the van pull away, stuffs the envelope back into the springs below the seat. "Is this really the one you want?" I say loudly, as Tall Neck approaches. Rebecca nods. "Well, Happy Birthday then."

"Oh Mama!" Rebecca squeals, and she throws her arms around me. She breaks away from my embrace to pump Tall Neck's hand up and down. "Thank you, oh, thank you so much!"

"I'll get the title," Tall Neck says, and he limps towards the concrete block building that must serve as an office.

Rebecca smiles until he closes the door behind him and then she turns to me. "Let's get out of this dump." She leans her head back against the seat and holds her hand to her throat. "Does anybody tap dance anymore?"

Tall Neck reappears with a manila envelope that looks much like the treasure under the seat, which makes me wonder if this isn't some stash of his he has forgotten about. I rifle through the cash. "You should really keep your money in a bank," I tell him. "You never know if you're going to get held up."

He laughs, showing spaces where he has no teeth. "Not out here. Tourists don't come to Poplar. And," he points to a shotgun propped next to the gas pump, "robbers know better."

I smile weakly. "Well," I say, wondering if he'll shoot at us as we leave, realizing he's left money in our car, "thanks for your help."

Rebecca has been moving all our possessions from the back of the station wagon. She takes the duffel bag out of the back seat and the maps from the glove compartment and tosses them in the tiny trunk of the new car. "Look for me in the movies!" Rebecca calls to the man. We pull alongside the station wagon, expecting to feel some sort of remorse, the way you feel like you are leaving a piece of yourself behind whenever you trade in an old car. But this one reminds me of Oliver, and of leaving, and I don't think I will miss it much at all.

"Mom," Rebecca urges, "we're going to miss the audition." She reaches her arms over her head as we plow back through the field, which is easier this time because we have cleared a path. The weeds climb right inside the car, since we have the top down, and Rebecca picks them as they whip her across the chest and the face, creating a bouquet in shades of purple. "This is some car," she screams, her words lost in the rush of the wind.

It is a lot of fun. It's less clunky than the station wagon, that's for sure—I keep looking in the rearview mirror and expecting to see another half-length of car. There is just enough room for me and Rebecca. "So whose money do you think that is?"

"I think it's ours now," Rebecca says. "Some mother you are. Turning me into a liar and a thief."

"You turned yourself into a liar; I didn't command you to do a tap recital. And as for being a thief, well, technically we bought the car, including anything that happened to be inside it." Rebecca looks at me and laughs. "Okay, so it's a little dishonest." A runaway reed scratches against my cheek, leaving a raised mark. "I think the money belonged to an heiress who had fallen in love with her groundskeeper."

Rebecca laughs. "You must write plots for *All My Children* in your spare time."

"So the groundskeeper sees the baron approaching with the body of the woman he loves and has to decide whether to take off with the car or to grieve over the woman. And of course he stays—"

"Of course."

"—and is shot by the baron, who then drives the car to a deserted town in Montana where it is not likely to be found, and moves his estate to Estonia under an assumed identity." I take a deep breath, proud of my story. "What do you think?"

"Number one, how did the money get into the car, then, if the woman never had a chance to get it before she was knocked off? Number two, no idiot in his right mind would take a bullet just because his girlfriend has been killed too. If he really loved her he'd go off and live the life they'd planned together." Rebecca shifts in her seat and inadvertently knocks the rearview mirror. "You're a hopeless romantic, Mom."

"Well, whose money do *you* think it is?"

Rebecca starts to throw the flowers from the bouquet she's collected in the air, one by one. They seem to fly away as if they have lives of their own. "I think that Indian guy put his savings account in the car a long time ago, so long that he's completely forgotten. He's probably after us in the blue Jeep right now."

"That's lousy," I tell her. "That's hardly a good story at all."

"If you want to spice it up, then maybe he got the money from robbing a bank. Which would explain why he doesn't keep his cash there in the first place." Rebecca cocks her head to one side. "Now that we're rich, what are we going to do to celebrate?"

"What do you want to do?"

"Take a shower. Get another pair of underwear. And other luxuries like that."

"We should buy some clothes," I agree. "Not that the selection around here is going to match our style." Some style. I've been wearing the same dirty shirt of Oliver's for four days, and Rebecca has been sleeping in the bathing suit she wears all day.

"So we'll go shopping the next town we find."

"The next town that looks like a town," I clarify.

"The next town that has a *store*." Rebecca pushes her hands against her stomach. "When did we have breakfast?"

"Two hours ago," I say. "Why?"

Rebecca curls into a ball, her head on the armrest beside the stick shift. Here she doesn't have the room for movement the station wagon allowed her. "My stomach hurts. Maybe I'm not hungry. Maybe I ate a bad egg or something."

"Do you want to stop?" I turn to look at her; she's a little green.

"No, just keep driving." Rebecca closes her eyes. "It's not so bad. It comes and goes." She kneads her hands in a knot, and presses it against her stomach.

For about half an hour, Rebecca falls asleep, which makes me feel better because I know she is no longer in pain. This is the mark of a mother; I am able to feel what she feels, to hurt when she hurts. Sometimes I believe that in spite of the traditional birth, Rebecca and I were never disconnected.

She has not missed much, being asleep. We have passed the border into North Dakota, and we seem to be leaving the great purple swells of mountains behind us.

"Are we there yet?" Rebecca rolls into a sitting position, pushing her hair away from her face where it has unraveled into thin strings. She folds her legs into her habitual sitting position, and then she screams.

I swerve the car onto the shoulder of the road and brake violently. "What's the matter?"

Rebecca reaches between her legs and lifts her hand and on it there is blood.

"Oh, Rebecca," I say. "Relax. You just got your period."

"That's all?" she says, dazed. "Is that all?"

She starts to smile, and then she actually laughs a little. I help her stand up outside the car and we survey the damage: her bathing suit is covered with a spreading brown stain and there is some blood on the vinyl MG seat. I wipe this clean with a rag from the trunk, and then Rebecca and I take a walk further into the flatlands on the side of the road. There are no cacti or brush to hide behind here, but then again there aren't many passing cars either. We take my pocketbook, which Rebecca, thank God, had remembered to grab in San Diego, and rummage through it for a tampon or a sanitary napkin. I am hoping for a napkin; I don't want to have to explain the use of a tampon. When I find one I help Rebecca position it in the bottom of her bathing suit. "We'll get you something else to wear at the next store."

"This is disgusting," Rebecca says. "This is like a diaper."

"Welcome to womanhood."

"Listen, Mom." Rebecca looks at me sidelong. "Don't give me any of those talks about how I'm growing up, all right? I mean, I'm fifteen and I must be the last girl in school to get my period, which is bad enough. I know all about sex, so I don't want the responsibility lecture either, agreed?"

"No problem. But if you get cramps again, let me know. I'll give you Midol."

Rebecca smiled. "I've been wanting this to happen for so long, you know? So I could get boobs. I can't believe *this* is what I've been waiting for."

"Someone should tell you when you reach twelve that it's no great shakes."

"I feel like an idiot. I thought I was dying."

"When it happened to me I said the same thing. I didn't even tell my mother. I just went to lie down on my bed and folded my arms across my chest and expected that I would die before the day was out. Joley was the one who found me, and got your grandmother, and then she gave me all those lectures you don't want me to give you."

We reached the car and Rebecca hesitates before sitting down. "Do I have to sit there?" she says, although it is clean.

"You're the one who wanted the sports car." I watch her climb in and adjust herself in her seat several times, getting used to the sanitary napkin. "Okay?" I ask, and she nods without looking at me. "Let's find a place to go shopping."

Rebecca leans her head against her arm, propped on the open window. There is so much I wish I could warn her about; the chain reaction that is a consequence of this event. The acquisition of hips, for example, and the discovery of men, and falling in love, and falling out of it.

Rebecca, suddenly self-conscious, sifts through the glove compartment she has already inventoried. She is looking for something, or pretending to look for something, that isn't there at all. She closes her eyes, letting the wind unleash her hair and blow the garbage twist-tie in the direction of Montana.

30 REBECCA *July 18, 1990*

The people wearing white T-shirts marked CREW ask us to join the line of cars. It stretches like a snake along the dock in Port Jefferson. While we are waiting my mother makes up stories about the people she passes in surrounding cars. A woman with a baby beside her is going to visit her long-lost aunt in Old Lyme, the one for whom the baby is named. A businessman is really a government spy, checking on the U.S. Coast Guard. Sometimes I wonder about my mother.

"This way," a man yells. My mother puts the car into gear. She rolls it up a side ramp and into the hinged mouth of the ferry. It is like we are driving right into the jaws of a great white whale.

We are beckoned by another crew member and told to park the car halfway up a steep ramp on the side. There are two symmetrical ramps, and cars are parked on them and beneath them. I had been wondering how they would fit us all in.

It is a one-hour-and-fifteen-minute ride. We spend it on the upper deck, lying on our backs on the compartment that holds life jackets. Between this and the convertible I am starting to get some color. Even my mother is looking tan.

"Well," she announces, "we'll be in Massachusetts first thing in the morning. We should get to Uncle Joley's by noon."

"It's about time. It feels like we've been gone forever."

"I wonder what it is he does on an apple orchard?" my mother says. "We didn't even have a garden as kids. Well, we tried, but everything kept dying. We blamed it on the New England soil."

"How did he get it?"

"Get what?"

"The job. How did he get a job, without any experience farming?"

My mother flips onto her back and shields her eyes against the sun. "He didn't quite tell me. Something to do with a visit, I think, and this guy hired him. The guy who runs the place. Supposedly he's younger than Joley, even. He took over from his father." She sits up. "You know the types. The real ambitious ones, who've wanted to be farmers ever since they were knee-high to a beetle."

"A grasshopper. Knee-high to a grasshopper."

"Whatever," my mother sighs.

"How can you pass judgment," I say to her. "You don't know the man, and you don't know anything about growing apples."

"Oh, Rebecca," my mother laughs. "How hard could it be?"

The ferry is gushing a backwash and slowly turning 180 degrees. That way, when we dock, we can drive right off. From what I can see, Bridgeport does not look like someplace to write home about.

It seems as if every other line of cars gets to drive off before we do. Plus, since we are halfway up a ramp we cannot see if the line is moving. We cannot see anything but the Ford Taurus in front of us. It is very dusty and someone has etched "WASH ME" on the back window. Finally a man wearing a CREW shirt points to the car and motions that we can move ahead. But the Taurus in front of us, instead of pulling forward, has shifted into reverse. It slams us squarely on the front fender. I can hear the metal crunch.

"Jesus Christ," my mother says. "It figures."

"Well, aren't you going to stop?" The man in the CREW shirt is yelling something I can't hear. The overall gist of it is: Move, lady. My mother pulls off the boat with the fender hanging half on and half off. She drives to a spot out of the way, on the right, where the Taurus is waiting.

She gets out of the car and walks in front to see the damage. "We can drive. We just won't look very pretty." She tries to bend the fender back into place with her bare hands. "I suppose you can't ask for much when you've paid five hundred dollars."

The driver gets out of the Taurus, which hasn't been damaged. "Oh, dear," he says. "I'll certainly pay for this. I can give you cash, right now, if you like. Or we can exchange licenses." He wrings his hands in front of himself, so upset that it is almost funny.

"Well," my mother says, "it would probably cost at least four hundred dollars to fix. Don't you think so, honey?" she calls to me.

"At least. And the car being brand new, and all."

"Brand new?" the man gasps. He doesn't notice all the rust spots, apparently. "I am so sorry. I can't tell you how sorry. I didn't mean to put it into reverse. Stupid, stupid me." He bends down over our twisted fender and smooths his fingers over it. "I don't have the money on me, but if you follow me I can get it. And I don't mind giving the cash up front, not at all. Less points on the old insurance, after all."

"We really don't have a lot of time," my mother says.

"Oh, it's just up the road. I'm Ernest Elkezer, the curator for the Barnum Museum on Main Street here. It's after hours, but I'll let you look around while I open the safe. It's the least I can do."

My mother gets into the driver's seat and starts the ignition. "Can you believe this? The car was free, and now we're getting a bonus four hundred dollars." She turns her face towards the sun. "Rebecca, baby, the gods are smiling on us today!"

The P. T. Barnum Museum is next door to a modern city building. It is strange, walking up to this huge door which is locked and being let inside. I feel like I am doing something I shouldn't. "You know Bridgeport was the birthplace of General Tom Thumb," Mr. Elkezer says. "Full-grown he was only twenty-eight inches tall."

He switches on the lights—one, two, three—and the dark hall comes to life. "Make yourselves at home. Plenty of interesting circus memorabilia here. You won't want to miss the third floor."

The third floor is almost entirely covered with a miniature display of a big top. Three red rings sit in the sawdust center. Suspended over one is a net for the trapeze artists. There are heavy drums tucked into the corners for the elephants to stand on. A thick, knotted tightrope is stretched overhead. "If it was a little bit larger, I'd try it out," my mother says, one foot already in the display. When I close my eyes, I can see the audience. Red flashlights on lanyards, circling over the heads of kids.

I leave my mother and walk around the perimeter of the mock circus. There is a display about Jumbo the elephant, whose skeleton (it says) is on display in the Museum of Natural History in New York City. Now that would be something interesting. I lean closer to see the photograph taken of the huge skeleton, which has a man standing beside it as a reference measure. The man is Ernest Elkezer himself. Just as I am reading the caption, Elkezer approaches with a wrinkled manila envelope.

"Jumbo was my favorite," he says. "Came over a century ago, on a ship called the *Assyrian Monarch*. Barnum paraded him up and down Broadway, with a big brass band and all the fanfare you could imagine."

My mother walks over, and Elkezer hands her the envelope absentmindedly. "Back then, most people had never seen an elephant. So it wasn't really that he was so tremendous, but that he was *here*. And then three years later he was hit by a speeding freight train. Other elephants that were crossing the tracks got knocked out but survived. Jumbo, though, well, Jumbo didn't make it."

"He was hit by a train?" I say, stunned.

"*You* lived through a plane crash," my mother points out.

"Barnum carved up the beast and gave pieces to different

museums. He sold the heart, even. To Cornell University, for forty dollars. Can you imagine?"

"We'd better be going," my mother says.

"Oh, all the money is there," Elkezer says. "You can count it if you like."

"I'm sure that isn't necessary. Thank you."

"No, thank *you.*" We leave him standing on the third floor, lightly touching the photo of Jumbo.

As we close the heavy door of the museum behind us, my mother rips open the envelope. "We're rich again, Rebecca," she sings. "Rich!"

We get into our car and pull out of the parking lot. The fender scrapes like a rake against the pavement. We pass little boys playing handball and a fat woman with skin the color of molasses. We pass a deal going down on a street corner: a man in a leather cap unfolding a small wrinkled square of paper. In spite of this I can still picture the heavy dance of a motorcade, the oompah of a tuba, the slow-foot sashay of those elephants down Main Street.

31 JANE

We celebrate Rebecca's birthday at the geographical center of North America. Right outside of Towner, North Dakota, I give her a Hostess cupcake with a candle stuck in it, and I sing "Happy Birthday." Rebecca blushes. "Thanks, Mom. You didn't have to."

"Oh, I've got a present too," I say, and I pull an envelope out of my back pocket. We both recognize the envelope—the scruffy manila one that held the money under the MG's seat. Inside, on motel stationery, I've written an IOU.

Rebecca reads it out loud. "IOU anything you want (within reasonable limits) on a shopping spree." She laughs, and looks around. We've pulled over at a road sign that announces this geographical center, and with the exception of a superhighway beside us, there is nothing as far as the eye can see. "I guess I'll have to wait till we hit civilization again to go shopping," she says.

"No! That's the point. Today's driving is going to be wholly devoted to finding a suitable place to buy clothes. God knows we need them." The old shirt of Oliver's I've been wearing is covered with engine grease and food stains. My underwear can stand by itself. And Rebecca doesn't look much better; the poor kid didn't even take a decent bra along. "So how does it feel to be fifteen?" I say.

"Not much different than it felt to be fourteen." She hops into her side of the car: she has this down to a science by now. Me, I still have to crawl over the door, and I usually jam my foot on the handle.

"Okay," Rebecca says, settling herself with her feet swung over the passenger door. "Where to?"

Towner, I suppose. It's the place that Joley had directed us towards, although I have discovered that even a filling station and maybe three wooden houses can be classified as a "place" in North Dakota.

Rebecca guides me down a dirt road. We drive for a mile without seeing any signs of life, much less commerce. Finally a dilapidated barn that leans decidedly to the right looms into view. On it is a hex sign, two lovebirds in all the primary colors. "Eloise's?" Rebecca says.

"This can't be a store. This doesn't even qualify as a home." But there are several cars parked outside, cars so old and faded I have the sense I have arrived in a 1950s movie set. Tentatively, I pull over and climb out of the car.

The barn doors are propped open by long poles burning citronella candles. Inside are rows of barrels with flip-up tops. They are labeled: FLOUR, SUGAR, BROWN SUGAR, SALT, RICE. There is a strong sheet of smell that hits you when you cross the threshold, like molasses being burned. In a pen to one side of the barn is a tremendous sow collapsed on its side, most likely from its own weight, and ten spotted pigs jockeying for a better position at her teats. Next to the pigpen is a long, planed board propped on makeshift trestles, and on the board is a cash register—the silver kind where the buttons pop into the window: 50¢, $1, *No charge.*

"May I help you?" a woman says. She has been bent into the

pigpen so neither Rebecca nor I noticed her. Rebecca is deeper into the barn, exploring darker corners, so that leaves me to answer. "Well, actually," I say, "we're looking to get some new clothing."

The woman claps her hands together. She has stiff red spitcurls and a triple chin. She cannot be more than four and a half feet tall. When she walks, her shoes squeak as if her socks are wet. "You have come to the right place," she says. "We have a little bit of everything."

"So I see."

"My motto is, buy one only of each item. It helps the customer make up his mind more quickly."

I am wary of buying something at Eloise's. True, she has one of everything, but not necessarily things you would ever want.

"Mom," Rebecca says, sweeping towards us. She is holding a sequined evening gown. "What do you think? Pretty sexy, huh?"

It has spaghetti straps and too much lycra. "Wait till you're seventeen," I tell her. She groans and disappears behind a bolt of calico.

"Excuse me," I call to the woman who is leading me on this serpentine journey. "Miss?"

"Call me Eloise. Everyone else does."

Rebecca, who is still holding onto the sequined black evening gown (where do you wear that in a place like Towner?), has culled a pile of clothing. "You finding what you want, dear?" Eloise calls. Then she turns to me. "Are you two together?"

"Very much so," I say, and I walk over to Rebecca's pile.

Rebecca peeks at the tag on a pair of red walking shorts. "Check out the prices, Mom." She holds up the shorts. "Do you have these in a three?"

"What we have in stock is on the sales floor. I'd be happy to move these items to a dressing room for you." She waddles around a corner, led by a sixth sense, I imagine, since the clothes are piled over her head. "You're in room number six," she calls to Rebecca. I peer around the corner at the fitting rooms. Cow stalls.

"Mom." I walk over to where Rebecca stands, eyes shining. "This—" she holds out a pair of designer jeans, "—this is only three dollars," she says. "This bathing suit is made by La Blanca, and it's only one-fifty."

I finger the white price tags. The numbers are written in crayon. "Maybe we'll come here to do all our shopping from now on."

I begin to leaf through the racks myself. At these prices, what have I got to lose? Eloise is a prudent businesswoman. She orders her stock in one of each size. So the bottom line is, if a pair of striped Liz Claiborne trousers come in, you can expect to find one of each size: 4, 6, 8, 10, 12, 14 and 16. If you happen to be a ten, and another ten has gotten here before you, you are out of luck. This is what happens in several cases for items that catch my eye; I'm an eight and I guess in North Dakota that's a popular size. Those, and the sixteens, seem to be selling the best. Rebecca has her pick of the racks, still sporting a preadolescent figure.

Eloise crosses in front of me holding out a cute yellow jumper. "I saw her face and I thought of this. You said size three, dear?"

"What she really needs is a bra and some underwear. Do you stock that as well?"

Eloise leads me to another row of barrels, marked by size. I reach into the bin marked *Four* and pull out a handful of panties in pink, fuschia, black lace, and white with green flowers. "Wonderful," I say, taking all but the black lace. As I am looping them over my wrist for safekeeping, Eloise returns with a neatly packaged bra. I take these over to Rebecca. "You might as well put on some underwear," I tell her. "Since we're going to buy it anyway."

"Ma . . ." she says, hanging her head over the swing door of the stall. "*You* know."

"Oh." I rummage in my bag for anther maxi-pad. There are no garbage pails to be seen. I lean close to Rebecca. "Just bury it under the hay or something."

Rebecca puts on a fashion show for me and Eloise. We are sitting on the underwear barrels with our legs crossed when Rebecca comes out in the yellow jumper. "Oh, how darling!" Eloise says.

Rebecca does look cute. She has braided her hair to get it out of her face, and it swings over the Peter Pan collar of the matching striped jersey shirt. The straps of the jumper criss-cross in the back and are secured with buttons in the shapes of crayons. She is barefoot. She twirls around, letting the skirt fly up.

"Let me guess." Eloise says, pointing to Rebecca's feet. "Size seven?" She shuffles off in another direction, back towards an area where an Old Town canoe is suspended from the rafters.

Rebecca ends up with six pairs of shorts, eight casual tops, a pair of jeans, a pair of white cropped pants, crew socks, black shoes, white shoes, various and sundry items of underwear, a nightgown covered in teddy bears, a pullover cotton sweater, a blue polka-dotted bikini and two grosgrain ribbon barrettes for her hair. "I can't believe this," she says, coming out and seeking the stack of clothes Eloise has neatly folded. "This is going to cost a fortune."

I doubt it; I've been keeping a mental tab and I don't think we'll even break fifty dollars. "Well, it's your birthday. Enjoy."

"So," Eloise says, as Rebecca throws her arms around me. "What about for you?"

"Oh, I shouldn't." I cross my legs nervously, and then uncross them.

"I'm not going to let you travel with me, looking like that," Rebecca says. "Not now that I'm dressed to kill."

"Well, I could certainly use some underwear," I admit. I have been sitting on the size seven bin. I jump off and open the lid, lining up several pairs on my arms. The last pair I pull out is a G-string, a leopard print.

"Oh, that's you, Mom. You've *got* to get that pair."

"I don't think so. It has its appeal, the way garter belts and thigh-high silk stockings have always held my interest. I like the idea behind them, but in reality I know I wouldn't have a clue about how to put them on, so I do not bother.

Rebecca runs with Eloise around the racks, collecting cotton sundresses and khaki shorts and silk tank tops. It is harder to find such close matches because, like I said, I wear a popular size. "Really, you don't have to do this."

"Oh, just go get undressed," Rebecca says, pointing to the cow stall. I walk inside and kick off my sneakers. The hay tangles in between my toes, prickling. Eloise sticks her head inside, which makes me embarrassed. I cross my arms in front of my chest. "Hello," I say shyly.

Eloise throws two shoeboxes on the floor, a pair of leather

woven sandals and a pair of black heeled shoes. They are both size eight. How did she know?

I check the price on each item of clothing before I try it on, a habit from shopping in expensive California boutiques that really is pointless here; nothing costs more than five dollars. The first dress I try on is too tight across the chest. I throw it onto the hay, disappointed. Somehow I had hoped that everything would look as perfect on me as it did on Rebecca.

The next piece of clothing is a cotton jumper along the same lines as the one Rebecca tried on. It is red and splashed with blue and pink flowers. There is a matching white linen top with buttons down the back and embroidered flowers on the collar and sleeves. I try it on with the sandals Eloise has given me and walk out of the stall. Rebecca claps. "You really like it?" There are no mirrors, so the only reflection I have is Rebecca's opinion.

The last thing I try on is a lycra stretch tank dress, black. I put it on with heels. I don't need a mirror for this one. The way it hugs my body, I know it's bad. I can imagine sight unseen the places where my hips bulge out and where my tummy bloats. This is a dress for Rebecca's body, not mine. "You want a laugh?" I say, calling to Rebecca.

She jumps off her underwear barrel and walks to the stall, holding the door open so that I don't have to walk out. "Who'd believe it? My own mother is a fox."

"Tell me you don't see my hips or my butt. Tell me my stomach doesn't look like a tire."

Rebecca shakes her head. "I wouldn't tell you this if I didn't think you looked good." She points to my hip and addresses Eloise. "What do you do about those panty lines?"

Eloise holds up a finger, runs to the underwear barrel, and retrieves the leopard G-string. She snaps it at me, as insubstantial as milkweed. "No way," I say to Rebecca. "I'm not getting into that."

"Just try it. You don't have to get it if you don't like it."

I sigh and pull up the slim skirt. I wiggle my underpants off over the shoes and hold the leopard ones up to the light. "The little patch of fabric goes in the front," Rebecca says.

"How do you know that?" I stand on one leg and then the

other. I pull up the G-string and discover, to my surprise, comfort. Between my legs I can barely feel the thin material of the underwear, covering me. I wriggle the skirt back down, and pace a few steps to get used to the feel of fabric against the skin of my rear end. Then I open the door.

"What a knockout," Eloise says.

Rebecca turns to her. "We'll take that."

The whole ensemble costs no more than four dollars. "We will *not*. Where am I going to wear something like that?" I strip the skinny slip of material off my body so that I am standing braless, in this G-string. "It's a waste of money."

"Like four dollars is going to break you," Rebecca says.

As we are arguing, Eloise reappears with a flimsy rose-colored sheath. "I thought you might like this. You didn't buy a nightgown, after all."

I lift the negligee from her hands. Soft, it slips to the floor, spilled on the hay like a broken flower.

Do you know the way there are certain things you try on, once or twice in a lifetime of shopping, and before you even see yourself you are convinced you have never looked so good in your life? I did not feel that way about the black dress, which Rebecca raved about. But this satin sheath, with its braided spaghetti straps and slit up the side, breathes with me.

Before I step outside to show Rebecca I run my hands up my sides. I touch my own breasts. I spread my legs apart, enjoying the way satin slides across hot and bothered skin. So this is what it feels like to be sexy.

I wore something like this on my wedding night, a white teddy with lace at the neck and six fabric buttons down the front. Oliver and I checked into the Hotel Meridien in Boston. Upstairs, Oliver did not comment on the teddy. He ripped it during foreplay, and after we had checked out I realized we had left it on the floor of the honeymoon suite.

I know before I open the door to reveal myself to Rebecca that I am taking this. If I could, I'd wear this one out of the store, and drive down the highways of the Midwest feeling the satin rub in between my thighs each time I shifted gears. I strike a dramatic pose, arched against the back wall of the cow stall.

Rebecca and Eloise applaud. I take a bow. I close the door behind me and very slowly pull the negligee over my head. Talk about a waste of money. The truth is, I've left the only man I've ever slept with. So who am I going to wear it for?

I start to pull on a pair of the cotton underwear I am going to buy when I stop, and step out of it, and try on the G-string instead. I pull my shorts over this, and button them and zip the fly. When I take a step forward to lace up my sneakers, there is a forbidden sensation of freedom. I feel like I am hiding a secret that no one has to know.

32 Oliver

Now that I have ascertained that Jane and Rebecca are on their way to Iowa, I am much less worried by my situation. Today, in fact, I took two spare hours and called the Institute, taking messages down on a small bedside pad at the Holiday Inn.

I will not pat myself on the back yet; it is not the mark of a good scientist to congratulate himself before he comes to a conclusion, an endpoint. But nonetheless I consider this my finest work to date. Starting with next to nothing, I have beat Jane to the punch, if you will—I've discovered where she is headed before she even realizes she is headed there. Jane is the type who will be driving through Iowa, and then, having remembered her daughter's plane crash, will turn off the road at the spur of the moment. Of course it no longer matters. Because when she turns off the road I will be there, and I will take her back to San Diego. It is where she belongs. If my calculations go according to plan, I will be home in time to catch the start of the humpback migration to the breeding grounds of Hawaii.

This morning I spoke to Shirley at the office and asked her to help me with some research. The poor girl was near tears when she heard my voice, for Christ's sake, it's only been four working days. I told her to ask a reference librarian in town to help her find microfiche files on the crash of Flight 997, Midwest Airlines, in September 1978. She was to record as much precise information about the site of the crash as possible. Then she was to take the data and call the State Department of Iowa, and using the Institute's clout, find out the names of the owners of the surrounding farms. Presumably, in two days when I contact her again, I will know whose land I have to stake out.

And so the next challenge, having mastered their route, is to be able to read from a distance the role I have to play. I will need two speeches: one as a penitent husband, and one as a dashing savior. And I will need to assess practically on sight which of these two categories I must fill.

Have I always been this good an analyst?

It is only noon, but I feel like celebrating somehow. I am on top of the crisis. I have at least found all the pieces of the puzzle, if I am still somewhat muddled about fitting them together. I know that I must be back on the road by two in order to reach the next Holiday Inn in Lincoln by dinnertime. Checking my watch (a nervous habit, I don't really need to see the time), I wander into the hotel lobby to find the bar.

These lobbies all look alike: blue and silver, carpets with a pattern, a *de trop* glass elevator and a fountain in the shape of a dolphin or cherub. The staff behind the desk even starts to clone from city to city. The lounges are always done in maroon, with round leatherette chairs that look like teacups and spotty highball glasses.

"What can I get you?" the waitress says. Are they called waitresses or barmaids these days? She is wearing a silver plate over her left breast that reads MARY LOUISE.

"Well, Mary Louise," I say, sounding as pleasant as possible, "what do you recommend?"

"Number one, I'm not Mary Louise. I'm wearing her apron because mine got stolen last night along with my car and my house keys by my no-good motherfucker of a boyfriend. Number two," she pauses, "this is a *bar*. Our specialties of the house are whiskey straight and whiskey on the rocks. So do you want to have a drink or are you just wasting my day like every other sorry asshole in this place?"

I look around, but I am the only customer. I decide she must be distressed over her misfortune of the night before. "I'll have a gin and tonic," I say.

"No gin."

"Canadian Club and ginger."

"Look mister," the girl says. "We've got Jack Daniel's and a faucet of Coke. Take your pick. Or come back after the truck delivers more stock today."

"Well, I see. I'll have Jack Daniel's, straight up."

She flashes me a smile—she is sort of pretty, actually—and walks away. Roach clip earrings swing in her ears. Roach clips. Rebecca taught me that. We had been walking on a boardwalk at the beach and I picked up this long, trailing feather-and-bead creation. I was trying to place it as an Indian artifact, or a new tourist item from over the border. "That's a roach clip, Dad," Rebecca had said casually, taking it from me and throwing it into a trash bin. "You use it to smoke pot."

The waitress comes back with my drink and fairly tosses it onto the table so that it spills in a clear amber puddle. Rather than face her wrath, I mop it up with a napkin. HOLIDAY INN! the napkin says, in embossed gold letters. The waitress climbs onto a bar stool and rests her cheek on her hand. She stares at me.

I take a sip of my drink and try to put this woman out of my mind. I do not normally look at women, they tend to confuse me. But this one is different. Not only is she wearing those feather-type earrings; she also sports a red leather skirt that barely covers her buttocks, and a studded bustier. Her stockings, which are white, are covered with fat black polka dots that stretch over the muscles of her thighs. She is wearing far too much makeup, but there is an art involved; one eye is done in violet, the other in green.

I try to think of Jane in such a get-up and I laugh out loud.

The waitress gets off her stool and walks up to me. She points a red fingernail at my throat. "You listen to me, pervert. You get your eyes back in your head and your dick back in your shorts."

She says this with such hatred, with such conviction, although she does not know me, that I feel obliged to reply. She has already turned on her heel when I say, "I'm not a pervert."

"Oh yeah? Then what are you?" She does not turn around.

"Well, I'm a scientist."

The waitress spins and sizes me up. "Funny. You're better looking than those polyester pants types."

I look down at my trousers. They are wool, summerweight. The waitress snorts, a laugh. "I'm just yanking your chain." She pulls a compact mirror out of I don't know where exactly—it looks like her pantyhose—and bares her teeth. When she finds a spot of lipstick she rubs it vigorously with her thumb.

"I'm sorry to hear about your car," I say. "And your boyfriend."

The waitress snaps the mirror shut and stuffs it, this time, into the crevice of her bustier. The pink plastic edge juts out a bit from between her breasts. "He was a louse. Thanks." She looks in the direction of the front desk, and when she decides that nobody is paying attention, she swings her leg over one of the leatherette chairs nearby and sits down. "Mind if I join you?"

"Not at all." I have always wondered about women like her, the kind you find superimposed on X-rated videocassettes or packages for sexual aid devices. There have been several women for me other than Jane—two before and one during the marriage, for a brief stint, a diver on one of my marine excursions. None of them, however, acted or looked like this. This waitress is more than a woman, she is a specimen. "Have you worked here long?" I care nothing about the answer. I just want to watch the way her lips move, fluid, like coagulating rubber.

"Two years," she says. "Just during the day. At night I work in a twenty-four-hour mini-mart. I'm saving to move to New York City."

"I've been there. You'll like it."

The waitress squints at me. "You think I'm some Nebraska field girl," she says. "I was *born* in New York. That's why I 'm going back."

"I see." I pick up my drink, and swirl it around. Then I dip my finger in and run it lightly around the edge of the glass. When my fingertip reaches a certain level of dryness the friction causes a sound to moan out of the glass. A sound that, frankly, reminds me of my whales.

"That's cool," the girl says. "Teach me."

I show her; it isn't difficult. When she gets the hang of it her face lights up. She gets three or four more glasses and fills them to varying levels with Jack Daniel's. (Why tell her it works with water, if I can get a free drink?) Together we create a melancholy, screeching symphony.

The waitress laughs and grabs my hands. "Stop! Stop, I can't take it anymore. It hurts my ears." She holds my hands for a second, looking down at my fingers. "You're married." A statement—not an accusation.

"Yes," I say. "She's not here, though."

I do not mean anything by that; I am just stating the facts. But this girl (who I imagine is closer to Rebecca's age than mine) leans forward and says, "Oh, *really*." She is so near that I can smell her breath, sweet, like Certs. She lifts herself out of the chair and creeps forward on the table, led by her hands, which reach over the boundary of decorum and grab the collar of my shirt. "What else can you teach me?"

I have to admit that I have a vision of this waitress naked, with a tattoo somewhere unspeakable, telling me in her rough and husky voice to do it to her again, and again. I see her in my safe aqua suite in this Holiday Inn, reclining in her leather bra and her polka-dot hose, just like a cheap movie. It would be so incredibly easy. I have not told her my name, or my profession: it would be an opportunity to be somebody else for just a little while.

"You can't leave here," I say. "You're the only one working."

The waitress wraps her arms around my neck. She smells of musk and perspiration. "Just watch me."

I have been given two room keys. I slip one out of my pocket, along with a five dollar bill for my drink. She deserves a hell of a tip. The key hits the rim of the whiskey glass, and rings. Then I stand up, like I imagine very suave men in Hollywood do, and without turning back or saying a word I walk to the bank of elevators in the lobby.

When I am inside the elevator, with the doors closing, I lean back and breathe quickly. What am I doing? What am I doing? Is it infidelity, I wonder, if you are pretending to be someone that you aren't?

I let myself into the hotel room and I am relieved by its overwhelming familiarity. There is the bed on the left, and the bathroom behind the door, and the thin sanitary strip around the toilet that the maid leaves every morning. There is the folding stand for luggage, and the room service menu, and the wavy patterned curtains made of some flammable substance. Everything is just as I have left it, and there is some solace in this.

I lie on the bed, my hands at my sides, completely naked. The air conditioner, making the obligatory hum that all hotel cooling units do, stirs the hair on my chest. I picture the face of this waitress, her lips moving down the length of my body like water.

Although we had been dating, I did not have intercourse with Jane for four and a half years. There were two women on the side, women who meant nothing. You know the phrase: there are certain women you sleep with, and others you marry. It was quite clear which category Jane fit into. Jane, who smelled of lemon soap, and who matched her headbands to her handbags. I had been working for a while at Woods Hole by the time Jane entered her senior year at Wellesley, and I got into a routine. I'd see her every weekend (the commute was too draining for anything more) and we'd go out. I'd feel her under her bra and then take her back to her dormitory.

That last year, though, something happened. Jane stopped fighting my hands as they groped through layers of clothes in the dark. She started to move my hands herself, so that they would touch certain places and slide with certain rhythms. I did everything I could to stop her. I believed that I knew the consequences better than she.

We had sex for the first time in the balcony of an old movie theater. She had been provoking me to distraction downstairs, where we were surrounded by other people. I pulled her to the balcony, which was roped off for renovation at the time. When I took off her clothes, and she was standing in front of me haloed in the light from the projector, I realized I wasn't going to fight her any longer. She rubbed herself against me until I was certain I would explode and then I grabbed her hips and pushed myself into her. I started to lose control, the warm sponginess like a closing throat, and then I realized that Jane had stopped breathing. She had never had intercourse before.

I know now I must have scared her to death, but I wasn't thinking rationally back then. Once I had tasted honey, I was not about to go back to bread and water. I began to call Jane daily and make the commute from the Cape two or three times a week. I was working with tide pools then, and I spent the day staring at them, at the hard-shelled invertebrates and the kelp, entire societies that were devastated in the ruthless blast of a wave. I turned over the horseshoe crabs and unraveled the tentacles of the starfish without interest. I took no notes. And when a mentor at Woods Hole confronted me about my attitude, I did the only thing I could: I stopped seeing Jane.

I was not going to make a name for myself if I spent the day thinking about being in the throes of passion. I told Jane many things: that I had the flu; that I had switched to a project on jellyfish and had to do background research. I spent more time devoted to my job and I called Jane occasionally, with distance keeping us safe.

About this time I witnessed a miracle: the birth of a pilot whale in captivity. We had been studying the mother's gestation and I happened to be in the building when she started labor. We had her in a huge underwater tank for easy visibility, and naturally when such a marvel occurs everyone stops what they are doing and comes to see. The baby spit out of its mother in a stream of entrails and blood. The mother swam in circles until the baby had become oriented to the water, and then she swam beneath it in order to buoy it to the surface for air. "Tough break," said a scientist beside me. "Being born underwater to breathe oxygen."

That day I went into town and bought an engagement ring. It had not occurred to me before: the only thing that could be better than becoming famous in my field was to do it with Jane by my side. There was no reason I could not have my cake and eat it too.

She possessed all the qualities I knew I would never grow to espouse. By having Jane, I had hope. I understood sacrifice.

Jane. Lovely, quirky Jane.

Would she believe in second chances?

Suddenly mortified by my behavior, I cross my hands in front of my groin. I pull on my clothes as quickly as possible and zip up my suitcase. I have to get out of here before this waitress comes. What have I been thinking? I drag the suitcase down the long hallway and into an elevator, hiding behind balustrades to make sure she isn't coming. Then, calmed by Muzak, I take deep breaths and plummet to ground level, thinking of Jane. Jane, only of Jane.

33 REBECCA *July 15, 1990*

According to Indianapolis Jones, the DJ on this radio station (and no relative of ours), the temperature has reached 118 degrees. "One hundred and eighteen," my mother repeats. She lifts her hands off the steering wheel as if it too is boiling. She whistles through her front teeth. "People die in this kind of weather."

We have stumbled into a drought and a heat wave, mixed. It also seems that time is passing much more slowly here, although I imagine that could be due to the temperature. We are destined for Indianapolis, but I don't think we will ever make it. The way things are going this car will explode in the heat of its own gas before we get there.

It is so hot I can't sit up anymore. I never thought I'd say it but I wish we had the old station wagon back. Inside, there was plenty of room to create shadows. In an MG there's no place to hide. I'm curled into the smallest ball I can manage, with my head pointing down on the floor mat. My mother looks at me. "Embryonic," she says.

Sometime before we actually cross into the city of Indianapolis the temperature rises another three degrees. The vinyl in the car begins to crack, and I point this out to my mother. "You're being ridiculous," she tells me. "That was cracked to begin with."

I feel the pores on my face breathe. Sweat runs down the inside of my thighs. The thought of entering a city—concrete and steel—disgusts me. "I mean it. I'm going to scream." I summon up every morsel of strength I have left and shriek, a high-pitched banshee sound that doesn't seem to originate from any part of my body.

"All right." My mother tries to put her hands over her ears but she cannot do this and drive at the same time. "All right! What do you need?" She looks at me. "A Sno-cone? Air-conditioning? A swimming pool?"

"Oh yes," I sigh, "a pool. I need a pool."

"You should have said that in the first place." She nudges over the suntan lotion that sits on the seat between us. "Put this on. You're going to get skin cancer."

According to the Indianapolis Department of Tourism, there is no city pool, but relatively nearby is a YMCA where we could probably pay admission to swim. My mother gets directions and (after stopping off for Uncle Joley's letter) drives to the building. "What if it's an indoor pool?" I whine. But then I hear it: the screams and the splashes of kids, towels dragging on concrete. "Oh, thank God."

"Thank Him after you get inside," my mother murmurs.

You know the way your body feels on the hottest day of the summer, when you actually get within swimming distance of a cold, blue pool? How you feel more relaxed than you have in the seven hours you've suffered from heatstroke—as if all you had to do to cool off was imagine that you would finally be able to dive in? This is exactly the way I feel, waiting with my back pressed up against the cinderblock yellow walls of the YMCA. My mother is negotiating. It is not their policy, the woman says, to let in nonmembers. "Join," I whisper. "Oh, please join."

I don't know if it is mercy or fate that makes the woman let us in for five dollars each, but soon we are standing at the edge of heaven. The cement burns the balls of my feet. There is a lesson going on in the shallow end. The lifeguard keeps calling the kids her guppies. They are doing rhythmic breathing, and only half are following instructions.

"Aren't you going to go in?" I ask my mother. She is standing next to me, fully clothed, and she hasn't even taken her bathing suit in from the car.

"Oh, you know me," she says.

I don't care; I don't care. I don't have time to argue with her. As the lifeguard yells and tells me not to, I dive into the deep end, into the heartbeat of ten feet.

I hold my breath for as long as I can. For a moment, drowning seems better than having to face the heat above. When I burst to the surface, the air wraps around my face, as solid as a towel. My mother has disappeared.

She is not at the car. She is not under one of the umbrellas, with large ladies in flowered bathing suits. I drip my way into the YMCA building.

I pass a Tai Chi class. This amazes me: why would anyone be doing exercise on a day like today? Down the hall I see a blue door marked LADIES LOCKER. It is steamy and humid inside. A gaggle of women are crowded into the showers. Some are behind the showers with curtains but most choose the open showers with no privacy. Three women are shaving their legs and two are shampooing.

The woman farthest on the right is young and has a tattoo over her left breast. It is a tiny red rose. "What do you have going for this weekend?" she says. I jump but she is not talking to me.

The woman under the nozzle behind her reaches for her towel to wipe her eyes. She is tremendous, with patches of cellulite waffling across her arms and her thighs. Her stomach forms a furrowed *V* that hangs over her private parts. She has painted toenails. "Oh, Tommy's coming out with Kathy and the baby."

"Tommy is the youngest?" the tattoo woman asks.

"Yeah." The other woman is older than I thought at first; without the shampoo her hair is speckled, gray and black. She sounds Italian. "Tommy is the one who got messed up with this girl who's been divorced. I keep telling him, You do what you do, but you don't marry her. You know what I mean?"

The other three women in the shower nod vigorously. One is shaped like a pear and has bleached hair. The next one is very old, and wrinkled all over like a giant raisin. She kneels on the floor of the shower, letting the spray hit her back, as if she is praying. The last woman has long white hair and is round all over: round shoulders, round hips, round belly. Her nipples are pushed-in, and stay that way. "Why do you let him come to the house, Peg?" she says. "Why don't you tell him he comes alone or he don't come at all?"

The enormous woman shrugs. "How do you tell that to a kid?"

One by one the women leave the showers until the only person left is the old woman. I begin to wonder if she is a permanent fixture. Maybe she needs help. This is what I am thinking when the curtain opens from the shower across the way and my mother steps out. "Well, hi honey," she says. She acts like it is perfectly normal to find me standing there.

"How come you didn't tell me you were coming inside? I was worried about you."

All the ladies are watching us. When we turn towards them, they pretend to be doing other things.

"I did tell you," my mother says. "You were underwater, though." She unwraps the towel from her body; she is wearing her bathing suit. "I just wanted to cool off."

I'm not going to fight her. I walk through the twisted lines of lockers. My mother stops in front of Peg, who is hoisting up her underwear. "Give Tommy time," she says. "He'll come around."

Outside my mother sits on the edge of the shallow end, dangling her feet. When she really gets hot she sits on the first step of the pool and lets her butt get wet. When I see her there I swim up underwater and grab her ankles. She screams. "You shouldn't sit here," I tell her. "All the little kids pee in the shallow end."

"Think about it, Rebecca. Won't it make its way to the deep end, then?"

I try to remind her that this is a concrete pool; that she will be able to grab the edge of it the entire way around if she chooses to get wet above her waist. "It's less deep than the Salt Lake, and you were doing the backfloat there."

"I did that against my will. You tricked me."

She exasperates me. I breaststroke away from her, diving over the blue and white bubble-string that separates the shallow from the deep end. I slide my belly down the concrete ramp and touch the drain of the pool. I run out of air and push off the bottom, roll onto my back. The clouds are stuck in the sky. I can make out all kinds of shapes: beagles and circus acts, lobsters, umbrellas. With my ears tucked under the surface of the water, I listen to my pulse.

I backfloat until I crash into a woman wearing a bathing cap with plastic flowers. Then I tread water. My mother isn't on the steps anymore, and she isn't sitting on the edge of the pool. I glance around wildly, wondering where the hell she's gone this time. And then I see her, chest-high in the water. With one hand she's grabbing onto the ledge of the pool, and with the other hand she's grabbing the blue and white string of buoys. When she gets to the other side she lifts the heavy line and ducks under it. I'll bet she doesn't hear the kids squealing, or the slap of thongs on puddles. I'll bet she isn't thinking of the heat. She grabs onto the edge of the pool again and slides one foot down the ramp of the deep end, testing her limits.

34 SAM

"So these two guys open a bar together," Hadley says, and then he stops to take a drink of his beer. "They go through this whole big deal cleaning up the place and stocking it and then comes the big opening day. They're waiting together for a customer, and in walks this grasshopper that's six feet tall."

"Here we go," says Joley.

Hadley laughs and sprays beer all over my shirt.

"Jesus, Hadley," I say, but I'm laughing too.

"Okay, okay. So there's this grasshopper—"

"Six feet tall—" Joley and I yell out at the same time.

Hadley grins. "And it sits down at the bar and orders a vodka tonic. So the guy who's waiting on him goes up to his buddy and says, 'I don't believe this. Our first customer is a grasshopper.' And they have a few laughs and then he goes back to the grasshopper with his vodka tonic. And he says, 'I can't believe it. You're our first customer and you're a grasshopper.' And the grasshopper says, 'Yeah, well.' So the bartender goes, 'You know, there's a drink named after you.' "

Joley turned to me. "This is going to be a disappointment. I can feel it."

"Shut up, shut up!" Hadley says. "So the bartender goes, 'You know—' "

"There's a drink named after you," I say, prompting him.

"And the grasshopper says, 'That's ridiculous. I've never heard of a drink called an Irving.' " Hadley finishes the joke and then hoots so loud the whole place is looking at our table.

"That's the dumbest joke I've ever heard," Joley says.

"I have to agree," I tell Hadley. "That was pretty stupid."

"Stupid," Hadley says, "but real fucking *funny*."

Of course anything's funny when you've had about ten beers apiece and it's after midnight. We are onto our stupid joke contest: the one to come up with the stupidest joke gets out of paying the tab. We've been here for a while. When we first got here, around nine-ish, there was next to no one in the bar, and now it's packed. We've been keeping tabs on the women that come in—no real lookers, yet, but it's been getting darker, and everyone's getting prettier. It will probably keep up like this for another hour: we'll tell dumb jokes and talk about the women behind their backs and none of us will do a damn thing about it, so we'll leave just the three of us and wake up alone with hangovers.

We come here every few weeks—everyone's welcome who works in the fields, to talk about their gripes at a place where it's common knowledge the boss is buying. Some of the guys make up complaints just for the free beer. The meeting starts unofficially at nine, and usually by eleven-thirty most of the others have cleared out. From nine to ten we actually do discuss the business of the orchard: on my end, I tell everyone about the revenues and the new costs, or about meetings I've had with produce buyers, and the guys from the field talk about getting a new tractor, or division of labor. They're the only guys I know of in an orchard who haven't unionized, and I think it's because of these conversations. I don't know that much ever gets done—money's tight—but I think they just like knowing that I am willing to listen.

It always ends up with me, Hadley and Joley—most likely because we all live in the Big House, we all drive down here together, and we all have nothing better to do. We participate in the obligatory dumb joke event. We put quarters in the jukebox and talk about whether or not Meatloaf songs really belong with the oldies—Joley says yes, but he's five years older anyway. Hadley finds some girl and talks to us for about three hours about how he'd like to dance with her and do other unmentionable things, but he chickens out halfway to her table and we get to rib him about it. If Joley has enough to drink, he'll do his Honeymooners imitations and his best turkey call. Is it any wonder that I'm always the one who drives us home?

"So tell us about your sister," I say to Joley, who returns from the bar with three more Rolling Rocks.

"Yeah," says Hadley. "Is she a babe?"

"For Christ's sake. She's his *sister*."

Hadley lifts his eyebrows—this is a real effort for him by now. "So what, Sam? She's not *my* sister."

Joley laughs. "I don't know. I guess it depends on what you call a babe."

Hadley points to a girl in a red leather dress, leaning on the bar and sucking on an olive. "That's what I call a babe," he says. He purses up his lips and makes kiss noises.

"Will somebody get that boy laid?" Joley says. "He's a walking gland."

We watch Hadley stand (almost) and make his way towards the red-leather girl. He uses the backs of chairs and other people to steer by. He makes it all the way to the bar stool next to her, and then turns to look at us. He mouths, *Watch this*. Then he taps the girl on her shoulder and she looks at him, grimaces, and flips the olive into his face.

Hadley reels back to our table. "She loves me."

"So your sister will be getting here soon?" I ask. I haven't any idea, really. Joley brought it up once, and that was it.

"I figure five more days, maybe."

"You looking forward to seeing her?"

Joley sticks his thumb into the neck of an empty green bottle. "Like you don't know, Sam. It's been so damn long, with her out in California."

"You guys pretty tight?"

"She's my best friend." Joley looks up at me and his eyes are bare, the way they get that makes people so uncomfortable around him.

Hadley sits with his cheek pressed into the table. "But is she a babe? That's the question."

Joley pulls Hadley's head up by a chunk of hair. "You know who's a babe? I'll tell you who's a babe. My niece. Rebecca. She's fifteen, and she's gonna be a knockout." He lets Hadley's face fall back down, slapping against the formica.

"Jailbait," Hadley murmurs.

I look at Hadley. "You gonna get sick, Hadley? Do you need to get to the john?"

Hadley tries to shake his head without lifting it off the table. "What I really need, is another beer." He waves his hand in the air. "Gar-konn!"

"That's garçon, you idiot. He's pathetic," I say to Joley, like I do every week.

"So tell me about this Jane." Someone's got to hold up a conversation.

"Number one, she's on the run. I figure her husband will show up at the orchard some time after she gets there."

"That's nice," I say, sarcastic. "Nothing like a scandal in Stow."

"It's not anything like that. The guy's an asshole."

"What are we talking about?" Hadley says.

I pat him on the shoulder. "Go back to sleep," I say. "But isn't he a famous asshole?"

"I guess." Joley rolls his empty beer bottle on its side. "That doesn't make him any less of an asshole."

"If he's such an asshole why is he coming after her?"

"Because she's a babe," Hadley says, "remember?"

"Because he doesn't know how to let go. He doesn't understand that she'd be better off without him because he doesn't know how to think about anything but himself."

Joley looks at Hadley, who says, "This is too fucking deep," and leaves to go to the bathroom.

"Sounds like a soap opera to me," I say. "Couldn't she just have stopped off in Mexico for a divorce?"

"She can't do anything until she comes here and talks to me. This hasn't only got to do with Oliver. This has to do with us, when we were kids, and the whole way she grew up. She *needs* me," Joley says, and for his sake I hope she does.

I am trying so hard not to pass judgment on Joley's sister. I mean, I don't even know her, right? And for all practical purposes I should feel about her the same way I feel about Joley. Joley's proven himself. He loves to watch things grow, same as me. But every time I picture his sister, I see her like every other girl who looked down her nose at where I came from; what I wanted to be.

A little while after Joley started to work at the orchard we realized I had dated a girl, Emily, who lived two houses down the street from him as a kid. She had long black hair that hung to her waist and eyes like emeralds, and to top it all off, she had tits like a Playboy bunny's. I was watching her at a hardware store, and she asked if I could help her with the difference between a nut and a bolt. I now suspect this was all a ploy. Of course I took her home and on that street where Joley was growing up, she gave me my first hand job.

Emily invited me to a party at some friend's house. I remember I came wearing the clothes I wore for church, and she was dressed in this skin-tight purple skirt. I spent the first two hours of this party gawking at the cathedral ceilings and stained-glass windows of this mansion. Then Emily grabbed me and asked me to dance. She pushed us into the middle of this parquet floor, next to another couple. She wheeled me around so I was looking into the face of a tall guy in a tennis sweater, and then she burst into tears. "You see what you've done to me!" I thought she was talking to me, and I looked down to see if I was stepping on her feet. But she was talking to this guy, who it turned out had dumped her a couple of weeks before. "Because of you," she cried, "look at what I have to go out with!"

What, not *who.* I stopped dancing with her there and then, and with all those rich kids looking at me like I had three heads, I ran out the heavy beautiful door of that house and drove back to Stow. Joley mentioned that Emily's older sister and Jane were friends. That they all moved in the same circles. It is quite possible Jane was even at that party.

This is what comes to mind when Joley brings up his sister: that maybe she saw me, and will walk up to me the minute she sets foot on my orchard, and laugh her head off. "Aren't you—?" she'll say, and on my own land, she'll make me feel as worthless as I did when I was just a kid.

"Earth to Sam," Hadley says, coming back from the bathroom. He's got the red-leather girl in tow. "Look who wants to buy us all beers." He winks at the girl. "I'm just kidding. I told her *you* wanted to buy her a beer."

"Me." I smile at the girl. "Um. I—I—"

"He's engaged," Joley says. "This is his bachelor's party."

"Oh," says the girl. "A kind of Last Supper?" She leans across the table.

"*I'm* not getting married, though," says Hadley.

"Look, the truth is, I'm not getting married. The truth is, he's going to blow a fuse unless you dance with him. He's likely to become violent. Please do us this one small favor." Hadley, on cue, drops to his knees and assumes a begging position.

The girl laughs and grabs Hadley's hand. "Come on, Fido." She looks at me as she's leaving. "You owe me one, and don't think I'm not going to collect."

Joley and I watch Hadley dancing with the red-leather girl. The music is Chubby Checker's "Twist," but Hadley is slow dancing. His face is buried in the girl's neck. It is difficult to see if he is standing, or if she is holding him up.

After the dance, the girl slips away in the direction of the bathrooms and Hadley comes back over to us. "She's in love with me," he says. "She told me."

"We gotta get him out of here before he fathers a child," I tell Joley.

"Hey," Joley says, "I never got to tell *my* stupid joke."

Hadley and I look at each other. There's always time for another stupid bar joke.

"Okay." Joley rubs his hands together. "There are these three strings, standing outside a bar."

"Strings?"

"Yeah, strings. And they want a drink. So the first string goes into the bar and hops onto the bar stool and says to the bartender, 'Good evening, sir. I'd like a drink.' The bartender says, 'I can't serve you. You're a string!' and he kicks him out of the bar."

"A string," Hadley says. "I love it."

"The second string goes into the bar, and decides to try another approach. He sits down on the stool and slams his fist on the table and says to the bartender, 'Gimme a drink, Goddammit!' And the bartender looks at him and laughs and says, 'I'm sorry, but I can't serve you. You're a string.' And he boots this guy out of the bar too."

The red-leather girl comes back and sits on Hadley's lap.

"So by now the third string sees what's going on. He looks at his two friends and says, 'I've got it.' Then he reaches up by his head and unravels himself a little and then he twists himself up. He walks into the bar and sits upon the bar stool. 'Hi,' he says to the bartender, 'I'd like a drink.' And the bartender sighs and says, 'Look, I've told you once, I've told you twice. I can't serve you. You're a string.' And the string takes offense. He squares his shoulders. He looks the bartender in the eye. And he says, 'I'm a frayed knot!' " Joley starts to crack up. "You get it? I'm *afraid not?*"

I start to laugh. Hadley either doesn't understand it or he doesn't find it funny.

The red-leather girl purses her lips, trying not to laugh. "That's the stupidest joke I've ever heard."

"Oh! You hear that!" Joley reaches for the girl and kisses her on the mouth.

She laughs. "It was really stupid," she says, "really."

"Mine was more stupid," Hadley insists, banging the table.

"I don't know," I tell him. "This one was really dumb."

In the background, the bartender announces last call. Hadley and Joley look at me, their eyes glinting with competition. About those dumb joke contests: I'm the judge. The categories are the content, the punch line, the delivery. Oh, and the confidence the joke teller has in his story. I hem and haw for effect, but this time I have to agree with the girl. Hands down, Joley is the winner.

35 JOLEY

Dear Jane—

Do you remember when the Cosgroves' house burned down? You were in high school, and I was still a little kid. Mama came into my room in the middle of the night, and you were with her—she'd just woken you up. She said, "Mr. Cosgrove's place is on fire," really calm. The Cosgroves were the neighbors behind us, through the backyard and the woods. Daddy was already dressed and downstairs. We had to get dressed too, even though it was three in the morning. As we came into the kitchen the telephone rang. It was Mrs. Silverstein, across the street. She saw the orange flames, like a halo, behind our house, and she thought our place was on fire. "No," I remember Daddy saying, "it's not us."

When nobody was looking, you and I stole into the backyard, where the small forest behind was exploding. We walked through the woods, through the cool, tall birches, across the wet pine carpet. We got as close to the house as we thought we could. The Cosgroves' den faced the woods, and when we got near we could hear the fire breathing like a lion. It sucked all the air away and sent sparks into the night, millions of new stars. You said, "How beautiful!" and then, realizing the tragedy, covered your mouth.

We tried to walk around the house, towards the street, to where the firemen were working to put out the fire. We saw windows explode in front of us. Some kids we knew from the neighborhood were standing on the flat, inactive fire hoses. When the firemen opened the hydrants, the water would pulse through them like arteries, popping the kids off one by one. We decided there wasn't that much to see, especially because the Cosgroves were huddled in a pocket on that side of the house, crying in their bathrobes.

Daddy was back at our house rigging up hoses and buckets, convinced that the fire was going to spread to the entire neighborhood, what with the houses so close together. He was spraying our roof. He figured, if you keep it wet, it won't ignite.

The fire didn't spread. The Cosgroves' house was gutted. They tore it down, and started to build the exact same one, something my mother didn't understand, with all the money they got from the insurance company.

That week, another catastrophe happened in Boston. The new windows of the John Hancock building spontaneously started to pop out. They'd fall fifty stories to the ground, shattering so dangerously that the police roped off entire blocks surrounding the building. It seemed the windows were not treated for the lower pressure experienced so high up, and the air in the building was pushing out the windows into the sky. Eventually at great expense the windows were removed. The next thing we knew, the Cosgroves had a huge pane from the Hancock building in their new home. It was fine for a home, they said. Just not right for a skyscraper.

Just before Route 2 takes you into Minnesota, get off on Rte. 29 South. Take it to Fargo and get on 94 East. This highway should take you directly to Minneapolis. Make sure you are there by seven A.M. *Saturday morning. I won't tell you what's going on, but let's just say you've never seen anything like it.*

I hope Rebecca enjoyed her birthday—how many kids her age get to turn fifteen at the geographical center of North America? Speaking of which, you will be heading towards Iowa next. I think you know where you have to go.

Give my love to the kid.

Joley

36 JANE

Although Joley hasn't mentioned where I should go in Minneapolis, I have no trouble finding what it is I am supposed to see. Rebecca and I have been up since four A.M. to ensure that we will reach the city by seven, but for the last hour and a half we have been sitting in traffic.

Policemen in white gloves are directing people and blowing whistles. There are lots of teenagers here in souped-up cars. They put their Camaros into park, and sit on the roof, smoking. "I've had it," Rebecca says. "I'm going to ask what this is all about."

She jumps over the passenger door before I can tell her not to and runs up to a young policeman with a crew cut. He takes the whistle from between his lips and says something to her, and then she smiles at him and runs back to the car. "They're blowing up the old Pillsbury building."

I am not sure if this really explains the commotion, so early on a Saturday. Do people really come out of the woodwork to watch catastrophes?

It takes us another twenty minutes, but we inch towards the policeman who spoke to Rebecca. "Excuse me," I say, leaning over the windshield. "We don't really know where we're going."

"Not too many places you can go, lady. The whole city's roped off for the demolition."

We drive along a barricaded path, following other cars blindly. We pass the central post office and drive through its parking lot. We cross a river. Finally we get to a point where other people have stopped and are parking haphazardly. I find myself wondering how we are ever going to get out of here, now that six other cars have flanked our own, like petals. A fat man walks by selling T-shirts: *I Knew Minneapolis Before They Changed the Skyline*.

"Well, let's go." I climb out of the car and start to follow the people who are skipping eastward, like a pilgrimage. Whole families are going, the fathers carrying the youngest on their shoulders. We reach an area where people have stopped moving. Bodies start to settle on steps and railings and billboards, anywhere you can find a spot is okay. The woman next to us stops abruptly and hands the man she is with a Styrofoam cup. She pours coffee from a thermos. "I can't wait," she says.

Rebecca and I find ourselves standing next to a large ruddy man in a flannel shirt with cut-off sleeves. He is holding a six-pack of Schlitz. "Beautiful day for wrecking," he says to us, smiling.

Rebecca asks if he knows exactly which building is the Pillsbury building. "It's this one now." He points to a large skyscraper fashioned of chrome and glass. "But it used to be this one here." He moves his finger across the skyline to a stubby grey building, a sort of eyesore next to all the modern ones. No wonder they want to knock it down.

"Did they try to sell the building?" Rebecca asks.

"Would you buy it?" The man offers her a Schlitz, and she tells him she is underage.

"Well," he snorts. "Could've fooled me." He is missing a tooth in the front. "You're sure here at a historic moment. This building has been here forever. I remember when it was one of the only skyscrapers in Minneapolis."

"Things change," I say, because he seems to be waiting for a response.

"How are they going to do it?" Rebecca asks.

At this, a woman on the other side of Rebecca turns her head towards our conversation. "Dynamite. They've layered it on every other floor, so the whole thing's gonna crumble systematically."

Over an unseen loudspeaker, a voice booms. "*We cannot demolish the building until everyone is standing behind the orange line.*" The voice repeats itself. I wonder where this orange line is. If it is as crowded up front as it is back here, the bystanders should not be blamed. They probably can't see their own feet.

"*You must move back behind the orange line before the demolition begins!*" At this second warning, the crowd begins to press itself tightly together, like a thick knit sweater. I find myself pushed into the soft belly of the larger man. He uses my shoulder as a coaster for his beer.

"*Ten . . . nine . . . eight . . .*" the loudspeaker booms.

"Fuckin' A," the man says.

"*Seven . . . six . . .*" Somewhere, a fire engine screams.

I do not hear the final five numbers. The building caves in, in sequence, top down. It is only after the second layer falls that I hear the dynamite howl. The cinderblock crumbles floor by floor.

Boom! We hear the next explosion after the fact, after an entire section has been leveled. They are erasing history in one swoop. It takes no more than five minutes, the blasting, and then nothing's left but a hole in the skyline.

The crowd begins to jostle and shove, and Rebecca and I get thrown into this flow. People, pulsing like blood, rush beside us.

About halfway to the car I realize why everything looks so different. Dust has settled over everything that has been immobile. Grey-white, like the artificial snow you see on television. Rebecca tries to pick some up but I brush it out of her hand. You don't know what's in that stuff.

I don't even recognize the MG when we reach it: because we haven't put up the top, it too is chalky. This dust gets on our clothes and between our fingers and we have to blink to keep it from getting into our eyes. The dust keeps coming, drifting over from the demolition site like nuclear fallout. Rebecca and I pull up the convertible top, something we haven't done since we bought the car.

I know I still have to get Joley's letter but I am reticent to walk the streets of Minneapolis. What if the other buildings fall? I suggest to Rebecca that we go out for breakfast.

Over bacon and hash I tell Rebecca that we are going to go to Iowa. To the place where her plane crashed. I tell her that I've been thinking about it. Since we're out here anyway, I say. I tell her we can go right up to the ruins. From what I hear, they are still in the cornfield. I wait for her to raise an objection.

Rebecca doesn't say what I am expecting. There is no resistance, really. Maybe Joley is right; she is ready for this after all. She asks, "Why are they still there?"

37 Rebecca

Uncle Joley talked my mother into joining the self-help group for abused wives when she returned to California after my plane crash. He said when you're with other people living the same life as you, you feel better—and as always, she believed him.

In this case, it was a good idea. She never told my father, and since I was still practically a baby she took me along. She'd pick me up from preschool and we'd go to a therapy session. There were seven women. I'd crawl around the floor playing between their shoes with my toys. Sometimes a red-headed woman with bright jewelry would pick me up and tell me I was pretty; I think she was the psychologist.

The way the sessions began was what I liked: women who were almost always crying lifted up clothing to reveal welts and bruises in the shapes of kettles and pelicans. Other women would hum softly, or touch the less tender parts of the bruise. They were hoping to heal. Those, like my mother, who had no physical signs to show, brought their stories. They had been yelled at, put down, ignored. At this early age I could see the differences between physical and verbal abuse. I'd stare at the splits and swellings of the battered women. My mother always told a story. In comparison I thought we were lucky.

Within several weeks my mother stopped going to the group. She told me things were fine again. She said there was no reason to continue. My mother did not keep in touch with these battered wives. As mysteriously as we had met those women, we never saw them again.

38 JOLEY

Dear Jane—

You may not want to hear this but I have been thinking about why Rebecca survived.

The day her plane crashed, I was in Mexico. I was working on translating some Incan document, I think—part of my Grail ordeal. I knew you were at Mama's; I had talked to you there a couple of days before. Anyway, I called to see how you were doing and you started to tell me what Oliver had done. He was going to send the FBI, you said, and even though I told you he didn't have the clout for that you said you had put Rebecca on a plane that morning. "You're an idiot," I told you. "Don't you see you've just played your ace?"

You didn't understand what I meant by that, but then again you didn't really see Rebecca the same way I did. I'd known it from the minute I first held her as an infant: She belonged *with you; she* was *you. All my life I had been trying unsuccessfully to explain to people the wonderful combination of elements that made up my sister, and then, without even trying, you created a replica of yourself. Sending her back to Oliver; well, that was making the same mistake twice.*

I argued with you about whether or not I should drive up to California (I could just about make it by the time the flight arrived) to intercept Rebecca before Oliver got her at the airport. You told me I was being ridiculous, that Oliver was after all the baby's father and it was none of my business. I am pretty sure that you knew how hard it was for me to put calls through from Mexico, but you slammed the phone down and hung up on me anyway.

This is what I figured out: At the moment we were talking, Rebecca's plane was exploding over the cornfields of Iowa. And it is my hypothesis that the very reason she is still alive today is because you and I were fighting about her. Only souls that are at peace can go to Heaven.

I tried to call you when I heard about the plane crash that afternoon. But like I said, it was almost impossible to put calls through to the States and anyway, you were on your way to Iowa. I heard through Mama that you and Oliver had arrived at the hospital at the same time. The next time I spoke to you, everything was fine. "We're back to normal, Joley," you told me, and you didn't want to discuss Oliver, or if he apologized, or the fact that he hit you in the first place. You shut me out. You acted just like you did when this kind of thing first happened, when we were kids.

I decided to let sleeping dogs lie. And this is why, Jane: because this time, you had Rebecca to consider. I know that when you were a kid you kept quiet about Daddy because of me, but this wasn't Daddy and this wasn't me. Oliver was different; even the way he hurt you was different. More important, Rebecca was different. I kept hoping, silently, that you would want to save her like you hadn't been able to save yourself.

I have waited years for you to see that you had to get away. I know you think that because you threw the first punch you are at fault, but I believe in histories, and Oliver was the one who started this a long, long time ago. So this is why Rebecca survived that plane crash: she was spared twelve years ago so that she could save you now.

When I first came back from Mexico, before I went to visit either you or Mama, I stopped in What Cheer, Iowa, to see the remains of Rebecca's plane, and I realized why that farmer had never bothered to remove the wreckage. It had nothing to do with posterity, or tribute. It was simply that the ground was dead. Nothing will ever grow there again.

I don't expect this will be easy for either of you to see. But it means that you have come more than halfway, that you will be at the apple orchard before you know it. Take Route 80 to Illinois, to Chicago, to the Lenox Hotel. As always, there will be a letter.

With love,
Joley

39 REBECCA *Friday, July 13, 1990*

Midwest Airlines flight 997 crashed on September 21, 1978, in What Cheer, Iowa—a farming town sixty miles southeast of Des Moines. Newspaper reports I have read say there were 103 passengers on the plane. There were five survivors including me. I do not remember anything about the crash.

You get the feeling that anybody in What Cheer would be able to direct us to Arlo van Cleeb's farm. This is the place where the plane crashed and in fact it was Rudy van Cleeb, the man's son, who took the famous picture of me running away from the plane and waving my arms. He is also the one who drove me to the hospital. I would like to thank him but it turns out he is dead. Killed in some accident that involved a combine.

Arlo van Cleeb is very surprised to see me. He keeps pinching my face and telling my mother how nice I grew up. We are sitting in his living room, and I am listening to my mother tell him the story of my life. We are only up to age eight, when I played a molar in a school play about dental hygiene.

"Excuse me," I say. "I don't mean to be rude but maybe we should just go on out there."

"The good Lord loves patience," Mr. van Cleeb says.

Seventy million years later, my mother stands up from the flowered couch. "If you don't mind."

"Mind!" Mr. van Cleeb says. "Why would I mind! I'm flattered that you've come."

Corn is a funny thing—it's much higher and thicker than I'd expected. When you drive through Iowa, you have to inch out at the intersections because cars coming in the other direction can't see you through the thatch of stalks. I can see why we didn't decide to just wander out here on our own. Most likely, we never would have found our way back. Mr. van Cleeb turns and cuts through the corn like there are actually paths. Then he spreads the final wall of stalks.

It is a wide open area about the size of a football field. The ground is jet black. In the middle of this is a rusted frame, cracked at the middle and the seams like a lobster. One wing sticks out like an elbow. There are several sections, too, sitting here and there: a row of seat skeletons, the huge fan of an engine, a propeller the size of my body.

"May I?" I ask, pointing to the plane. The farmer nods. I walk up to it, touching the rust and rubbing it between my fingers. It comes off orange and powdered. Although it is broken into pieces, it still looks like a plane. I crawl through a gash in the body and walk down what is left of the aisle. There are weeds wrapped around the metal.

It still smells like smoke. "Are you okay?" my mother yells.

I count down the holes where windows used to be. "This is where I sat," I say, pointing to a hole on the right side. "Right here." I step down into the place where the seat used to be. I keep waiting to feel something.

I walk the rest of the way down the aisle. Like a stewardess, I think, only the passengers are ghosts. What about all those people who died? If I were to dig through some of the twisted steel at my feet would I find carry-ons, jackets, pocketbooks?

I cannot remember anything about the crash. I do remember being in the hospital, and the nurses who sat with me and read me nursery rhymes. Jack and Jill went up the hill, they'd say, and they'd wait to see if I could finish the rest. I slept for a long time when I got to the hospital and when I woke up both my parents were there. My father had brought a yellow teddy bear, not one from home but a new one. He sat on the edge of the bed and my mother sat on the other side. She brushed my hair and told me how much she loved me. She said the doctors wanted to make sure I was just fine and then we would all go home and everything would be better.

Because it was a special circumstance, my parents were allowed to stay overnight in the hospital. They slept on the little bed next to mine. A few times during the night I woke up to make sure they were there. At one point I had a nightmare; I don't remember about what. I had lost that yellow bear because my arms relaxed in sleep. But I woke up terrified and looked over to the other bed. There wasn't much room there so my parents had curled into a little ball. My father's arms were wrapped around my mother, and my mothers lips were pressed against my father's shoulder. I remember staring at their hands, at how they were locked together. I had been asleep and I couldn't hold onto that stupid bear, so I figured this was something truly special. My parents were holding onto each other. It just looked so, well, solid, that I closed my eyes and forgot about my nightmare.

I cannot remember anything about the crash. I crawl out from another gash in the metal and sit on the edge of the wing. I close my eyes and try to imagine fire. I try to hear screams, too, but nothing comes. Then there is a wind. It sings through the metal like a giant flute. The corn begins to whisper and when it does I know where all those people are, all the people who have died. They never left here. They are in the earth and wound around the frame of the plane. I stand and run away from the wreck. I press my hands over my ears, trying not to hear their voices, and for the second time, I outdistance Death.

40 JANE

Midwest Airlines flight 997 crashed on September 21, 1978, in What Cheer, Iowa—a farming town sixty miles southeast of Des Moines. The entire crew died but the black box tapes suggest the crash had something to do with a failure of both engines. The pilot was trying to land in Des Moines.

These are all things I have read, and told my daughter. They do not prepare me in any way for what Arlo van Cleeb shows me in the middle of his cornfield.

It is a black snaking skeleton stretched over one hundred yards of black ground. In several places the rain and mud of twelve years has covered parts of the plane. Half of the tail is now buried, for example. There are large pits and gaps where the metal was broken or torn to remove the corpses. The red and blue logo of Midwest is scarred with moss. When Rebecca moves towards the frame of this airplane, I reach out to grab her but then I stop myself. As she crawls through a cockpit window the farmer speaks to me. "You can't figure out what's missing, can you?" I shake my head. "It's the fire. There's no fire, and no water gushing all over the place. This plane is just dead, now. It's not the way you remember from the pictures."

I suppose he is right. When I think of the plane the image I have is one made by the media: firemen pulling wounded people from the wreckage, scarred farmland, flames that reach as high as God.

"Rebecca," I call, "are you okay?" It smells like smoke. Rebecca sticks her head out of a hole in the frame. I wave at her. I don't know, I keep expecting this monstrous metal creature to swallow her whole.

I wonder if she will get upset. Start to cry. She never really has. She's never really spoken to anyone about it. She claims she cannot remember a thing.

Oliver and I had this pact when we got married: we weren't going to have children right away. We were going to wait until Oliver got a promotion, at least until he moved back to the East Coast. We expected that we would have to go to California, but we didn't think it would be permanent. I guess I was too young at the time to really have given much thought to whether or not I wanted a baby. Anyway, Oliver didn't.

But when he got promoted and we moved to San Diego, it became apparent that this was not a case of paying one's dues to get back to Woods Hole. San Diego's Oceanographic Institute was far more prestigious. Maybe Oliver knew that all along and maybe he didn't. But it became clear to me that I was three thousand miles away from my friends, from my home. Oliver was too involved in his new job to pay attention to me, and we couldn't afford for me to get a master's degree in speech pathology, and I started to get lonely. So I poked pinholes in my diaphragm.

I got pregnant quickly and things started to change. At first, Oliver actually seemed excited by the idea. For a few months he did the usual things: told me to stay off my feet, and held his ear to my belly. Then work got very busy for him, and he got a promotion earlier than expected, and he started to travel with other researchers. He missed Rebecca's birth, but by that time I didn't really care. I had a daughter and I truly believed she was everything I could ever want.

When the plane crash happened my first thought was that this was my punishment for tricking Oliver. Then I thought it was my punishment for leaving Oliver. Whatever the reason, it was clearly my fault. My father had been watching a baseball game on TV and it was interrupted with a special bulletin on location in Iowa. He yelled into the kitchen that some plane had crashed and I didn't even have to hear the flight number. I knew. It is that way between mothers and daughters.

I flew to Iowa and I remember looking at the other people on the flight. Were any of them relatives of other people on the Midwest plane? What about the woman in the pink jumpsuit? She was crying on and off. Did it have to do with the crash in What Cheer?

By the time I arrived in Des Moines the survivors of the crash had been taken to a hospital. I met Oliver at the front door; he was pulling up in a taxi too. We ran through the green corridors, calling out Rebecca's name. I would not go into the morgue to identify bodies. Oliver did that for me, and came out smiling. "She's not there," he said. "She's not there!"

We found a Jane Doe in pediatrics. They had been calling her Jane all this time; I found that very strange. She was asleep, heavily sedated, when we were let into her room. "Came out hardly with a scratch," one nurse said. "She's a lucky little girl."

Oliver held my hand as we walked over to Rebecca, so tiny and white against the dotted hospital sheets. She had a breather tube in her nose, and a kidney-shaped bruise on her forehead. Oliver had brought her a yellow teddy bear. I started to cry, realizing that Edison, Rebecca's old teddy bear, had probably burned in the crash. "It's all right," Oliver said, holding me against him. He smelled of the shampoo we had at home in San Diego. It took me several minutes to realize that the whole time, he was crying too.

She was released two days later. We went back to the site of the crash. I don't remember it looking like this; I wonder if some of these pieces—the seats, the engine, what have you—have been moved as the years went by. I excuse myself to Arlo van Cleeb and begin to circle the remnants of this plane.

Metal ribs poke into the sky at odd angles, and although many of the hinges are intact, the doors of the plane are nowhere to be found. There are pretzeled knots of black steel at the sides of the wings. All the windows are gone. I remember hearing they exploded due to the change in pressure, when the plane was plummeting to the ground. Suddenly I realize I cannot see my daughter. I run around the plane trying to peek through the holes and the gaps, trying to catch a glimpse. Then I see her coming towards me. Her eyes are shut tight and her hands are pressed against her head as if she is trying to keep it from splitting. She is running so fast her feet are kicking up a stream of mud. I do not think she realizes it but she is screaming at the top of her lungs. "Rebecca!" I cry out, and Rebecca's eyes fly open, that startled shade of green. She crashes against me, demanding to be protected, and this time I am waiting there to catch her.

41 OLIVER

Midwest Airlines flight 997 crashed on September 21, 1978, in What Cheer, Iowa—a farming town sixty miles southeast of Des Moines. When the pilot realized he would not be able to land in Des Moines he coasted into a farmer's cornfield. The plane landed on its own fuel tanks and exploded.

These are the reports, as faxed to me by my secretary, that lead me to the site of the crash. It was not easy to find a facsimile machine in What Cheer, Iowa, either, but I have had two days' advance time.

I know of Arlo van Cleeb but I have never been a fan of intermediaries. Therefore I set up shop in his cornfield without him ever noticing. I have a small folding beach chair and a thermos of coffee. A portable clip-on fan; the heat gets intense at this elevation. I sit behind a fringe of cornstalks, hidden by the greenery and yet strategically able to peer through the vertical bars. For two days I have been waiting for Jane and Rebecca, binoculars in hand.

It has not been an entirely idle forty-eight hours. You see, the partially obscured view I have of the wreckage gave me a slightly different perspective from the one splashed across the oily faxes of the front page of the *New York Times* and the *Washington Post*. When I first perceived the airplane's frame, blackened by fire and age, it was through the haze of corn that forms my camouflage.

And quite honestly, at first glance I thought it was a beached whale. Enormous in proportions, with the sun glinting off its slightly sunken tail—have you ever noticed the parallels between humpbacks and airplanes? The elongated body, the hub of the cockpit and the whale's jawbone, the wings and the fingered fins, the cross section of the tail and the fluke? I have never thought of whales in terms of aerodynamics but of course it makes sense. What is streamlined underwater serves the same purpose in flight.

It has been a tedious trip here, and I have to say I'm glad it's all coming to an end. I can take my family home with me; I can get back to my research.

I am just pouring my second cup of coffee (a lousy habit I've picked up on this tracking voyage, I'm sorry to say), when I see the farmer van Cleeb push his way through the cornstalks. Then out of this sea of green steps Rebecca, her hair pulled away from her face. Following her, in close pursuit, is Jane.

She stands tall with her hands on her hips, talking to the farmer. She seems to be holding a conversation but her eyes betray her, running over the framework of the plane, assessing it; carefully checking the movements of Rebecca. She has this down to an art, I think. How is it I have never really watched her act as a mother?

Rebecca points to the plane and then moves closer. She steps into the gashes in the metal body, as I did two days ago. She runs her hands over everything, it seems, cataloguing and processing the information. Her eyes are wide, and from time to time she bites her lower lip. She is standing only feet away from me when she says, quite clearly, "This is where I sat. Right here."

I push my hand through the stalks in front of me and pull them aside so that I can really see her face. She looks like me, in many ways. My hair, my eyes. And she has always been able to hide her emotions. Even after the crash, she would not talk about it. Not to me, not to Jane, not to the psychiatrists. They tried to get her to act the crash out on dolls and models, but Rebecca refused. At the time I thought it interesting to find such willfulness in a four-year-old. Now I have my doubts.

I could take my daughter in my arms and tell her it is all right.

And she will smile like the sun itself, so surprised to see me. Like she used to do as a child when I came home from Brazil or Maui, wherever. I'd hide toys in my pockets, and shells and small bottles of sand. I told her I would always bring her back a piece of the place that took me away from her.

I am ready to push through the corn when I see Jane from the corner of my eye. She is calling Rebecca. She starts to walk towards me.

I let the corn free, a shade. I am breathing arhythmically. I am terrified of speaking to Jane.

For one thing, I haven't any idea what I am going to say to her. I know, I am supposed to have prepared something elaborate, something akin to wooing, but everything that has crossed my mind in the past two days has simply disappeared. What I am left with is how I feel, and what am I supposed to do about it? I want to just walk up to Jane and say that I miss the way she flips pancakes. That no one but her has ever left me a love note on a steamed-up shaving mirror. I want to tell her that sometimes, when the sun is setting over the unfurled fluke of a humpback, I wish I had her beside me. That when I give a speech, I wish I could see her face in the first row. How stupid you are, Oliver, I think. You can write circles around any scientist in your field. You've published more than any researcher your age. You are supposed to be the expert. But you don't know how to tell her that you can't live without her.

The week before Rebecca's plane crash, Jane and I had a terrible argument. I do not remember what it was about, but it could not have been any less ludicrous than this latest one about Rebecca's birthday. The next thing I knew she had driven me to such a point that I hit her.

It was a slap, not a punch, if distinctions matter. And after I did it I thought I would die. I knew about her childhood, her father. I knew what I wasn't supposed to be.

Jane took Rebecca to her parents' place in Massachusetts. I wanted her back so badly I could taste it. But, like now, I did not know what to say. I just knew that where Rebecca went Jane would follow: she lived for Rebecca then, as she does now. So I threatened litigation if she didn't send the child back. I expected her to come too, even if I didn't say so directly.

When I heard about the crash over the car radio, I started to shake so badly that I had to pull off the highway. This has not happened, I told myself. You have not lost your entire family at once.

I drove to the airport and parked at a two-hour meter, the illogic of which struck me only after I had purchased a ticket to Iowa. I picked up a teddy bear—wishful thinking?—before I boarded. I looked around the plane wondering who else was headed to Des Moines because of the crash. When I arrived in Iowa, the wounded had already been shuttled to a hospital. My taxi pulled up directly behind another taxi, and Jane stepped out. I almost fell to my knees, seeing her there with mascara running down her face and her nose dripping. I stared at her and all the words defining forgiveness caught in my throat and for the life of me I couldn't understand why Rebecca had not come out of that taxi as well. Stupefied, I asked where Rebecca was. I did not know that Jane had not been on fight 997; I did not learn that until several minutes later, and then only by deduction.

We were asked to go to the morgue, along with the other frantic relatives, to survey the bodies that had been pulled from the wreckage. Jane stood outside, cleaving to a fire extinguisher on the wall, while I crept into the refrigerated rooms. I do not remember looking at the bloodied shrouds of infants and children. If Rebecca's body had been there, I am not certain I would have admitted it to myself or the coroners, anyway.

We found Rebecca in pediatrics, tangled in wires and tubes. I lifted Rebecca's arm and tucked the cheaply-made yellow bear underneath it. I pulled Jane close to me, burying my nose in her hair and rubbing my palms against her familiar shoulder blades. I never really had to say anything to get Jane to come home. I do not think I read the signals wrong when I believed that she understood.

Jane comes around the plane and stands almost directly in front of the spot where I am hidden. This is my chance. I am going to tell her. I am going to start by speaking her name.

She is close enough to touch. Wind breathes through the

wreckage of the plane. It shrieks, an unnatural note. I reach my hand through the blind of cornstalks and stretch out my fingers. "Jane," I whisper.

But at that moment Rebecca emerges from the twisted gyves and fetters of metal. Her hands are pressed against the sides of her head. She is screaming, running from the body of the plane with her eyes closed. Jane holds out her arms. She says something I cannot hear and Rebecca's eyes open. I push aside the cornstalks, revealing myself, but I do not think Rebecca, who is facing me, notices. She falls against Jane's breast, clutching and gasping. Her eyes pass right over me and they do not see a thing, of that I am sure. Jane smoothes our daughter's hair. "Sssh," she says. She sings something very softly, and Rebecca's breathing turns even again. She grabs fistfuls of Jane's shirt, over and over.

I stand only three feet away, but it could be three hundred. I am not privy to this. I cannot heal. If given the chance, Rebecca would not run to me. I am not even sure that Jane would run to me. I let the corn close in around my face and I turn my back to them. Even if I could get Jane to listen to me, get her to understand why it is that I cannot live without her, it is not enough.

It hits me: I am not part of this family. I would never say I am a scientist without offering proof. How can I say that I am a father, a husband?

Jane is murmuring to Rebecca. The words get softer and softer and I realize they are walking in the opposite direction. And this is when I make what could possibly be the greatest—and most difficult—decision of my life. I will not call to them when I do not know what to say. I won't reveal myself without having anything to show. I have much thinking to do, but right now I act purely on instinct. It is hard as hell, but I let them go.

42 JANE

After we check into the only motel in What Cheer, I find myself remembering things that I have not thought about for years. I could understand it if I were replaying the crash over and over in my head—that would make sense to me. But instead I am seeing my father, plain as day. He moves around the edges of the motel room, picking up glass tumblers and straightening the bathroom mirror. He flushes the toilet, twice. I do not dare fall asleep; I do not dare fall asleep. Then, just as I have expected, he starts to walk towards my bed. But he changes course and sits instead on the other bed, next to Rebecca. He breathes clouds of scotch and tugs the blanket away, revealing, ripe, my daughter.

I was nine the first time it happened. My mother and father had a fight, and my mother left to stay with my aunt in Concord. I did everything I was supposed to: I made dinner for Daddy and Joley; I cleaned up the kitchen; I even remembered to put the hose into the sink when I ran the dishwasher. We all avoided talking about Mama.

But because she was away, and because I felt I had earned it, I decided to go into her room, to her perfume tray. Mama smelled different every day: like oranges and spice, or fresh lemon pies, or cool marble, or even the wind. When she left the room she left a memory, a scent, behind her.

I knew what I was looking for, a little red glass bottle in the shape of a berry that was called Framboise. The word was etched right on the glass. My mother did not let me wear perfume. Little girls who wear perfume, she said, turn into big girls who are tramps.

I was very careful with the fragile bottle because I didn't want to spill a drop. I turned it over on my finger the way I had seen her do every morning, and then I touched this finger, wet with the smell of raspberries, to my throat and my wrists and behind my knees. I turned around and around in a circle. How wonderful, I thought. It is with me no matter where I go.

I stopped myself by catching my arms around the post of my parents' bed. Standing at the door was my father.

"What the hell have you been doing?" he said, sniffing the air. He leaned closer to grab my shirt and the smell of whiskey cut through the thickness of berries. "You will bathe. Now!"

He made me strip naked in front of him, although I hadn't done that in five years. He watched me from the door of the bathroom with his arms crossed. The entire time, I cried. I cried when the shower, too hot, scalded my skin and I continued to cry when I stepped onto the bath mat and toweled dry. "Go to your goddamned room," my father said.

I pulled a flannel nightgown over my head and turned down the covers of my bed. I told myself aloud this was like any other night, and I tried not to lie awake waiting for punishment.

Joley came into my room on his way to bed. He was only five, but he knew. "Jane, what did you do wrong?" And I told him as best I could explain that I had stupidly been pretending to be Mama.

"There's nothing you can do," I said. "Get out before he hits you too."

I waited the longest time that night, but my father did not come up to spank me. Maybe that was the worst part: imagining what terrible thing he was thinking up downstairs. A belt? A brush? When I heard him, heavy, coming up the stairs, I dove beneath the covers. I pulled my nightgown tight around my ankles, a drawstring. I counted to one hundred.

At seventy-seven my father turned my doorknob. He sat down on the edge of the bed and waited for me to pull away the covers from my face.

"I'm not going to punish you tonight," my father said, "and do you know why? Because you were such a good little cook. That's why."

"Really?" I asked, amazed.

"Really." He took off his shoes and asked if I would like to hear a story.

"Yes," I said, thinking this might not be so bad after all. My father started to tell me a story—a fairy tale—about an evil woman who kept her daughter locked in a closet with mice and bats. The girl's father tried to get to this closet but the woman had huge guard dogs protecting it and he had to kill her, and then the dogs, before he could rescue his daughter.

"And then what?" I asked, waiting to see what would happen.

"I don't know. I haven't come up with the ending."

"You can't just leave a story hanging," I protested, and he said we should try to think of one together. But he was getting tired, so could he lie down next to me?

I moved over on the bed and we talked about the ways the girl's father might kill the evil woman. Stakes through the heart, I suggested, but my father was leaning towards poisoned tea. We came up with other things that might be lurking in the closet: ghosts and tarantulas and man-eating piranhas. Maybe the girl should try to get out by herself, I suggested, but my father insisted that was not the way it would happen.

When he got cold he crawled under the covers, so close that when he spoke my hair fluttered. "What do you think will happen to that girl, Jane?" he said, and as he did that he put his hand on my chest.

It wasn't right, I knew that, because every muscle in my body tensed at once. It wasn't right, but then again he was my father, wasn't he? And he had been so nice. He could have hit me tonight, but he didn't.

"I don't know," I whispered. "I don't know what should happen."

"Well, what about this? The father drives stakes through the heart of the evil woman and drugs the Dobermans with poisoned tea. That way both of our ideas come into play." Without hesitation, like he was proud of it, he slipped his hand between my legs, coming to rest like a weight on my vagina.

"Daddy."

"Do you like it, Jane?" my father whispered. "Do you like the ending?"

I did not move. I pretended that this was some other little girl, someone else's quivering body, and then when I heard my father's breathing come deep and even, I slid away. I got out of bed without creaking the mattress and turned the doorknob like a whisper. I started to run as fast as I could. At the bottom of the stairs, I tripped and hit my head. Blood was running down my face when I flung open the front door and ran into the night, barefoot, no longer sure about anything, including who or what I was supposed to be.

A policeman found me in a neighbor's yard early the next morning, and brought me back to the house. He held my hand and rang the doorbell and my father came to answer the door. Daddy was wearing his best suit and even Joley had on a nice Sunday shirt and a button-on tie. "We just called the station," my father said, beaming. "Damn quick service." He joked with the policeman and invited him in for coffee. He looked at the cut on my forehead and tried to rub over the dried blood with his finger but I pulled away. "Suit yourself, Jane," he said. "You can take care of it upstairs." As I crawled up the steps, with Joley behind me, I heard my father talking to that policeman. "We don't know what the problem is," he was saying. "It's those nightmares."

"What did he do, Jane?" Joley asked when I had locked the bathroom door behind us. I wouldn't tell him, but I let him watch as I cleaned my cut with Bactine. He stripped the Band-Aid for me. It did not surprise me that the cut was the shape of a cross.

I told Joley I had to pee and pushed him outside. Then I locked the door again and pulled my nightgown over my head. I ripped it into shreds and threw it in the garbage pail. On the back of the door was the full-length mirror Mama used when she got all dressed up to go out. I could hear my father downstairs, laughing. I gazed into the mirror, expecting to find outlined the very parts that I could say I hated—but I was standing tall, thin, arms at my sides. I knew from this alien rhythm in my heart that I had become a different person. I did not understand how, under the circumstances, I could possibly look the same.

43 JANE

I've told Rebecca she can plan whatever she'd like for our day in Chicago. Me, I don't much feel in the mood. I didn't get much sleep last night, and because I screamed through the nightmare, neither did Rebecca. When I woke up she had her arms around me. "Wake up, wake up," she said over and over. When I came around I did not tell her what my nightmare was about. I said it had to do with the plane crash. And then, in the morning when she was showering, I called Joley.

After speaking to him I was inclined to drive straight through to Massachusetts. To hell with Joley and his letters; to hell with my problems charting direction. We could be in Massachusetts by tomorrow morning, according to the legend of the U.S. map. In the car, I asked Rebecca what she thought about this. I expected her to jump at the chance: I'd seen her counting the states left to cover when she thought I wasn't looking. But Rebecca looked at me and her mouth dropped. "After all this, you can't just quit halfway!"

"What's the big deal?" I said. "The point all along was to get to Massachusetts."

Rebecca looked at me and her eyes clouded. She settled into her seat, and she crossed her arms over her chest. "Do whatever you want."

What could I do? I drove to Chicago. Even if we decided to drive straight through, we still had to go to Chicago.

My first choice would have been the Art Institute or the Sears Tower Skydeck, but Rebecca opts for the Shedd Aquarium, an octagon of white marble on the edge of Lake Michigan. The brochure Rebecca picks up on the way inside boasts that it is the largest indoor aquarium in the world.

Rebecca runs ahead to the huge tank in the center of the aquarium, the Caribbean coral reef complete with rays and sharks and sea turtles and eels. She jumps back as a sand shark lunges at a piece of fish in the hand of a diver. "Look at its belly. I bet they always keep it full. Why bother to eat when you aren't hungry?"

The shark rips its teeth into the fish, biting it in half. As it takes the second part, it is more gentle. The diver strokes the shark on its nose. It seems to be made of grey rubber.

Rebecca and I walk through the saltwater exhibits, where fish congregate in bright splashes like kites against an open sky. They come in the most incredible colors; I have always been amazed by this. What is the point of being fuchsia, or lemon, or violet, when you are stuck under the water where no one can see you?

We pass polka-dotted clownfish and blowfish that puff up like porcupines when the other fish come too close. There are fish here from the Mediterranean and the Arctic Ocean. There are fish here that have traveled the world.

I am stuck in front of a magenta starfish. I have never seen anything so vivid in my life. "Come look at this," I tell Rebecca. She stands beside me and mouths, *Wow.* "Why do you think that leg is shorter?" I ask.

A passing woman in a white lab coat (marine biologist?) hears me and leans over the small tank. Her breath fogs the window. "Starfish have the power of regeneration. Which means if a leg gets cut off or ripped in some way, they can grow a new one back."

"Like newts," Rebecca says, and the woman nods.

"I knew that," I say, primarily to myself. "It has to do with their habitat, tide pools. In a tide pool, waves come and destroy the marine equilibrium every few minutes, so nothing ever really gets a chance to settle."

"True," the woman says. "Are you a biologist?"

"My husband is."

Rebecca nods. "Oliver Jones. Do you know him?"

The woman sucks in her breath. "Not *the* Oliver Jones. Oh, my. Would you mind very much if I brought someone here to meet you?"

"Dr. Jones isn't with us on this trip," I tell her. "So I don't know as I'd be all that interesting to one of your colleagues."

"Oh, you most certainly are. By association, if nothing else."

She disappears behind a panel that I didn't realize was a door. "How did you know about tide pools?" Rebecca asks.

"Rote memorization. They're all your father talked about when we were dating. If you're a good girl I'll tell you about hermit crabs and jellyfish."

Rebecca presses her nose up to the glass. "Isn't it awesome, that someone in Chicago would know Daddy? I mean, it kind of makes us celebrities."

In the oceanic community, I suppose she is right. I hadn't even associated this aquarium with Oliver, at least not on a conscious level. These delicate fish and quivering invertebrates are so different from the hunkering whales Oliver loves. It's hard to believe they exist in the same place. It's hard to believe that a whale wouldn't take up all the space, all the food. But then again I know better. These tropical fish are in no danger from the humpbacks, which are mammals. Whales don't prey on them. They screen plankton and plants through their baleen.

I have a vision of a sample falling two stories in a Ziploc bag, smashing against the blue Mexican tiles of the foyer in San Diego. Baleen.

"Mom." Rebecca tugs on my T-shirt. Standing in front of me is a bookish man with a goatee and the thinnest eyebrows I have ever seen on a male.

"I can't believe this," the man says. "I can't believe I'm standing here face to face with you."

"Well, I haven't done anything, really. I don't work with whales at all."

The man smacks himself on the forehead. "I'm such a jerk. My name is Alfred Oppenbaum. It's an honor—an honor!—to meet you."

"Do you know Oliver?"

"*Know* him? I *worship* him." At this, Rebecca excuses herself and ducks behind a tank of zebra fish to laugh. "I've studied everything he's done; read everything he's written. I hope—" he leans forward to whisper, "—I hope to be as prominent a scientist as he."

Alfred Oppenbaum cannot be more than twenty, which tells me he has a long way to go. "Mr. Oppenbaum," I say.

"Call me Al."

"Al. I'll be happy to mention your name to my husband."

"I'd like that. Tell him my favorite article is the one on the causality and sequence of themes in humpback songs."

I smile. "Well." I hold out my hand.

"You can't leave yet. I'd love to show you the exhibit I've been creating."

He leads us into that panel of the wall that masquerades as a door. Behind are twenty-gallon tanks filled with crustaceans and fish. Several nets and small receptacles hang from the sides of each tank. From this angle we can also see the backs of the tanks that are displayed in the aquarium.

Everyone wears white coats that turn faintly blue under fluorescent lights. As we pass by, Al whispers to his colleagues. They spin around, their mouths agape. "Mrs. Jones," they all say, like a line of servants as royalty passes by. "Mrs. Jones. Mrs. Jones. Mrs. Jones."

One of the bolder scientists steps forward, blocking my path. "Mrs. Jones, I'm Holly Hunnewell. And I wonder, do you know what it is Dr. Jones is researching now?"

"I know that he was planning to track some humpbacks on their way from the East Coast of the States to the breeding grounds near Brazil," I tell her, and there is a resounding, *Oh.* "I don't know what he's going to do with the research," I say, apologetically. Who knew Oliver had such a following?

Al leads us to a blinking set of tubes. "Doesn't look like much, does it? It works under black light." With a nod to a colleague, the room goes dark. Al pushes a button. All of a sudden his voice fills up the room, a commentary over the yips and churrs of humpback whales. The frame of a whale appears out of nowhere, neon blue, and unfurls its fluke. "In the 1970s Dr. Oliver Jones discovered that humpback whales have the capacity, like humans, to develop and pass down songs from generation to generation. With extensive research, Dr. Jones and other colleagues have used whale songs to identify different stocks of whales, have used the songs to track the movement of whales over the oceans of the world, and have speculated about the changes these songs undergo yearly. Although their meaning still remains a mystery, it has been discovered that only the male whales sing, leading the foremost researchers in the field to believe that the songs may be a way to woo mates." Fade out of Al's voice, crescendo the ratchets and oos of a whale.

"Oliver would be proud," I say finally.

"Do you really think so, Mrs. Jones?" Al asks. "I mean, you'll tell him about it?"

"I'll do more than that. I'll tell him he has to fly here to see it himself."

Al almost passes out. Rebecca puts down a small box turtle she's been tickling and follows me back into the exhibit hall.

When we are safe in the dark aquarium, I sit down on one of the marble benches that spot the floor. "I can't believe it. Even when your father isn't here, he manages to ruin a perfectly good day."

"Oh, you're just cranky. That was really kind of neat."

"I didn't know people in the Midwest knew about whales. Or cared about whales."

She grins at me. "I can't wait to tell Daddy."

"You're going to have to wait!" I say, a little too sharply.

Rebecca glares at me. "You did say I could call him."

"That was back then. When we were closer to California. He's not home now anyway. He's on his way to find us."

"How come you're so sure?" Rebecca asks. "He would have found us by now, and you know it."

She's right. I don't know what is taking Oliver so long. Unless he is jumping the gun by flying to meet us in Massachusetts. "Maybe he went to South America after all."

"He wouldn't do that, no matter what you think about him."

Rebecca sits back down and scuffs her sneakers on the edge of the bench. "I bet he misses you," I say.

Rebecca smiles at me. Behind her I can make out the silver fins of a paper-thin fish. Oliver would know its name. For whatever it is worth, Oliver would know the names of all of these.

"I bet he misses you too," Rebecca answers.

44 Oliver

The first time I ever saw Jane I was waist-deep in the murky water at Woods Hole. She did not know that I was observing her on the ferry pier, jackknifed over the rotten railing, with the fine madras print of her sundress blowing against the curve of her calves. She did not know that I witnessed her watching me; if she *had* known this, I'm sure she would have been mortified. She was very young, that much was evident. You could see it in the way she chewed her gum and traced patterns with the toe of her sandal. I was studying tide pools at the time, but she reminded me of a gastropod; a snail in particular—remarkably vulnerable if removed from its external casing. I was overwhelmed; I wanted to see her exposed from her shell.

Because I wasn't very good at those sorts of social overtures, I pretended that I hadn't noticed her at all; that I hadn't seen her glance back at me when she boarded the ferry to Martha's Vineyard. As simple as that I assumed she had tripped through my life, and I would never cross her again. But I stayed at the docks recording observations two days longer than was necessary, just in case.

I knew that the purse that floated by me was hers before I even opened it. Still, I was shaking when I popped the snap and retrieved the dripping identification card. So, I thought, her name is Jane.

At that time in my life I was driven by my goal: to dedicate myself to the study of marine biology. I had gone through an accelerated program at Harvard that graduated me in three years with a baccalaureate degree as well as a master's, and at twenty, I was the youngest researcher at Woods Hole.

I did not have many friends. I did not distinguish weekdays from weekends; it always surprised me when I saw the crowds at the Woods Hole ferry, embarking on their forty-eight hour holidays. I spent days on end in a blue wetsuit, reaching for starfish and mollusks and arthropods that lived in hollow pockets on the bottom of the ocean. I did not date.

And so I was surprised that something as mundane as a laminated identification card from this slip of a girl could move me so violently. As I showered and dressed in preparation for the long drive to Newton, I kept track of the odd physical reactions I was undergoing. Palpitations. Perspiration. Nausea. Vertigo.

The Liptons lived on Commonwealth Avenue in Newton, in one of the smallest mansions that in today's market sell for several million dollars. I pulled into the driveway and rang the doorbell, which roared like a lion. I was expecting a maid, but Mary Lipton herself answered the door—Jane's mother, I assumed, remembering her from the pier. She was a small, fragile woman with auburn hair wrapped into a French knot. Although it was July, she was wearing a wool sweater. "Yes?" she said.

It took me several minutes to remember the English language. "Oliver Jones," I said. "I'm with the Woods Hole Oceanographic Institute." I assumed, incorrectly, that having a title would award me a certain amount of prestige in a situation like this. "I found this purse and thought I would return it."

Mary Lipton took her daughter's purse and turned it over in her small hands. "I see," she said, measuring her words. "You drove all the way up here?"

"I was passing through."

She smiled then. "Won't you come in, Mr. Jones," she said. "The children are in the backyard."

She led me through the parlor: carved oak paneling bordering the marble floor, a fresco on the ceiling. On impulse I turned around and looked back at the door; a large stained-glass window filtered diamonds of light onto the cool marble. I had grown up in Wellfleet, on the Cape, in a home that was large and expensive by the standards of the summer tourists, but that could not hold a candle to Bostonian finery such as this. As we walked, Mary drilled me on my breeding, my profession, and my education. She led me past a library, a sitting room, and through French doors into the backyard.

We stopped on the porch, which overlooked a small hill of grass that shaded into a thicker forest behind. Two bright red towels stained the lawn like blood. A boy and a girl sat upon them: Jane and, presumably, Jane's brother. They looked up, almost instinctively, when their mother approached the wooden railing. Jane was wearing a bikini, yellow. She pulled a T-shirt on and ran up to the porch.

"Mr. Jones brought back your purse," Mary said.

"How kind of you," Jane replied, as if she had practiced the phrase.

I held out my hand. "Please, call me Oliver."

"Oliver, then," Jane said, laughing a little. "Can you stay a while?" When she laughed, her eyes brightened. They were a remarkable color, like a cat's.

Mary Lipton called to the boy on the lawn. "Joley, help me get some lemonade."

The boy came closer, and even at eleven he was easily the best-looking male I'd ever seen. He had thick hair and a square jaw, a quick smile. "Lemonade," he said, brushing Jane as he passed by us. "Like she can't carry it herself."

"I can stay a little while," I said. "I have to get back to the Cape."

"You work there?"

It returned, the vertigo. I leaned against the cool wood of the porch. "I'm a marine biologist."

"Wow. I'm in high school."

Perhaps if I had known better I should have ended it then and there. Age differentials tend to become less pronounced as one grows older, but during adolescence, five and a half years is an entire lifetime. I saw Jane looking at me, well, like I was old. As if her eyes had played a trick on her at Woods Hole; as if she had been seeing through a haze someone who turned out to be not at all what she had expected. "I'm twenty," I said, hoping to make her understand.

She relaxed, or at least I perceived her relaxing. "I see."

I didn't know what I was supposed to say. I was not accustomed to interfacing with people; I spent most of my time beneath the surface of the ocean. But Jane drew me out. "What were you doing at the ferry dock?"

So I told her about tide pools, about the hearty crustaceans that survive such adverse living conditions. I told her I was going to study them for several years, and write my dissertation. "And then what?" she asked.

"And then what?" I had never even considered what might happen after. So much hinged on that final step.

"Will you move to something else? I don't know, flounder, or swordfish, or dolphins maybe?" She grinned at me. "I like dolphins. I mean, I don't know anything about them, but they always look like they're smiling."

"So do you," I blurted out, and then closed my eyes. Stupid, stupid, Oliver. I opened one eye at a time, but Jane was still there, waiting for me to answer her question. "I don't really know yet. Maybe," I said, "I'll study dolphins."

"Good."

"Good," I repeated, as if my fate had been settled. "I have to go now, but I'd like to see you again. I'd like to go out sometime."

Jane blushed. "I'd like that," she said.

At those words, I felt as if a tremendous weight had been lifted. It was similar to the euphoria I had experienced when, as an undergraduate, my first scholarly article had been published. The significant difference was: that time, the euphoria left me pondering *me*—where I would go from here? Now, as high-spirited as I felt, all I could think about was Jane Lipton.

A man came out to the porch. Of course I know better now but back then I attributed to imagination my sense of Jane stiffening. "Jones?" The man said, a big, cavernous voice. "Alexander Lipton. Wanted to thank you for bringing back Jane's wallet."

"Purse," Jane whispered. "It's a purse."

"It was nothing," I said, shaking her father's hand.

He was a large, overbearing man with tanned skin and narrow eyes. His eyes, in fact, disturbed me even then: jet black. I could not see where the iris ended and the pupil began. He was dressed for golf. He walked over to Jane and put his arm around her. "We don't know what to do with our Jane," he said.

Jane squirmed out of her father's embrace and murmured

something about seeing what had happened to the lemonade. She opened the door to the house so quietly it didn't even swing on its hinges. She left me outside, alone with her father.

"You listen to me, Jones," Alexander Lipton said. His face metamorphosed into that of a hard-line criminal lawyer, unwilling to give an inch. "When Jane turned fifteen I told her she could date whomever she'd like. If she likes you, that's her business. But if you do anything to hurt my daughter, I swear I'll string you by the balls from the Old North Church. I know your kind—I was a Harvard man, too—and if you so much as lay a hand on her before she turns seventeen, let's just say I'll make your life miserable."

I thought, this man is psychotic. He doesn't even *know* me. And then, as if it were a passing thunderstorm, Alexander Lipton's face softened into that of a middle-aged man of means. "My wife tells me you're a marine biologist."

Before I had a chance to answer, Jane and her mother came through the door with a tray of glasses and an icy pitcher of lemonade. Jane poured and Mary handed out a glass to each of us. Alexander Lipton drank his lemonade in a single chugging gulp and as soon as he was finished, his wife was at his side to relieve him of the glass. He excused himself and left, and Mary followed behind him.

I watched Jane drink. She held the glass with both hands, like a child. I waited until she was done and then repeated that I really had to leave.

Jane walked me to the car. We stood in front of the old Buick for a moment, letting the sun beat onto our scalps. Jane turned to me. "I threw my purse into the water on purpose."

"I know," I admitted.

Before I got into the car I asked if I could kiss her goodbye. When she acquiesced I took her face in my hands, the first time I ever touched her. Her skin sprang back at my touch, slightly greasy with suntan oil. Jane closed her eyes and tilted her head back, waiting. She smelled of cocoa butter and honest perspiration. There was nothing I wanted more than to kiss her, but I kept hearing the voice of her father. I smiled at my good fortune; and, thinking I had all the time in the world, I pressed my lips against Jane's forehead.

45 JANE

Dear Joley—

If Daddy could see me now. I spent the morning with Rebecca at the Indianapolis Speedway, at an auto museum filled with Nascars and racing paraphernalia. Do you remember when we used to watch all five hundred laps with him, every year? I never understood what it was that made auto racing such a biggie for him—it's not like he ever tried the sport himself. He told me once when I was older that it was the absolute speed of it all. I liked to watch for crashes, like you. I liked the way there'd be a huge explosion on the track and billows of ebony smoke, and the other cars would just keep a straight course and head right for the spin, into this sort of black box, and they'd come out okay.

I practically had to drag Rebecca onto a bus that drove right along the speedway. I closed my eyes, and I tried to imagine that speed that enchanted Daddy. It wasn't easy, lumbering along at 45 mph, on a track that's meant for 220 mph. When we got off the bus, we were each handed a card signed by the track president: "I hereby certify that the bearer of this ticket has completed one lap around the Indianapolis '500' Mile Speedway." I laughed. It isn't much, you know? But Daddy would have hung it over his desk, on the SAE fraternity bulletin board Mama was always trying to take down.

This is the best part, though: after we got that card, I thought about all the things I could do with it. I certainly wouldn't hang it up on the refrigerator, or on any bulletin board, and I didn't care enough to keep it in my wallet. I considered taking it to Daddy's grave when I got to Massachusetts. And no sooner had I thought that very thought, than my fingers just released the card—just let go, like they belonged to someone else's body—and the wind carried the card up to the clouds. It was a beautiful day, today, too—those big puffy clouds with ironed-flat bottoms, like you were looking at them from underneath a glass table where they had been arranged. The card crept higher and higher towards the sun, and when I realized I wasn't going to see it again, I started to smile.

I don't know why I felt it was important to tell you this; I suppose this letter is part-this and part-apology for the way I sounded when I called you the other day. Sometimes I act like it's your fault Daddy never went after you, and I'm the martyr. Maybe it's the way I try to make sense of it.

There are things that happened that I've never told you about, at least not in so many words, that I'm sure you've figured out by now. And there was a reason I never did tell you. When he started to come into my room at night, even though it was only once a month or so, I thought I was going crazy. Daddy was so incredibly nice to me when it was all happening. He told me over and over what a good girl I was, and I believed him. Still, when he turned the doorknob my fingers would curl around the edges of my mattress and my blood would run thick. It got to a point where the only way I could let him do the things he did was by pretending this wasn't me at all. I would pretend to be in some other part of the room, like a corner or a closet. I'd watch. I could see everything that happened, which wasn't nearly as bad.

One morning I faked being sick so that I wouldn't have to go to school. While Mama was making me lunch I told her that Daddy had been coming into my bedroom at night, and she dropped the can of tuna all over the floor.

"You must have had a bad dream, Jane," she said. We were both crouched over the linoleum, wiping up the runny oil and the flakes of fish.

I told her it had happened over and over, and I didn't like it. I started to cry, and she held me, getting fingerprints of grease on my nightgown. She promised me it would never happen again.

That night Daddy did not come into my room. He went into his own, and had a tremendous fight with Mama. We heard crashes and loud shrieks; in the middle of it all you came into my room and crawled under the covers. The next morning Mama had her arm bandaged, and the frame of their pine bed had been split.

The next time that Daddy came to my bedroom, he told me we had something very serious to discuss. "Here I am, spending all this special time with you," he said, "and what thanks do I get? You run and tell your mother you don't like to spend time with me." He told me I'd have to be punished for what I'd done. He wanted to spank me, but he made me pull down my underpants before he started. As he struck me, he told me not to tell anyone again. He said he wouldn't want anyone to get hurt. Not Mama, not Joley, not anyone.

In retrospect I believe I was very lucky. I have heard stories from the social workers at the San Diego schools about children younger than I who have sustained much more violent sexual abuse. It never got beyond the point of touching, and it only lasted for two years. When I was eleven, just as strangely as it all had started, it stopped.

So I wanted you to know why I never told you what I am sure you already have deduced. Perhaps now Daddy won't be able to hurt you.

Please do not be angry with me. Please do not—

I stop writing here, and I reread the letter. Rebecca turns on the water in the shower and starts to sing at the top of her lungs. On second thought, I rip the paper into shreds. I rip it so many times there is no more than one word on each piece. I toss them into a garbage pail. And then, taking the matches the housekeeping staff has placed beside the bed, I set the shreds on fire. It is a plastic trash can and the flame scorches the sides. It will never be seashell pink again, I think. It is probably ruined forever.

46 JOLEY

Dear Jane,

When you were twelve you had a rabbit named Fitzgerald, you'd seen the name on the shelf at the library at school and liked the word. The rabbit wasn't as interesting as the circumstances that surrounded it—Daddy had actually broken two of Mama's ribs and she'd been hospitalized and you got so distracted by it that you refused to eat, sleep, whatever. In the long run Daddy broke the spell by bringing home this rabbit, striped like an Oreo, whose ears couldn't quite stand up.

Unfortunately this was February and rather than building the rabbit a hutch you insisted we keep it safe and warm indoors. We took a thirty-gallon aquarium tank from the attic and put it on the floor of the living room. We filled it with wood chips that smelled of forests and then we dropped Fitzgerald in. He ran in confined circles and pressed his nose up to the glass. He pawed at the clear corners. All in all, he was a rotten rabbit. He chewed through telephone cords and socks and the edge of the rocking chair. He bit me.

You loved that demonic rabbit. You dressed it in apple-spotted baby clothes; hid it in your shiny, stooped church purse; you sang it ballads by the Beatles. One morning the rabbit was stretched out on its side—a revelation—we discovered the rabbit was male, but you felt this change of position was a bad omen. You made me stick my hand in Fitzgerald's cage and when he didn't nip me you knew he was sick. Mama refused to take him to the vet; she wouldn't get close enough to the rabbit to drive it anywhere. She told you to be sensible and get ready for school.

You kicked and cried and tore the upholstery on a certain loveseat but in the end went to school. That day, however, as if God was involved, a nor'easter was predicted. When snow came down so heavily we couldn't see the playground from our classrooms, we were dismissed. By the time we got home, Fitzgerald was dead.

It's a funny thing, we'd never experienced death before this and yet both of us were pretty much matter-of-fact about it. We knew *the rabbit was dead, we* knew *there was something to be done, and we did our best. I went to get a shoe box from Daddy's closet (the only one large enough to fit a rabbit corpse in) and you found Mama's sterling silver serving spoons and stuffed them in your snowsuit. We put on our down bibs and boots and then it came time to put the body in the shoe box. "I can't," you told me, and so I wrapped a dishcloth around Fitzgerald's cold legs and lifted.*

There were three inches of snow on the ground by the time we left the house. You led me to the school playground—the spot where the window of your classroom met the outdoors, a place where you could see the grave all day long. Taking a spoon out of your pocket, you began to chip at the frozen earth. You gave me a spoon, too. An hour later, when the brown ground had opened itself like a raw mouth, we set Fitzgerald to rest. We said an "Our Father" because it was the only prayer we both had memorized. You made a cross in the snow out of the stones we'd unearthed and began to cry. It was so cold the drops froze on your cheeks.

Take Route 70 to Route 2, and then to Route 40. Your endpoint is Baltimore. If you get there before five, you'll be able to tour the medical museum at Johns Hopkins—a favorite of mine.

Afterward, you denied that you ever owned a rabbit. But this is what I remember about the incident: it was the first time I ever held your *hand when we were walking, instead of the other way around.*

Love,
Joley

47 JANE

It's empty, except for the twenty teenage boys who wear T-shirts emblazoned with the interests they have at stake. *Medical Explorers*, the shirts read. They are outlined with the faint black cartoon of a skeleton. *Boning Up on the Future of Physiology*. Apparently they are a division of the Boy Scouts, devoted to the study of medicine.

If that's true—if these well-meaning young kids are planning to be doctors—I'd never bring them to this museum. Set off from the campus of Johns Hopkins like a quarantined captive, the building is even more dismal inside than it is outside. Dusty shelves and dimly lit glass exhibition cases form a maze for visitors.

Rebecca runs up to me. "This place grosses me out. I think Uncle Joley got it mixed up with somewhere else."

But from the looks of things, I'd say this is just up Joley's alley. The meticulous preservation, the absolute oddity of the collection. Joley collects facts; this is cocktail party conversation for a lifetime. "No," I tell her, "I'm sure Joley got it right."

"I can't believe the things they've got in here. I can't believe someone would go to the trouble of *saving* all the things they've got in here." She leads me around the corner, to a gaggle of Medical Explorers who are bent over a small glass case. Inside is a huge overgrown rat, bloated and patchy, its glass eyes frozen towards the north. The card says it was part of a research experiment, and died from the cortisone shots. At death, it weighed 22.5 pounds, approximately the same as a poodle.

I stare at the gummy features a few minutes longer until Rebecca calls me from across the room. She waves me over to a wall-length exhibit of stomachs that have been frozen in time. Floating in large canisters of formaldehyde, the anomalies are tagged. There is a series of hair balls in the stomachs of cats and humans. There is a particularly disgusting jar with a stomach that still contains the skeleton of a small animal. *Amazing!* the tag reads. *Mrs. Dolores Gaines of Petersborough, Florida, swallowed this baby kitten.*

How awful, I think. Was it possible that she didn't know she was doing it at the time?

The next wall of the maze holds shelves of fetal animals. A calf, a dog, a pig, which Rebecca informs me she will dissect next year in biology class. A human, in several stages: three weeks; three months, seven months. I wonder who willed their own children to this museum. Where the mothers are today.

Rebecca stands in front of the human fetuses. She holds her forefinger up to the three-week specimen. It doesn't even look like a baby, more like a cartoon ear, a pink paisley amoeba. There's that red dot, like Jupiter's storm, that is an eye. It is just the size of the nail on Rebecca's pinky. "Was I really that small," she says rhetorically, and it makes me smile.

By the time the baby is three months, you can really start to see that it is a baby. An oversized head, transparent, carries thin blood vessels to the black hooded eye. Stick-figure arms and webbed fingers and Indian-crossed legs stick out from the body, which is little more than a spine. "When do you start to look pregnant?" Rebecca asks.

"It depends on the person," I tell her, "and I think it depends on whether you are having a boy or a girl. I didn't show until about three months."

"But it's so tiny. There's nothing to see."

"Babies seem to carry a lot of extra baggage. When I was pregnant with you, I had been doing a practicum towards a masters as a speech pathologist at an elementary school. And back then you weren't allowed to teach and be pregnant. Well, you were allowed, but it wasn't common practice, and you'd certainly be out of a job when you gave birth. So I kept getting bigger and bigger and to hide the pregnancy I wore these hideous tie-dyed caftans. All the faculty kept telling me, 'Jane, you know, you're putting on a little weight,' and I'd say, 'Yeah, I don't know what I can do about it.' I'd run out of faculty meetings and student consultations to throw up. I told everyone I kept contracting different strains of the flu."

Rebecca turns around, fascinated with this story of herself. "And then what?"

"School ended," I shrug. "I had you in July, two weeks after school was finished. I still had six months of student teaching to do in the fall, so your father took care of you. And then, when I finished, I stayed home with you till you went to nursery school, when I continued my coursework and graduated."

"Daddy stayed home with me for six months?" she says. "Alone?" I nod. "I didn't know that."

"Actually, I'd forgotten."

"Did we get along? I mean, like, did he know how to change diapers and stuff?"

I laugh. "Yes. He knew how to change diapers. He also burped you and bathed you and held you over his back upside-down from your ankles."

"You let him do that?"

"It was the only way you'd stop crying."

Rebecca smiles shyly. "Really?"

"Really."

She points to the seven-month fetus, complete with tiny toes and a nose and a bud of a penis. "Now that's a baby," she says. "That's the way they are supposed to look."

"They get bigger. You'd think natural selection would have found an easier way of reproduction. Childbirth is like trying to get a piano through your nostril."

"Is that why I don't have a brother or sister?" Rebecca asks.

We've never talked about this. She's never asked, and we didn't volunteer. There's no real reason we didn't have any other children. Maybe because the plane crash scared us. Maybe because we were a little too busy. "We didn't need any other kids," I say. "We got it perfect the first time."

Rebecca smiles again, looking like Oliver in this dismal light. "You're just saying that."

"Yeah, in fact, your father and I have already willed you to this exhibit. For the extra cash. Three weeks—three months—seven months—fifteen years!"

Rebecca throws her arms around me. As she speaks I can feel her chin, shaped exactly like mine, pressing into my shoulder. "I love you," she says, plain and simple.

The first time Rebecca said she loved me I burst into tears. She was four and I had just rubbed her dry with a towel after a romp in the snow. She was very matter-of-fact about it. I am sure she does not remember but I could tell you that she was wearing red Oshkosh overalls, that there were hexagonal snowflakes caught in her eyelashes, that her socks had come off, bunched and burrowing in the toes of her boots.

This is why I became a mother, isn't it? No matter how long you have to wait for her to understand where you come from, no matter how many bouts of appendicitis or stitches you have to suffer through, no matter how many times you feel you are losing her, this makes it all worth it. Over Rebecca's shoulder there are brains of monkeys and eyes of goats. There is a thick brown liver curled inside a glass cylinder. And there is a line of hearts, arranged in order of size: mouse, guinea pig, cat, sheep, Saint Bernard, cow. The human, I think, rests somewhere in the middle.

48 OLIVER

They have two tapes at the Blue Diner in Boston—the Meat Puppets and Don Henley, and they alternate them over and over, the entire twenty-four hours that they remain open. I know because I have been here at least that long, having noticed the same waitresses repeating their shifts. I can sing most of the words from each tape. I have to confess I had never heard of either, and I've been wondering if Rebecca knows them.

"Don Henley," Rasheen—the waitress—says, refilling my coffee cup. "You know. From the Eagles. Ring a bell?"

I shrug, singing along with the tape. "You've got that down," Rasheen says, laughing. From the greasy grill, Hugo, the short-order cook who is missing a thumb, cheers. "You got a nice voice, Oliver, you know?"

"Well." I stir in a packet of sugar. "I'm known for my songs."

"No shit," Rasheen says. "Wait, let me guess. I got it. Blues. You're one of those white-bread trumpet players who thinks he's Wynton Marsalis."

"You got me. I can't keep anything from you."

I have been on this stool, at the Blue Diner on Kneeland, for so long now that I am not certain I could use my legs to stand. I could certainly have taken a room at the Four Seasons or the Park Plaza

Hotel, but I haven't been overcome with the desire to sleep. In fact I haven't slept since I left Iowa, three and a half days ago, and drove continuously through to Boston. I would have gone straight to Stow, but in all truth, I'm terrified. She is a supernatural force with which I have to reckon. No, scratch that. She isn't the problem at all. I am the problem. But it is easier to blame Jane. I have been doing it for so long that it is the first explanation to spring to mind.

The Blue Diner management has been kind to me, neglecting to report me to the authorities for loitering. Perhaps they can see I am a distressed man by my rumpled suit jacket, or the circles beneath my eyes. Perhaps they can tell by the way I eat my food—three meals a day, the specials, reassembled in geometrical patterns on my plate until Rasheen or Lola or pretty Tallulah decides it is cold enough to take back to the kitchen. When anyone will listen, I talk about Jane. Sometimes when no one is listening I talk anyway, hoping my words will find an audience.

It is almost time for Rasheen to go home, which means Mica (short for *Mon*ica) comes on. I have begun to tell the time by the arrivals and departures of the Blue Diner staff. Mica is the late-night waitress; a dental hygiene student by day. She is the only one who has actually asked me questions. When I told her the story of Jane's exodus, she propped her elbows against the speckled white countertop and rested her cheeks in her hands.

"I got to go now, Oliver," Rasheen says, pulling on an army-surplus jacket. "I guess I'll see you tomorrow."

Just as she is walking out the door Mica blows in in a flurry of paper, pink uniform, and leatherette coat. "Oliver!" she says, surprised to see me. "I was hoping you'd be gone by now. Couldn't sleep last night?"

I shake my head. "I didn't even try."

Mica waves to Hugo, who, oddly enough, doesn't seem to sleep either. He has been here the same length of time as I. She pulls up a stool beside me and grabs a Danish from beneath a scratched plastic dome. "You know, I was thinking about you during lecture today, and I think Jane would be very impressed. From what you've said, I think you're a changed man."

"I'd like to believe that," I say. "Unfortunately, I haven't the same conviction as you."

"Don't you just love the way he talks." Mica says this to nobody in particular. "It's like you're British or something."

"Or something," I say. Although she's asked, I've refused to tell her anything about my life with the exception of the fact that I come from San Diego. Somehow I think that finding out I am a Harvard man, that I lived on the Cape as a child, would crush the mystique.

"No wonder Jane fell for you." Mica reaches over the counter to pour herself some coffee. "You're such a kidder."

After our wedding ceremony, the reverend led us into the library at Jane's parents' house. He told us we could probably use a few moments alone; it would be all the peace and quiet we'd have that day. It was a nice gesture but I had no pressing information I had to share with Jane; it seemed to be a waste of time. Don't misunderstand me: I loved Jane, but I did not care much about the wedding. To me, marriage was a means to an end. To Jane, marriage was a fresh beginning.

When Jane said her vows, she had given a great deal of thought to the ideas behind the words, which I cannot say I'd done at all. And so for those few moments in the study, she was the one who did the talking. She said she was the luckiest girl in the world. Who would imagine that of all the women around, I would pick *her* to spend forever with?

She said it easily but I think it took her a few months to understand what she meant. Jane settled easily into a routine: taking shirts to the dry cleaners, registering for courses at San Diego State, grocery shopping, paying the telephone bill. I must admit, she was well suited to marriage, making my own experience much better than I had imagined. Every morning she'd kiss me goodbye and hand me a brown-bagged lunch. Every night when I came home from the Institute she'd have supper waiting, and she'd ask me how my day had been. She liked the role so much she won me over. I started to act like a husband. I would tiptoe into the shower when she was washing her hair and grab her from behind. I checked her when she got into the car to make sure she was wearing her seat belt.

We were dirt-poor, but Jane didn't seem to notice or care. One night over dinner she clattered her fork and knife against the side of her china plate and smiled, her mouth full of cheap spaghetti. "Isn't life wonderful?" she said. "Don't we just have it all?"

That night she woke up screaming. I sat up, temporarily blind in the dark, and felt my way across the bed for her. "I dreamed that you died," she said. "You drowned because of a problem with an oxygen tank in your diving gear. And I was left alone."

"That's ridiculous." I said the first thing to come to mind. "We check all our gear."

"That's not it, Oliver. What *if* one of us dies? What happens then?"

I reached around and turned on the light to see the clock: 3:20 A.M. "I suppose we'd remarry."

"Just like that!" Jane exploded. She sat up in bed, facing away from me. "You can't just pick a wife off a shelf."

"Of course not. I just meant that if I happened to die young I'd want you to be happy."

"How could I be happy without you? When you get married, you make the biggest decision of your life; you say you're going to spend eternity with one person. So what do you do if that person leaves? What do you do once you've already committed yourself?"

"What do you want me to do?" I asked.

And Jane looked at me and said, "I want you to live forever."

I know now that I should have said, "I want you to live forever too," or at least I should have thought it. But instead I retreated back to the security blanket of scientific discovery. I said, "Oh, Jane, 'forever' depends on gradients of time. It's a relative term."

She slept on the couch that night, wrapped in an extra sheet.

At this point, Mica interrupts me. "My uncle was hospitalized for a broken heart. Swear to God. After my Aunt Noreen was hit by a truck. Two days later, my uncle went into spasms."

"Technically it was cardiac arrest," I say.

"Like I said," Mica insists, "a broken heart." She arches her eyebrows, as if to say, *I told you so.* "What happened after that?"

"Nothing," I tell her. Jane got up and made me lunch and

kissed me goodbye like nothing had happened. And since neither of us died, we never had to test the theory.

"Look," Mica says, "do you think you can fall in love more than once?"

"Of course." Love has always seemed to me such an ethereal issue one cannot pin it down to singular circumstances.

"Do you think you fall in love more than one way?"

"Of course," I say again. "I don't want to talk about this. I don't like talking about things like this."

"There's your problem right there, Oliver," Mica insists. "If you'd given yourself a little more time to think about it, you wouldn't be sitting in this stupid diner crying into your coffee."

What does she know, I think. She's a goddamned waitress. She watches soap operas. Mica walks around to the other side of the counter so that she is facing me. "Tell me what it was like in the house after she left."

"It was nice, actually. I had a lot of free time, and I didn't have to worry about letting my work get in the way of other things."

"What other things?"

"Family things. Like Rebecca's birthday, for instance." I take a sip of coffee. "No, I really didn't miss them much at all." Of course I couldn't get any work done, either, because I was crazed with anxiety. I couldn't stop picturing Jane. I picked up and left an important research excursion just to get them back home.

Mica leans forward so that her lips are inches from mine. "You lie." Then she pulls on her apron, and heads in the direction of Hugo. "I don't listen to liars."

But I've been waiting for her all day. I've been waiting for Mica to listen. "You can't leave me."

She turns around on her heel. "Can't stand to be deserted twice, can you?"

"Do you want to know what it was really like without her there? I could still feel her in the house. I can now. The reason I won't go to sleep is because sometimes I wake up in the middle of the night and I can sense her, if that means anything. Sometimes when I'm alone I think she's standing behind me, watching me. It's like she never left. It's like it always was." Oh Jane. I lean my cheek against the cool counter. "For fifteen years I kissed her hello and goodbye and I didn't make anything of it. It was a habit. I didn't even notice when I was doing it. I couldn't tell you what her skin feels like, if you asked. I couldn't even tell you what it's like to hold her hand." All of a sudden I'm crying, something I haven't done since I was a child. "I don't have any memories of the important things."

When my eyes focus again Mica is talking to Hugo, and pulling on her faux leather coat. "Come on," she says, "I'm taking you back to my place. It's in Southey, and it's a hike, but you can make it." She puts her arm around me, almost as tall as I am, and I lean on her to get off the stool. It takes us fifteen minutes to walk there and the whole way, as idiotic as I imagine I look, I can't keep myself from crying.

Mica opens the door to the apartment and apologizes for the mess. Strewn across the floor are empty pizza cartons and textbooks. She leads me into a sideroom barely large enough to be a walk-in closet, which holds a white futon and a floor lamp. She loosens my tie. "Don't get the wrong idea," she says.

I let her take off shoes and my belt and then I practically collapse onto the low futon. Mica gets a washcloth and a bowl of water and leans my head in her lap, sponging my temples. "Just relax. You need to get some sleep."

"Don't leave me."

"Oliver," Mica says, "I have to go to work. But I'll be back. I promise you that." She leans close to my face. "I have a good feeling about this."

She waits until she thinks I am asleep, and then she edges my head off her lap and creeps out of the room. I'm pretending because I know she needs to go back to the diner. She needs the money. She turns off the lights and closes the front door behind her. I have every intention of getting up and walking around, but suddenly my body has become so heavy it is a hardship. I close my eyes and when I do I can perceive her there. "Jane?" I whisper.

Maybe this is the way it would be if you had died. Maybe I would be crying, wishing there had been one extra minute. Maybe I would spend my time and money contacting mediums, reading up on the spiritual world, in hopes of finding you so that I'd have the chance to tell you things I hadn't. Maybe I would look twice in the reflection of mirrors and store windows, hoping to see your face again. Maybe I would lie in bed like I am now, with my fists clenched so hard, trying to convince myself you are standing, flesh and blood, before me. But in all likelihood, if you were dead, I wouldn't have any chance at all. I would not get to tell you what I should have been telling you every day: that I love you.

49 JANE

With the moves of a practiced dancer, the man twists the ram onto its side, catching its haunch in the crook of his leg and rolling it, a cross between a pas de deux and a half-nelson. With the ram breathing evenly, he peels away the fleece. It falls away in one continuous piece. It's white and clean, the underside.

When he finishes he tosses the shears on the ground. Pulling the ram to its feet, he leads it by the neck out of the fenced gate. He slaps its behind and it runs off, naked.

"Excuse me," I say, "do you work here?"

The man smiles. "I suppose you could say that."

I take a few steps closer, watching the wet hay to see that it doesn't stick on my still-white sneakers. "Do you know someone named Joley Lipton?" I ask, looking up. "He works here too."

The man nods. "I'll take you to him in a minute, if you'd like. I've got one more to shear."

"Oh," I say. "All right." He asks me to help, to make it go faster. He points to the door of the barn. I turn to Rebecca, mouthing, *I don't believe this*. I follow him into the barn.

"Hey little lady," the man whispers, "hey my pretty little lamb. I'm gonna come a little closer. I'm gonna come a little bit closer." As he says this he is creeping forward, and then with a shout he sinks his hands into the wool of the sheep's back. "Take this side. She's young and feisty, and she'll get away."

I do what he has done, and hunch over with my fingers roped into the fleece. All three of us walk out to the brown mat. "Where would you like me to put this?" I ask, wondering if I should just go off on my own to find Joley. God only knows how long this will take.

"Put her over here," the man says, nodding his chin several feet forward. He lets go of his side, and, following suit, I do the same. The sheep takes a quick look at me and runs away. "What are you doing! Catch her!" the man yells.

Rebecca lunges at the sheep but it darts in the other direction. The man stares at me, incredulous. "I thought it would just stay put," I say, explaining. The least I can do is catch the damn thing. I run to a corner of the pen and try to sink my fists into the wool of the sheep's neck again. But suddenly I've lost my balance and though I reach for the fence, for Rebecca, I grab at nothing at all. I fall with an audible squelch and gag. "Rebecca," I choke out, "get over here."

The man is laughing in the distance. He grabs the sheep like it is no trouble at all and hoists it onto the brown cloth mat. He shears the thing in seconds, while I am trying to shimmy sheep manure off of my legs. I can't get away from the smell.

"Tough break," the man says, walking over.

I've had about as much of this asshole as I can take. "I'm sure this isn't appropriate behavior for a field hand," I say, putting on my most educated cocktail-party voice. "When I tell Joley about this, he'll report you to the person who runs the place."

The man offers his hand to me, but takes it away when he sees what's covering my fingers. "I'm not too worried about that. I'm Sam Hansen. You must be Joley's sister."

This *idiot*, I think, this *fool* who's gone out of his way to humiliate me; this is the Boy Wonder Joley raves about?

I turn away, from embarrassment or sheer anger or whatever, and whisper to Rebecca, "I want to clean up."

Sam takes us up to the Big House, as he calls it, the modest mansion of sorts that overlooks the hundred acres of apples. He rattles off dates and facts that I imagine are meant to impress us: it was built in the 1800s, it is filled with antiques, blah blah blah. He leads me up the spiral staircase to the second room on the right. "Your stuff still in the car?" he asks, as if this is my fault as well. "This was my parents' room. You'll fit into my mom's stuff. Check in the closet."

He walks out and closes the door behind him. It is a pretty room with a four-poster, a night table stacked with curly maple Shaker boxes, and curtains and a comforter in wide blue-and-white awning stripes. There are no dressers or bureaus or armoires. I lean against the wall and wonder where Sam's parents put their clothes, and when I stand up again the wall juts open, hinged from the inside, pressing open into a hidden closet the size of a room itself. "How neat," I say to myself. When you close the closet, the wallpaper matches so exactly—blue cornflowers—you'd never know there was a door. I press against the wall again and it springs off its magnetic hook. Inside are four or five sundresses and skirts, not half as dowdy as I'd imagined. I pick a pretty madras, which turns out to be two sizes too big, and I belt it with a bandanna that has been tied to a hook inside the closet.

I am tempted to leave the dirty clothes on the floor of this room but something tells me there won't be maid service. So I gather them into my arms, inside out, and head downstairs. Rebecca and Sam are waiting. "What should I do with these?"

Sam looks at me. "Wash them," he says, and then he turns and walks out the door.

"He's a hell of a host," I say to Rebecca.

"I think he's pretty funny." She shows me where the washing machine is.

"Thank God. I was expecting a scrub board."

"Are you coming or what?" Sam yells through the screen door. "I don't have all day."

We follow him through the orchard, which I have to say really is beautiful. Trees spread their arms in octopus embraces, jeweled with waxy green leaves and bud necklaces. They are planted in neat, even rows, with plenty of room between them. Some have grown so big their branches entwine with the tree beside. Sam tells us which parts of the orchard are retail and which are commercial. Each patch of trees is cut by several roads, and the markers on the roads tell you what's grown where and to whom it gets sold.

"Hey Hadley," Sam yells approaching a tree, "come meet Joley's relatives."

A man steps off a ladder, which has been hidden by the trunk of the apple tree. He is tall, and he has an easygoing smile. I'd put him at the same age as Sam, by the looks of things. He grabs my hand and shakes it. "Hadley Slegg. It's nice to meet you, ma'am."

Ma'am. Such decorum. He's obviously not a close relative of Sam's.

He walks with us towards the lower quarter of the orchard, where I imagine we'll find Joley. I can't wait to see him—it has been so long, really, I don't know what to expect. Will his hair be longer? Will he speak first, or just hug me? Will he be different?

"So I hear you've done quite a bit of traveling," Sam says.

I jump; I've forgotten he's here. "Yes," I tell him. "All across the country. Of course I've also been to Europe and South America, with my husband's research." I stumble a little over the word *husband* and I catch Sam looking at me. "Lots of interesting places, actually. Why? Do you travel?"

"All the time. In spirit, at least." He leaves it like that, cryptic, for a moment, long enough to make me wonder if there is more to him than meets the eye. "I've never been outside of New England, but I've probably read more books on travel and exploring than anyone."

"Why don't you take a trip?"

"You don't get time off when you run a place like this." He has a nice smile; he just doesn't seem to use it a lot. "The second I set foot away from here, I think about all the things that are going wrong. It's easier now that your brother's here. Between him and Hadley I've split a lot of the responsibility. But it's not like a regular business. You can't reschedule a tree bearing fruit like you'd reschedule an appointment."

"I see," I say, not really understanding at all. We walk a few yards without saying anything. "So where would you really like to go?"

"Tibet," Sam says without hesitation. It surprises me. Most people say France or England. "I'd like to bring back some of the Asian strains of apples and propagate them in this climate. In a greenhouse, if need be."

I find myself staring at him. He is young—younger than Joley—but he already has the beginnings of lines around the corners of his mouth. He has thick dark hair and a strong square chin and what looks like a perpetual tan. As for his eyes, you can't tell anything from them. They are neon, really, blue but not like Oliver's. They burn.

Sam looks up and, embarrassed, I turn away. "Joley tells us you've run away from home," he says.

"Joley told you that?"

"Something about a fight with your husband."

Sam is bluffing, I think. Joley wouldn't tell people that. "I don't think it's any of your business."

"Well, in a way it is. What you do is what you do, but I don't want any trouble going on here."

"Don't worry. If Oliver shows up there won't be a Tombstone showdown. No blood. I promise."

"Too bad," he says. "Blood's good for fertilizer." He starts to laugh, surprised that I don't find this funny at all. He clears his throat. "So, what do you do for a living?"

I tell him I'm a speech pathologist. I look at him. "That means I go to schools in the San Diego area and diagnose children with speech problems caused by lisps, cleft palates, what have you."

"Believe it or not," Sam says sarcastically, "I *did* go to school." He shakes his head and walks faster.

"I didn't mean it like that," I say. "A lot of people don't know what a speech pathologist does. I've just gotten used to explaining it."

"Look, I know where you're from. I know what you think about guys like me. And to tell you the truth I don't give a shit."

"You don't know anything about me."

"And you don't know anything about *me*," Sam says. "So let's just leave it at that. You want to come here to visit your brother, that's fine. You want to stay a while, okay. Let's just say I'll do my thing, and you can do yours."

"Fine!"

"Fine."

I cross my arms and stare over the flat calm of the lake in the valley. "I want to know why you didn't help me up back there."

"In the manure?" Sam leans close to me and I can smell sweat and sheep and the honey of hay. "Because I knew exactly who you were."

"What does that mean?" I call after him. He's already begun to walk off, long carefree strides. "What the hell does that mean!" He squares his shoulders. "Pig," I say, under my breath.

I take just two more steps and then I see the ladder propped against the tall budding tree. "It's Joley," I shout. "Joley!" I pick up the long skirt of Sam's mother's sundress and run across the field.

Joley is wrapping some kind of green electrical tape around a branch. His hair is still light and curling around his ears. He is wiry, strong, graceful. He opens his eyes, with their long dark lashes, and turns to me. "Jane!" he says, as if it truly is unexpected to find me standing there. He smiles, and the world turns inside out.

He jumps off the ladder and folds me into his arms. "How are you doing," he whispers into my neck.

I blink back tears. I've waited so long.

Joley holds me at arm's length, passing his eyes gently over my face and my shoulders and my hips. Still holding onto one of my hands, he walks over to Rebecca. "Looks like you survived the trip," he says, and kisses her on the forehead. She bends in close, like she is receiving a benediction. He grins at Sam and Hadley. "I assume you've all met."

"Unfortunately," I murmur. Sam glowers at me, and Joley looks back and forth between us but neither of us will say a thing.

Joley claps his hands together and locks his fingers. "Well, it's great that you're here. We've got a lot of catching up to do."

Sam, in a stroke of unexpected kindness, gives Joley the afternoon off. We stand in front of each other, just staring, until everyone else disappears. *My baby brother,* I think. *What would I do without him?*

Joley walks me over to a fat stunted tree with low branches. From the looks of the tree, which is blackened and leafless, it is not going to make it. "I'm doing my best," he says, "but you're right. I'm not sure about this one at all." He straddles one of the bent arms and pats the space beside him for me to do the same. We look at each other and both begin to talk at the same time. We laugh. "Where are we going to start?" Joley says.

"We could start with you. I want to thank you for getting me here." I smile, thinking about his reflective letters, on yellow ruled paper, words written without margins, precipitous, as if they would have fallen right off the page without the adhesive structure of sentence. "I certainly couldn't have done it without you."

"I'm glad you didn't have to. You look great. You're prettier than you've ever been."

"Oh, that's a crock," I say, but Joley shakes his head.

"I mean it." He smiles at me, and he holds one of my hands, kneading it with his fingers as if that is the way to start resuscitation.

"Are you happy here?" I ask.

"Look at the place, Jane! It's like God just dropped down this gorgeous hill and lake, and I have the good fortune to work here. If you can call this work. I fix the unfixable. I bring trees back from the dead." He looks into my eyes. "I've become mythic. The god of second chances."

I laugh. "Sounds right up your alley. No wonder I'm here."

"Which brings us to you." Joley looks at me, waiting for me to start talking.

"I don't know where to begin."

"Start anywhere," Joley says. "It'll come to center."

"I can tell you this." A nervous laugh. "I didn't leave because I had thought long and hard about it. I left on impulse. Just like that." I snap my fingers. "I don't know what I'm doing anymore."

"What made you hit Oliver, then?" Joley smiles. "Don't get me wrong. Not that I don't think it was a wonderful idea."

"You know the textbook answer to that. Abused child grows up to be an abuser herself. I've been thinking so much about Daddy lately. It's classic, isn't it? The sins of the fathers are visited upon the children?"

Joley stretches my hand out on the leg of his jeans. "Do you think he's on his way here?"

"I give him ten days at most." I twirl my wedding band, which I am still wearing, to my own surprise. "Unless of course he just decided to take off to South America like he had planned. In which case I get a grace period of a month."

"I hate to admit it myself, but you *used* to love him."

Joley comes to the heart of the matter faster than anyone I know. "I loved the idea of being in love with him," I say, "but that can be a poor substitute for a life." I stare at my brother. "I already told you this isn't about Oliver. It's about me. I just snapped when we were having that fight. I mean, we were arguing about whether shoe boxes or files should go in my closet. That doesn't ruin a marriage." I look into my lap. "I'm scared. I've spent fifteen years cutting up fruit the way Oliver likes it, folding his laundry, wiping clean his messes. I've done everything that I was supposed to. I don't know what made me hit him that day. Maybe it was just a way out."

"Is that what you've been looking for?"

"I don't know what I'm looking for." I sigh. "I got married young. I had a baby young. So when people asked me who I was, I'd answer by saying 'a wife,' or 'a mother.' I can't tell you at all what *I'm* like, what *Jane* is like."

Joley's eyes do not leave my face. "What is it you want?"

I close my eyes, and try to picture it. "Oh, Joley," I say, "I'll go home and be the ideal wife, the perfect mother. I'll do everything I've been doing and I won't ever bring this up again. I'll live the most ordinary life there ever was, just as long as you promise me that I'll get five minutes of wonderful before it's all over."

50 SAM

From the beginning there's friction. I know she's coming, but I'm not looking forward to it, and sure enough she shows up just when I'm in the middle of shearing. So I see her get out of the car with the little girl, but I pretend I haven't heard her drive up. I am working the ram when she comes into the pen. I can't tell much about her because I am facing the sheep, except that she has pretty good legs. I try to concentrate on running straight rows of fleece, on peeling the wool back from the sheep's side like filleting a bass. Good wool is seventy-five cents per pound these days, belly wool goes for something cheaper. When my mother was alive she'd card and spin it, and then knit something out of it: a sweater, an afghan. But these days we just sell the fleece to the town pool. From time to time, I'll buy one of the blankets they weave from everyone's sheep.

She's stepping around on the hay like it's a mine field. For Christ's sake, it's just manure. Half the vegetables she eats at the supermarket have probably been mulched with the stuff. She asks me if I know Joley.

Maybe I shouldn't give her such a hard time. After all, I don't really know her. What I'm going on is an assumption. Still, I can't resist. Just because I want to watch her out of her element, I ask her to help me get the next ewe, and she follows me into the barn. I'm figuring on a good laugh, and then I'll tell her who I am.

She follows my actions, digging into the fleece like she is knotting her fingers into a net, and we walk slowly, hunched, with the sheep between us. She follows me out to the ledge where I've been doing the shearing. I steal a look at her, then, impressed. She isn't afraid to get her hands dirty, at least. She has a high forehead and a little nose that goes up at the end, like it's too small for her face. I wouldn't call her a knockout, but she's all right. In a fresh, just-washed way. Of course, I'm not seeing her all done up. Back where she's from, she probably wears all that makeup and chunky jewelry and suits with crazy angles.

I have to keep myself from smiling: she's doing a good job. I let go of the sheep to grab the razor and all of a sudden the ewe bolts, heading straight for the girl. "What are you doing!" I yell, the first thing that comes to mind. "Catch her!"

The girl—Rebecca, that's her name—dives for the sheep but it runs in the opposite direction. I turn to Joley's sister. I absolutely can't believe someone would be stupid enough to let go of a sheep before shearing.

"I thought it would just stay put," she says.

All it takes is common sense, for God's sake. She looks up at me with this apologetic gaze and when she sees that isn't going to work she runs after the sheep herself. She lunges for the ewe, but doesn't see the manure heaped onto the hay. Naturally, she falls, smack in the middle of it.

I didn't mean for anything like this to happen, honest. I expected to have a little fun with her, make the ol' Newton girl see what a working farm is really like, and then I was going to take her down to Joley. But now that it's happened, really, it's a riot. To keep myself from laughing, I catch the sheep and throw all my attention into shearing her. I rub the shears up the belly, across the hinds, between the legs, around the neck. I use my legs and knees to pin her on her side while I run the shears over her flanks, letting the wool roll off like a carpet of snow. It's perfect, from the inside, white with only a few spots of lanolin. It springs back at the touch, crimped with natural oils from the skin. In a few minutes when I am finished with the sheep, I slap her lightly on her hind leg. She springs up, looking back at me once, a little angry. She bolts away, down into the field with the other sheep.

I walk over to where Joley's sister is rubbing her back up against the split rail. She's doing everything she can to keep from touching the stuff. That does it for me; I laugh in her face. She smells awful; even her hair is encrusted with manure. "Tough break," I say. What I really mean is: I'm sorry.

She looks so out of place and incredibly miserable that I rediscover my conscience. I'm about to tell her who I am, and how I didn't really mean for this to happen, when she undergoes this transformation. It's a physical thing–her shoulders square up and her chin lifts and her eyes get very dark. All of a sudden she has this attitude. "I'm sure this isn't appropriate behavior for a field hand," she tells me. "When I tell Joley about this, he'll report you to the person who runs the place."

"I'm not too worried about that," I say dryly and I tell her who I am. I hold out my hand, and then on second thought, take it back. The girl introduces herself. She's laughing, which makes me think she'll turn out all right. "Come on," I say. "You can get cleaned up at the Big House."

I show them their rooms, figuring it's the least I can do after that fiasco, and tell Jane she's welcome to the clothes my mother left in her closet. They'll be big, but she can figure it out. She near about slams the bedroom door in my face, and I walk downstairs to Rebecca again, who's peeking into each of the drawers of an antique apothecary chest that came from my mother's mother. "Nothing in there," I say, catching her in the act.

She jumps a few feet into the air. "I'm sorry," she says, "I didn't mean to be doing that."

"Sure you did. It's okay. This is your house now. For a while, anyways." I pull open one of the drawers myself, and take out an Indian head penny, 1888. I wonder if she knows that means good luck.

Rebecca starts to wander into the other rooms: the parlor and the blue tiled kitchen and the library, with wall-to-wall books, mostly on exotic places, that I've picked up over the years. "Wow," she says, lifting a coffee-table book on the Canadian Rockies. "You've been to all these places?"

I walk into the library behind her. "You know what a mental traveler is?"

"It's what I was before this summer." She smiles at me, real open, like she's got absolutely nothing to hide. I like her.

"I'm just going to sit outside. You can check out anything you'd like." I leave her staring at an antique sextant propped over the mantel. "It's for navigation," I say, on my way out. She moves closer after I turn away, the old floorboards sigh under her weight.

It's warm out, but not oppressive: it's been that kind of a summer. I stare at my watch, impatient, which isn't fair. It's only been about four minutes since I left Joley's sister, and she has to wash off anyway, and when you get right down to it it's my fault she's filthy. I glance over the orchard, which you can pretty much see in total from the Big House, trying to find Joley or Hadley or someone else who can take them off my hands. I'm not much good with visitors; I never know what to say. Especially in this case; I don't expect a California woman to understand my life any more than I could make heads or tails of hers. My eyes run over the roads that separate the different stocks in the orchard, noticing which groups of trees need to be sprayed, which need to be pruned. I'm staring at these even rows, but I keep seeing her. Standing in the closet, pulling off her shirt. I jam my hands into my pockets and start to whistle.

When she comes downstairs, she's wearing my mom's madras sundress. It's all these crazy peach colors, like a hot muggy sunset, and Dad gave her so much trouble about it being an eyesore she left it behind when she moved. It's true, it looked too showy across her wide hips, but on Joley's sister it's almost elegant. It pinches at the waist where she's wrapped it with an old handkerchief—can that possibly fit around her? Her arms, which are kind of thin for my taste, peek out pale from the too-big cap sleeves. And those peach colors show up again in her cheeks, which makes it all seem to match.

She's holding all the dirty clothes. "What should I do with these?"

My voice is not my own. It's hoarse and it comes out uneven. "Wash them," I say, and I turn and walk down the path before she notices the way I sound.

They catch up quick enough, and I try to keep from holding a conversation by telling them about the orchard. As Lake Boon comes into view at the foot of the orchard, I tell Rebecca it's great for swimming, and just in case she fishes, I let her know there's bass. I catch Jane looking around at the thick older trees in this section of the orchard—the McIntosh stock—and then taking note of the pond. When I walk past her I can smell lemons and fresh sheets. Her skin, even this close, reminds me of the inner edge of a crab apple blossom, flawless.

"Hadley!" I say. He steps off a ladder behind a tree he's been pruning. When I introduce him, he does everything I didn't do at the barn. He takes Jane's hand and pumps it up and down; he dips his head towards Rebecca. And then he gives me this look, like he knows right there and then he's already outdone me.

He immediately drops behind to talk to Rebecca—it figures, Hadley's a pretty quick judge of character—leaving me to hold a conversation with Jane. I think about just walking the next ten acres without saying a word, but I've been rude enough today. Well, Sam, I tell myself, they've just come from across the country. Surely you can think of something pertaining to that. "So," I say, "I hear you've done quite a bit of traveling."

She jumps, just like Rebecca did when I caught her looking in the apothecary chest. "Yes," she says, sort of guarded. "All across the country." She looks at me as if she wants me to evaluate what she's said, and then that look comes over her again, that haughty *I'm-leagues-beyond-you* look. "Of course I've also been to Europe and South America with my . . . my husband's research." That's right, Joley's told me about the whale guy, and why Jane left in the first place. "Why?" she asks, "Do you travel?"

I smile and tell her I've gone all over the place, at least in spirit. But I can't tell what she thinks of that, until she asks me flat out why I don't just take a real trip. I try to explain why running an orchard is different from running any other business, but she doesn't understand. Not that I'd expected her to.

"Where would you really like to go?" she asks, and right away I have an answer. I'd love to go to Tibet, just because of what I could bring back. I know technically it takes months to import agriculture products, and I'd never clear customs with a tree, but if I got a small enough series of grafts I could hide them in my luggage without a problem. Can you imagine what it would be like to bring back an original Spitzenburg, or an even older stock, and make it come alive again?

I realize I've been doing way too much talking, and I turn to find her staring right at me. I'm caught off guard, and like an idiot, I say the first thing that pops into my mind. "Joley tells me you've run away from home."

All the blood goes out of her cheeks, I swear. "Joley told you that?"

I mention I think it had something to do with her husband. I don't mean anything by it, but her eyes get violent, all the light parts filling in black like a cougar's. She straightens up and tells me it's none of my business.

God, she has some attitude. It's not like I've mentioned some big secret. I'm just retelling what her own brother told me. If she wants to get all pissy, she should take it out on Joley, not me.

I don't have to take this, not on my own land. I should have known better to begin with. Nothing's changed between the likes of her and the likes of me: certain trees just cannot be grafted; certain life-styles just do not mix.

She folds her arms across her chest. "You don't know anything about me."

"You don't know anything about *me,*" I say, almost hollering now. "Let's just leave it at that. You want to come here to visit your brother, that's fine. You want to stay a while, okay." I can feel the sweat starting to run down the sides of my face. "Let's just say I'll do my thing, and you can do yours."

She jerks her head, so a strand of her ponytail lands across her mouth. "Fine."

"Fine." That settles it. I have a policy with Joley and Hadley: whoever they want to bring up here as a visitor is their business, and they're more than welcome. So if Joley wants his sister to stay a while, I'm not going to cross him. But I'm sure as hell not going to babysit her.

"I want to know why you didn't help me up back there."

"In the manure?" I say, and then I grin, satisfied. Because of all the times your friends pointed at me when I was in high school. Because of that party, where I was just a kid and a girl just like you was using me. Because I could look but I wasn't allowed to touch. "Because," I tell her, "I knew exactly who you were."

Triumphant, I walk off in the direction of the commercial section. Then I hear her voice, fluted like a cardinal's. "Joley!" she cries. "It's Joley!"

It's remarkable to watch them from this distance, this guy I've come to trust like a brother and this woman who has done nothing but give me grief from the moment she's arrived. Joley doesn't hear her at first. He's got his hands pressed around a tree he's been grafting; his head bent almost reverently, willing it to live. A second later, when he lifts his head in that way he has, kind of dazed, he sees Jane and jumps off the high rungs of the ladder to meet her. He picks her up and swings her around and she wraps her arms around his neck and clings to him like she's been drowning and just found a sure call for safety. I've never seen two people so different fit together so perfect.

Hadley and me and Rebecca are all watching this and getting kind of uncomfortable. It's not just like *we're* intruding; it's as if everything—the orchard, the lake, the sky, God Himself—should be giving these two a little privacy. "Why don't you take the rest of the afternoon off, Joley," I say softly, "on account of you never see your sister."

I start to walk back in the direction of the barn, figuring I can clean up after the shearing. I need to separate that last ewe's wool, and tie the bags and get them into town sometime this week. I leave Hadley in charge of Rebecca, figuring the two of them are getting along all right. And then with the sun burning against the back of my neck, I make my way across my orchard.

I have never disliked someone so much so quickly. I'd say I wasn't being fair to her, with the shearing accident and all, but I certainly gave her plenty of chances to see that I didn't mean it on purpose. Ten acres back to the barn is a long ways, and the whole time I'm thinking of Jane Jones, and her face flushed to the same color as Ma's dress, and the way one minute she could act so self-righteous, but the next minute she needed to cling to Joley for support.

I try to do a few things back at the greenhouse, but I'm not concentrating well. I keep remembering stupid things from high school—dumb incidents with city girls who, most likely, Jane used to hang around with. I seemed to always go for that type: the ones who looked like they'd just scrubbed their faces so hard they'd turned pink at the cheeks; the girls who had straight shiny hair that, if you came close, gave off the scent of raspberries. I went crazy over them at first sight, my heart going a mile a minute and my throat getting all hollow until I got up the nerve to go over and try one more time. You never know, I used to tell myself. Maybe this girl won't know where you're from. Maybe she won't be the kind who cares. Eventually I knew better. They didn't have to say it outright; their message came through loud and clear: stick to your own kind.

So that was my first mistake with Jane Jones. I should have just let her go her own way. I should have pointed her in Joley's direction and I shouldn't have asked her to help out with the shearing in any way, shape or form. I started out just doing it for a laugh but that wasn't right. She's not like us. She wouldn't get the joke.

I realize then that I have left the greenhouse without noticing, and I'm standing in front of a dead apple tree, staring at Joley and his sister. Joley notices me and waves me over. From the other direction, Hadley and Rebecca approach. "Where have you guys been?" Joley says. "We were getting ready to have lunch."

I open my mouth but nothing comes out. "We were down by the lake," Hadley says. "Rebecca was telling me all the stupid things you did at family Christmas parties." He's got a gift for situations like this. He can take knots and unravel them, smooth the kinks, put everyone at ease.

"Sam," she says. She's talking to me. "Joley says you have a hundred acres." She looks directly at me, bright and friendly.

"You know anything about apples?" I say, too gruff. She shakes her head, so that her ponytail bounces on her shoulders. A ponytail. You don't see many grown women with one; *that's* what it is about her. "It really wouldn't interest you."

Hadley looks at me, as if to say, *What the hell's gotten into you?*

"Sure it would. What varieties do you grow here?"

When I don't say anything, Hadley and Joley go through the rigamarole of reciting all the stocks and varieties at the orchard. I walk up to the dead tree, within inches of her, and pick at the bark of a branch. I pretend that I'm doing something important.

Jane walks to a nearby tree. "And what are these?"

She picks a Puritan, holds it up to the warm noon sun, and then presses it up against her lips, getting ready to bite. I see this from behind, and I know what she is about to do. I also know that this section was sprayed with pesticides this morning. I move quickly on instinct, throwing my arm over her shoulder so that her back presses against me, sharp and warm. I manage to swat that apple out of her arm so it rolls out of her tight hold, settling heavy, like an overturned stone.

She whirls around, her lips inches from my face. "What in God's name is your *problem?*"

I am thinking: Get in your car; go back where you belong. Or else leave your big ideas behind and let me run my place the way I know it should be run. I am thinking: Here, I am the big fish in the pond. Finally I point to the tree where she picked the fruit. "They were sprayed today," I say. "You eat it, you die." I push past her, past the catch of perfume that hangs about her and the warm outline of air that hovers inches from her skin. I brush her shoulder as I pass, and I step on the goddamned apple with the heel of my boot. I fix my eyes on the Big House; I keep walking. I don't look back. Out of sight, I tell myself, is out of mind.

51 JANE

Because the Big House was built in the 1800s, all the plumbing's been restored. Naturally, they have bathrooms but not many. Everyone upstairs has to share one master bathroom, one claw-footed tub with a pull-around shower curtain, one ancient toilet with an overhead chain-pull tank.

Today, I get up so late I'm sure that everyone else has already gone down to the fields. There's no one in the bathroom, so I just walk in and turn on the shower. I let the room fill up with steam and then I'm singing the melodies of doo-wop songs, so I don't hear the door open. But when I peek my head out to reach for a towel so

I can wipe soap out of my eyes, I see Sam Hansen standing in front of the mirror.

He's rubbed a little part clear, and he's got shaving cream all over his face. I'm so shocked that I just stand there, stark naked, with my mouth hanging open. There's no lock on the bathroom door, so I could understand him walking in. But actually staying? Shaving?

"Excuse me," I say, "I'm taking a shower."

Sam turns to me. "I can see that."

"Don't you think you should leave?"

Sam clicks his razor three times against the porcelain of the sink. "Look, I've got an appointment in Boston this afternoon, and a meeting in Stow in three-quarters of an hour. I don't have time to wait for you to finish your three-hour stint in the bathroom. I needed to get in here to shave. It's not my fault you picked such a goddamned inconvenient time to take your shower—practically afternoon, now."

"Wait just a minute." I turn off the water and pull the towel into the bathtub. I wrap it around myself and then I throw back the curtain. "You're intruding on my privacy. Do you *always* walk in on people who are in the bathroom if you're running late? Or is it just me?"

"Give me a break," he says, running the razor down his cheek. "I told you I was coming in."

"Well, I didn't hear you."

"I knocked, and then I told you I had to get in there. And you said 'Mmm-hmm.' I heard it with my own two ears. Mmm-hmm."

"For God's sake, I was *humming*. I wasn't inviting you in here; I was singing in the shower."

He turns to me and holds up the razor, making a point. "And how was I supposed to know that?" He stares at me, his mouth surrounded with white foam, a perverse version of Santa Claus. Almost imperceptibly, his eyes flicker, just quick enough to take in my body, shrouded in its towel, from head to toe.

"I don't believe this," I say, and I open the door to the bathroom. A cool blast of air rushes in and makes the skin on the back of my neck prickle. "I'm going into the bedroom. Please let me know when you're through." I stomp away, leaving wet pressed footprints on the Oriental runner in the hall.

I go to my bedroom and lie down on the bed, unwrapping the towel and spreading it out underneath me. On second thought, I rewrap it. With my luck, he'll just walk in here. There's a loud thud on the heavy wood door. "It's all yours," Sam says, his voice muffled.

Shaking my head I go back into the bathroom and this time I push the barrel used as a clothes hamper in front of the door. It isn't heavy enough to keep someone from getting in, but I'd be sure to hear it fall over. I step into the shower and wash the shampoo out of my hair. I finish my song.

When I shut off the water and go to pull the shower curtain away, I notice for the first time how thin and white it is. I hold my hand up in front of it and I can see straight through. It's practically transparent, which means he probably saw everything. Everything.

I rub a corner of the mirror dry so that I can check my face for new or deepening wrinkles. I stare at myself a little longer than usual, paying attention to the look in my eyes. I start to wonder what exactly Sam saw. I wonder if he liked it.

"Wait!" I call down from the bedroom window. "Don't leave without me!" Joley, who's standing outside with Hadley and Rebecca, waves—he's heard. I run past the mirror, tucking a stray hair behind my ear, and head for the stairs.

As I am going down I pass Sam going up. He grunts at me. I don't make much of an attempt to acknowledge him, either. I can feel my whole face turning red.

"Where are we going today?" I say, stepping onto the bright brick patio that overlooks the orchard.

Joley smiles when he sees me. "Not too far. I've got to go into Boston with Sam this afternoon to meet a produce buyer." He's wearing a shirt I sent him last year for Christmas—Polo, with wide rugby stripes in plum and orange. It's faded, which makes me happy: he must have liked it. "How'd you sleep?"

"Fabulously," I say, and I'm not lying. This is the second night we've stayed in the Big House, and for the second night I've been fast asleep by the time I hit the pillow. Part of it might be all the time we've been spending in the sun, letting summer catch us off guard. But part of it also has to do with the bed itself: a double four-poster with a feather mattress and an eiderdown quilt.

Hadley is showing Rebecca how to twist the stem of a cattail around its furry head, and then pop the head off, a projectile. He hits me on the leg. Rebecca thinks this is just delightful. "Oh, show me again," she says. I walk towards them, a moving target.

"She made me do it, I swear," Hadley shields his eyes from the sun.

I like him. I did right off the bat, but part of that was due to the contrast between Hadley and Sam. Hadley's simple: what you see is what you get. And he's been awfully nice to Rebecca. Since we've come to the orchard, he's adopted her. She follows him like a puppy, watching him prune trees or do bud-grafting things or even chop wood. Every time I've seen Hadley recently, I've seen Rebecca.

Rebecca wraps the stem of the cattail, with Hadley's help. "Now just put your fingers in the loop," he says, gently moving her hand, "and pull." She bites down on her lower lip as she does it. The head of the reed shoots over my head and lands on Joley.

Joley moves towards us, his hands buried in the pockets of his shorts. "So where are we headed today, crew?"

"We could take them into town," Hadley suggests. "We could take them to the supermarket so they can see where our apples end up."

"That sounds like a thrill a minute," Joley says.

"Don't feel you have to entertain me," I say. "I'm happy just hanging around here. If you two have things to do we can occupy ourselves." I spent all of yesterday with Joley, trailing him from tree to tree as he worked. He said there was no reason he couldn't graft and talk at the same time. We talked about the places I'd seen en route to Massachusetts. We talked about Mama and Daddy. I told him what Rebecca's grades were last spring; what Oliver had been planning to do off the coast of South America. And in return he taught me the names of the apples grown at Hansen's. He showed me how you can take a young budding branch and make it become part of a tree that has been dying. He showed me trees that have survived this process and trees that haven't.

It is so good to be with him. Just standing at his side reminds me how empty it is when he isn't around. I really believe that we can think directly into each other's minds. Many times when we are together, we don't bother to talk at all, and then when one of us *does* begin to speak, we realize we have both been wallowing in the same sharp memory.

Joley and Hadley are talking about what's going on this afternoon at the orchard. It turns out Hadley will be busy too, as acting supervisor when Sam's gone. I assume, though, like Joley, he'll offer to take Rebecca along with him while he works. They both look at each other, and then they say simultaneously, "Ice cream."

"Ice cream?" Rebecca says. "What about it?"

"We should definitely take them to Buttrick's," Hadley says, "no question about it. They have Holsteins penned up in the field, the ones whose milk they use for the ice cream."

"It's only eleven." I haven't even had breakfast.

"That's all right," Joley says. "They open at ten."

"I don't know."

Joley grabs my hand and starts pulling me towards the blue pickup truck in the driveway. "Stop being such a mother. Live a little."

Hadley offers me the passenger seat in the cab, saying he can ride in the flatbed with Rebecca. Joley turns over the ignition and just as he shifts into reverse, Hadley leaps off the truck. "Wait a second," he yells, and he runs into the garage. He comes back with two bright striped folding beach chairs, and tosses them to Rebecca.

I peer through the tiny window in the cab and watch Hadley set up the chair for Rebecca. With a grand sweeping stately gesture, he helps her into it. She's laughing; I haven't seen her so happy in a long time. "He's a nice guy."

"Hadley?" Joley says, backing up the hill and turning the truck around. He looks in the rearview mirror, presumably to check what's going on in the back of the truck. Rebecca's chair, which is sliding, crashes her into Hadley's chair, and she lands awkwardly, splayed across his lap. "He *is* nice. I just hope for everyone's sake he isn't being *too* nice."

I check through that dusty little window, but it all seems innocent. Hadley, laughing, helps Rebecca back in her chair, and shows her how to anchor herself by holding on to the sides of the truck. "She's just a kid."

"Speaking of kids," he says, "or for that matter, their parents—you never did tell me what your game plan is here."

I fiddle with the glove compartment, opening it and then locking it and then opening it again. There's nothing in there but a map of Maine and a bottle opener. "What game plan? I thought we were on vacation."

Joley looks at me out of the corner of his eye. "Sure, Jane. Whatever you say."

I find myself slouching down in the passenger seat and putting my feet up on the dashboard, the very thing I tell Rebecca not to do. We pull up to a stop light, and I can hear Hadley's and Rebecca's voices carrying. "Eighty-two bottles of beer on the wall," they sing.

Joley glances at me. "I won't bring it up anymore. But sooner or later—probably sooner—Oliver is going to show up at the orchard and demand an explanation. I'm not sure you've really got one, yet, either. And I'm positive you won't know what to say when he orders you to get back in the car and go home with him."

"I know exactly what I'm going to say," I announce, to my own surprise. "I'm going to tell him no."

Joley slams on the brakes and I hear the thump of two chairs against the back wall of the cab. Rebecca says, *Ow*. "You've got a little girl back there who doesn't know what's going on in your head. Do you think it's fair to waltz her out of her home and then spring on her the surprise that she's not going back? Or that she's not going to live with her father? Have you asked her what she thinks about all this?"

"In not so many words," I say. "What would you do?"

Joley looks at me. "That's not the issue. I know what *you* should do. Don't get me wrong: I love having you here, and I can be all selfish about that, but you don't belong in Massachusetts now. You should be back in San Diego, sitting at your kitchen table with Oliver, talking about what went wrong."

"My brother the romantic," I say dryly.

"The pragmatist," Joley corrects. "I think fifteen years is a lot of time to chalk up to a mistake."

Hadley informs Joley he's just missed the turn. Joley backs up into a dirt driveway and turns the truck around. "Promise me you'll think about it. Even if good ol' Oliver is standing on the porch when we get back, you won't open your mouth until you hear what he has to say."

"Hear what he has to say. Jesus, Joley, I've been doing that for a lifetime. When do *I* get to talk? When is it *my* turn?"

Joley smiles. "Let me tell you something I've learned from Sam."

"Do you have to?"

"He's a hell of a businessman. He's not a man of many words, and just because of that he creates a presence for himself. He forces whomever he's up against to do the speaking, to talk in circles. And the whole time he just sits there and listens. It gives the appearance of absolute knowledge, of total control. I mean, I know Sam pretty well, so I can see that sometimes he's scared shitless. But that's not the point. The point is, he knows how to turn that to his advantage. He waits, and he absorbs the whole situation, and he's so quiet that when he *does* open his mouth, you can be damn sure the whole world is listening."

I loll my head against the side of the seat belt. "Thank you for sharing that tidbit of advice with me."

"Pretend it has nothing to do with Sam," Joley says, grinning. "It's valuable, in spite of what you think of him."

Before I know it we are speeding across a gravel area, kicking up a storm of dust. BUTTRICK'S, the hand-painted sign reads. The building is shaped like a T. A line of girls in yellow checked dairy outfits are waiting, pen and pad in hand, to take orders. On the roof, above the sign, is a big plastic cow.

"You like the cow?" Hadley says to Rebecca, helping her out of the truck.

She nods. "I've never seen anything like it."

Hadley leads her over to a split-rail fence, with an extra layer of barbed wire running above the top rail. It encloses a large grassy meadow dotted with Holsteins. It looks like they have been arranged by a photographer, really. "This place reminds me of New Hampshire," Hadley says. "That's where my mom lives now."

He hops over the fence, which almost grabs the attention of the lazy cows. One actually turns its head. He holds his hand out to Rebecca and helps her climb over the barbed wire so that she is in the field too. "When are you going to be back?" I ask my brother.

"Dinnertime," Joley says, "with all the traffic."

Hadley takes Rebecca by the hand and leads her up to a placid cow. It is sitting, its knees folded up underneath. Rebecca, guided by Hadley's hand, holds her fingers out to the cow, which starts to lick them. Rebecca laughs and steps back. "You get many of these in San Diego?" he asks.

Rebecca shakes her head. "What do *you* think?"

"They have four stomachs. I don't know what they do with each one, though."

"Four stomachs," Rebecca says, awed. "*Wow.*"

Hadley takes a step back; you can tell he isn't used to being revered as an expert on much of anything. "And you can't keep them in the same field as sheep, because the sheep eat the grass too low and then the cows can't wrap their tongues around it to rip it up." He is visibly enjoying this. "They only have one set of teeth, the bottom." For a girl who never cared about livestock, Rebecca is hanging on his every word.

"They have this ear language," Hadley says, even more animated. "Two ears back is happy, two ears forward is mad. One forward and one back means, 'What's up?'" Hadley laughs. "If you lived here," he says, dropping his voice a little, "if you lived here for real I'd get you a calf." He holds Rebecca with his eyes for a few seconds, and then he turns away.

"I'd like that," Rebecca says. "A calf. I'd call it Sparky."

Hadley, who has been walking in a circle, stops in his tracks. "No kidding," he says, his mouth dropping open. "I had a cow named Sparky as a kid."

He stares at Rebecca with such curiosity she looks down at her hands. "So what are the spots for?" she asks, shy.

"Camouflage."

"Really?" Rebecca traces the side of the cow, a blotch in the shape of a teapot.

"Actually, they never draft cows to the front line. Just bulls." He waits until Rebecca laughs with him. Then he leans closer and whispers something to Rebecca I can't hear.

Whatever it is, it gets Rebecca running. She steals a look at Hadley and then starts to chase him around the field, leaping over some of the rocks and dodging the cows, which have been frightened into standing. "Is this dangerous?" I ask.

"They move quicker than the cows," Joley says. "I wouldn't worry."

It's a game of tag. Hadley overcomes Rebecca—after all, he's got much longer legs. He tosses her into the air. Rebecca, out of breath, tries to pull Hadley's hair, beats her fists against his shoulders. "Put me down!" she yells, laughing. "I said, put me down!"

"He's good with kids," Joley says, finishing his cone.

Rebecca stops fighting Hadley so that he's holding her in the air, his hands caught under her armpits, like a ballerina and her partner. Rebecca's arms go limp and Hadley slowly lowers her down to the ground. Rebecca stops laughing. Hadley turns away from her. He rubs the back of his neck. Then he motions towards me and starts to walk back. "Wait!" Rebecca cries, running after him. Hadley doesn't answer. "Wait for me!"

In the afternoon, when everyone is gone, I spend time walking around this rolling stretch of land and thinking about Oliver. It's remarkably hot out; too hot really, to be outside, but there's even less to do inside the Big House than there is to do out of it. The orchard is boring without Joley around; I haven't seen Rebecca since we've come back from Buttrick's, and I'm not about to spend time with the field hands. So I take off my shoes and walk around the land that borders the lake.

I start to think about Oliver only because my skirt is singing his name. With each step it swishes back and forth, catching in the air like a nursery rhyme: *Ol-i-ver Jones. Ol-i-ver Jones.*

What is the rule, anyway? Can two people change so much in fifteen years that a marriage can be past the point of no return? What is it called in divorce cases—irreconcilable differences. I wouldn't say we have that. Sometimes, it's true, Oliver can look at me and make me think I'm back on the pier at Woods Hole, watching him waist-deep in the water, arms covered in mud, tenderly holding a quahog. Sometimes when I look at Oliver, I can fall into those pale aqua eyes. But the truth is those times are few and far between. The truth is that when I *do* feel like that, I'm actually surprised.

Suddenly I realize Rebecca's standing in front of me. I put my arm through her arm. "You can feel the heat just hanging here, can't you," I say. "It's enough to make you want to go back to California."

She's knotted her T-shirt into a halter top and rolled the sleeves, and she's still got a line of sweat running down her chest and her back. She's braided her hair to get it out of her face, and wrapped it with a dandelion's stem.

"Not much to do here, is there. I was off with Hadley but he's ignoring me today." She shrugs, as if she doesn't really care—of course, I know better. I saw what happened at the ice cream place: Rebecca got too close, and Hadley, respectably, stepped back. She's crazy about Hadley; a summer crush. And like Joley said, he's good with her; brushing her off with an excuse about work hurts much less than saying she's just a kid. Rebecca purses her lips. "He's acting like a big shot with Sam gone."

Sam. "Oh, please," I say, hoping the story of this morning's escapades in the bathroom will cheer up Rebecca.

Rebecca's face lights up. "Did he see you?"

"Of course he saw me."

Rebecca shakes her head and leans closer, staring at me knowingly. "No," she says, "did he *see* you?"

At least I've piqued her interest. "How should I know? And why should I care?"

She goes on to tell me the same old blah-blah story I've heard from Joley already: how Sam is God's gift to business, how he built up this orchard from nothing, how he's the exemplary benchmark of success for the community. I'm sure she can tell I'm not listening. So she tries to grab my attention. "Why do you and Sam hate each other so much? You don't know him well enough for that."

I laugh, but it comes out a snort. "Oh yes I do. Sam and I grew up with these stereotypes, you know?" I tell her about what Newton girls thought of the guys at Minuteman Tech—how absolutely wrapped up they were in their vocational schooling, when we all knew the value of a truly good education. "There's no denying that Sam Hansen is an intelligent man," I tell her, "but don't you think he could do better than *this?*" I gesture with my arm, but when I really start to look at what I'm pointing to I stop. Even I have to admit it is lovely, spattered with the colors of the season. It may not be for me, but that doesn't mean it isn't worth something.

Rebecca starts to pick at the grass. "I don't think that's why you hate Sam. My theory is you hate him because he's so unbelievably happy."

I listen to her go on and on about simpler things in life, and achieving all your goals, and then I raise my eyebrows. "Thank you Dr. Freud." I tell her that I'm not here because of Sam, anyway; I'm here because of Joley.

That's when she catches me off guard: she asks me what we are going to do next. I hem and I haw, telling her that we'll just stay a while until we come to some decisions, and then she rolls up on one elbow. "In other words," she says, "you have absolutely no idea."

I lean towards her. "What is this all about, Rebecca? Do you miss your father?" She is the one thing I haven't really considered when it comes to Oliver and me. Where does she fit in?—half me, half him. "You can tell me if you do," I say. "He *is* your father. It's natural." I try to remain as nonjudgmental as I can, for her sake.

Rebecca looks up at the sky. "I don't miss Daddy," she says. "I don't." Then the tears start to roll down her face. I pull her closer and hold her to me. That's when I remember her the day we left California. She was the one who was sitting in the car. She was the one who had packed a bag. Long before I had realized I was trying to leave, she'd been planning.

At some point when I was growing up I realized that I had no love left for my father. It was as if each time he hit me, or came into my room at night, he'd draw a little of it out of me, like blood.

It didn't hurt to feel nothing for him. I assumed, as I grew up, that he had done this to himself. I *had* to become desensitized; if I had continued to feel as strongly as I had when I was little, I would have surely died that first time he came to my room.

I can tell from Rebecca's face, and even from the temperature of her skin, that she is thinking about what it means to love your father, and whether or not he is worth it. Because once you get to that point, I am not sure you can return.

"Sssh," I say, cradling her head. I'd do anything to keep her from having to get there. I'd go back to Oliver. I'd make myself love him.

In the distance a Jeep drives up. I can just see it, a dot far off by the barn. I see Joley get out of the car; the other person I know must be Sam. Even from this far away, my eyes connect with Sam's. Although I cannot tell what is going through his mind, I find myself trapped, entirely unable to turn away.

52 SAM

For the past two days, I've had a headache. Not a normal headache, either—but one that starts back by my ears and works its way across my eyes, over the bridge of my nose. I've never had a headache this bad, not in twenty-five years. Which makes me believe it's all on account of Jane Jones.

This morning I walked in on her in the shower, and she took it all the wrong way. I had an appointment to get to, and when I'm running late and Joley or Hadley is showering, they don't care much if I come in and do my business. Maybe I'm just not used to having ladies in the house. But anyway, *this* one happens to keep getting underfoot.

Joley and I are on our way back from Boston, where we've had one hell of a successful meeting with a buyer from Purity who renewed our Red Delicious contract. I can't say I much like Regalia—she's fat and always eats more at lunch than I do—but she signed us on again. "I think this is the start of a very long, prosperous relationship for both of us, Sam," she said today over her quiche. She lowered her eyes, giving me this look. It's funny, I started taking Joley along to meetings with the female buyers or supermarket chains because he always turns a head and knows how to lay on the charm. He's got all that social finesse I never was good at. But Regalia has a thing for me. So, being the businessman, I smiled at her and winked. Sometimes I think it's dishonest to do that—but then again, one in a million produce buyers is a woman, and I might as well use what I've got to cut a deal.

Joley's driving. We've just passed the hand-painted sign that welcomes you to Stow when he starts to speak—he's been quiet since we left Boston. "I want to talk to you about my sister, Sam."

"About what?" I say, drumming my fingers on the dashboard. "There's nothing to talk about. You're having a good time with her. Enjoy it."

"Yeah, well, I figure I'd better get in all the time I can before one of you kills the other one."

"You've got it all wrong, Joley. There's nothing going on with us. We're just steering clear of each other."

"What made you get off on the wrong foot?"

"Oil and water don't mix," I tell him, "but that's no reason they can't both sit in the same jar."

Joley sighs. "I'm not going to push you, Sam. I'm sure you've got your own ideas about this. But—for my sake—I wish you'd cut her a little slack."

"There's no problem," I say.

Joley looks at me. "All right."

He pulls into the driveway, and when we get out of the Jeep, we can see Jane and Rebecca in the distance. I catch Jane's eye. It's like we're locked together; neither one of us is about to break away first. That would mean losing. "Are you coming?" Joley asks, heading off in their direction.

"I don't think so," I say, still staring at his sister. "I'm going to start dinner." I swallow hard and turn away, feeling her still staring, boring through my back.

Inside, I hack at zucchini and potatoes, setting them into pots, ready to boil. I quarter two chickens and dip them in flour and then fry them up. I slice up almonds for the vegetables and I shell fresh peas. These are all things I have learned from my mother. I do almost all the cooking here; if I left it to Hadley or Joley we'd be eating Chef Boyardee.

Three-quarters of an hour later, I ring the rusty triangular bell on the porch for dinner. Joley and Jane and Rebecca come in from the east side of the orchard, Hadley comes in from the west. They file upstairs to the bathroom to wash up and then one by one fill in the places around the table. "Dig in," I say, helping myself to a chicken breast.

Joley tells his sister all about Regalia Clippe, a conversation I tune out. After all, I was there. I concentrate on watching Hadley, who's being awfully quiet. Usually at the dinner table you can't get him to shut up long enough to eat. But tonight he's pushing his peas around on his plate, colliding them with the mashed potatoes.

We all go on eating for a while so that the only noise is the scraping of silverware against my mom's old country plates. Joley holds up his drumstick and waves it at me, nodding, his mouth full. When he swallows, he tells me how good it is. "You know, Sam," he says, swallowing, "if the orchard ever folds you could go into gourmet catering."

"I don't call fried chicken gourmet. Besides, it's just food. No reason to make a big deal about it."

"Sure there is," Rebecca says. "*She* doesn't cook this well." She lifts her elbow in the direction of her mother, who puts down her knife and fork and just stares at Rebecca.

"So what did you two do today?" Joley asks. Jane opens her mouth but it's clear that Joley's talking to Rebecca and Hadley. Hadley's face reddens to the top of his neck. *What* is going on here? I try to catch Hadley's eye but he's not looking at anyone. My fork slips out of my fingers, hitting the edge of my plate.

The noise makes Hadley jerk his head up. "We didn't do anything," he says, testy. "All right? I had a lot of stuff I had to get done." He mutters something, and then crunches his napkin into a ball and aims for the garbage pail. He's off by several feet, so he winds up hitting Quinte, the Irish setter. "I've got somewhere I have to go," he says, and then he almost knocks his chair over getting up from the table. He slams the door when he leaves.

"What's his problem?" I say, but nobody seems to know.

The disruption makes everyone sort of quiet again, which is just fine with me. I'm not one for talking through dinner. Then out of the clear blue Joley's sister starts to speak. "Sam," she says, "I was wondering why you don't grow anything but apples."

I exhale slowly through my nose. I've fielded this question at least a million times from dumb, pretty girls who thought this was a good way to act interested in what I do. "Apples take a lot of time and effort," I say, knowing damn well I haven't answered her question.

"But couldn't you make more money if you diversify?"

That headache starts to come back. It's near enough to drive me crazy. "Excuse me," I say to Jane, "but who the hell are you? You come in here and two days later you're telling me how to run things?"

"I wasn't—"

The pain is shooting now, straight down the back of my neck. I start sweating. "If you knew a damn thing about farming maybe I'd listen."

Maybe I've been talking rougher than I should have. She looks up at me and she's practically crying. For a second—just a second—I feel awful. "I don't have to take this," she says, her voice thick and hoarse. "I was just making conversation."

"Sam," Joley says, a warning. But it's too late. Jane stands up and runs outside. What is *with* these people today? First Hadley, now Jane.

It is just the three of us around the table. "Any more chicken?" I say, trying to break the ice.

"I think you overreacted. Maybe you could apologize," Joley says.

I can tell it's going to be two against one, here. I close my eyes to make that headache go away and I see Jane wandering around the orchard, which is not very well lit. She's liable to hurt herself.

What am I thinking? I shake my head hard, getting back my senses. "She's your sister," I tell Joley. "*You* invited her here. She just doesn't belong in a place like this." I sort of smile. "She should be wearing high-heeled shoes and clicking along some marble parlor in L.A."

Rebecca leaps out of her seat. "That's not fair. You don't even know her."

"I know plenty like her," I say, looking right at Rebecca. For a minute I think she's going to cry too. "Okay," I say, "would it make it all right if I went out there and apologized?" I want to do it for my own conscience, but they don't have to know that. I'm not about to lose face in front of Joley, though, so I set my chin and pretend to sigh. I say, "Shit. For a little peace and quiet." I push away from the table heavily. "So much for a happy little family dinner."

Outside the crickets are sounding a symphony. It's a humid night, so all the wildflowers around the house are drooping, exhausted. I hear noise coming from the shed where we garage the tractor and the rototiller, next to the barn. It's a high-pitched mechanical scream and then the sound of something being shattered. I walk in the direction of the noise and turn the corner to find Jane Jones presiding over my box of clay pigeons, the orange ones I used for target shooting. She reaches into the box and grabs a disc, then whips it like a frisbee against the red wall of the barn about twenty feet away. By the time it explodes into splinters and dust, she's got another disc in her hand, ready to go.

I have to give her credit for this: she's got determination. I can see it in the way her whole body goes into the throw, as if she's pretending it's me she's hurtling into the barn. Here I was thinking she was getting into some kind of trouble. She's something else.

I try to keep my footsteps quiet as I walk up to her. "It's more challenging with a gun," I say.

She turns around fast, her eyes adjusting to the dark clearing where I'm standing. When she focuses on me, her face falls. "I didn't know anyone was here." She points to the mess in front of the barn wall. "I'm sorry about that."

I shrug. "They're cheap. I'm glad you didn't get pissed off in the parlor. There's antique china in there."

Jane wrings her hands in front of herself, fidgeting. You'd never guess she was ten years my senior; she looks like a little kid. From what I've seen, she acts like one more often than her own daughter. Maybe I've been too hard on her. "Look," I say. "About what happened at the table. I'm sorry. I've had this headache, and I overreacted." She looks at me strangely, as if she's never seen my face before. "What?" I say, self-conscious. "What is it?"

"I've just never heard you talk without sounding angry," Jane says. "That's all." She walks towards me, swinging her arms at her sides. She is still holding two clay pigeons. Just in case I get out of line? "Tomorrow morning Rebecca and I will check into the closest hotel."

I feel that headache coming back. If she does that, I'll never hear the end of it from Joley. "I told you I was sorry," I say. "What more can I do?"

"You're right. It's your house, your farm, and I shouldn't be here. Joley imposed on you. He shouldn't have asked you to do something like this."

I smirk. "Thank you, I know what 'imposed' means."

Jane throws up her hands. "I didn't mean it that way." She turns in such a way that the light from the barn falls over her face, enough to let me know she's on the verge of crying again. "I don't mean anything the way you take it. It's like every sentence I say goes through your head the reverse of the way I intended it."

I lean against the shed and start to tell her about my father. I tell her how I used to fight with him about how the orchard ought to be run. I tell her how the very minute he moved to Florida, I was digging up trees and replanting them where I thought they should go.

She listens patiently, her back to me. Then she says, "I get your point, Sam." But she doesn't know anything about the way I run my business. And what's worse; she doesn't see it as a business. To her, an orchard is another form of farming. And working with your hands, to a born and bred Newton girl, is sure-fire second-class. I feel at that moment something I haven't felt since I left Tech: shame. Running an apple orchard isn't what people do in the real world. If I was really someone, I'd want to make a lot of money. I'd own more than one suit, and I'd drive a Testerosa, not a tractor.

"No," I say to her, "you don't. I don't give a shit if you think this orchard should grow watermelons and cabbage. Go tell Joley and tell Rebecca and whoever the hell you want. And the day I die if you can convince everyone else, go ahead and replant the place. But don't you ever tell me to my face what I've done so far is wrong." I lean closer to her, so that our faces are inches apart. "It would be like—like me telling you your daughter is no good."

When I say that, she takes a step back, like I've hit her. Her face goes white.

She looks up at me with incredible force—that's the only way I know how to describe it. It's like she could physically move me with the strength of her eyes. And as for me, I look at her, and I really see her for the first time. That's when I see something written all over her face—*Please.*

She opens her mouth to speak, but she can't seem to find her voice. Then she clears her throat. "I wouldn't plant watermelons," she says.

I smile, and then I start to laugh, and that makes her laugh too. "Let's start over. I'm Sam Hansen. And you're . . . ?"

"Jane." She smooths her hair back from her forehead, as if she's concerned about this first impression. "Jane Jones. God, I sound like the most boring person on earth."

"Oh, I doubt it," I say. I hold my hand out to her and feel quite clearly the pattern of her fingerprints when she presses her palm against mine. When we touch, we both get a shock—probably static electricity from moving around on the dusty floor of the shed. We both jump back, equal distance.

The next morning Jane is sitting in the kitchen when I come downstairs. It's early, and this surprises me. "I wanted to make sure I was out of the shower," she says, smiling.

"What have you got planned for today?" I ask, pouring myself a glass of juice. I hold the bottle out to her. "Do you want some?"

Jane shakes her head, pointing to a mug of coffee. "No thanks. I don't know what I'm going to do today. Joley was asleep by the time we got back in last night, so I haven't asked him what the plan is."

After we talked last night, I walked Jane around the grounds of the orchard. It is careful going in the dark, but if you know it as well as I do there's nothing to really be afraid of. I showed her which apples would go directly to Regalia Clippe, which ones would be seconds for the public stand in the fall. We even placed a five-dollar bet on one of Joley's latest grafts; she said it would take, and I said it wouldn't. The tree's past hope, the way I see it—and even Joley can't work miracles all the time. Jane asked me how she was going to get her money if the graft took after she'd left Massachusetts. "I'll mail it," I said, grinning at her. She said I'd forget. "No I won't," I told her. "If I say I'll stay in touch, I'll stay in touch."

On the way back to the Big House, we talked about what everyone else thought must have happened to us. We agreed they probably figured we'd killed each other now, and they were waiting till day to find the bodies. And then, halfway there, a woodchuck crossed our path. It stopped a second to look at us and then leaped down a hole. Jane had never seen one before. She crept up to the hole and stuck her face close, trying to get another glimpse. Most women I know who see a big old ugly woodchuck run in the other direction.

I watch her swirling her coffee in her cup. "I was thinking today I'd take you down to Pickerel Pond. There's this really nice area to go swimming."

"Oh," Jane says, "I'm not much for swimming, but Rebecca would love it. It's hot enough."

"You can say that again." Now, barely seven in the morning, it's at least eighty-five degrees outside. "I was thinking I'd do a little fishing before everyone else gets up." I slide into the seat across from her at the table. "I usually take Quinte, but I think you'd make better company."

"Fishing," Jane says, like she's weighing it in her mind. She looks up at me and smiles. "Sure. I'd like that."

So I take her out to the sheep pen and overturn a mound of soil with a spade. Underneath all this manure there's more worms than I know what to do with. I pick ten long juicy ones and put them in a canning jar. To my surprise, Jane gets down on her hands and knees. She reaches right into the soft earth and pulls out a thick wiggling worm. "Is this a good one?"

"You don't care about touching them?"

"Not really," she says, "but I'm not going to thread your hook."

I run to the shed for my fishing stuff and then we walk down to the shore of Lake Boon. I've got an old wooden rowboat there, one I've had since I was a kid. I keep it turned upside down on the yellow reeds, with the oars underneath. It's green, because that was the color of the primer I used when I was twelve and decided to paint it. Except I never got around to buying the paint.

This is my favorite time of the day at the orchard. The water sings to us as I row into the center of the lake. Jane sits across from me, prim, with her hands in her lap. She's holding the jar of worms.

"It's nice out here," Jane says. Then she shakes her head. "That's an understatement."

"I know it. I come out here almost every Sunday if I get the chance. I like feeling that I'm part of this picture, kind of."

"I must be ruining the harmony, then," Jane says.

I open up the tackle box and take out a hook and a leader. "Not at all. You're just what this place needed." I point to the jar. "Hand me a worm?" Jane unscrews the lid and pulls out a fat worm without a second thought. "You should try catching the first bass." I hand her the fishing rod. "You know how to cast?"

"I think so." I tell her to aim for the lily pads behind me. She stands up precariously, balancing the boat under her feet, and releases the catch on the reel. She whizzes the line over my head; a really good cast, actually. Then she chokes up on the line a little and sits back down. "Now I just wait?"

I nod. "They'll be here soon. Trust me."

I like fishing because it reminds me of Christmas, when you're handed a box and you don't know what's inside. You get a tug on your line and you have no idea what you're going to pull up—bass, sunfish, pickerel, perch. So you reel in, but slowly, because you don't want the excitement to be over too quick. And then there's something thrashing on the end of your hook, scales catching the sun, and it's yours, all yours.

We sit in the calm cradle of the rowboat, letting the sun drip down the necks of our shirts. Jane holds the cork grip of the rod lightly, and I think, please God, don't let her drop it if it she gets a bite. The last thing I want to do is to lose my lucky rod overboard. She leans back against the bow of the boat, balancing her elbows just so. The backs of her legs rest on the seat, supporting the rest of her. "I should have told you this before," I say, "but I hope you know you're welcome to use the phone. If there's someone you need to call in California. Your husband, or whoever."

"Thanks." Jane gives me a perfunctory smile, and rolls the fishing rod around in her palm. If you ask me, she should call that scientist guy. He's probably going out of his mind wondering if she's all right. At least I know that's the way *I* would be if my wife up and left me. But I don't say anything. If I've asked Jane not to interfere in the way I run my life, I'm sure as hell not going to meddle in hers.

Jane asks me when everyone else gets up on Sundays, and I'm about to answer when the tip of the rod jerks down violently. Her eyes fly open, and she grabs tight onto the rod while the bass starts running with the line. "It's strong!" Jane cries, and as she says this the bass leaps arching its back, trying again to make a getaway. "Did you see it! Did you see it?"

I reach over the side of the rowboat and pull the end of the line up. The fish comes out of the water, blue-green. The hook is caught in the corner of its jaw, and still it does not give up without a fight.

"Well," I say, holding up the bass. Its hinged mouth, a perfect round *O*, is translucent. You can see right through to its insides. Its tail flaps back and forth, curving the body into such a half-circle it seems impossible the fish could have a spine. I hold it up on the line in such a way that one filmy green eye stares at me, and the other one at Jane, taking us both in at the same time. "What do you think of your fish?"

She smiles so I can see all her teeth—neat and white and even, like the small rows on Silver Queen corn. "He's delightful," Jane says, poking a finger at the tail. As soon as she touches the fish it thrashes in her direction.

"Delightful," I repeat. "I've heard them called 'huge,' or even 'feisty,' but I can't say as I've ever heard a fisherman talk about a 'delightful' catch." As I talk I run my free hand down the slippery body of the fish. I can't touch it too much because then it'll smell like human when I release it back into the water. I edge the hook back out of its hatched jaw.

"Watch this," I say, and holding the fish over the water, I release it. It floats for a second near the surface of the lake, and then with a mighty whip of its tail it dives so deep we lose track of its movements.

"I like the way you set it free," Jane says. "How come you do that?"

I shrug. "I'd rather catch it again for sport than fry up such a tiny fillet. I only keep the fish if I know I'm going to eat it."

I hold the rod out to her again, but she shakes her head. "You try," Jane says.

So I do, pulling up in rapid succession a sunfish, two small-mouth bass and another large-mouth. I hold each one up into the sun, glorifying the catch, and pointing out to Jane the differences between each. It's only when I cut the last bass free that I realize Jane's not really listening. She's holding her right hand with her left, cradling it in her palm, and squeezing her forefinger. "I'm sorry," she says when she sees I'm looking at her. "I've just got a splinter, that's all."

I take her hand and after holding the cool fish I'm surprised at the heat of her skin. It's a deep splinter, fairly far below the surface of her skin. "I can try to get it out now," I say. "You don't want it to get infected."

She looks up at me, grateful. "You've got a needle in there?" she asks, nodding towards the tackle box.

"I've got clean hooks. That'll do."

I take a brand new hook out of its flimsy plastic wrapper and bend it so that it is straight, like a little arrow. I don't want to hurt her too much, but the point of a hook is constructed to grab onto whatever flesh it catches, so that a fish can't free itself. Jane closes her eyes and turns away, offering her hand. I scrape at the surface of her skin with this needle. When blood comes, I dip her hand into the water to clean it.

"Is it over yet?"

"Almost," I lie. I haven't even come close to the splinter. I dig and dig through the layers of her skin, looking up from time to time to see her wince. Finally I nudge the sliver of wood up, and then using the hook, I push it to an upright position. "Easy now," I whisper, and then I bring my teeth to her forefinger, pulling out the splinter. Holding her hand under the water, I tell her she can look now.

"Do I want to?" Jane says.

Her upper lip is quivering, which makes me feel awful. "I'm sorry it hurt, but at least it's out." She nods bravely, looking just like a little kid. "I guess you never wanted to be a doctor."

Jane shakes her head. She pulls her hand out of the water and looks critically at her finger, assessing the damage. When the pit of skin begins to fill with blood, she closes her eyes. I watch her take her finger and stick it in her mouth, sucking the wound dry. I should have done that, I think. I would have liked to have done that.

53 OLIVER

It takes several seconds to hone in on my faculties of perception. I have never in my life blacked out; I have never in my life awakened in strange environs and not been able to account for my whereabouts. And then, blinking at the fringed curtain of that waitress Mica's apartment, the whole grisly situation starts to come back to me.

Mica herself is sitting cross-legged on the floor, several feet away. At least I remember her name. "Hello," she says shyly, holding out the chain she is making from gum wrappers. "You've given me some scare."

I sit up and to my surprise discover I am wearing nothing but my boxers. I gasp, and pull a woolly brown afghan over myself. "Did anything . . . ?"

"Happen?" Mica says, smiling. "No. You've been entirely faithful to the long-suffering Jane. At least for the time you've been here."

"You know about Jane." I wonder what I've told her.

"She's all you talked about before you passed out for three whole days. I took off your clothes because it's a hundred degrees outside, and I didn't want you to get sunstroke while you were catching up on your beauty sleep." She pushes the gum wrapper chain at me, and, since I know of nothing else to do with it, I hang it around my neck.

"I've got to get to her," I say, trying to stand. But unfortunately I change positions too quickly, and the room starts to spiral. Mica is quickly at my side, pulling my arm around her neck for support.

"Easy," she says. "We've got to get some food into you."

However, Mica is not one for cooking. She picks up a photo album and hands it to me. Inside are take-out menus for everything: pizza, Thai, Chinese, barbequed chicken, health food. "I don't know," I say. "You pick."

Mica studies these. "I think Thai is definitely out, since you've been off solid food for three days. My guess is some hummus and a tofu dip from 'Lettuce Eat.' "

"Sounds wonderful." I prop myself onto my elbows when I feel my body can take the strain. "Mica," I ask, "where have you been sleeping?" If memory does not serve me wrong, this is a one-bedroom apartment with very little extra space.

"Next to you on the futon," she says noncommittally. "Don't worry, Oliver. You're not my type."

"I'm not?"

"You're too—I don't know—*preppy* for me. I like guys a little more BoHo."

"Of course. How stupid of me."

Mica calls the vegetarian restaurant. "Fifteen minutes."

It strikes me that I am indeed starving. I hold my hand to my stomach. "I wonder," I say, "you don't know of any apple orchards around here?"

Mica rolls her eyes. "Oliver, you're in the heart of Boston. The closest I come to an orchard is Quincy Market."

"This place is in Stow. Or Maynard. Somewhere like that."

"Out west. With every other apple orchard in Massachusetts. You're welcome to call information."

So I roll onto my stomach and reach for the phone. "Yes," I say when a rhythmic voice answers, "in Stow. I'm looking for Joley Lipton." The woman informs me she has no one there by that name. Nor in Maynard, nor in Bolton.

"Didn't you say he's working for someone?" Mica says, and I nod. She's paring her toenails with a brass clipper. "What makes you think he would have his own phone listing?"

"It was a stab in the dark, all right?"

She holds her foot out in front of her. "Oh. This is rude, isn't it? I'm sorry. I suppose for all practical purposes you're a stranger. It's just that with you passed out, I've been doing all kinds of things with you in the room. Changing, calisthenics, what have you."

Changing?

"If it were me," she says, "although it's not—I'd drive out to Stow and ask if anyone's heard of him. I mean, Stow isn't Boston. He's liable to have run into a mom-and-pop grocery store or a neighborhood barber, or whatever things they have out in the boonies."

"Oh, Mica." She's hit on it. I have no choice but to canvass that section of Massachusetts and hope for the best. I grab her hand, which is nearby, and kiss it.

"Who says chivalry's dead?" she says. Then the doorbell rings, and she's up to collect the tofu.

It all starts coming back to me: how I hadn't slept since Iowa; how I believed Jane was near me all the time; how much I wanted to tell her. With renewed energy I jump from the futon and collect my clothes, strewn orgiastically around the tiny bedroom. I turn on the television with the remote, automatically set for the mid-day news. I pull on my trousers and zap through the stations until I find an anchorperson with a soothing voice. "Well, Chet," she says, as Mica reapproaches with a vegetable cornucopia, "efforts continue to free the humpback whale tangled in fishing nets off the coast of Gloucester."

"What?" I whisper, sinking to my knees. Mica rushes over to me, afraid no doubt that I will pitch forward into the television set.

"Scientists from the Provincetown Center for Coastal Studies have been working for the past four hours to free Marble, a humpback whale, from a gill net left behind by a fishing boat." The anchor smiles into the camera, behind her a stock photo of a humpback surfacing. "We'll have more on this heroic story on the six o'clock news, when, we hope, Marble will be swimming free."

I grab the remote and flip to a second station, which is reporting with coverage live from Gloucester. According to the commentator, the whale was only recently found, and scientists are now trying to determine the best and safest method to free her. In the background I can see a man I knew when I worked at Woods Hole. "That's Windy McGill."

"Isn't it sad," Mica says, pursing her lips. "I hate to see these whale stories."

"How do you get to Gloucester from here?"

"You *drive*."

"Then you've got to tell me where my car is."

"I thought your priority was getting to Stow."

Jane. I sigh. "Okay. This is the problem. I'm a marine biologist. I know humpback whales probably better than any person in the United States. If I get to Gloucester, I'll be able to rescue that whale. On the other hand, if I get to Stow, I have an outside chance of rescuing my marriage."

"Oliver," Mica says, "you don't need *me* to tell you what's more important."

I pick up the phone and call the center in Provincetown—a number which, after so many years, I can still remember. "This is Oliver Jones. I need directions to the stranded whale, and I need you to wire ahead to Windy and tell him I'm on my way and I'll need two Zodiacs with outboard motors and my own diving suit." The secretary jumps at my command. It is gratifying to know that, over such distance, I can garner respect.

Mica is staring at me. "Isn't this what got you in trouble in the first place?"

"Mica," I say, lacing my shoes, "I don't make the same mistake twice." I lean down and kiss her on the forehead. "I appreciate your generosity and your caretaking. Now I've got to give a little of that kindness back."

"Oliver, don't take this wrong. I mean, I hardly know you. But make sure you don't get all wrapped up in this. Promise me you'll be in Stow, looking for your wife, within twenty-four hours."

I button my shirt and tuck it in, then I rush a brush of Mica's over my hair. "I promise," I tell her. I mean it, too. I'm not losing sight of the bigger picture here, meaning my family. I don't know where they are, and rather than searching for a needle in a haystack, I can use the media coverage to call Jane and Rebecca to come forward. Besides, maybe it will make Jane proud of me. Doing research for my own advancement may not win points with her, but helping a dying animal will get her cheering.

Mica takes me to my car, which is in such a seedy area I am shocked to find it intact with all its hubcaps and accessories. She bequeaths me a map of the north shore of Massachusetts, and a postcard of the Blue Diner with her name and phone number. "Let me know how it works out," she says. "I love happy endings."

54 Jane

I've been with Sam all morning, and I can't ever remember feeling so strange. He teaches me things I've never imagined knowing. If he said the thrill of my life would be doing handsprings across an open field, I'd probably follow his lead.

Which is all very well and good for me, but more than once today I have seen Rebecca staring at me as if she isn't certain I am the same person I was three days ago. In all likelihood I may not be—I have to admit it's been a radical transformation—I'm in much better spirits. I owe her an explanation. Every time I've looked at her today I've seen a reflection of Oliver in her eyes, which makes me feel guilty. Don't get me wrong: we're just friends, Sam and I. We have fun together; surely that's not a crime. After all I am a married woman. I have a daughter to think about.

"Penny for your thoughts," Sam says, looking across the truck at me.

"My thoughts? A penny?" I grin at him. "Ten bucks and you're on."

"Ten bucks? That's robbery."

"That's inflation."

Sam leans his elbow out the open window. "How about I pay for your ice cream?" He is driving us—me, Joley, Rebecca and Hadley—to yet another ice cream stand, en route to the pond where we can go swimming. Joley, Rebecca and Hadley are in the back of the truck, sitting on T-shirts to keep the hot metal from burning their legs, singing at the tops of their lungs.

"I've been thinking of how to explain to Rebecca why all of a sudden we stopped arguing," I say.

"I don't see why it's any of her business."

"That's because you don't have children. I *owe* her an explanation. If I don't give her one, she loses trust in me. If she loses trust in me, she won't listen, and she'll wind up as another fifteen-year-old pregnant teenager smoking crack."

"That's an optimistic way to look at it. Why don't you just tell her you finally succumbed to my charm?" He flashes a smile at me.

"Right. Very funny."

"Tell her the truth. Tell her we had it out last night and called it a truce."

"Is that what we did?"

"In a manner of speaking," Sam says. "Didn't we?"

I stick my head out the window, turning halfway around in the seat. Rebecca spots me and waves vigorously. Then all of a sudden I can see Hadley's face and Joley's, as they slide over from the other side of the flatbed. I turn around and lower myself back inside the cab. "But it's more than that," I say, and I'm not sure I should go on. What if it's all in my head?

We come to a stop sign, and Sam pauses a second longer than he has to. "Jane," he says, "you know why we were fighting so hard, don't you?"

I do, but I don't want to. I look up, and find Sam's eyes on me. "If we didn't like each other," he says, "then there was nothing to be afraid of."

I can feel the temperature in the truck. My forehead starts to perspire. "You know," I say quickly, licking my lips, "I read somewhere that if it's ninety-seven degrees out, but it's seventy percent humidity, it feels like it's a hundred and fifty-five degrees. It was in the *Times*. They had this fancy chart."

Sam looks in my direction and smiles. He relaxes his shoulders and he shifts in his seat so he is that much farther away from me. "Okay," he says, softly. "Okay."

At the ice cream stand, I watch Sam from a distance. He is leaning against a telephone pole, beside Hadley and Joley, pointing to features on an all-terrain bike. Since we have been left alone, Rebecca will not look me in the eye.

I decide to lay it on the line. "Rebecca," I say. "About Sam. What do you think? Really." Rebecca's eyes open wide, as if this is the last topic she expected me to bring up today. "Well, it's pretty obvious that we've patched up our differences, and I imagine you've been wondering about it."

"I don't know him really well. He seems nice enough."

"Nice enough for what?"

I move in front of her so that she is forced to look at me when she speaks. "If you mean, 'Should I screw him?'" she says, "then, if you want to, yes!"

"*Rebecca!*" I grab her arm. "I don't know what's gotten into you here. Sometimes I think you aren't the same kid I brought out East." I shake my head, and when she turns her face up to me I can see it again: Oliver.

I take a deep breath. "I know you think I'm betraying your father."

The truth is: when I'm with Sam, I don't think about Oliver. And I *like* that. It's the first time since we've left California that I've felt really free. On the other hand, I've never really considered what constitutes faithfulness in a marriage. I've never had to. Is it being unfaithful to Oliver if I spend time with a man who makes me forget about him?

"I know that I'm still married to him," I say. "Don't you think that every time I see you in the morning I think about what I've left behind in California? A whole life, Rebecca, I've left my whole life. I've left a man, who, at least in some ways, depends on me. And that's why sometimes I wonder what I'm doing out here, in this godforsaken farm zone with this . . . this . . ." I stop, catching sight of Sam in the distance. He winks at me.

"This what?" Rebecca says, her voice quiet.

"This absolutely incredible man." It just slips out and after it does I know that I am in trouble.

Rebecca takes a few steps away from me, rubbing her chin as if she has been struck. Her back is facing me, and I try to imagine the expression she will have in her eyes when she turns. "So what's going on between you and Sam, anyway?"

I can feel myself blush from the tip of my neck up to my eyebrows. I hold my hands up to my cheeks, trying to stop it from happening. "Nothing," I whisper, upset that she would think such a thing. My own daughter. "Absolutely nothing." *But I've been having some crazy thoughts.*

"I didn't think you two got along."

"Neither did I. I guess compatibility isn't the issue." So, I think. Then what *is?* Joley is at the front of the line, juggling several ice cream cones. "We should head back," I suggest, but I don't make a move to go anywhere.

"You've got the hots for Sam," Rebecca says, matter-of-fact.

"Oh please. I'm a married lady," I say, "remember?" The words come to my lips automatically. Married.

"*Do* you remember?"

"Of course I remember. I've been married to your father for fifteen years. Aren't you supposed to love the person you marry?"

"I don't know," she says. "You tell me."

I narrow my eyes. "Yes, you're supposed to." It remains to be seen, though, whether you can continue to love the person you marry. But that isn't what is at stake, here. "Sam is just a friend," I say emphatically. "My *friend*." If I say it over and over I will start to believe it.

The ponds opens out of nowhere in the middle of a thicket. It is square and sparkling, surrounded on three sides by short sunburned grass and on one side by a makeshift beach. Sam tells me it's a sandy bottom. "It doesn't matter to me," I say cheerfully. "I'm not planning on going in."

"I bet you change your mind," he says.

"I bet she doesn't," Joley says. "I've been trying to get her into the water for twenty years." He lays the ukulele he's been playing on his towel, and strips off his T-shirt. He is wearing faded madras bathing trunks. "I'm coming," he calls to Hadley and Rebecca, who are already waiting at the brink of the water.

I start to arrange the towels neatly on the beach. I do it the way I like best: all towels touching, so that no sand gets through.

"At least come down to the edge of the water with me," Sam says.

I look up just in time to see Hadley doing a nicely executed swan dive from one of the two docks that run into the middle of the pond. "All right." I leave the towels half-arranged. "But just to the edge."

Hadley and Rebecca are standing in the more shallow water. He swims underneath her and puts her feet on his shoulders, and then stands so that she towers like a giant and dives. She surfaces, and slicks her hair back from her face. "Do it again!" she cries.

Before I know it Sam has me standing ankle deep in the water. "It's not so bad, is it?"

It is warmer than I expected. I shake my head. I stare down at the blue-tinted water and this is when I see them.

If I didn't know better I would say my ankles were surrounded by a million squiggling sperm. I nearly jump out of the inch of water

I'm standing in, and Sam pushes me back. "They're just pollywogs. You know. They turn into tadpoles."

"I don't want them near me."

"You don't have a choice. They were here first." Sam lowers his hands to the water. "When we were little we used to take tadpoles home in a bucket. We'd try to feed them lettuce but they always died."

"I'm not one for frogs," I say.

"Just worms?"

"Just worms." I smile.

"Frogs are remarkable, you know," Sam says, taking my hand. "They breathe air *and* water. They breathe through their skin. Experts say that frogs are the missing link in evolution. They say humans came from the seas, and frogs make the transition between water and earth."

"How do you know all this?"

Sam shrugs. "I pick it up here and there. I read a lot." In the background, I hear Rebecca scream. Instinctively my head jerks up, and I find her safe on the floating dock, where Hadley is trying to push her over the edge. Sam watches this, and then turns to me. "It must be incredible being a mother."

I smile. "It's pretty incredible. You find that you have this raw animal instinct. I could pick out Rebecca's scream from any other kid here, I bet." I watch Rebecca gracefully bellyflop off the dock.

Sam lets go of my hand and points to the water. I find that I am standing in it again, this time up to my thighs. I hadn't even noticed we were walking in. I jump a little, but we are so far away from the edge of the beach that there's really nowhere for me to go. "That was a dirty rotten trick," I say.

Sam grins. "I suppose, but it worked."

I can feel him looking right through me, so without glancing up I turn away. "I'm going to finish setting up the towels. You go ahead in."

It doesn't take long to set up six towels, however, so I sit on the corner of one and watch them all horse around in the pond. Hadley and Rebecca are working on finding her center of balance. It is somewhere near her hips; I could have told them that. Rebecca takes a running start in the shallow water towards Hadley, and then he lifts her high into the air, trying to hold her up by her pelvis, and then inevitably one of them breaks and they both collapse into the water. Joley is doing a lazy backfloat, his favorite summer stroke, pursing his lips and spouting a fountain. And Sam is showing off. He runs down the length of one of the wooden docks, springing into the air, tucking his taut, tanned form into a double somersault. He's just like a kid, I think, and then I remember that he *is* a kid.

He pulls himself onto the dock and takes a bow. Everyone, even the lifeguard, claps. Sam dives into the water again and swims the entire length of the pond underwater. He comes towards me on the towel, and shakes his hair out all over me. It feels nice, being wet. "It's no fun in there without you. Come on in, Jane."

I tell him the story about Joley, and how he almost drowned, and how I haven't gone underwater since then. Every now and then when it gets very hot I'll take a dip into a pool, or let the ocean run over my ankles. But since Joley, I will not—*cannot*—go beneath the surface. I won't risk the consequences.

Sam stands up and cups his hands around his mouth. "Hey Joley!" he yells. "Do you know you're the reason she won't go in?"

Rebecca and Hadley are on the dock, sunning themselves. I wonder how they can possibly be comfortable on the hard wood, without a towel or a T-shirt under their heads. I see them partially obscured through Sam's legs, but when he sits back down to dry off I have a clear view of my daughter. She is so thin her ribs are raised against the red fabric of her bathing suit. Her feet point sideways, a hereditary trait. And her hand, on the dock, smoothly covers Hadley's.

"Sam," I say, pointing this out. "Is there something going on I should know about?"

"No. Rebecca's just a little kid. And Hadley's no fool. Look at them—they're fast asleep. They probably don't even know they're doing that."

I could swear I see Rebecca's eyes slit open then, slick and green, but maybe I am mistaken.

I forget all about this and sit on the edge of the beach, vicariously swimming through Sam. He has me call out a stroke, and then he does it. Midway I'll call out another stroke, and he'll switch.

When he looks like he's having too easy a time of it, I call out the butterfly. I watch his arms crest out of the water, and his torso emerge, his mouth round and gasping for air.

When lunch is over, Sam dives into the water, and I think this means he's forgotten about me. But after he gets wet, he walks back out to the beach. "You made me a promise," he says. "After lunch, you said."

"Oh, Sam, you're not going to make me do this."

"Do you trust me?"

"What does that have to do with it?" I say, starting to fight him.

"Do you?"

I am forced to look up at him. I would walk through coals, I would dance in fire. "Yes," I say.

"Good!" Sam scoops me into his arms, as if he is going to carry me over a threshold.

I am so fascinated at first with the feel of his skin against mine that I do not pay attention to where we are going. Up until now only our hands have brushed, but now, all at once, I can feel his arms, his chest, his neck, his fingers. With the exception of Oliver, I have never been this close to a man. Sam takes long, high steps towards the water. *I am losing control*, I think. I have to get away from him. "Sam," I say. "*Sam*. I can't," I say. I start panicking: I will drown. I will die. In another man's arms.

He stops so abruptly and speaks so casually I forget for a moment where we are; what we are doing. "Can you swim?"

"Well, yes," I admit, getting ready to explain. Well yes, *but*. Sam's feet hit the water. "No!" I shout.

But he will not stop. He clutches me tighter and moves steadily. The water reaches my toes. I stop kicking when the water begins to splash up in my face.

What I see in those last few moments is my brother, flailing in the tide at Plum Island, caught in a dragging undertow. "Don't do this to me," I whisper.

Somewhere, as if it is happening across a long distance, I hear Sam telling me not to worry. He tells me I can go back if I say the word. He tells me he will not let go. And then I feel this heavy water pressing in around me, changing the shape of my body. At the last minute I hear Sam's voice. "It's me," he says, "I'm not going to let anything happen." He fills my lungs with those words and I go under.

55 JOLEY

When Jane and I were very small, before the swimming accident at Plum Island, we used to build cities in the sand. Jane was the engineer; I was the slave labor. We fashioned pagodas and English castles. She'd form the furrows and I'd come after her with a bucket of ocean water. "The waterfall," I'd announce. "Construction of the waterfall ready to begin!" Jane did the honors, pouring the water in for the moat, or digging rivulets that ran right into the ocean, a permanent source. We drew windows with light pieces of driftwood, and we edged gardens made of stones and shells. Once we made a fortress so big that I could hide inside and toss tight-lipped mussels at people walking by. Even after we were finished playing, we left our buildings standing. We swam in the waves and we bodysurfed, keeping an eye on the slow destruction of our handiwork.

This is what runs through my mind, like a grainy home movie, as Sam lifts my sister and brings her into the pond. This, and how slowly things change, and how malleable are boundaries. He picks her up and she is fighting, like we all expected.

I may be the only person in this world who understands what Jane needs. And perhaps I don't even know the half of it. I have seen her cut and bleeding on the inside. It is me she always turns to, but I am not always the one who can help.

Jane stops kicking and resigns herself to the fact that she is going underwater. Sam says something to her. It's there in her eyes, too, whether or not she will choose to admit it to herself.

I learned a doctrine long ago from an ancient Muslim in

Marrakesh: in this world, there's only one person with whom you are meant to connect. This is a God-woven thread. You cannot change it; you cannot fight it. The person is not necessarily your wife or your husband, your long-term lover. It may not even be a good friend. In many cases it is not someone with whom you spend the rest of your life. I would hazard a guess that ninety percent of all people never find the other person. But those lucky few, those very lucky few, are given the chance to grab the brass ring.

I have believed in Jane for so long, and I have loved her so. I could never find anyone that measured up to her, which is why I've kept from marrying. What is the point of love unless I can have the ideal?

Take her, *I find myself whispering to my friend Sam. The water closes in over their heads. I tell myself I am the lucky one, to have given Jane away twice. I wonder why, this time, it hurts so much more.*

56 SAM

And then we burst through the surface of the water, gasping, and I'm still holding Jane tight. "Oh!" she cries. "This is so wonderful!" She looks at me, blinking water from her eyes. Her hair is sticking up in the back; her T-shirt is plastered to her body. She tentatively takes her right arm away from around my neck; then her left arm, and just like that she's treading water. "I can do it," she says, and she dives under the water again, coming up about eight feet away.

Some of the people on the shore are clapping, having watched the whole ordeal. I wave to them while Jane tries out her sea legs. I follow her around—just in case—while she goes through all the antics a kid would the first day of summer at the beach. At this rate, I think, she'll be doing a back flip off the dock by the end of the afternoon. She tells me she really likes swimming underwater the best, then jacknifes to touch the bottom.

I go under, too. She's got her eyes wide open, trying to see through the murky blue dye they've added here for health reasons. Basically, it keeps you from seeing anything farther away than five inches. I lean in close to Jane, letting her hair swim around my head like a mermaid's. God, I'm close enough to kiss her. Her skin is translucent, nightmare blue. But then there is a flood of bubbles between us–I think I hear the muffled, deaf-man's sound of Jane saying my name–and the moment's gone by.

I've fallen asleep on the towels, but I drift in and out of consciousness enough to know that Jane and Rebecca are whispering about Hadley. In spite of what I've said to Jane about Hadley's good intentions, she doesn't believe me. She keeps telling Rebecca he's up to no good, and that she's too young. I'm tired and sun-dazed, but I try to do the calculations in my head. There are ten years between Hadley and Rebecca. There are ten years between Jane and me.

"I'm fifteen," Rebecca whispers. "I'm not a kid."

"You're a kid."

"How old were you when you started to go out with Daddy?"

I want to hear this. I open my left eye a slit. "It was different then," Jane says. Well, isn't that something, I think. The old proverbial apple doesn't fall too far from the tree. I try to imagine Jane at fifteen, but it's hard. First off, I know she didn't look anything like Rebecca, so that's that. Second, when she was fifteen is ten years earlier than when I was fifteen. She lived through the early Beatles and civil rights. I watched the soldiers come back from Vietnam. She was in fourth grade before I was even born.

Rebecca's voice starts to get louder. I wonder if Hadley is asleep, or if he's faking it too. "You can't just keep yourself from falling for a person. You can't turn off your emotions like a faucet."

"Oh," Jane says. "You're an expert?"

I consider sitting up here, before somebody gets hurt. But I wait until Jane finishes talking. "You can steer yourself away from the wrong people. I'm just warning you before it's entirely too late."

I make a big act of stretching and yawning before I sit up. I rub my eyes with my fists. "So," I say, grinning from Rebecca to Jane, "what did I miss?"

"Nothing." Rebecca stands up to take a walk. "I'm going somewhere."

Jane calls after her. "Don't worry about her," I say. "She can't go all that far without the keys to the truck." I reach lazily for her hand, the one with the splinter from this morning. "How's your war injury?"

Jane laughs. "I think I'll live."

"The rowboat's back at the dock. We can take it out, if you're up for a little more fishing."

Pickerel Pond is glacial, formed by a massive chunk of ice that carved the valley. It's bordered by two orchards, competitors, and the fertilizer they use has run into the lake, making lily pads spring up all over the place. In about ten more years, they'll choke the pond. For right now, though, they're the best bets for fishing. I hand Jane the fishing rod. "Ladies first."

Jane picks out a shiny Mepps spinner and threads it on the end of the line. I never did ask her how she knows about fishing, but I'd assume it has to do with her husband, and his interest in the ocean. And right now, I don't much feel like bringing him up. She casts and gets tangled in a fallen log, and has to tug to free the line. "I'm sorry," she says, reeling in. She casts again, a good one, landing just where I would have placed it in the dark shadow of a cluster of lily pads.

"Are you mad at me for taking you swimming?" I ask.

"No. I should have done that a long time ago." A cormorant cries, and a flock of starlings, frightened by the noise, dart out of a willow tree. Jane reels in and casts again, the same spot.

"I was hoping we could talk," I say. "Even though I'm not one for talking much." I stare over the edge of the rowboat to a rock several feet ahead that rises out of the water with such pride you'd think it was a tiny mountain. "I wanted to bring up what we were discussing on the way over here."

"Boston radio DJs?"

"Not quite." I look up at her, she's smiling. "This isn't real easy, you know."

"We don't have to talk. Why ruin a good thing?"

We both stare at the purpled weeds that have swallowed the gold hook. We stare as if we are expecting some miracle to happen. "Look," I say.

Jane interrupts me. "Don't. Please. I've got a home to go back to." She looks at me for only a second, then turns away. "I've got Oliver's daughter."

"She's your daughter too."

"Sam, I like you. I really do. But that's where it ends. I'm sorry if I gave you the wrong idea."

"The wrong idea," I say, getting my guard up. "What did you think I was talking about anyway?"

A wave, coming out of nowhere, tenderly swings the boat. "Sam," she says, her voice cracking.

I don't know what she has planned to say, because at that moment her line begins to run back and forth in front of the lily pads and underneath us. "It's a sunfish," I say, forgetting everything in the thrill.

"What do you think of that?" Jane says, swinging the rod in my direction so that I can release the fish. "I'm two for two."

"You're luckier than I am, even on a good day. I should take you out with me more often." I don't look at her when I say this; I smooth my free hand over the spiky scales of the sunfish until it stays limp on the hook. Then I quickly pull up and out and hold it over the edge of the rowboat, watching it leave faster than my eye can follow.

Jane leans against the bow of the boat, watching me. I don't think she's noticed that fish at all. "You don't want to get involved with me, Sam. Everything is going so well for you now, and I'd only be trouble." She looks down, twisting her wedding band around her finger. "I don't know what I want. Please don't push me, because I don't know how strong I can be. I can't even tell you what I'm going to do tomorrow."

I move closer. "Who's asking for tomorrow? All I wanted was today."

She pushes me off with her hands. "I'm an old lady."

"Yeah," I say, "and I'm the Pope."

Jane is still holding me at bay. Inches. "Is it adultery if you just kiss?" she whispers. She presses her lips against mine.

Oh, God, I think, so this is what it can be like. She tastes of sassafras and cinnamon. I move my tongue between her lips, over the neat barricade of her teeth. She opens her eyes then, and she smiles. My mouth, on hers, smiles too. "You look different up close." When she blinks, her eyelashes brush against my cheek.

I press my palms against the back of her head and her shoulders. I tear my mouth away from hers, gulping in the stale air of the lily pond, and fall to my knees in front of her. I've forgotten we're in a boat, and it pitches from side to side, so that we both have to keel ourselves. I kiss her along the line from her ear to her neck and I move one hand from her back to her breast. Jane loosens her arms from around my neck and grabs onto the gunwale of the rowboat. "No," she says, "you have to stop."

I sit back obediently on the low rowboat seat, watching the ripples we've made in the pond. We are left staring at each other, flushed, with all that has happened hovering in between. "You just say the word," I murmur, breathless, and I lightly let go.

57 OLIVER

Windy meets me on the shore of the weathered little beach at Gloucester. He hands me a neoprene wet suit and a yellow Helly-Hansen cap. Although he is a garrulous man by nature, in the midst of this throng of television and radio correspondents, he says nothing. He waits until I have stepped into the fifteen-foot inflatable Zodiac, until he has revved the outboard, and only then does he smile at me and say, "Who the hell would have expected Oliver Jones to be *my* guardian fucking angel?"

Windy McGill and I worked together at Woods Hole before it was fashionable to be involved in the cause of whales. We were the two gofers for the prestigious scientists; we were expected to fit in our own doctoral research around the time spent analyzing data or getting coffee for these other biologists. We discovered quite by accident that we had both been graduated from Harvard the same year; that we were both researching tidal communities for our doctorates; that we had been born a day apart at the same Boston hospital. It almost came as no surprise that our research turned in the same direction: towards humpbacks. Of course we've taken different tacks. Windy steers clear of whale songs; he's worked on different methods of identification of humpbacks. At this point, he's credited for the Provincetown research that is used to catalog entire generations of whales.

Windy pulls a bottle out of his pocket—cough medicine—and offers me a swig. I shake my head, and lean back against the bubbled bow of the little boat. Zodiacs tip at the drop of a hat, but I manage to strip and get the wet suit over my body. Windy watches me out of the corner of his eye. "Getting a little thick around the middle, Oliver?" he says, patting his own ribs. "Goddamned cushy California jobs."

"Fuck you," I say good-naturedly. "Tell me about this whale."

"Her name is Marble. White markings on her neck and her fluke. Three years old. Got herself all tangled up in a gill net some asshole left behind." He squints, and adjusts the rudder to the left. "I don't know, Oliver. It took us two days just to *find* her out here. She's testy and she's tired, and I don't know how much longer she'll hold on. I'll tell you this," he says, "I'm glad you're here. If I'd known you were back in Massachusetts, I would've called you in a minute."

"Bullshit. You hate it when I steal your thunder."

Windy and I discuss our intended course of action. The most pressing problem is knowing where exactly the gill net has become entangled on the whale. Windy's primary observation—"around the jaw"—isn't precise enough. Once this has been determined, it will be much easier to cut away the net. The assessment, however, is the most dangerous aspect of a whale rescue: one slap of a fluke or a fin is deadly. Last year, in northern California, a colleague was killed when he dove beneath a whale to determine the points of entanglement.

As we get farther away from the Massachusetts shoreline, I begin to feel the prickling to which I am accustomed; the heady excitement of the unexpected. Few humans have seen it, the look in the eyes of a beached whale one has redirected towards the black ocean. Few humans understand that relief transcends verbal communication; that gratitude is not limited to our genus and species.

I spot the second Zodiac before Windy and direct him towards it. Four students are crowded into the little raft, along with Burt Samuels, a biologist who is getting too old for this. Twenty years ago, this man would command us to scrub sea lion shit from decaying study tanks and we would jump at his beck and call. And now we are defining the pace.

Marble rolls miserably on her side, feebly fanning the water with her dorsal fin. One of the students calls out to Windy—apparently three whales have been hovering nearby, waiting to learn the fate of Marble. One circles closer and sidles up to Marble, who rolls onto her belly. The second whale disappears beneath the water, unfurling the edges of its fluke. Gracefully, gently, it strokes Marble's back with its tail. It caresses her several times, and then sinks and vanishes.

"I'm going in," I say, pulling a mask over my face. We stop alongside the second Zodiac, which is slightly larger and which has an oxygen tank, ready to go. I adjust the harness and check my gauges, and then with the help of one of the students, I sit on the edge of the inflatable boat. "On three." The oxygen mists against my skin. I look out through the mask, that familiar perspective of being on the inside of a fishbowl. One. Two. Three.

The rush and light of the world sizzles and then smoothes underwater. I adjust to breathing below the surface of the water; and then I blink and concentrate on finding the green gill net tangled about this massive wall of whale. I hear Marble moving, pendulous, creating unnatural currents. She sees me out of the corner of her eye, and she opens her mouth, creating a rush of seaweed and plankton from which I have to kick away.

I circle her tail first. I move quickly and steadfastly, noting mentally where the net is tangled (right fin, clear of the fluke). I hold my breath when I swim beneath her, praying to a God I am not sure I believe in. She is over thirty feet long, and she weighs well over fifty thousand pounds. *Do not dive,* I whisper. *For God's sake, Marble, do not dive.*

I lie beneath her on my back, floating motionless. I know that I should get out of the way as quickly as possible, but what a view. It makes you hold your breath, such beauty. Right there, the creamy white of her belly, nicked with scars and barnacles and grooved at the jaw like a zinc sinkboard.

What I would give to be one of them. For a little while, I could trade in my legs for a massive form, a mighty tail. I could run with them along the mountains of the ocean, calling out, understanding. I could sing in the quiet of night with absolute certainty that there would be someone waiting to hear me. I could find her; I could mate for life.

With three sharp kicks of my fins I swim up to Marble. Keeping my distance, I mark where the gill net has tangled in her mouth, caught no doubt across the baleen. I do not think we will be able to cut it entirely without compromising our own safety. Most likely we will have to rip the net so that she is at least free, and then Marble will have to adapt. Whales have an incredible propensity for adaptation. Think how many have spent years living with broken harpoons in their thick skin.

When I surface I am pulled into the second Zodiac by two young marine biology students. I roll onto my stomach on the floor of the boat, which shivers like Jell-O with every twitch of Marble's body. I pull the mask off, unhook the harness with the tank. "It's tangled around her right fin and pretty much woven through her baleen," I say. Then I notice the television camera looking down at me. "What the hell is this?"

"It's okay, Oliver," Windy says, "Anne's from the Center. She's videotaping for our files."

I sit up, panting. I watch the lens zoom closer. "Do you mind?" Still dripping, I crawl into Windy's Zodiac. I instruct the students in the other boat to start hanging buoys around the whale in any manner they can—looping, hooking, anything, just so it doesn't hurt her anymore. The idea here is to tire her out, keep her floating at the surface so that we have a chance to cut away the net. Windy and I rope a few large sailing buoys around Marble's tail.

"Okay," I say, surveying the whale, now edged in pink floating balls like a decorated Christmas tree. "I want you to get the hell out of the way." I say this expressly to Samuels, although I mean everyone in his boat. One of the students backs the second Zodiac several hundred feet away, leaving Windy and me alone alongside Marble.

I lean out of the boat, an arm's length away from the soft surface of Marble's skin. At this point she is so exhausted she doesn't try to fight as I snip at the net with a grappling hook, leaving entire chunks of it still tangled in her baleen. "You need to get closer to her," I say, as we approach her fin. "I can't reach the net."

"I can't get any closer without going right over her."

"Then go over her. Just watch your engine."

Windy and I argue this point, but in the long run he does move the tiny craft over the tip of Marble's fin. I am confident that at this point she is tired enough to let us go about our business. I lean out of the boat and try to unravel the gill net.

Suddenly I am pitched backward. Marble exhales through her blowhole, a fetid combination of stale water and algae, and whacks the edge of the boat with her fin. She hits us twice so forcefully that the Zodiac rises and pitches, on the verge of overturning. "Fuck," Windy cries, holding onto the rubber handles on the inside of the boat. The students in the other Zodiac begin to scream, and I hear it quite clearly, as if their voices have been attached to a speaker in our boat. Then I realize our Zodiac has been thrown into the air. I am tossed onto my back, on top of Windy, who is lying face down in the boat. It is purely by chance that the inflatable raft landed face up, rather than face down, in the freezing depths of this ocean, in the nether region of a whale. "Get off me," Windy says. He sits up gently and rubs his arm. "I told you we shouldn't go over her."

"Is the engine all right?"

"Screw the engine. Are *you* all right?"

I grin as he takes inventory of his limbs. "I'm better than you," I say.

"You are not."

"Always was."

"Bullshit," Windy says. He fiddles with the Evinrude and starts it again. "Where do you want to go?"

This time, Windy approaches from the back of the whale, sneaking up between the fin and the lower half of the body. After several passes with the grappling hook Marble is free. Windy and I pass around the perimeter of the whale one last time, unhooking the buoys. Then we rev the boat's engine backward, floating several hundred feet north of the whale. It takes Marble several minutes to realize she is unencumbered, and then finally she sinks several feet below the surface of the water and swims off. About a quarter mile away, she is joined by a small group of whales. As they are leaving, Marble arches and dives, holding up the underside of her fluke and slapping it against the water with such force that we are all caught in the spray.

Windy and I watch Marble swim away into the swirling eddies of Stellwagen Bank. "Christ, that's beautiful," he says, and I put my hand on his shoulder.

"I'm only going to say this once," he says, smiling, "so you'd better listen up. I want to thank you, Oliver. I couldn't have done it without you."

"Sure you could have."

"You're right. It just wouldn't have been as much fun." He laughs and guns the engine toward the shore. "You're a crazy son of a bitch. I would have taken a dive to check the location of the net, but I sure as hell wouldn't have taken a nap under the belly of a twenty-five-ton whale."

"Yes you would," I say. "When an opportunity like that presents itself, you don't fight it."

"You're still crazy."

"You're jealous. You wish *you* could fight off the paparazzi."

Windy rubs his forehead with his hand. "Christ. All the reporters. I forgot. How come nobody gives a damn about a whale until it's in trouble, and then it becomes a national event?"

I smile. "I don't mind talking to the networks."

"Since when?"

"Since I'm trying to find Jane." I don't look at Windy when I say this. "Jane left me. She took my kid and she left. I'm under the impression she's in Massachusetts, but I don't know where for sure. So I figure if I make myself into a media hero, I can ask her back over the nightly news."

"Jane left you? Jane *left* you?" He cuts the engine so that we are sitting in the middle of the Atlantic, the other Zodiac speeding off ahead of us. "I'm sorry you came here at all. You should have been looking for her."

"You didn't ask me," I remind him. "I invited myself."

"Is there anything I can do? You know you're welcome to stay with me as long as you want."

"Thanks, but no thanks. The only thing you can do for me right now is get me back to all those cameras and microphones." The boat rocks back and forth, tossed by a passing wave. "I've got to get her back, you know," I say, more to myself than to Windy.

"You will," he says.

When we come closer to shore Windy lifts up the engine and lets us drift in with the tide. The crowd of newspeople runs down to the edge of the beach. "Dr. Jones," they call. "Dr. Jones!"

I have heard that sound so many times; the pitch of twenty, thirty voices singing my name. I can feel the old college rush of adrenaline when I consciously register that it is me they are all waiting to meet. I used to hear that marvelous sound and think that this was my ticket to the top. Then I would go home and tell Jane, and she would ask all the right questions: How many reporters were there? Did you talk long? Will it be on the news? Were any of them pretty?

None like you, Jane.

I step off the boat seconds before Windy, who walks me up the beach with his arm around my shoulders. "Ladies and gentlemen," he says, interrupted briefly by a hacking cough, "I'd like to introduce Dr. Oliver Jones, affiliated with the San Diego Center for Coastal Studies. Dr. Jones is singularly responsible for the rescue of Marble, the humpback that has been entangled in fishing nets for several days."

It comes in a rush, the push of the microphones and the incoherent babble of twenty different questions being asked at once. I hold up my hands and take a deep breath. "I'll be happy to answer," I say quietly, knowing well that first impressions last the longest, "but you need to speak one at a time."

I point to a young black man in a yellow rain slicker. "Dr. Jones, can you describe the procedure used to disentangle the whale?" As I start to answer, I see Windy pass behind the throng of reporters. He signals an O.K. sign to me. He takes his cough syrup from his pocket and makes his way towards the group of students who were in the other Zodiac.

I tell them where the net was caught. I tell them we used a grappling hook to cut it away. I tell them about the whale that came up to Marble and stroked her gently, and I let them know such tenderness is often exhibited among humpbacks. I tell them everything they want to know and then finally someone asks the question I have been waiting to hear.

"Dr. Jones," the man says, "was this a case of being in the right place at the right time? Or did you come here expressly to help the whale?"

"I didn't know about the whale until I heard of its plight through the efforts of you good folks. I'm in Massachusetts on a different sort of rescue mission. I have been traveling across the country looking for my wife Jane and my daughter Rebecca. I have reason to believe that they are in Massachusetts; unfortunately, it is a very big state and I don't know where. If you'll indulge me, I was hoping you'd allow me to send a message to them."

I pause long enough to let the cameras start rolling again. I clear my throat and look as honestly as one can into the blind eye of a TV camera. "Jane," I say, and I realize that it comes out sounding like a question. "I need you. I hope you can see this, and I hope you and Rebecca are all right. I can't stand being without you. I don't blame you if you don't believe me, but I came to save this whale because I knew you'd hear about it on the news and I wanted you to see me. I wanted you to remember how it used to be—we postponed our honeymoon because of a whale, don't you remember that? Don't you remember how we cheered and hugged each other when we saw it swimming again, miles off the coast? Well, I saved a whale today. And I want you to know it wasn't any fun without you. If you're watching this, I hope you'll let me know where you are. Call the Provincetown Center for Coastal Studies—they'll know how to get in touch with me."

A reporter interrupts. "Do you have a picture?"

I nod and pull my wallet out of my pocket. I open to a photo taken of Jane and Rebecca less than a year ago. "Can you get this?" I hold it up towards the cameras. "If anyone out there has seen my wife, or this little girl, please call in." I stare at the grey cataract eyes of the television cameras. Jane's eyes are grey too, I think, surprised that I can still picture them so vividly. "I love you," I say. "I don't care if the whole world knows."

58 JANE

For a long time I watch the different digits materialize on the face of the clock beside the bed. I wait until it says 1:23, and then I stand up and walk around this borrowed bedroom. There's no moon tonight, so there is no natural light. It is only through the practice of several nights that I do not bump into the dresser, the post of the bed, the rocking chair, as I make my way out the door.

I hold my breath as I walk down the hall. When I pass Rebecca's bedroom, I press my ear against the door and I listen to her steady, even breathing. Satisfied by this small thing, I amass enough courage to walk seven steps farther down the hallway, to his room.

Having practiced for twenty minutes on the doorknob of my own bedroom, I find it easy to let myself inside without making a sound. When I open the door, a slice of light from the hall spills onto the floor of his room, illuminating a runway that leads to the foot of the bed. From where I stand, I can see the tangled sheets and blankets.

I take a deep breath and I sit on the edge of the mattress but all I hear is the sound of my own throat pounding. "I know you're awake," I say. "I know you can't sleep either." *Jane,* I tell myself, *you are not leaving until you say what you've planned to say.* "I've never been with anyone but Oliver, my whole life," I say, turning the words over and over in my mouth. "I've never even kissed anyone but him. Really kissed. Well, you know, except for this afternoon." I spread my fingers out in front of me, wondering if there is something there for me to touch. "I'm not saying that today was your fault. I'm not saying there's anyone to blame. I'm just telling you I don't know if I'm any good at this." I wonder why there is no response. What if he hasn't been thinking these things at all? "Are you awake?" I ask, leaning into the night, and then the air closes in from behind me.

It envelopes me and wraps itself so tight that I start to scream, until I feel the hand press against my lips and I try to bite it but that's no use, and it pushes me down against the bed, rolling me onto my back and pinning me by my shoulders and this entire time I am trying to scream, and then my eyes clear and inches away from me is Sam.

He relaxes his hold on my mouth. "What are you doing?" I whisper, hoarse. "Why aren't you in bed?"

"I was in the bathroom. I stopped there on the way to *your* room."

"You did?" I sit up on the edge of the bed, and he is still holding my hands. Our fingers rest, entwined, on top of my leg.

"And by the way," Sam says, "I think you *are* very good at this."

I look down at my lap. "Oh, how much did you hear?"

"All of it. I was waiting at the door, listening. You can't get mad at me for eavesdropping, either, because you thought I was over there." He points to the lump of blankets and pillows that have been balled into the center of the bed. Then he takes one of my hands and turns it over in his own, rubbing the warm skin of my palm with his thumb. "So what are you doing in my room?" He leans close.

I sink down into his pillows. "I'm waiting for the guilt. I figure if the guilt comes, then I can punish myself and feel better. I keep waiting, you know, and I think about you, but no matter what I don't feel guilty. So then I start to believe that I'm not the person I thought I was at all. And *then* I figure if I'm awful, I don't deserve to be thinking about you." I sigh. "You must think I'm crazy."

Sam laughs. "Want to know why I was headed to your room? To talk about marriage. Honest to God, I was. I wanted you to know that you were driving me nuts, because here I was thinking about things that I shouldn't be, knowing you've got a family and all. And the worst part of it is: I believe in marriage. I haven't gotten married because I haven't found the right woman. My whole life I've been waiting for something to just click, you know. And tonight I was lying here, thinking about what you might have looked like the day you got hitched to Oliver Jones, and it all just connected for me. Don't you get it? He's taken the woman that I'm supposed to marry."

"When I got married, you were the same age as Rebecca. You were just a kid."

Sam lies down on his side so that he is facing me. He is wearing a T-shirt and polka-dotted boxer shorts, and when he sees me looking at them he reaches for a sheet and wraps it around his hips. "I'm not a kid now," he says.

He reaches his hand towards my face, and traces the length of my cheek and chin with his finger. Then he grabs my hand and holds it to his own cheek. He runs it over the coarse field of stubble, over the break of his jawbone and the soft, dry line of his lips. Then he lets go.

But I don't pull my hand away. I keep my fingers against his mouth as it opens to kiss them. I run them lightly over Sam's eyelids, feeling his eyes moving wild behind. I comb over his lashes and down the bridge of his nose. I explore him as if I have never seen anything of the kind.

He doesn't move as I slide the palms of my hands over his shoulders and his arms, over the indentation where his muscles join, into the hollow of his elbow. He lets me trace the sinews of his strong forearms, turn his hands over in my own, feel for the calluses and cuts. He helps me pull his shirt over his head and when I throw it, it lands on the night table.

If I keep it like this, like an exploration, then I have nothing to be afraid of. It is only if I move to a different level, to intimacy, that I will have to worry. Sex has never been mystical for me. The earth doesn't move, and I don't hear angels, or bells, or all those other things. I am always a little too self-conscious. With skeletons such as mine in the closet, I never expected making love to be magic. The way I saw it, I *had* done something extraordinary: I had pushed the worst memories out of my mind. The first time was the hardest for me, and having hurdled that with Oliver, I never expected to have to face that problem again.

But when I feel Sam wrap his arms around my waist, and gently run his fingers over my ribs; when I feel him already hard, pushing against my thigh, I start to cry.

"What is it? What's the matter?" Sam pulls me against him. "Did I do something?"

"No." I try to catch my breath. I cannot tell him. I haven't told anyone. But suddenly I don't want to carry it around anymore, like Atlas's weight. "When I was little," I hear myself murmur against his skin. My voice sounds foreign, like I am listening, again, from that far corner, but as I speak I seem to be coming closer.

Sam holds me at arm's distance then, and I witness the most amazing thing. He is staring at me, puzzled, waiting for me to tell him about my father. But all I have to do is raise my eyes to his, and look at him, really look at him. And I realize from his gaze that he isn't waiting for an explanation anymore. "I know," he says then, sounding surprised at his own words. "I know about your father. I don't know why, but just then I could tell what you were going to say." He swallows hard.

"How?" My mouth forms the word but there is no sound.

"I—I don't know how to explain it," Sam says. "I can see it in you." Then he winces, and draws back, as if he has been stricken. "You were just a kid," he whispers.

He holds me tight, and I hold him back. He is shivering, having found pieces of me that have been missing, having found parts of himself he didn't know existed. The whole time, I cry like I have never cried before; tears I did not cry when I was nine and Daddy came into my room, tears I did not cry at my father's funeral. Sam unbuttons the silk nightgown I am wearing, and slides it off my shoulders. He guides my hands to inch off his shorts. Our skin is iridescent in the dark. Sam reaches his hand between my legs. I cover his hand with my own; I urge him. He slips one finger inside me, moist and blossoming, and all the while he is watching my face. *Is this all right?* Just like that, he has found my center. Sam kisses away my tears, and then he kisses me. Like salt, I can taste my pain, my shame, on his lips.

59 SAM

She is so beautiful, lying here on my bed. And so sad. She keeps trying to turn her face, to hide in the pillow. But I can't let her do that, not knowing what I now know. I am taking Jane with me every step of the way.

I close my eyes and kiss her neck, her breasts, the curve of her hip. I breathe lightly inside her thighs, knowing she can feel it. That is when she takes my hand, guides me inside her. I watch her face the entire time. I ask her if this is all right. But she holds my wrist, insisting, and so I go as tenderly as I can. Inside is hot, pulsing. I can feel myself getting harder; I rub against her leg. When I think I am going to lose control I pull away, and run my tongue over her nipples. Her eyes are open, but she isn't looking at anything. She does not make any noise. Sometimes I think she is forgetting to breathe.

Then she sits up and reaches for me. She slides her palms up and down. Her touch is feather-light, teasing. When I can't take it anymore I fall down on the bed, grab her roughly and kiss her. She tastes of mint and honey. Once I begin I cannot stop; I crush my mouth against hers, bruising. She pushes me away, gasping, and then she kisses me again. She rubs against me, wrapping her arms around my hips. I will not let her go. I drink her in, every inch that I can touch, and I watch to see her back arch, knotted by pleasure.

We become a twist of arms and legs. It takes a moment to see that she is moving, tunneling low, running her fingers over my body like the feeding seam of a sewing machine. She stops, looks up at me once, and then takes me into her mouth.

It is like a warm sponge, wrapped around, and she moves up and down, and the wonderful thing is: I can feel the line of her teeth; I can feel the nut of her tongue. I try to reach for her; to do something for her that feels as good as this does for me—but all I can touch are her shoulders. Her hair is spread over my hips like a dark fan. She begins to go faster and faster. I close my eyes, thinking of rhythm. I move my hips with her. This is going to be it; this is going to be it, but I want more.

Gasping, I pull her hands from my sides to slide her up my body and that is when I see her ring.

It has been there the entire time, but I didn't notice. It's thin, gold. It looks permanent. She follows my gaze to her left hand. "Throw it out," she whispers, "I don't care." She rolls away from me and tugs it off, setting it spinning on the nightstand. She rubs her finger, as if she is trying to erase the memory. But there is a thin white line where she hasn't tanned.

She takes that hand and brushes hair away from my face. I can't help it, I flinch—it's got me thinking again. She leans over to kiss my chest, and then she buries her face in a blanket. "I just want to be yours," she says.

I turn her so that she is facing me again. We start to kiss, touching together with the sound of a sigh. This time, our eyes are open, because we don't want to miss seeing each other. I become aware of her hands on my hips, lowering me. She wraps her legs around me, and eases me inside her, and that is when I understand what it is to feel whole.

She closes around me like a soft throat. So this is what love is like. So this is the way all the pieces come together. All my blood is pouring towards my hips, pounding out of rhythm. I cannot press any closer to her, but I'm trying. I want to be contained, to come through to her other side. We cling to each other, heat steaming from our bodies.

I start to feel it building up, insistent and demanding. She opens her eyes wide, looking at me in wonder. This is the image that I carry when I crush her to me, and feel myself explode just as she tightens around me.

We stay like that for a long time. Neither of us wants to speak. I kiss her on the forehead. Astonished, that's the way she's watching me. And I suppose it's the way I'm watching her too. When she shifts under my weight I move, wincing as we are ripped apart. It just doesn't feel the same. Now that I know what it is like to feel complete, it's no good to be by myself.

60 REBECCA *July 7, 1990*

This diner has velvet Elvises on the walls. Two waitresses are sharing a cigarette and talking about Elvis. The place is empty.

"Vera saw him," the fat waitress says. "A party in Blue Dome."

"Well Glory Be for Vera. He's dead, I tell you. D-E-A-D. Dead." The waitress turns to us. She has a nose ring. "Can I help you?"

"We can seat ourselves," my mother offers. The waitresses are already ignoring her.

My mother and I don't bother to read the menu. We've memorized it. We're listening to these waitresses, and taking in the seventeen pictures of Elvis. They are the kind you buy on highways and they hang over each booth. In the one above our heads, Elvis wears a white jumpsuit and a belt whose buckle spells LOVE. He is gyrating, even on velvet.

"Elvis died when you were three," my mother says, and both waitresses stare at us. "Well, *theoretically.*"

We order three sandwiches between us: chicken cutlet, meatball parmigiana, and tuna with swiss. We order Cokes and onion rings, potato skins. While this is all being cooked we go to the restrooms and wash up. Then while we eat our food, we plot the route from Idaho to Fishtrap, Montana, with spoons and forks and sugar packets. "It won't take us more than a few hours," I say, and my mother agrees.

"I figure we'll be in Massachusetts in a week," she says. "We'll probably celebrate your birthday in Minnesota, at this rate."

Minnesota. My birthday. I forgot about that. As the fat waitress brings us our food, I think about what my birthday might have been like. A big surprise party, maybe, out in our backyard. Maybe even a night cruise on one of my father's Whale Watch boats from the Institute. With a DJ and a parquet dance floor laid down. Or maybe there'd be a huge wrapped package waiting at the foot of my bed when I woke up. Inside, a red dress with spaghetti straps and sequins, the kind I always want but my mother says makes me look like a child prostitute. And my father would promenade my mother into my bedroom—she'd be wearing a taffeta gown and he'd have on his fancy tuxedo with the pinstriped bow tie. We'd walk down to the limo, and we'd be off to the fanciest restaurant for steamed lobster. And at the table, the waiter would be young and blond and gorgeous, and he'd hold out my chair for me and unfold my napkin and bring me a drink without questioning my age.

It won't happen in Minnesota. But it probably wouldn't have happened in San Diego, either. My father wouldn't have been around for my birthday, or we wouldn't be here in the first place. He wasn't home when I tried to call last night from the motel. I tried when my mother was in the bathroom, but she probably knew. I can't hide those things from her, no matter what.

It's not so much that I miss him. I think if he'd picked up the phone I would have hung up anyway. Still, it would have been nice to hear his voice. To hear him say he missed me, even. I would like to think he wasn't home because he's on his way to find us. I have these Hollywood visions of him begging on his knees for my mom to come home, and then sweeping her up in his arms for a long movie-style kiss. I have these visions, but I know better.

My mother, who has been rummaging through her wallet, starts to empty her entire pocketbook on the crummy table. "What's the matter?"

She looks up at me. "We can't pay. Simple as that."

She's got to be kidding. We have plenty of money. We would have noticed before now. My mother leans across the table and whispers to me. "Ask if they take checks."

So I sidle up to the fat waitress and in the most precious sugar-coated voice I can summon, I ask if a check is okay. "We're just trying to ration our cash," I say. The fat waitress says it's okay, but a voice from the grill in the back yells out it isn't, not one bit. Too many travelers come through. Too many checks bounce.

I walk back to the booth. Will they make us scrub the floors with a toothbrush? Wait tables? I tell my mother we are out of luck.

"Wait," she says. "There's five dollars in the glove compartment."

This gets me all excited—can you imagine, going crazy over five bucks? Then I realize I've been using that money for tolls. My mother glares at me and counts the change in her purse. We have one dollar and thirty-seven cents.

My mother closes her eyes and wrinkles up her nose, the way she does when she is creating A Big Plan. "I'll go out first, and then you make an act out of coming to get me. That'll look natural."

Sure it will, I think. What kind of mother are you, to leave your kid behind when *you* are stupid enough to run out of cash? I scowl at her as she stands and peers into a compact mirror. "I've left my lipstick in the car," she says in this bird-chirpy voice to all seventeen Elvises. "Diana?" She stomps on my right foot, just in case I haven't picked up my cue.

"Yes, Aunt Lucille?"

"Wait here. I'll be right back."

She smiles at the waitresses on the way out. I drum my fingers on the formica. I slurp my empty Coke. I count the rows of glasses behind the counter (twenty-seven) and try to invent names for the waitresses. Irma and Florence. Delia and Babs. Eleanore, Winifred, Thelma.

Finally I sigh. "I don't know what she's doing but we're going to be late for ballet class," I say loudly, wondering if Idaho girls take ballet lessons. I approach the waitresses. "Could you just watch our stuff for a minute? I think my aunt's gone and gotten lost!" I smirk a stupid teenage smirk and put my hands palms up, *What can you do?*

"Sure honey. No problem." I walk out the door, blood pounding behind my knees. I wonder how you get a criminal record. I wait until I think I am out of sight from the diner door and then I run like hell.

My mom has the car pulled up and I jump in. She screeches out of the parking lot. For a few miles I lean forward in my seat, my eyes wide. Then I relax. My mother is still paralyzed with fear, panic, I don't know what. I touch her hand where it rests on the radio dial, and all the air goes out of her like a deflating tire. "That was close," she says.

My mother wipes her upper lip with the collar of her shirt. I don't know if she's laughing or crying. I unroll the window, wondering what comes next. I smile, but only because this keeps the wind from hurting my eyes.

61 JANE

That night I have my flying dream. I have had it often: when I was a very little girl, when I first married Oliver, days before I gave birth to Rebecca. The dream is always the same: I run as hard as I can, and then I jump up high with both feet, and I can fly. The higher I get the more scary it is, but I always make it just above the tree line. Below, people look tiny and cars seem like toys, and just at that point I start to lose control. I worry about how I am going to land and sure enough I crash through the trees at an astounding pace, hurtling towards the ground, and land a little too hard. But it is a wonderful dream. When I was little I hoped each night I would have it. I figured if I dreamed it often enough, eventually I would learn how to land.

"Hello," Sam says as I'm waking, and it's the most beautiful word I've ever heard. He comes into his room with a wicker tray, balanced with melon and cereal and fresh-picked raspberries. "I didn't know if you like coffee."

"I do," I tell him. "Cream, no sugar." He holds up a finger and disappears, then returns with a steaming mug and sits on the edge of the bed. He watches me while I am drinking, and under his gaze I wait for embarrassment, but nothing comes. In fact I've never felt better. I could climb a mountain today. I could hike forty miles. Or I could just follow Sam around, that would be fine.

"Did you sleep all right?"

"Fine," I say, "and you?"

"Fine." Sam looks up then, and catches my eye, and turns red. "Look, I wanted to say something about last night."

"You're not going to apologize, are you? You don't think it was a mistake?"

"Don't you?" Sam says, looking at me. I can't concentrate when he does that; he takes my breath away.

Those eyes. My God. "I think," I say, halting, "I think I love you."

Sam stares at me. "I'm taking the day off."

"You can't. You've got an orchard to run."

"I've noticed lately that when I'm near you—fighting or kissing, it doesn't matter—I don't give a damn."

"Everyone will start talking. Rebecca can't know."

"She'll find out. She isn't stupid. Besides, I deserve a break. That's what I've got Hadley for. What good is hiring someone to be second in command if you never leave the post?" He leans over me and kisses my forehead. "I'll tell them we're going back to bed."

"Sam!" I call out, but to my surprise, I am not upset. I want the world to know I feel like this; that I am capable of it. I move the tray onto the floor, picking at the fruit. Then I stretch across the tangled sheets of the bed. My nightgown—that pretty silk from North Dakota—is on inside-out.

There is a knock at the door. I slide off the bed and open it. "Sam?" I say, and there is Rebecca, her voice chiming with mine, asking for him too. She does a double take, checking to see if she has the right bedroom. I pull the neck of my nightgown closed, feeling the telltale tag inside-out on the collar. "Sam's not here," I say quietly.

Rebecca keeps looking around the room like she is searching for evidence. Finally she meets my eyes. "I was looking for you, actually. I wanted to know if he knew where you were. Apparently," she says, "he does."

"This is not what you think," I say too quickly.

"I bet it's exactly what I think." I feel a stab in my heart, and this makes me feel better—isn't that what I have been waiting for? "I came to tell you Hadley and I were going into town this afternoon. I wanted to know if you'd like to come." She peers over my shoulder again. "I guess you have better things to do."

"You can't go into town. Well, Hadley can't. Sam was going to tell him he's in charge of the place today."

"Is that so?" Rebecca says, hands on her hips. "Straight from the boss's mouth?"

"You'd better watch it," I say quietly.

"*I'd* better watch it? *Me?* I don't think I'm the one who's got the problem. I'm not the one who is cheating on my husband."

Instinct: I raise my hand to strike her. Then, shaking, I bring my arm down to my side. "We can discuss this later."

"I think you're disgusting!" Rebecca yells, her hands balled into fists at her sides. "I can't believe you'd do this to Daddy! I can't believe you'd do this to me! Whatever you think, he still loves you. He's coming here, you know. And then what are you going to do?" She turns around and thunders down the stairs.

Sam finds me in the open doorway. "She came in here," I say. "Rebecca. She hates me now."

"She doesn't hate you. Give her a little time." But nothing he says can keep me from crying. He puts his arms around me, he rubs my shoulders—all of which worked wonders last night, but this is different. This is a rift between my daughter and me. This is something he could not possibly heal.

Eventually Sam leaves me alone for a while. He says he's going to make sure Joley knows what's getting sprayed with what today. He kisses me before he leaves, and tells me I'm beautiful. On his way out he turns around. "Your nightgown's on wrong."

I move to the window that looks out onto the brick patio in front of the house. When my cheek is pressed against the sill my face doesn't feel half as hot. I've been so selfish. All right, Jane, I think. You've had your moment in the sun. Now just put it behind you. You have to work with your loose ends and see what you can make of them. When Sam comes back, I'll tell him this. I will say that it might have worked in another time or another place. If I was ten years younger; if he worked behind a desk. And then I'll go out and find my daughter. *You see?* I'll say. *You have to love me again. Don't you see what I have given up for you?*

Absentmindedly I watch Hadley walk up the hill. He's wearing a blue flannel shirt that makes me think of the dark shade of Sam's eyes. Suddenly the front door on the Big House opens and Rebecca flies out of it. She is still crying; I can tell from the way her shoulders quiver. She runs to Hadley and presses herself against him.

For just a minute, I remember that Hadley and Sam are the same age.

Hadley cranes his neck, taking a look around. When I see him surveying the upstairs windows I duck back. Then I peek over the edge of the sill. Hadley is kissing the tears off my daughter's face.

It must be minutes that this goes on. I watch every move they make. She's a baby. She's just a baby. She doesn't know any better—how could Hadley *do* something like this? The way she arches her neck and the curve of her eyebrows, and the way she moves her hands across Hadley's back—there is something very familiar about this. Then it comes to me. Rebecca. When she is making love, she looks like me.

I think I am going to scream, or vomit; so I fall away from the window, out of sight. Sam comes into the room then; I wonder if he has seen them as well. "You look like you've seen a ghost," he says. But by the time he crosses the room to look outside, Hadley has pushed Rebecca away to a safe distance. At least a foot of space separates them.

"What?" Sam says. "What's the problem?"

"I can't do this. It isn't fair to you; it isn't fair to my daughter. I can't just think about myself. It's been wonderful, Sam, but I think we should just go back to being friends."

"You can't go backward." Sam moves away from me. "You don't tell someone you love them, and send them flying, and then trash them the next time you see them." He comes closer and puts his hand on my shoulder, but when I feel it starting to burn I shrug him away. "What's gotten into you?"

"Have you seen them? Hadley and Rebecca? He's the same age as you, Sam. And he was practically screwing my daughter."

"Hadley wouldn't do that. Maybe Rebecca egged him on."

My jaw drops. "Whose side are you on?"

"I'm just saying you should look at this logically."

"Let me put it to you this way," I say. "If I see him near my daughter again I'll kill him with my own two hands."

"What does this have to do with us?"

"If I hadn't been so wrapped up in you," I say, "I might have noticed what was going on between Rebecca and Hadley." Sam starts to kiss my neck. It strikes me that this was the exact pose in which I just spied my daughter and Sam's best friend. "You're distracting me."

"I know. I planned to." I start to protest but he holds his hand up to my mouth. "Just give me one more day. Promise me that."

When we leave the orchard, I haven't even seen Joley yet. Sam tells me he's down spraying organic pesticides on a section of the commercial grove. I want to find Rebecca one more time before I go, but she is nowhere to be seen.

Sam drives the blue pickup truck to a nature sanctuary about thirty miles west of Stow. Run by an Audubon spin-off, it is a large penned-in area where there are deer, great horned owls, silver foxes, wild turkeys. The paths wind through natural habitats: ponds with fallen logs, tall gold grasses, antlered branches. We walk around holding hands; there is nobody here who knows us. In fact because it is a weekday there is almost nobody here. Just some elderly people, who watch us as much as they watch the wildlife. I hear one old woman whisper to her friend as we walk by. *Newlyweds*, she says.

Sam and I sit for three hours on the brink of the deer habitat. Inside, the sign says, are a doe and a buck. We can spot the buck easily because it is drinking in the lake, but the doe is indistinguishable from the mottled foliage. We try to find her for a half-hour, and then we give up for a while.

Instead, we sit facing each other on a low log bench and try to catch up on the rest of our lives. I tell Sam about the house in Newton, about Joley's trek to Mexico, about cocktail parties at the Institute and about a little girl with a cleft palate who has been my favorite student now for three years. I tell him about the time Rebecca needed stitches in her chin, and about the plane crash, and finally, about how

Oliver and I met. Sam, in return, tells me about his father in Florida, and about giving speeches at Minuteman Tech, about the almost extinct apple he's been trying to recreate genetically, about all the places he has read about and wishes he could go. We say that we will travel together, and we make up a list as if it is truly going to happen.

"There are all these things I used to say I wanted to do that I never got to do," I tell him.

"Why not?"

"I had Rebecca," I say, matter-of-fact.

"She's old enough to take care of herself."

"Apparently not. You didn't see her this morning. You can't decide these things for yourself when you're only fifteen."

Sam grins. "Didn't I hear right that you met old Oliver when you were fifteen?"

I start to say that was different, but I change my mind. "And look where that got me."

"I think you're overreacting."

"I think you aren't her mother," I snap. I take a deep breath. "I want you to fire Hadley."

"Hadley?" Sam says, incredulous. "I can't do that. He's my best friend."

I stand up, searching for that doe. "It's just wrong. I know he's wrong for Rebecca as much as I've known anything. He's ten years older than her, for God's sake." I pause, and then turn to Sam. "Don't say it."

Suddenly I see her, stepping through the trees with the grace of a ballerina. The doe lifts her legs high, sniffing with her head delicately bowed. Behind her is a caramel-colored fawn. Nobody said there was a fawn. "I'm not going to be here very long, Sam," I say softly. "You know that and I know that."

Sam stands up, his hands in his pockets. "You're giving me an ultimatum."

"No I'm not."

"You are," Sam insists. "If I want you, I've got to do something about Hadley. And even so, it would be a temporary victory."

"What do you mean by that?"

Sam grabs my shoulders. "Tell me you'll leave him. You and Rebecca can stay with me in Stow. We'll get married and we'll have a zillion kids."

I smile sadly. "I've already got a kid. I'm too old to have babies."

"That's bullshit," Sam says. "You know that. We'll live in the Big House and it'll be perfect."

"It'll be perfect," I say, repeating his words. "It's nice to think that."

Sam wraps his arms around me. "I'll talk to Hadley. I'll work something out." He leans his head on my shoulder. "Perfect," he says.

Only Joley is in the Big House when we return. It is late afternoon, and he's come in for a cold drink. As we walk into the house, Sam is grabbing at the waistband of my shorts. "Stop!" I laugh, swatting his hand away. That's when I see my brother. "Oh," I straighten up—we've been caught with our hands in the cookie jar.

"Where have you two been?" Joley says, amused. At least he's not shocked, like Rebecca. Where is she?

"At the nature sanctuary," Sam says. "Where is everyone?"

"Finishing up. Rebecca's down there too."

"Can I talk to you, Sam?" Joley asks, and Sam looks at me: *We knew it was coming*. He leads Sam into the kitchen and starts the faucet running, no doubt to keep me from listening.

I walk into the den, where the television is on. The five o'clock local news. I swing myself sideways in the armchair so that my feet dangle over the edge. The anchorwoman is reporting on a fire that killed three people in Dorchester. Then a familiar logo appears on the screen behind her. Why do I know it? "And now," the anchorwoman says, "we take you to Joan Gallagher, reporting from Gloucester, where rescue efforts have been underway for the past three days to save a humpback whale tangled in a fishing boat's gill net. Joan?"

"I don't believe this," I say out loud. "This stuff *follows* me."

"Thanks, Anne," the reporter says dutifully. "Behind me is Stellwagen Bank, a major East Coast feeding ground for several groups of humpback whales. Many people have been following the plight of Marble, a humpback who became tangled three days ago in a gill net left behind by a fishing vessel. Sighted once by the Coast Guard, it took forty-eight hours to find the exact location of Marble again. Today, Dr. Windy McGill, director of the Provincetown Center for Coastal Studies, undertook the rescue of the desperate humpback."

The reporter cuts to footage of an inflatable boat being tossed about on the ocean. There are two people on board. "Dr. McGill was joined by a colleague, Dr. Oliver Jones, a prominent marine biologist whose research on humpbacks is world-renowned." They zoom in on Oliver's face, bent low as he untangles a nylon rope. I sit absolutely still. "Dr. Jones, who studies whales off the coast of California, just happened to be in the Boston area and offered his help when he heard of Marble's dilemma. These two scientists bravely made the twenty-three mile trip in a Zodiac raft to the location of the whale."

They show the boat being pitched up, regaining its balance, slapping back against the ocean. "Oliver," I say, covering my mouth with my hand.

By now Sam and Joley have come out of the kitchen. They stand on either side of me, watching the footage. "Isn't that . . . ?" Joley says, but I hush him.

The camera refocuses on the reporter. "After three and a half hours of dedicated and dangerous work, Marble swam free. She was joined immediately by several other whales. And perhaps the most touching twist to this story was that the foremost rescuer, Dr. Oliver Jones, is in need of some help himself."

"Jones?" Sam says.

The camera closes in on Oliver's face, on his pale eyes, his Kahlua skin. "Jane." His voice is shaking, hoarse. "I need you. I hope you can see this, and I hope you and Rebecca are all right. I want you to know something. I can't stand being without you."

"Don't tell me," Sam says.

Oliver takes a picture out of his wallet, one of Rebecca and me. It's not even a good one. "If anyone out there has seen my wife or this little girl, please call in," Oliver says.

I have grabbed Sam's hand; I didn't even notice myself doing it. "That's Oliver. That's my husband."

Oliver stares at me, painfully honest. I wonder how much he can see. I wonder if he knows what I have done. "I love you," Oliver says to me, just me. "I don't care if the whole world knows."

62 JOLEY

After the news broadcast, Sam takes off. He says he has something to do; he doesn't mention what it is. He doesn't say anything to my sister.

"Come on," I say, taking her hand. "Help me make dinner." She follows me into the kitchen, weak, easily led. She sits down on a ladderback chair.

"Oh, Joley," she sighs. "What have I done?*"*

I take carrots and lettuce from the refrigerator. I'm not gourmet, but salads are easy. "You tell me.*"*

She looks up, her eyes wild. "Maybe we can run away. If we leave now we'll be gone by the time Oliver gets here."

"You can't drag Rebecca away again. It's not healthy. She's just a kid."

"I'm not talking about Rebecca," Jane mutters. "I'm talking about Sam.*"*

I drop several carrots I have been peeling in the sink. "You knew Oliver would come to find you. You told me that yourself. And you didn't want to talk about what would happen when he got here."

"I don't want to talk about it."

"You're right. Maybe if we don't think about him, he'll disappear." I throw the vegetable peeler into the sink. "All right, then, let's talk about something else. Let's talk about Sam."

"I don't want to talk about Sam," Jane says.

"Look at me." She will not.

"What's going on?" When I spoke to Sam earlier, he gave me the runaround. I first heard from Rebecca, who came running to me in the morning, crying. Uncle Joley, *she sobbed,* I hate her. I hate her.

"Nothing," Jane says. Then she sighs. "I'm not going to lie to you. You know what's going on. Everyone knows what's going on."

"You tell me," I say. I want to hear it from her.

I am expecting her to tell me she slept with Sam. But instead she tilts her head, and says, "Sam's the person I was supposed to fall in love with."

"Then what is Oliver?"

Jane looks at me and blinks quickly. "Extra baggage."

"You've been with Sam for five days. How can you come to a conclusion in five lousy days?" He doesn't know you, I think. I've been by your side for thirty years. I'm the one to whom you are tied.

"Remember what I said to you when we first got here?"

"That Sam was a stubborn pig."

"Besides that," Jane says, smiling. "I did say that, didn't I? Well, I also said that I'd know what I was looking for when it hit me. I said that all I needed in my life was an instant of time when I could honestly say I was on top of the world, and not be lying. This is it."

"You also said that if you got those five terrific minutes you'd go back to Oliver. You'd live the life you started with and you'd never complain."

"But that was before. How do you know my five minutes are up? I said I'd go back when it was over. But it's not over yet. Not by a long shot, Joley."

I start to tell her about Rebecca, and what happened this morning. I tell her because it gets me off the hook; it keeps me from thinking about Jane and Sam, together. Rebecca came up to me, and told me what she had seen. She said, Does this mean my parents are getting a divorce? Does this mean I'm never going to go home?

I watched her standing in front of me, and I knew how she

felt. I remembered what it was like to crawl into the safety of Jane's bed, under the covers, and listen to the screaming going on downstairs between my mother and father. Nothing seemed so loud, or so awful, if I had Jane's arms around me.

Even my father started to go to Jane's room at night. At first I thought it was for the same security that I went there for. I figured everyone has something he is afraid of, something he needs to forget about, even Daddy. I began to piece together the differences slowly, and by the time I understood, Jane stopped letting me come into her room. It was right at the time when she started to change; when Jane sprouted breasts and I began to notice the hair under her arms and vined on her legs. She wouldn't let me in the room when she was dressing. She wouldn't let me under the covers. Instead we would sit primly on the bedspread and play Hearts.

It killed me when she went to college. She left me home alone. She'd visit, almost every weekend, but it wasn't the same. I always expected that she'd come back to me, but instead, she married Oliver Jones.

What I told Rebecca this morning is that Jane was always meant to be a mother. Look at how young she started taking care of me. But right now Rebecca would have to be the logical one. "Your mother will come around," I told her, but she winced as I said it. She wanted to know how long it would take. She wanted to know how many people would have to be hurt. Most of all she asked why Jane was the one who got to make the final decision.

What decision? *I asked Rebecca.*

To throw it all away, *she cried.* Can't you see that's what she's trying to do?

I tell my sister all this, and she nervously winds her hair around her finger.

"I don't get it, Joley. You spend your whole life as my biggest cheerleader. You're always there to tell me I'm not paying enough attention to myself; that I deserve better. So after fifteen years I finally take your stupid advice and you tell me I'd better

slow down. Make up your mind," she says. "I'm not going to lie to Rebecca. I'm going to tell her everything; I'm just not going to do it today. Give me a little time. I've never asked for anything my whole life. I've given and given and given. So can't I just get this one small thing?"

"No," I say, too quickly, and Jane explodes.

"What do you want me to do?"

"Come to me. I've always wanted you to come to me."

"I can't hear you," Jane says irritably.

I clear my throat. "I said I wanted you to come to me."

She throws her hands up. "I did come to you. I traveled three thousand miles to come to you. And all I've gotten is a lecture."

The day that Jane married Oliver, the day that she kissed me on the cheek and told me she was happier than she'd ever been, something happened to me. Quite concretely I felt my chest swell and then contract, and that's when I understood that you can clearly feel a broken heart. I turned away without saying anything to her, but she didn't notice, engulfed in a flood of guests. I promised myself that I wouldn't let myself get hurt like this again.

I have never stopped looking after Jane, but I have kept my distance. Almost immediately after she got married I started to travel, bouncing from college to college and then across the United States, into Mexico, to Bangladesh, Morocco, Asia. I put as many miles between us as I could allow, assuming this was the easiest way. I have always wanted the best for her because she means so much to me. So, when all this was beginning with Sam, I gave my blessing. I wanted him to have her. If it could not be me.

She puts her arms around me, and for a minute I'm back where I used to be, where love could be tucked in a pillow fold. "I'm sorry. I didn't mean to yell at you."

I used to think about dying and being cremated. I wanted my ashes placed in a leather pouch and I wanted Jane to wear it around her neck. I used to imagine her pulling on layers of clothing in the winter, turtlenecks and sweaters and bulky down parkas, knowing that I was the thing that came closest to her heart.

This is the most it will ever be, I think. "Don't worry about me." I smile at her. "I've always had trouble adjusting to your boyfriends."

Jane holds me at arm's length. She opens her mouth to say something—what?—but she closes it again, silent.

Just then Rebecca and Hadley swing into the kitchen. Hadley is giving Rebecca a piggyback ride, and she kicks the door open with her foot. They just make it over the threshold before Hadley loses his hold on Rebecca and half drops, half tumbles her onto the floor. They are both laughing so hard it takes them a minute to realize that I am in the kitchen, that Jane is in the kitchen. "Did we interrupt?" Hadley says, good-natured and grinning, dusting off the legs of his jeans.

"No," Jane says. "Not at all." He is staring at Rebecca, who has deliberately taken a good deal of time to get to her feet. Funny, she is exactly as tall as Jane.

63 SAM

You should have seen the look on her face when that guy came onto the television. I mean, she just shriveled up inside. I could tell from the way she almost fell out of the chair. She kept saying his name: Oliver.

I would have given anything then to tear her away from that TV. Give her a sedative, a stiff drink, I don't know what. Maybe I could just hold her. But seeing her like that knotted up my gut. I had to do something. And I couldn't very well just kneel down next to her, with her god-damned husband larger than life, swollen in technicolor. So I chickened out. I left; said I had something to do in the field. Instead, I'm taking a walk through the woods that border the orchard.

The mosquitoes are awful this time of year, and the land is swampy. Part of the woods has become a makeshift dump, even for neighboring farmers. There's an old enamel bathtub and a few dead washing machines at a certain point on the trail. But it's quiet, so quiet you can hear your mind snapping as it jumps from one idea to another.

I walk for quite a distance, because I come to the foundation of a house that must have burned to the ground. It's a small ring of stones with a crumbling fireplace at one end. My father used to say it dated to the 1700s.

When Hadley and me were kids we'd come out here a lot. When we were about nine, we made this our secret clubhouse, and we lugged beams and old boards from the barn all the way here, trying to hammer together some kind of enclosure. We had a password: Yaz, after our favorite player on the Red Sox. We'd meet every day at sunset, just so we could hear our mothers hollering from different edges of the woods, calling us to supper.

I've been hanging around with Hadley since we were seven. That's eighteen years. That's longer than Rebecca's even been alive. Under any other circumstance, I'd stand behind him. He's my best friend. He knows what he's doing; he wouldn't take a fifteen-year-old on a joy ride. But I know as sure as I know the boundaries of my orchard, what is happening to me now comes once in a lifetime. I can't stand to see Jane upset, and for selfish reasons: it hurts me to see her like that.

By the time I get back to the Big House, I've missed dinner. Joley's doing the dishes; he tells me Jane's upstairs. "Where's Hadley? I've got to talk to him."

"I think he went out on the back porch with Rebecca. Why?"

But I don't have time to answer him. I stroll out the back door, immediately feeling that I have interrupted something. Rebecca and Hadley are on the swinging bench, and when the door creaks open they fly to opposite ends. "Hey," I say, noncommittally. "You busy?"

They shake their heads. Rebecca's making me uncomfortable. I can feel her stare burning into the collar of my shirt. I pull at it, trying to let in some air. "What's up?" Hadley says. He's bolder now. He's got his arm around Rebecca, on the back of the bench.

"I kind of need to talk to you." I turn to Rebecca. "Alone." I open the screen door. "I'll just wait in here." I walk inside and let the door slam behind me. Hadley asks how long this is going to take. "I was figuring we'd go grab a beer, if that's okay with you."

I hear Rebecca say, "Do you have to?" but I can't tell what Hadley says in return. He walks into the house, that wide smile on his face, and slaps me on the back. "Let's roll. You paying?"

We go to Adam's Rib, a restaurant with a big bar section frequented mostly by motorcycle gangs. We don't go there much, but I don't want to have this conversation in a place I go to often, so that every time I walk in the door in the future I'll have a memory of the time I let down my best friend. Hadley and I take a table near the door, one that is really a Pac-Man game dotted with two napkins and an ashtray. A waitress with very high teased red hair asks us what we're drinking. "Glenfiddich," I say. "Two."

Hadley lifts his eyebrows. "You getting married or having a baby or something? What's the occasion?"

I lean my elbows on the table. "I got to ask you something. What's going on between you and Rebecca?"

Hadley grins. "What's going on between you and Jane?"

"Come on," I say, "that's not the question here."

"Sam, I don't mess in your business; you don't mess in mine." The drinks come, and Hadley lifts his glass and toasts me. "Cheers."

"She's really young. You've got Jane all upset."

Hadley scowls. "Rebecca's got a more grown-up head on her shoulders than either one of us. I wouldn't fuck around with a kid, Sam, if I didn't think it was right."

I take a long, deep drink of the whiskey. It burns the back of my throat, which makes me think the words may come easier. "I wouldn't fuck around, either, if I didn't know it was right." I swirl the liquid in the glass. "I think you'd better go away for a little while."

Hadley stares at me. "What are you talking about?"

"I'm saying I think you should take a vacation. Get away from the orchard. Go visit your mom," I say. "She hasn't seen you since Christmas."

"You're doing this because of her fucking mother."

"I'm doing it because of me. And you. I'm doing what I think is right."

"She told you to do it, didn't she? She's making you do this. You've known me all your life. You've known her for five days. I can't believe you're doing this."

"Leave Jane out of this," I say, floundering. "This is between you and me."

"Like hell it is. Jesus!" He kicks the table again, and then takes a deep breath and eases himself into his chair. "Okay," he says. "I want to know one thing. I want to know why nobody asked me or Rebecca what we think. I want to know why the whole goddamned world is voting on our future, everyone but us."

"It's not for long. A week, maybe two. I just want to give Jane a little time to herself. You don't know her, Hadley. She's not just some rich bitch. She's had a really rough life."

"Yeah, well, you don't know Rebecca," Hadley says. "Do you know what it's like when I'm with her? She believes in me more than my own folks ever did. Shit, I've told her things I've never even told you. No matter what I'm doing or where I am, she's in my head."

Hadley flattens his palms against the game table. "Have you ever even talked to her, Sam? She's lived through a plane crash. She takes better care of her mother than the other way around. She knows about you two, that's for sure. You think Jane's had a rough life? You should see the trip she's laid on her own kid."

Hadley drains his glass, and then reaches for mine. "So if you want to know, Am I in love with her, the answer's yes. If you want to know, Am I going to take care of her, I will. No one else seems to be doing a bang-up job of it." When Hadley looks at me, there's a purpose in his eyes I've never seen before. "Don't think about what I'm doing to Rebecca, Sam. Think about what *Jane's* doing to her."

"Look," I say. "I need you to do this for me. I'll make it up to you. I swear it."

Hadley swallows hard and blinks. He's looking for more to drink, but there's nothing left between us. "Yeah, right."

"Hadley—"

He holds his hands up to stop me. "I don't want your explanations. I don't want to hear about it at all, okay? And I want my back pay." I nod. "You listen to me, Sam. You'd better work this out good. Because you're making me leave behind someone I care about a lot. I'm going to come after her, sooner or later, no matter how long you keep me away. I'll find her. Tell Jane that, straight from my lips. I'm going to be with Rebecca no matter what."

For what seems like minutes, we sit facing each other, absolutely silent. Finally I break the tension. "You'll go in the morning."

"Fuck that," Hadley says, snorting. "I'm out of here tonight."

We leave just after that. We ride home in the pickup and I swear I notice every bump and grit in the road. I notice the way both of our bodies bounce up and down at the same time. It's gravity; we both weigh about the same. We pull into the driveway, and most of the lights downstairs in the house have been turned off.

Neither Hadley nor I make a motion to get out of the truck. The crickets slide the bows of their wings back and forth. "Who gets to tell her?" Hadley asks.

"Rebecca? You do. You should tell her." Hadley looks at me, waiting for me to say more. "Go ahead. Go on up there. Stay as long as you want. I won't tell Jane."

He opens the truck door, and it buzzes the way it does when the seat belts are off. The inside light goes on, so I know he sees me lean my head against the steering wheel. I don't feel like getting out of the car just yet. "She's not a kid, Sam," Hadley says quietly. "I'm not like that." When he shuts the door, it makes a jointed, neat sound.

64 OLIVER

God bless America. My heart goes out to every sympathetic, kind-hearted man and woman who has called the Provincetown Center for Coastal Studies since hearing my broadcast on the shores of Gloucester. The switchboard operator patches them into the tiny closet where Windy has installed a telephone for me, for privacy. I am told that Jane has been spotted at an Exxon station on the Mass. Pike. A man remembers Rebecca's face in his convenience store in Maynard. And last, but certainly not least, a young fellow who works at an ice cream stand in Stow calls in. He asks if I am the whale guy. He has seen my wife and my child. "Came in here with a local man who runs an apple farm." Victory.

"Do you know his name?" I ask, pressing him for more details. What was he wearing? How many people in his party? What type of car did he drive?

"Hey, that's it!" the young man says. "A blue pickup, really nice new truck, which is how come I noticed. And it said *Hansen's* on the door."

Hansen. Hansen. Hansen. None of the mailboxes on this road have that name; doesn't the man have any relatives in the town? Anything to appease my gnawing excitement? I have already plotted what I will do. It is barely five in the morning, and even a farm will still be asleep. So I will jimmy the lock and creep inside, and try to find Jane's bedroom. It should be easy; she sleeps with the door ajar because she is claustrophobic. And then I will sit on the edge of the bed, and touch her hair. I have forgotten its texture. I'll wait until she stirs and then I'll kiss her. Oh, will I kiss her.

Hansen's. I slam the brakes, sending the Lincoln spinning. I have always preferred big cars, but they fishtail at times like this. I right myself, and pull into the long, winding driveway. If I drive the entire way, they might hear me. So I park midway on the rutted gravel and walk to the large white house.

The porch creaks beneath me. I try the door—open—does anyone in the country lock their doors? Inside, I have to feel my way in the dark, but I do not mind. This is a good sign: no one is awake.

I became very good at cracking doors just a hair when Rebecca was a baby. If she heard the slightest sound, she'd wake and begin to cry, and God knows it was difficult enough to get her to sleep through the night. It's all in the wrist.

The farthest door on the right yields an empty room decorated with antiques and patchwork quilts. Jane's purse is in here, which leads me to deduce that this is indeed her room and she is probably sleeping with Rebecca out of fear or discomfort or loneliness. My heart is pounding when I open the next door, expecting to find my wife and my child together. But it is just Joley, snoring loud enough to blast granite.

When I open the next bedroom door, it too is empty, but the sheets are messed on the bed. Strewn around the room are Rebecca's clothes—I recognize her GUARD suit, the one she was wearing the day she left. A half-full glass of juice sits at the bedside, as if the room was left in a hurry. As if the occupant is coming right back. This worries me; I don't want her to see me before I have a chance to see and speak to Jane. So I duck into the hallway, and make my way to the last door.

It falls open without a sound. Jane is in the bed, curled onto her side. She is not wearing anything. She is smiling in her sleep. She is in the arms of another man.

I stagger forward, creating a loud noise that coincides with the crash of the door against the wall. They both jump up, blinking. Jane sees me first. "Oliver," she gasps.

I lunge for him, hauling him out of the bed. Jane is screaming for me to stop. I think she is probably crying. "Get the fuck away from her!" I shout, throwing the man onto the floor. I don't even know who he is. I'm ready to kill him, and I don't even known his name.

I kick him in the gut and in the balls and send him reeling backward. Jane jumps out of bed, wailing, naked, and throws herself across him. I have poison running through my veins. I want blood.

She cradles his head in her lap. "I'm all right," he says to her. "I'm okay now." He tries to get to his feet, to come after me.

"Come on," I say, beckoning. "I'll kill you. I mean it, I'll kill you." Suddenly Jane is in between us, and she throws herself into my arms, and it is so remarkably distracting that I lose my sense of purpose. She has wrapped herself in a sheet. She is so soft.

"Don't do this," she pleads. "For me. Don't do this, please."

"Let's get Rebecca. We're leaving."

Jane will not make eye contact with me. "No."

"We're leaving, Jane," I say authoritatively.

She stands directly between us, her hands knotted into fists, her eyes pressed shut. "No!"

And this is when Joley chooses to enter the room. "What the hell is going on?" He sees me, he takes note of Jane and this other asshole, leaning on the bedpost for support. "Sam, what happened?"

"Sam Hansen? *You're* the one who's been screwing my wife?" It all balls up inside my throat then, my shoulders. I grab for Sam's neck. I can break it in one swift move. I know human anatomy.

Joley pushes Jane out of the way. He grabs me by the collar of my shirt and wraps his arms around mine so that I am pinned. I struggle but he is too strong for me, and eventually I relax. "Where's Rebecca? I want to see Rebecca."

"She's next door," Jane says.

"There's no one next door."

"Of course there is," Joley says. "Where should she go at five in the morning?"

Jane's hands start to tremble, and she turns to Sam. *Sam.* "I told Hadley to leave," he says. "I told him last night. She must have found out. She must have gone after him."

Jane nods very slowly, and then she bursts into tears. "She knows it was me. She knows I told you."

Joley, for once in his goddamned life the voice of reason, walks towards Sam and practically shouts in his face. "Do you know where his mom lives now?"

"I know the town. It won't be hard to find."

"I can't believe this," I say. "I travel across the country to find my child has run away and my wife is in another man's bed." Sam and Joley continue to talk about some area of New Hampshire. I come closer to Jane and I take her hand. "I had so much to tell you," I say sadly. Her cheeks are red and swollen with the tracks of tears.

"Oliver," she whispers, hoarse. "I can't lose her. I can't lose her." She looks up at me. "I'm so sorry. I didn't want to hurt you."

I know they are watching, from across the room. I know they are watching and that is what makes it even sweeter. This has not been easy. I came across an entire continent to tell this woman I am in love with her. I came to tell her my life is nothing unless she's by my side. And I'm not about to throw that away, in spite of it all. I know how to forgive, now. I know how to forget, I imagine, too. It is up to me to put my family back together. I squeeze Jane gently. Then I close my eyes, and press my lips against hers. Her mouth is quivering. But she is kissing me back. This much I know: she is kissing me back.

65 JOLEY

When Oliver hugs Jane like that, Sam stirs next to me. I brace my arm, so he doesn't step forward and do anything stupid. He takes three slow measured breaths that rock his whole frame. Then he pushes past me. "Let's go," he says.

We've decided that since we know where Hadley's gone, we have a good chance of finding Rebecca there. If we get a start this early, we'll be there by lunch time. "I'm going with you," Oliver says. He lets go of Jane and she sags against the post of the bed. I think she might pass out, from the looks of things.

"Oliver." You have to feel bad for the guy. This isn't what he expected to find in Massachusetts, after all. "It won't do you any good to come with us. Someone has to stay here with Jane, anyway."

"This is not a question. I am telling you: I'm going with you to New Hampshire."

Sam takes a step forward. I can see Oliver's face change as he drinks in the tone of Sam's voice. "You know where Hadley's mom lives. You two go. I'll wait here in case she comes home."

"Like hell you will," Oliver says. It's about to come to blows again, so I step in between them. "I'm not leaving you here with my wife."

"You can't go by yourself," Sam says. "Half the roads there aren't marked."

Oliver leans towards Sam. "I can find places that are totally unmarked, you asshole. I do it for a living."

"This isn't the ocean."

Jane puts her hand on Oliver's arm. "He's right, Oliver. You can't go up there alone."

"Okay," Oliver says, pacing. He wheels around and points to Sam. "You. You go with me. Joley stays here with Jane."

"What a goddamned pleasure," Sam mutters.

"What did you say?" Oliver grabs the collar of his shirt, but Sam, now awake and probably ten times stronger than Oliver, shoves him with such force Oliver crashes into the door.

"I said it would be my pleasure." Sam walks over to Jane, who is crying again. He leans his forehead against hers, and puts his hand on her shoulder. He whispers something only she can hear, and she starts to smile a little.

"We can check the grounds but I don't think we'll find her. We'll take my truck," Sam says, and Oliver shakes his head.

"We'll take my *car," Oliver says.*

After we hear the car drive away, Jane sinks down to the floor and pulls her knees up to her chest. "You win, Joley. You were right."

"Nobody's won anything. They're going to find her."

Jane shakes her head. "I should have said something to her. I should have told her about Sam, and above all else I should have tried to understand what was going on with Hadley." She pulls herself upright, and walks into Rebecca's empty room.

I hear all the air rush out of her, like she's been punched hard. She touches Rebecca's bathing suit, her hairbrush. "The room smells like her, doesn't it?"

She picks up Rebecca's bra. "We bought this in North Dakota," she says, smiling. "She was so excited because it had a cup size." She winds the bra around her waist, snapping the elastic. "I have been so selfish."

"You didn't know this would happen." I sit next to her on Rebecca's bed.

"If she's hurt," Jane says, "I'll die. I'll never be able to forgive myself. If she's hurt, it will kill me."

Jane lies down on the bed. I rub her back. "She's fine. She's going to be fine."

"You don't know that," Jane says. "You don't understand how I feel. I'm her mother. *I'm supposed to protect her. I should be with her now. I should be with her." Jane rolls over and stares at the ceiling. There is a water mark that has spread in the shape of a lamb, and another in the form of a zinnia. She sits up. "Drive after them. I want to be there when they find her."*

"We can't do that. What if she comes back home? Someone has to be here. You *have to be here."*

Jane sinks back down on the bed. She crawls under the covers, and turns onto her side. "She sleeps like this," Jane says. "With her mouth open and her hand curled up on the side. She even slept like this as a baby, when all the other infants in the hospital were on their stomachs with their rear ends sticking in the air. You know when they brought her to me, after I had her, I was terrified. I didn't think I'd know how to hold a baby. But she was the one who let me off the hook. She was this little wiggling mess of arms and legs," Jane says, smiling. "But Rebecca looked up at me, and she seemed to be saying, Relax. We've got a long way to go.*"*

I do my best to listen, because I know that's what she needs.

Jane suddenly sits up very straight. "Rebecca was my tradeoff," she says. "I didn't meet Sam earlier, or marry him, even though I was meant to. Don't you see? It was one or the other."

"I'm not following you."

"She's my daughter. *As much as I say Sam is a part of me, so is she. She knows me just as well. She loves me just as much, in a different way." She shakes her head. "I didn't have Sam my whole life. Instead, I was given Rebecca."*

I am going to hate myself for saying this, I know. I look out the window, to where the field hands are gathering near the barn. Someone has to tell them what to do today. "If you didn't have Oliver," I point out, "you wouldn't have had Rebecca. She's part of him, too."

Jane follows my gaze out the window. In the distance the lambs are bleating. There are all these things to do. "Oliver," she says. "That's true."

66 SAM

We come to a quiet understanding, Oliver and me. We don't talk too much in the car on the way to the White Mountains. Oliver drives, and I fidget with the cigarette lighter button and the power window controls. I keep my space, and he keeps his.

From time to time I get to study his face. I do it in a curious, kind of jealous way. You know: What has he got that I don't have? He's very dark, tanned, I guess, but I work outside as much as he does and I don't look like that. Maybe it's the salt water. It's cut lines in his face, around his eyes and mouth, that make him look so tired. Or determined. It depends on the angle. He's got hair like Rebecca's and vacant blue eyes with tiny little pinpoint black pupils. I try, really, I do—but I cannot picture Jane with him. I can't even think of him standing next to her, without the picture looking all funny. She wasn't meant to be with someone like him; someone so stuffy, with his head up in the clouds. She was meant to be with someone like me.

I've got my eye on him when the car starts to choke. We're on 93. I think I remember passing Manchester, but I can't be sure. About all I know for certain is that we're running out of gas.

"Shit," Oliver says, maneuvering the car onto the shoulder of the road. "I didn't even notice I was low."

I fold my arms across my chest. "Don't suppose you have a gas can?"

Oliver turns to me and smirks. "As a matter of fact I do. And we're *both* going for a walk down the highway with it."

"Someone should stay with the car. You don't want to come back and find it towed. This isn't even really a shoulder, here. You can't just leave it."

"You're not staying here," Oliver says. "I don't trust you."

"You don't trust me. *What* am I going to do with a car like this?" But Oliver isn't listening. He's popped the trunk, and he takes a blue plastic gas can out. He sticks his head inside my window and tells me to get a move on.

We walk along the highway. It's hot, and there are bugs everywhere. "So," I say, as friendly as I can, "how's work?"

"Shut up. I don't want to carry on a conversation with you. I don't even want to believe that you exist."

"Believe me," I say, "hanging around with you isn't up there on my list of things to do."

Oliver mutters something I can't hear, what with an eighteen-wheeler zooming by. It ends with: ". . . you should tell me what exactly prompted my daughter to leave."

So I tell him about Hadley, and about what Jane said. He takes this all very well, kind of weighing the information before he comes to any early conclusions. I finish the story about three miles down the road, when we reach the exit. Then I look at Oliver to see his expression.

He looks up at me. "Are they sleeping together?"

"How the hell should I know? I doubt it."

"I thought you'd know everything that goes on under your roof," Oliver says.

"He's a good person." I point up the road at a Texaco. "He's a lot like me, actually."

The second after I say it I realize it was the wrong thing to say. Oliver looks at me with disgust. "I'll bet."

At the service station Oliver fills up the gas can while I buy a Mountain Dew from a vending machine. Next to Jolt cola, it's got the most caffeine out of any soft drink and I figure I'm going to need it. I sit on the curb at the edge of the road and count the cars that go by. When I close my eyes, I get this picture of Jane: last night, when I came to her, and she was a blue silhouette against the white curtains in the window. She was wearing that slinky silky thing with thin straps, you know what I mean. Those sexy nightgowns. I don't know where she got it; God knows my mother didn't leave any behind in her bedroom. But Jesus was she something. When I touched her the fabric spilled through my fingers, and to my surprise, her own skin was even softer.

I open my eyes and jump up about a foot. Oliver's face is inches from mine, purple and angry. "You're thinking about her," he shouts. "I don't want you doing that."

Like he could possibly stop me. I could pommel this guy to a pulp in a matter of minutes; I'm restraining myself because Jane would fall apart, and besides, he may be instrumental in getting Rebecca away from Hadley. "Did it ever occur to you that this didn't develop just because of me? Did it ever occur to you that Jane wanted to be with me too?"

Oliver raises his free hand, probably to punch me, but I stand up. I'm a good four inches taller than him, and both of us know that now I'm awake I could kill him. He puts his hand down. "Shut up," he says between his teeth. "Just shut up." He walks a few feet in front of me all three and a half miles back towards the car. He won't speak to me, and frankly I don't care. The sooner he's out of here, the sooner Jane and I are alone again, the better.

It costs Oliver sixty-five bucks to get his car released from the garage where it's been towed. We've had to walk another five miles because of this, in the other direction. It sets us back about another two hours. It is after three when we leave, having cleared the ticket with the police station in Goffstown. The attendant is an old guy with white hair that sticks up in tufts all over his head. He rubs his palm up against the windshield, which is filmy with dust. "Looks like you're outta gas," he says. "I'd do something about that if I were you."

Oliver pushes past the man. He empties the can he's been hauling around most of the day into the gas tank. It chugs, like it's gulping down a good imported beer. When he finishes he throws the can into the back seat and stares at me. "What are you looking at? Are you going to get in or what?"

"I've been thinking," I say. "You ought to let me drive."

Oliver leans across the hood of the car. "Give me one good reason."

"So we can find Rebecca tonight. We're going to be getting off the major highways really soon, and I barely know where to go. I can do it by feel but I couldn't really direct you." I shrug; it's the truth. I want this to be over with as soon as possible, so that I can call Jane and hear her voice on the other end of the line. Hear her tell me to come home.

We reach Carroll, Hadley's hometown, just after dinnertime. I'm driving, like I suggested. I take a couple of wrong turns, but I get us to the Slegg house. "Why, hello, Sam!" Mrs. Slegg says when she answers the door. "It sure is nice to see you. Hadley's enjoying his vacation." She gracefully sweeps her arm towards the hallway. "Won't you come inside?"

"I'm afraid I can't, Mrs. Slegg. This is my—this is Oliver Jones. We're trying to find his daughter, and I think she may have come here to visit Hadley."

Mrs. Slegg pulls her bathrobe tighter around her neck. "Hadley isn't in some kind of trouble, is he?"

"Not at all." I give my best happy-go-lucky smile. Hadley does it better, I think. "They're just good friends, and well, we figure she came up this way."

Mrs. Slegg flicks on the porch light from inside. "He's not here now. He went out to a bar with a friend. Someone came to the door, I don't *think* it was a girl but I can't say for sure. And he said he was going out."

Oliver steps in front of me. "Ma'am, do you mind if I take a look around? You can imagine what it's like . . . your own child running away, wondering if she's in some terrible danger."

Mrs. Slegg nods with Oliver. "Oh, please, heavens, yes. I understand. Really I do."

Oliver gives a quick grateful smile. "Do you know the names of the bars your son might frequent?"

"Oh," Mrs. Slegg says, surprised. I'm not even watching Detective Jones anymore. "I don't really know, exactly. I don't get out much myself into town. Come to think of it, Sam, I don't believe Hadley *knows* of any bars around here." She turns to Oliver again. "You see, ever since I moved, Hadley's been working with Sam back in Stow. I just came to live here after Mr. Slegg died; before that we had a farm too. Right near the Hansens, isn't that right? Hadley comes up here but a couple of weekends a year, and at Christmastime, so he's usually at home with his brother and me. He's a quiet boy, you know, he's not one of those rowdy types."

Oliver nods. "He's not at a bar," he tells me.

"How do you know that?" I say, more to disagree with him than anything else. "Why would he lie to his own mother?"

"If you can't answer that you're more stupid than I thought. Check inside. See if there are any traces of him leaving, or of my daughter. I'm going into the backyard."

Reluctantly, I trudge to the back end of the little ranch, to the room Hadley uses when he's home. Mrs. Slegg stands behind me. "I'm sorry about intruding. We'll be out of here very soon. And when Hadley gets home, maybe you can ask him to–" I stop, watching Mrs. Slegg run her hands over the bed.

"Isn't this the strangest thing?" she says. "I gave Hadley an extra blanket just last night because it was so cold up here in the mountains. It was a really old one, from my grandma, and I told him to take good care of it because it's an antique. And here it's gone."

I check under the bed, and in the closet and the empty drawers. Nothing. Running to the next room over, Hadley's brother's, Mrs. Slegg tells me the blanket's missing on his bed too. "Oh, Sam," she says, her voice wavering. "My boy's not going to get hurt, now, is he? You've got to promise me that!"

She reaches out to me. I've known her all my life. How can I tell her that her son's run away, with a minor, and we haven't a clue where they are? "Nothing's going to happen to Hadley. Trust me." I kiss her lightly on the cheek and dash outside, to where Oliver is crouched near the rocky wall that abuts the backyard. It's the bottom of a mountain, actually: Mount Deception. Hadley and I climbed it once when we came up here for a long camping weekend. I remember it being steep, with few places for good strong footholds. And beautiful. Once you get to the top, if you ever do make it, there's quite a view.

Oliver dusts the edges of some of the rocks that make up the looming wall. "See this? Dirt. Mud. And it's fresh. I'll bet you ten-to-one Hadley and Rebecca have climbed up there."

"There are two blankets missing from the house. I don't know if that proves anything."

Oliver cranes his neck. From this angle, right at the very bottom, it's impossible to see to the top of Mount Deception. It hurts to just think about it. He anchors one leg in the crevice of the rocks. "Give me a lift up."

"Oliver," I tell him. "You can't go climbing this mountain right now." He is pulling himself up, and the remarkable thing is his agility, given the fact that he's wearing street shoes instead of boots. "It's getting dark, and you're going to be stuck halfway up this mountain in the freezing cold. We'll get a ranger; we'll go first thing in the morning."

"She's going to be up there the whole night. God only knows what sort of shape she's in, and how she got here."

"I don't like it any more than you do," I say. And I don't. I wasn't planning on spending the night in the company of Oliver Jones. By now the sky has turned a milky color, like the background on blueprints. There are a few stars here and there. "Let's go find a ranger. The sooner we get there the better."

The nearest ranger station is at a campground about ten miles south of Hadley's place. When we get there two rangers are inside the little log shack, cooking a can of Heinz beans.

Oliver just walks right in without being invited. He sits down at the kitchen table and starts to tell the rangers about Rebecca and Hadley. I interrupt him after about five minutes of extraneous background history. "Look, I know we can't get up there tonight, but we'd really like to go there first thing in the morning. Maybe you can help us; a trail or something."

The ranger who is just coming on duty takes out a relief map of the area and asks me to show him where the Sleggs live. I mention that I've hiked the mountain once with Hadley; I might remember things as we go.

We sleep on the floor of the cabin and when the sun comes up, we begin to pick our way through several trails. Oliver walks first, then the ranger, then me. From time to time Oliver slides on the worn soles of his loafers, knocking over the ranger and me like dominoes.

At a certain point it starts coming back to me. The cliff, the winding path and the little clump of trees in the distance. "We camped there," I say. "Last time I hiked this mountain we camped in those trees. There's a little clearing there, and you're close to the water, so it makes a good site."

We hike up the eastern edge, keeping the increasingly deep drop just an arm's length away. We can hear the river splashing over the rocks. Oliver's jaw tenses up when he sees the cliff. I know what he is thinking: What if she's down there? We are all out of breath by the time the ground levels off in front of us. Straight ahead is the clearing, through the pine trees, and I think I can make out something blue. We tiptoe in through the maze of trunks, and there on a blanket are Hadley and Rebecca, wound around each other. They are still, so still I think maybe this was a suicide pact, but then I see Hadley's chest rising and falling. He's practically naked, except for his boxers, and Rebecca's just wearing his shirt. The funny thing is, they look really peaceful. Like you say about angels. They're holding each other so tight, even fast asleep, that it's as if the rest of the world couldn't possibly matter.

"Jesus, Hadley," I say, more out of shock than anything else. In spite of what Jane has told me about him and Rebecca, in spite of the fact that I repeated the story myself to Oliver, I didn't really believe he was carrying on with her. She looks about nine years old with her hair spread out in back of her like that, all skinny arms and legs. She certainly doesn't look old enough to be wrapped in Hadley's arms this way. I can tell Oliver isn't taking it too well, either. He is rasping, choking on everyday air.

Hadley sits up at the sound of my voice. He's got an erection, for Christ's sake. He blinks a few times and looks around like a captured animal. By now Rebecca is sitting up too. The thing I notice about her is that her eyes are all fuzzy, and she doesn't seem to be surprised. "Hadley," she says calmly, "this is my father."

Hadley pulls a blanket over his lap and holds out his hand. Oliver doesn't take it. Rebecca lies back down on the blanket. How far *have* they gone? I wonder. I stare at Hadley, but he's not revealing anything. As Rebecca hits the ground heavily, he crawls to her side. So does the ranger, for that matter. Hadley holds his hand under Rebecca's neck, incredibly tender.

"Get the hell away from her." Oliver says, finally. "Don't touch her."

Seeing this may be harder for him than seeing me and Jane together. There's a rotten, stale smell that's hovering: disgrace. "Do it, Hadley. Just move away. It's the best thing."

Hadley turns to me and he looks like he's been wounded. "What do you know?"

Oliver ignores what's going on between Hadley and me. He takes a step towards his daughter, holding out his hand but not quite touching her. "Rebecca, are you all right? Did he hurt you?"

Hadley looks at me, as if to say: Don't do this to me twice. Stand up for me, now. Please. Believe in me.

I keep eye contact with him, and he nods, just the slightest bit. I turn to Rebecca. There's something wrong here, any fool could tell that from the way she's just lying there. "Can you stand up?" I say, stepping close.

When Rebecca shakes her head, which looks like it takes up all her energy, Hadley moves back next to her. He props her up by her shoulders. "She came to me. She hitched. We were headed to your place today to work this all out." He's shouting, I wonder if he knows.

I look from Hadley's face to Oliver's. He's got this look in his eyes that I didn't see even yesterday morning. I have never seen it on a human. It's the way raccoons get, when they're rabid. They walk right up to you, even though normally they're scared shitless of people, and they just attack, scratching and biting and clawing. It's like they have no idea where they are, or how they got there. They've just absolutely gone crazy. "Hadley," I say real slowly, trying not to set Oliver off, "I think you'd better let Rebecca come home with us. And I think you'd better stay here for a while."

Hadley glares at him, a vein in his temple pulsing angrily. "You know me," he says. "You've known me forever. I can't believe . . . I cannot *believe* that you'd doubt me." He walks towards me, so close I could reach out and just touch him, tell him it's over. "You're my friend, Sam," he says. "You're like my brother. I didn't tell her to come here. I wouldn't do that." He swallows; I think he's about to cry. In all the years, I've never seen him do that. "I'm not going to turn my back. I'm not going to let you take her away." He looks at Rebecca. "Jesus, Sam, I *love* her."

He takes a step backward, towards the chasm, and I lean forward, worried about his safety, but Rebecca lurches forward between us and throws her arms around Hadley's knees. Hadley crouches, holding her and brushing back her hair.

It is at this moment that Oliver loses control. "Let go of her, you bastard!" I grab his arm and pull him back. "Let go of my daughter!"

I kneel, eye-level with Rebecca and Hadley. "Give her to us, Hadley," I whisper. "Give her to us."

Rebecca's face is pressed into Hadley's shoulder. He talks to her quietly, and from the words I catch over the calls of circling hawks, I think he is trying to convince her to come to us.

"You have to go with them," Hadley says. He lifts her chin with her finger. "Don't you want to make me happy? Don't you see?"

I start to wonder if this is going to turn out all right. Oliver stands with his fists at his side, watching Rebecca as if there is a wall between them. I imagine it is next to impossible to see your child grow up; even harder when it comes in a matter of minutes.

Rebecca and Hadley are struggling. She clutches him, and Hadley is trying to push her away. Watching them, I have started to believe. I think I am on their side, now. In spite of Oliver, in spite of Jane. For the last time, Hadley looks at me, and he's begging for just five minutes. Five lousy minutes.

Because I am looking into the sun to give them privacy, I don't really know what happens next. All of a sudden, Rebecca and Hadley tear apart. In the effort to push her towards me, he falls. I see all this through blind orange sunspots, my own fault. And then Rebecca is in my arms, tiny and hot with sweat, reaching back towards the cliff as Hadley falls over the edge.

I will remember many things about that day in years to come, but the thing that will stick with me most vividly is Rebecca. Just that second her eyes clear, and she begins to scream. It isn't a scream, though, not really; it's the howling of an animal. I recognize it as the sound of death, and it never surprises me that it comes from her throat instead of Hadley's. I will remember that noise, and the way Rebecca looks over the edge of the cliff when none of us have the nerve. She rips the shirt she is wearing at the buttons and rakes her nails over her chest. All three of us—three men—just stand there, not doing anything; not knowing what we are supposed to do. We are speechless. She tears at her flesh, scoring her legs and her arms. We all watch the blood from the marks she's made seep into the earth.

67 JANE

They bring her back to me swathed in bandages. Her eyes are open but she isn't looking at anything. Even when I stand right over her, she doesn't see me. From time to time she says things about fire and lightning. She stood up during the second night, screamed at the top of her lungs, and got out of bed. She walked around the room, stepping over obstacles that were not there, touching her hand and shrieking from the burns. Then she sat on the floor, crouched, her head bent over her lap. When she looked up she was crying. She was calling for me.

Sam and Oliver drift in and out of the room at different times. They have both tried to get me to leave her side, but how could I do that? What if she chose that minute to regain consciousness, and I weren't there?

When Sam comes in, he sits behind me and kneads my shoulders. We don't say much to each other; he is just a presence for me, and that's plenty. When Oliver comes in, he sits on the opposite side of the bed. He holds Rebecca's other hand. As if she completes the circuit, when we are like this we can talk. I tell him what I feel for Sam, and it doesn't hurt so much to reveal the truth. I tell him how it makes me feel to be in love like this. I do not apologize; it's too late for that. And as for Oliver, I have to say he does not accuse. Instead he accepts what I have to say, and he weaves tales for me. He has become an expert storyteller. He reminds me of mishaps that occurred when we were dating; of escapades on our honeymoon to retrieve lost luggage, to find long-dormant hostels. He tells me together we can survive anything.

Oliver is in the room when she comes to. I have been tracing the hand-painted design on the edge of the walls, wondering what Sam's mother is like, when Rebecca's fingers move in my hand. Oliver looks up at me; he has felt it too. Rebecca opens her eyes, bloodshot and crusted, and coughs violently. "What's the matter with her?" Oliver says. Anxious to do something, I press a towel against Rebecca's forehead. Oliver holds tissues against Rebecca's chin, catching the phlegm.

Finally, thankfully, Rebecca stops. She sighs—actually, it is more like she deflates. Oliver strokes her arm gently. "Baby," he says, smiling down at her. "We're going to go home. We're getting out of here." I do not say anything. I don't care what he says. I will do anything—if Rebecca comes back whole.

Rebecca makes a motion to sit up, and I quickly stuff a pillow behind her back for support. "Tell me this," she says. "Hadley's dead?"

I don't think Oliver has come to terms with this; with Rebecca's ability to fall in love. I would not have believed it either, but I was there to witness it. Oliver looks at me, and then he gets up and leaves the room.

I don't know why she has asked. Does she know for sure? Is she just looking for a corroborating witness? "Yes," I say, and just like that, all the light drains out of my daughter's face. I am afraid I am going to lose her again. Once you make the decision you want to die, nothing can bring you back. I start to cry, and I apologize to her. I'm sorry for thinking she was too young. I'm sorry for sending Hadley away. I'm sorry, just sorry, that it had to come to this.

I bury my face in the quilt on top of my daughter, thinking: this is not the way I wanted it to be. I was hoping to be the strong one, the one who would be there to help her stand again. But Rebecca holds her hand against my cheek. "Tell me everything you know," she says.

So I recount the horror of Hadley's death, his broken neck, his bravery. I tell her he felt no pain. *Not like you,* I think. I do not tell her that under slightly different circumstances of fate, Hadley might have lived. The rangers said the drop was but one hundred feet—not far enough to ensure death. What killed Hadley was the spot where he happened to land, the rocks that severed his spine. I do not tell Rebecca that inches away was the forgiving cushion of water. I say that Hadley's funeral is tomorrow. It took this long to raise his body from the narrow chasm.

"This long?" Rebecca asks. I tell her three days have gone by. "What have I been doing for three days?"

She has pneumonia and she has been sedated most of the time.

"You were gone when your father first arrived here. He insisted on going with Sam to find you. He didn't like the idea of Sam staying here with me."

I help her lie back down and tell her she ought to rest. She fights me, struggling to sit up. "What does he mean, 'We're going home'?"

"Back to California. What did you think?"

She blinks many times, as if she is trying to clear her mind, or remember, or possibly both. "What have we been doing here?"

She catches me so off guard that I don't stop her in time from pulling the quilt back from her chest. When she sees her sores on her chest, arms and legs, she gasps. Her hands, trembling, reach out for something. They find me. "When Hadley fell, you tried to climb down after him. You wouldn't stop." I take a deep breath, feeling my voice catch. "You kept saying you were trying to tear your heart out."

Rebecca turns her face so that she is looking out the window. It is dark now, and all she will see is the reflection of her own pain. "I don't know why I bothered," she whispers. "You'd already done that."

I used to think, before this whole incident, that parental love was supposed to be unconditional. I believed that Rebecca would naturally be tied to me because I had been the one to bring her into the world. I didn't connect this with my own experience. When I could not love my father, I assumed there was something wrong with me. But when they carried Rebecca in here from the stretcher of the ambulance, I came to see things differently. If you want to love a parent you have to understand the incredible investment he or she has in you. If you are a parent, and you want to be loved, you have to deserve it.

Suddenly I am dizzy with guilt. "What do you want me to say, Rebecca?"

Rebecca will not look at me. "Why do you want me to forgive you? What do you get out of it?"

Absolution, I think, the first word that comes to my mind. I get to protect you from what I went through. "Why do I want you to forgive me? Because I never forgave my father, and I know what it will do to you. When I was growing up my father would hit me. He hit me and he hit my mother and I tried to keep him from hitting Joley. He broke my heart, and eventually he broke me. I never believed I could be anything important. Why else would my father hurt me?" I smile, wringing her hand. "Then I forgot about it. I married Oliver and three years later he hit me. That's when I left the first time."

Rebecca pulls her hand away. "The plane crash," she says.

"I went back to him because of you. I knew that more than anything else I had to make sure you grew up feeling safe. And then I hit your father, and it all came back again." I swallow, reliving that scene on the stairs in San Diego. The whale papers fluttering around my ankles. Oliver cursing at me. "This time it was part of me," I say. "No matter how far I run. No matter how many states and countries I cross, I can't get it out of myself. I never forgave him, because I thought that way I would have the last laugh. But he won. He's in me."

When she tries to sit up gain, I don't stop her. I start to tell her about Sam. I let her know what it was like to give the stars we saw from the bedroom window the names of our ancestors. How he could finish the very thoughts I was thinking. "I didn't believe anyone else could feel the way I did. Including—*especially* my daughter."

I move to the edge of the bed, pulling the quilt back over her chest. I take her hand, counting her fingers. "I did this when you were a baby. Making sure there were ten. I wanted you to be healthy. I didn't care if you were a boy or a girl. At least I said I didn't. But it mattered. I used to hope I'd have a little girl, someone just like me. Someone I could go shopping with, and teach to wear makeup, and dress for the senior prom. But I wish now you hadn't been a girl. Because we get hurt. It happens over and over."

We stare at each other for a long time, my daughter and me. In the dim light of a sixty-watt bulb, I start to notice things about her that I have never seen. Everyone has always told me she looks like Oliver. *I* even thought she looked like Oliver. But here, and now, she has my eyes. Not the color, not the shape, but the demeanor—

and isn't that the most remarkable feature? This is my child. There is no denying it.

When I am looking at her, all of my decisions come clear. Love, I think, has very little to do with Sam, with Oliver, with Hadley. What it all boils down to is me. What it all boils down to is Rebecca. It is knowing that the memories I pass down to her will keep me from feeling pain the next time. It is knowing that she has stories of her own for me.

"Sometimes I cannot believe you are only fifteen," I say. I pull back the quilt from my daughter's chest and peel off the strips of gauze. In some places she starts to bleed again. Maybe this is good. Maybe something needs to be let out. I hold my hands across her chest, over her breasts. Her blood slips between my fingers. I want so much to heal.

68 OLIVER

I have one strong lasting image of you, Jane. It was the morning after our wedding night, and you looked lost in the large, king-size bed at the Hotel Meridien in Boston. I awakened before the five o'clock wake-up call just for the chance to watch you with all your defenses down. You have always been so lovely when you stop resisting. It is your face that I remember the most: alabaster, honest, the face of a child. You *were* a child.

You had never been abroad, do you remember? and you were so looking forward to Amsterdam, Copenhagen. But then came the phone call from Provincetown, about several beached whales that were stranded on the shores of Ogunquit. When the telephone rang, you rolled towards me. "Is it time?" you whispered, twining your arms around my hips, playing at this world of adults.

I decided to simply tell you the truth. Perhaps in retrospect I see that I embellished the plight of these whales to be in more dire straits than could be considered strictly truthful. But you surprised me. You did not frown, or sigh, or show evidence of regret. You began to get dressed in an old pair of jeans and a sweatshirt—not at all the pretty pink suit of which you'd been so proud, your going-away outfit. "Come on, Oliver," you said to me. "We've got to get there as soon as we can!"

Driving to Maine I stole glances at you, checking once again for signs of self-pity. You exhibited none. You kept your hand covering mine for the entire trip, and you did not comment on our forgotten honeymoon or the missed flight. We reached Ogunquit the same time that our plane was scheduled to depart.

You worked beside me that day, and the next, ferrying buckets of water up from the ocean, massaging the crusted fins of these whales. You and I were a team, united in purpose. I had never felt so close to you as I did on the beaches of Ogunquit, separated by the huge frame of a whale, and yet still able to hear the song of your voice.

We told you to step aside when it came to moving the whales. You refused. You worked directly beside me, pushing where I told you it was necessary, stepping back delicately when common sense told you you were too small to do any good. You knew the clear danger of being so close to such a powerful mammal. You heard the stories of broken limbs, and worse, of bring crushed. We saw three whales swimming back out into the ocean that day—two females and a baby. The baby had to be redirected several times; it kept trying to swim back to shore. But we watched them go free. It took my breath away, seeing success right before my eyes. I wanted to tell you this but you were not there. I had to look around to find you in the cheering crowd. You were crouched near the one whale we could not save. Already the sun had cracked and bleached the skin on its back, and you were splashing bucket after bucket of water upon it. "It's gone, Jane." I tried to pull you away. You leaned against the still side of the whale near the hot and blistered eye, and you cried.

I do not know how it happened; the way we drifted apart. I am happy to assume the blame for it if it can be left in the past. I woke up one morning, greying at the temples, engrossed in the pursuit of my research, and discovered that my family had disappeared. I must confess to you that even as I began to search for you and Rebecca, I did not have a clear goal in mind. The object was to stop the nonsense, to bring you back as quickly as possible and resume the life that had been interrupted. But when I saw you in Iowa—yes, I was in Iowa at the same time, just across the cornfield—when I saw you with Rebecca, I realized there was much more going on than I had allowed myself to recognize. Here was this amazing woman with whom I had constructed the fragile shape of fifteen years. Here was this child who came back from the edge of death for *something*.

I understand you have undertaken many changes yourself during this trip and although I cannot pretend this does not hurt, I will not blame you. I brought it upon myself. I drove you to find someone else. But you have to see, Jane, that I'm a different man. For every action, there is an equal and opposite reaction: imagine how different our lives could be. Oh, I want you back. I want you and I want Rebecca, and I want for once to act like a family. I will bend over backward; I will give you both all I have. I know you have your own issues to sort out, but don't you see? I need you, Jane. I love you. I know that the only reason I have become successful in other areas of my life is because of you—at your expense. And I still feel the way I did the day you willingly postponed your own honeymoon. I want you by my side.

It would be too much to ask you to believe in me. But I know you believe in second chances. You can't throw this all away. At the very least, all the basal elements are still there: you, me, Rebecca. We could tear down everything, yet we would still have those building blocks. And my God, Jane, imagine the little world we three could create.

69 Joley

In all the years you've been coming to me for advice, I've never been able to get you to do something you didn't already have your heart set on doing. There: my secret's out. I'm not the sage I pretend to be; the fact is, Jane, you've got a mind of your own, and you only need me to pull the answers out from inside you. So I think you know what you are going to do. I think you understand, in this case, what would be the right thing.

Let me tell you a little something about love. It's different every time. It's nothing more than a chemical reaction, an arrow over an equation, but the elements change. The most fragile kind of love is that between a man and a woman. Chemistry, again: if you introduce a new element, you never know how stable the original bond is. You may wind up with a new union, with something left behind. I believe that you can fall in love many times with many different people. However I don't think that you can fall in love the same way twice. One type of relationship may be steady. Another may be fire and brimstone. Who is to say if one of these is better than the other? The deciding factor is how it all fits together. Your love, I mean, and your life.

The problem is that when you're old enough to really find a soulmate, you're already carrying around all this extra baggage. Like where you grew up, and how much money you make, and whether you like the country or the city. And sometimes, most of the time, you fall really hard for someone who you just can't squeeze into the limits of your life. The bottom line is: when your heart sets its sight on someone, it doesn't consult with your mind.

Most people don't marry the loves of their lives. You marry for compatibility; for friendship. And Jane, there's a lot to be said for that. It may not be a kind of relationship where you can read each other's minds, but it's comfortable, like a familiar warm spot on your favorite chair. That's just another kind of love, one that doesn't burn itself out, one that lasts in the real world.

You don't know how lucky you are. There's one person for each of us on this whole planet with whom we can really connect. And you found yours. I know how it feels too, you see, because I have had you.

I have always been your greatest fan, Jane. I can identify you in a room by the motion of the air around you. I knew it would be like this from the night that Daddy first crashed into my room. He flung open the door and saw you already sitting on the bed, holding a pillow up around my ears so that I wouldn't have to listen to the sounds downstairs of Mama crying. He told you to get the hell out of my room. You were no more than eight, all bones, and you hurled yourself at his groin with the force of a tropical storm. Perhaps it was just the region you hit that triggered his reaction, but I don't believe that. I can still see his head striking the sharp corner of the wooden bureau, and his eyes rolling back. You looked at him, whispered, Daddy*? "I didn't do that," you said, "you hear?" But even at four, I understood. "You're the only one who* could *have," I told you, and to this day that holds true.*

You have untapped strength, Jane. It's what got you through your childhood. It's what kept Daddy from going after me. It's what Oliver fell in love with, what Sam fell in love with, what I fell in love with. You came to me in Massachusetts, you said, because you couldn't remember who you were anymore. Don't you see? You're everyone's anchor. You are our center.

I want you to say it. Tell me what you are going to do.

Again.

You will not be sorry. I know; I have carried a memory of you wherever I have gone for thirty years now. That's the way it had to be. You will see. No matter what. You will take him with you.

70 Sam

Until now, I didn't know there was a down side to being able to read your mind. It's written all over your face, you know. I don't blame you. I should have known that you would go back to him. Back to California.

Later, when you are gone, it's going to hit me. Hadley, and then you, leaving at the same time. I won't blame you for what happened to him; I couldn't. But I haven't really grieved yet, not for him; not for you. In time, I'll make peace with myself for Hadley's death. With you, though, it will not be so simple.

It would be easy to say that when you leave I could just pretend this didn't happen. Truth is, you weren't here for all that long. I've always been sort of suspicious of immediate attraction, anyway, and I could just tell myself over and over that infatuation isn't the same as love. But you and I both know that would be lying. You can tell yourself anything you want, but you can't make what happened go away. It happened fast because we were making up for lost time.

When I picture you, it's a collage I see, not one whole picture. There's you sitting in the manure, doesn't that seem like a year ago? And talking to Joley under the shade of a Gravenstein tree, the sun casting shadows on your back. I think I knew I loved you then, no matter how I acted. Maybe I always knew.

I keep thinking we were so stupid. If we hadn't fought so hard when we first met, we would have had nearly twice as much time together. But then if we hadn't fought so hard I wonder if I could have loved you so damn much.

It sounds funny to say it here, just like that, in the light of day. I love you. You hear it so often, you know, on soap operas and stupid sitcoms that sometimes the words are just sounds, they don't mean anything. But God, I would shout it to the world day and night if it meant I could keep you with me. I've never tried to pack so much into one phrase in my whole life.

Is it different for you, because I am not the first man you've loved? I might as well say it, because it's true. You went first to Oliver. So what I want to know is: does your heart feel like it's being ripped out? Is it easier for you? Have you felt this way before?

I haven't either. I can't imagine ever feeling this way again. Not the pain, not now, that's not what I'm talking about. I'm talking about us. When I was with you nothing mattered. I could have watched this whole orchard get wiped out by blight. I could have witnessed massacres, a war, Armageddon. It wouldn't have made a difference.

I know that there will be other women, but they couldn't compare. Maybe I'll change, maybe love will change, but I think we were a once-in-a-lifetime. You could never leave me; that's why I am not more upset. You can't possibly break these feelings. They stretch, and they last. You're taking them with you back to Oliver, back to Rebecca. You will never be the same, because of me.

If I have to remember you, just for a second, it will be like this: you kneeling in front of me, at the windowsill, counting the stars. I don't remember why we decided to do that, it's an impossible, infinite task. Maybe because when we were together, we thought we had all the time in the world. You gave up at two hundred and six. That's when you started to name them, after grandparents, great-grandparents, distant ancestors. Antique names like Bertha and Charity and Annabelle, Homer and Felix and Harding. You asked me for family names, and I told you. We mapped the sky with our heritage. *Do you know what a star is?* I asked you. *It's an explosion that happened billions and billions of years ago. The only reason we see it now, is because it's taken that long for the light, the sight, to travel here into our line of vision.* I pointed to the North Star, and said I wanted to name it after you. *Jane,* you said, *too plain for such a bright one*. I said you were wrong. It was the biggest explosion, obviously, and it has taken many years to reach us, but it will be here for many more.

I will think about you every day for the rest of my life. It had to be this way; I can't see myself surfing on a beach any more than you can imagine raising sheep. We come from different backgrounds, and we happened to cross for a little bit of time. But what a time that was.

Don't say it. This is not goodbye.

Look at me. Hold me. I can get across so much more that way. There are things we need to say that there aren't words for, yet.

Oh I love you.

71 REBECCA *July 3, 1990*

I always pay attention to my parents' fights. They're incredible. It is hard to understand how so much anger could come from such indifference. When I picture my parents, I see them walking in concentric circles, in opposite directions. My mother's circle is inside my father's, for financial reasons. My father walks clockwise. My mother walks counterclockwise. Naturally they do not cross paths. From time to time they look up and see each other from the corners of their eyes. And it is this break in the line of vision that sparks an argument.

They are fighting, today, over me. My fifteenth birthday. My father is planning to be out of the country on my birthday. Out of fourteen birthdays, he has been here for seven. So it is not like this is something new. But my mother seems to have lost control. She yells at him in the kitchen, things I choose to ignore. I walk away from them on purpose, and turn up the game shows on TV.

But it is when they get upstairs that things begin to get interesting. My parents' bedroom is directly over the living room where I am watching TV. I can hear shouting. Then I hear very distinctly the thud of something being dropped. And something else. I jump up and throw my baseball cap down on the couch. I tiptoe up the stairs, hoping I can catch the tail end of this.

"I've had it," my mother shouts. She has a big cardboard box, the kind my father keeps his research files in. She lifts it with all her strength—she's not so big—and chucks it into the hall. I think she sees me on the staircase, so I duck. Then my father walks out into the hall. He takes the box my mother has thrown and rights it. He lifts it by its handles and sets it back inside the door.

For reasons I don't understand, my mother is faster than my father. A wall of cartons builds up so quickly that I cannot see much of anything at all. They have blocked off the access to their bedroom. "Jane," my father says. "That's enough."

I cannot see what my mother is doing. This makes me angry. So many days of the year I put up with them ignoring each other; the moments they connect, even fighting, are so rare. Anything, to watch them together. So I creep to the second floor of the house and shove the cartons a certain way. I push and rearrange them gently so that I don't make too much noise but I create a peephole. I see my father standing in a pile of loose papers and graphs. He looks helpless. He moves his hands in front of him, as if he can still catch them falling.

Then he grabs my mother's shoulders. I think maybe he is hurting her. She struggles back and forth, and with a force I didn't realize she had, she breaks away.

My mother lifts one of the cartons still out there and holds it over the banister. She rattles it like a maraca.

My father comes charging out of the bedroom. "Don't," he warns. Then the carton breaks. Slow-motion, I can see white bones in Ziploc bags, sharp strands of baleen, ribbons of charts and observation logs, all falling. Just like that, I stop breathing.

This is when, out of the blue, I remember the plane crash.

My father hit my mother once, when I was a baby. And she took me and flew to the East Coast. That's how the story goes. My father insisted she bring me back, so she put me on a plane headed to San Diego. But the plane crashed. I tell it like this, matter-of-fact, because I do not remember it. I was, as I say, a baby. What I know of the crash I have learned from reading newspaper articles, many years later.

I don't think about this crash much—it was a long time ago—but I believe that it has crossed my mind *now* for a reason. Maybe it is the thing that gets me to stand up and turn away. Maybe it is the reason I walk into my bedroom and pull out clothes and underwear, stuffing them into a small bag. Don't get me wrong, I have no master plan. I keep my face turned away from my parents when I run out of my room and into the bathroom. I grab some dirty clothes of my mother's from the hamper, and then I run down the stairs. My heart is pounding. All I want to do is get away. I hear my father say, "You bitch."

When I was around twelve I thought about running away. I suppose all kids do at some point. I got as far as our backyard. I hid underneath the black vinyl cover of the barbeque, but it took my parents four and a half hours to find me. My father had to come home early from work. It was a big deal when my mother lifted up the vinyl cover. She hugged me and told me I had scared her half to death. *What would I do without you?* she said, over and over. *What would I do without you?*

Sneakers. I grab mine from the living room, my mother's from the hall closet. They are what she calls her "weekend shoes." So I am packed. Now what do I do?

When the plane crashed, I was brought to a hospital in Des Moines. I was in the pediatrics ward, of course, and all I can really remember is that the nurses wore smocks with smiley faces. And hair nets with Ernie and Bert on them. I didn't know where my parents were, and all I really wanted was to see them. It took a while, but they came. They came in together, I remember. They were holding each other's hands, and that made me so happy. The last time I had seen them my mother was crying, and my father was yelling very loud. It had been very scary, the crash. But it was what had to be done. It brought my parents together again.

Just as I am thinking about this, I hear the sting of a slap. It's a sound you can recognize from any other, if you have heard it before. It brings tears to my eyes.

I slide the front door open on its hinges. I run to my mother's car, parked at the edge of the driveway. She has a clunky old station wagon that has been around forever. I perch on the edge of the passenger seat. They say history repeats, don't they?

My mother comes out of the house like a lost soul. She is looking into the sky and she is wearing nothing but her underwear. As if it is a magnet, she is being drawn towards this car. I am sure she doesn't see me. She holds some clothes in her left hand. When she gets into the car she slides them on the seat between us. She has red welts on her wrists from where he grabbed her. I don't know where he hit her this time. I put my hand over hers; she jumps in her seat. "I have everything," I say. My voice sounds too high and thin. My mother is looking at me as if she is trying to place the face. She whispers my name, and sinks back against the seat. So do I. I take a deep breath; wonder how long it will be before I see my father again.

72 Jane

The human body can withstand so much. I have read accounts of people who have survived extreme cold, brutality, bludgeoning, terrible burns. I have read the testimonies of these survivors. They all make it sound so simple, really, the ability to keep on living.

We all stand on the upper part of the driveway, where the gravel is a little thin. Sam has just carried Rebecca to the car. Oliver is standing a respectable distance away. Joley stands in front of me, holding my hands, trying to get me to look at him. Hadley is not here, and I cannot forgive myself.

It is a beautiful day by any other account. It's cool and dry, with a see-through sky. All the apple trees have fruit. I don't know where the birds have gone.

Joley smiles at me and tells me for the hundredth time to stop crying. He lifts my chin. "Well," he says, "under any other circumstance, I'd say, 'Come back soon.'"

My brother. "Call me," I say. I don't know how to tell him the things I really want to say. That I couldn't have lived through this without him. That I want to thank him, in spite of the way this has turned out.

"Tomorrow," Joley says, "go to the post office in Chevy Chase, Maryland. There are two. You want the one in the center of town." He makes me laugh. "That's better." I don't mean to, but just knowing Sam is in the foreground, my eyes dart over to his. Joley hugs me one last time. "This is my going-away present," he whispers. He takes several steps towards Oliver. "Hey, I don't think you've had a chance to see the greenhouse here, have you?" He claps his arm around Oliver's shoulders, and pushes him, forcefully, down towards the barn. Oliver turns around once or twice, reluctant to leave us like this. But Joley isn't about to let him off the hook.

So then it is just Sam and I. We move a few feet closer but we do not touch. That would be dangerous. "I've packed something for you," he says, swallowing. "In the back seat."

I nod. If I try to speak, it's all going to come out wrong. How can he look at me? I have killed his best friend; I have broken all my promises. I am leaving. I can feel my throat swelling up at the bottom. Sam smiles at me; he tries. "I know we said we weren't going to do this. I know it's just going to make it worse. But I can't help it." And he leans forward, wraps his arms tight across my back, and kisses me.

You don't know what it is like to touch him like that, our skin pressed together at the thighs, the shoulders, the cheeks. Everywhere Sam is, I feel a shock. When he pushes me away, I am gasping. "Oh, no," I say. He holds me at a distance, and that is supposed to be the end.

I have to stop shaking before I remember where I am. The little MG we bought in Montana is sitting next to the blue pickup truck. We are leaving it with Joley. Joley is leaning into the window of Oliver's Town Car, speaking to Rebecca. I am not sure she is up to traveling. I would have liked to give her one more day. But Oliver feels she ought to be home. She ought to recuperate where she doesn't have to think of Hadley every time she looks at something, and in this he is right.

Just then I am sure I will faint. I can't feel my knees anymore and the sky begins to spin. Suddenly Oliver is beside me. "Are you all right?" he asks, as if I can answer that in one simple sentence. "Okay," he says. "Then this is it."

"This is it!" I say, repeating his words. I can't seem to come up with any of my own. As I slide into the passenger seat, Joley gives Oliver directions back to Route 95. I unroll my window.

Oliver starts the car and puts it into gear. Sam moves so that he is standing across from my window, at just the distance where it is easy for us to look at each other. I do not let myself blink. I concentrate on his eyes. We are imprinting each other, etching an image so that when we meet again—ten months, ten years from now—we will have no choice but to remember. The car starts moving. I crane my neck, unwilling to break first.

I have to turn around in my seat, looking over Rebecca's head through the lines of defogger tape, but I can still see him. I can see him all the way past the welcome sign for this orchard, past the mailbox.

Then I realize how it will be. Like metal pounded to a thin foil, spreading in distance but not compromising its strength. It has simply changed shape, changed form.

Oliver has been talking but I haven't really heard what he's been saying. He is trying so hard; I have to give him credit. I open my eyes, and there is my daughter. Rebecca stares at me, or maybe right through me, I cannot tell. She pulls a blanket back from the floor of the car. Apples. Bushels and bushels of apples. This is what Sam wanted me to have. I find myself silently mouthing the names of the different fruits: Bellflower. Macoun. Jonathan. Cortland. Bottle Greening. Rebecca takes a Cortland and bites hard into its side. "Oh," Oliver says, looking in the rearview mirror. "You took some with you, did you?"

I watch Rebecca with this apple. She peels back the skin with her teeth and then sinks into the white flesh of the cheek. She lets the juice drip over her chin. Just watching her, I can taste it. When she sees me looking, she pulls the fruit away from her mouth. She offers the other half to me.

As I take the apple from her our hands touch. I can feel the ridges of her fingertips brush against mine. They seem to fit together. I raise the apple to my mouth, and take a huge bite. I take another bite, not having finished the first. I stuff my cheeks with the meat of this apple as if I have been starving for weeks. That's why he sent them. Even after Sam's apples are gone, they will remain part of my body.

As Rebecca watches, I toss the core onto the road, staring at the hand that so easily let it go. It is missing a wedding band. I left it at Sam's. Of all the things for him to have.

I wonder what Oliver and I will do when we get home. How one goes about getting back on track. We cannot pick up where we left off. I will not be able to put Sam out of my mind entirely when I am with Oliver. But then, did I ever really forget about Oliver when I was with Sam?

I was in love with Oliver once, when I was a different person. I did not know then what I know now. I saw him standing waist-deep in a pool of water and I pictured a life together. I had a child with him; remarkable proof of being in love. She is the best of both of us. Which means that there is a very good strain in me. And a very good strain in Oliver.

You can take dead trees in an orchard, and bring them back to life. You can take two different strains of apples and they will bear fruit on the same tree. Grafting: the science of bringing together the unlikely; of bringing back what is past hope.

Oliver squeezes my hand, and I squeeze his back. This surprises him; he turns to me and smiles hesitantly. Rebecca is watching all this. I wonder what she sees when she looks at us together. I roll up my window and turn sideways in my seat. I want to be able to see both Oliver and Rebecca.

Oliver slows at a toll booth. Already we have reached a highway. I smile confidently at my husband, and at my daughter. Rebecca breathes in deeply and reaches for my free hand. Oliver turns west towards California. Rebecca and I are both passengers this time, and together we follow the jagged, winding line of trees on the highway. I turn to watch her taking in the change of scenery. It is the first time I can remember having my eyes wide open while I look at my future.

SONGS OF THE HUMPBACK WHALE

Jodi Picoult

A Readers Club Guide

Introduction

Jodi Picoult's richly literary novel *Songs of the Humpback Whale* tells the story of a fragile family and one woman's voyage toward self-discovery. When an explosive argument with her husband, Oliver, prompts Jane and her daughter, Rebecca, to abruptly leave their California home, the two head east armed with little other than a few dollars, the clothes on their backs, and their love for each other. Traversing their way across the United States, following the directional clues provided to them by Jane's brother Joley, Jane and Rebecca inch their way toward Massachusetts while Oliver, an expert whale tracker, follows close behind.

When Jane and Rebecca arrive at a Massachusetts apple orchard, they both meet new people who will challenge them and force them to reconsider their life choices. Sam, a small-town apple farmer, pushes Jane to unveil the secrets of her past, finally enabling her to open her heart in the present. When Rebecca witnesses her mother and Sam's burgeoning love affair, she finds solace in Hadley, who offers her the support and nurturing she has so often yearned for from her own parents. Once Oliver arrives at the orchard to reclaim his family, Jane must finally decide whether to abandon her newfound love in order to return to California and fulfill her responsibilities to her husband and her daughter. Only after a tragic accident can the Jones family finally return home, together again but forever changed.

Questions and Topics for Discussion
Warning: Spoilers Ahead

1. Discuss the novel's structure. How did the alternating voices enhance or detract from the reading experience for you? Did you find that the characters' differing accounts of the events of the novel added to the dramatic tension, and how so? Similarly, Rebecca is the only character to narrate the novel's events backward chronologically. How does this affect the reading experience?
2. So much of the novel is about voice and people finding themselves through their voices: Jane is a speech therapist, Oliver tracks whale songs, Joley's words guide Jane and Rebecca across the country. Which relationships in the novel are founded on spoken connections and which are based on something other than language? How are these relationships different? How do these different relationships affect the characters?
3. When mentioning his research, Oliver proposes that the personal histories of whales—"who the whale is, where he has been sighted, with whom he has been sighted—tell us something about why he sings the way he does." Discuss how each of the characters in the novel is shaped by his or her past.
4. The relationship between Jane and Rebecca is one of the most complex in the novel. Although Jane is Rebecca's mother, it often seems that Rebecca is the more mature person—Hadley even tells Sam that Rebecca "takes better care of her mother than the other way around." Rebecca similarly comments that she and Jane are "more like equals." Discuss their relationship. Why do you think they relate to each other this way?
5. Although it is Rebecca who packs up, gets in the car, and urges her mother to run away from Oliver, she also misses her father and her home while she and her

mother are traveling across the country. Speculate on what Rebecca really wants for each of her parents. Do you think she wants to return to California? Why or why not?

6. The relationship between Joley and Jane is one of the most meaningful in the novel. Although Jane spent most of her childhood protecting Joley, it is Joley who cares for Jane in her adult life. Discuss the bond between them. What is it based on? Does Joley's love for Jane seem illicit at times? Why or why not?

7. Joley tells Jane and Rebecca that he will write them across the country, sending them "to places he thinks they need to go." Discuss the different geographic locations of their voyage. Why do you think Joley sends them to each place? How does each location affect them?

8. Sam comments that "if you leave things to their natural course, they go bad." Discuss Sam and his life choices. In what ways has he struggled against the natural course of his life, and in which ways has he accepted that he is living the life he was destined to?

9. When Sam and Jane first meet, each assumes certain things about the other—Jane assumes that Sam is a simple farmer, and Sam assumes that Jane is no different from other wealthy Newton girls. In what ways do Sam and Jane live up to each other's assumptions, and in what ways does each defy the other's preconceived notions?

10. Chapters 39, 40, and 41 offer Rebecca's, Jane's, and Oliver's perspectives on the plane crash. Although these chapters all begin the same way—"Midwest Airlines flight 997 crashed on September 21, 1978, in What Cheer, Iowa—a farming town sixty miles southeast of Des Moines"—each offers a different perspective on the same event. Discuss these perspectives. What do the differences and similarities reveal about

each character and the impact that event had on the rest of his or her life?

11. At the site of the plane crash, Oliver finally finds Jane and Rebecca. Though he is sitting close enough to touch them, he finds that he cannot bring himself to announce his presence. What is Oliver thinking? How does this moment motivate him to change? By the end of the novel, has he successfully transformed himself?

12. When Oliver goes to save Marble, the whale tangled in nets in Gloucester, it seems that he is temporarily calling off his search for his wife and daughter. How did you react to his decision? Do you think that Oliver was motivated only by a desire to get on camera and to make a public plea for Jane and Rebecca, or did you think that he may have been reverting to his old ways?

13. At the end of the novel, Jane abandons her love for Sam, choosing instead to honor her responsibilities to her husband and her daughter. How did you react to that choice? Did you find it surprising? Frustrating? What clues did Picoult provide throughout the novel to signal that Jane would eventually make this choice?

14. Jane comments, "You can take dead trees in an orchard, and bring them back to life." Discuss the final moments of the novel. In what ways have Jane, Rebecca, and Oliver changed? Do you think that the conclusion of the novel is ultimately hopeful about the family's future? Why or why not?

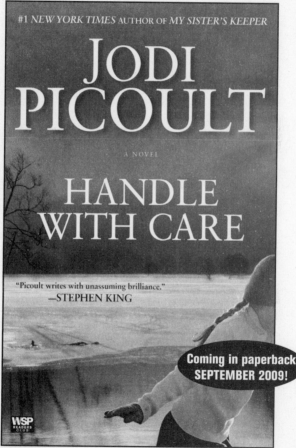

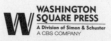